Praise for Patr...

"*The Inn at Harts Haven* is filled with delightful and complex characters that readers will adore. Hope, romance, and suspense combine perfectly in this heartfelt story from one of my favorite Amish fiction authors."
　　　—Jennifer Beckstrand, *USA TODAY* bestselling author
　　　　　　　of *First Christmas on Huckleberry Hill*

"Patricia Davids has done it again. *The Inn at Harts Haven* might just be my favorite of her books, and I've loved all of them. But a bit of suspense mixed with a romance full of conflict and torment had me reading long after I needed to get to bed! If you love Amish fiction, this one will go on your keeper shelf."
　　　—Lenora Worth, *New York Times* bestselling author

"Patricia Davids is one of the best writers in the Amish fiction genre. She's now on my must-read list!"
　　　—Shelley Shepard Gray, *New York Times* bestselling author

"Patricia writes with heart, integrity, and hope. Her stories both entertain and edify—the perfect combination."
　　　—Kim Vogel Sawyer, award-winning, bestselling author

Also by Patricia Davids

The Amish of Cedar Grove

THE PROMISE
THE HOPE
THE WISH

Look for Patricia Davids's next novel
A Match Made at Christmas
available from HQN.

For a complete list of books by Patricia Davids,
visit www.patriciadavids.com.

PATRICIA DAVIDS

The INN at HARTS HAVEN

HQN

HQN

ISBN-13: 978-1-335-42757-1

Recycling programs
for this product may
not exist in your area.

The Inn at Harts Haven

First published in 2022. This edition published in 2022.

Copyright © 2022 by Patricia MacDonald

For questions and comments about the quality of this book,
please contact us at CustomerService@Harlequin.com.

HQN
22 Adelaide St. West, 41st Floor
Toronto, Ontario M5H 4E3, Canada
www.Harlequin.com

Printed and bound in Barcelona, Spain by CPI Black Print

This book is lovingly dedicated to my youngest brother, Gary. I love that you like cats and that you gave a giant stray dog like Mika a home. I love how much we laugh when we get together. I adore that I can call you with research questions for my book, like "Can illegal drugs be baled into straw and transported on trucks?" I love that you respect wildlife and keep them in mind when you're farming by leaving cover and crops for them. You're a good man and I'm proud to be your sister. Any time you need me to help you rope two bucks with their antlers locked together and free them again, just call.

The INN at HARTS HAVEN

One

This has got to work. God, I'm so scared.

Victoria Abigail Worthington used one trembling hand to pull some of her curly long blond hair forward to obscure her face. She rubbed her damp palms on the sides of her jeans, took a deep breath then burst out of the restroom at the last possible moment to catch her bus.

Hurrying across the terminal in the Kansas City station, she dashed out to the bus departing for St. Louis. Her heart hammered in her chest when she was forced to stand behind a man huffing as he hauled a suitcase up the two steps. She expected to feel a hand grab her shoulder at any second.

Finally, she entered the vehicle. The door closed behind her. She looked back for the first time. The bus station was busy with travelers coming and going. She didn't see anyone she recognized, but she didn't know all her father's men. No one appeared to be searching for someone. For her.

The knot in her stomach loosened. Her pounding heart slowed. She moved to the back of the bus and sank onto a vacant seat two rows from the bathroom. So far, so good, but this was only a single step in her escape plan. Step one had been getting out of her father's estate undetected. Step two had been getting on this outbound bus without being stopped. The trip to St. Louis would take just over four hours. The bus would make a brief layover in Columbia in two hours' time. That would be step three, and the most crucial one to throw off any pursuit. She had a long way to go.

She didn't breathe easy until the bus left the city and was heading east on the interstate. As the suburbs fell away behind her, she briefly closed her eyes. She needed rest but couldn't afford to let her guard down. Her father and her ex-boyfriend Logan would do everything in their power to get her back. Stopping a bus and having her hauled off would be a piece of cake for men with their connections. All she could do was pray her absence wouldn't be noticed for at least four hours. A four-hour lead was crucial for her plan to work.

An hour and fifty minutes later she glanced around carefully. It was almost midnight and everyone she saw was nodding off, staring out at the night or reading by the light of the little overhead spots. No one paid any attention to her as she made her way to the restroom at the back of the bus.

Inside the stall that reeked of industrial-grade air freshener over less pleasant odors, she opened her backpack and pulled out a change of clothes. Her fingers shook as she slipped out of her faded jeans and bright pink T-shirt. She pulled on a dress that she had sewn from a set of her dark blue sheets. It reached to her midcalf and was gathered slightly at the waist with three-quarter-length sleeves, a style worn by thousands of Amish women. She slipped a matching apron over her shoulders and tied it in back. Next, she ruthlessly brushed her frizzy blond curls into sleek submission, parted her hair in the middle and twisted it up to the back of her head and pinned it in place.

Turning her yellow backpack inside out so that only the gray lining showed, she stuffed her jeans and shirt into it. She didn't have another pair of shoes. The serviceable black ones she had "borrowed" from one of the housekeepers were a half size too small but nondescript enough to escape notice. She then scrubbed every trace of makeup from her face with the dribble of cold water from the faucet and paper towels.

Finally, she settled a white Amish *kapp* on her head and smoothed the ribbons that hung loose on each side of her neck. It was the head covering her Amish grandmother, Miriam Martin, had made for her seven years ago. It was a treasured memento from the woman who'd loved her, and now it was a key part of her disguise.

She looked at her transformation in the cracked mirror. The heavily made-up woman with wild curly hair was gone. In her place stood a plain, modest, young Amish maiden. "Thank you, Grandma Martin."

No, she must speak *Deitsh*.

"*Danki*, Grossmammi." Her accent wasn't quite right, but no one would notice unless they were very familiar with the Amish. She tucked her brush in with her clothes. Picking up her backpack, she hooked the drawstring closure over her shoulder then opened the lavatory door and checked outside. Nothing had changed. No one was looking her way. She dropped Logan's credit card on the floor where anyone could find it. Proof that she had gotten on this bus and was heading for St Louis and then on to Miami, Florida, when in fact she was going back to Kansas. She glanced in the broken mirror one last time.

"Goodbye, Victoria Abigail Worthington. May *Gott* protect you."

She pressed a hand to her midsection and thought of the new life growing inside her. Her unborn babe was the reason she had found the courage to leave her father's house. She couldn't call it home. It had never been that, only her prison. "This is going to work, sweet one. I'll find a way to keep you safe. I promise."

The bus slowed down and turned. It came to a full stop and the intercom crackled. "Columbia." She stepped out and joined the trickle of passengers heading for the exit. She kept her head down in case there were cameras. It was essential to her plan that no one see Victoria getting off the bus.

Inside the terminal she saw people waiting in line to board the bus as the departing passengers met with others or left the building. Among the people leaving was a large Amish family. The father gathered up their suitcases as the mother shepherded the children toward the exit. It was good that she wasn't the only Amish person present. It meant she was less likely to stand out.

She went to the counter. "I'd like to purchase a ticket to Hutchinson, Kansas. I'll pay cash."

"Name?" A tired-looking, gray-haired woman slouched behind the counter.

"Abigail Martin." It wasn't the name she had been born with, but it was who she would become. Her grandmother had always called her Abby. She'd never liked the name Victoria. It was too *Englisch* sounding. Not a plain name. When Abby was older, she wondered if it wasn't really because she had been named after her father, Victor Worthington III, the man who had taken Miriam's only child away from her family and her faith.

"I'll need to see a photo ID." The booking agent looked up but didn't smile.

Abby hadn't planned for this contingency. Her father had never let her learn to drive. The Amish didn't drive and so didn't have licenses. She didn't think she would need an ID. "I'm afraid I don't have one."

"No ID, no ticket."

She had used one of Logan's credit cards and his laptop to purchase a "gift" ticket to Miami and had picked it up in the Kansas City terminal using the confirmation number instead of an ID. She wanted her father to track her all the way to Miami because she wouldn't be there when he came looking for her.

Now what? Panic rose like bile in her throat. "I must get to Hutchinson. It's important."

The woman's expression softened. "First time traveling, dearie?"

"Ja." Abby didn't have to fake the catch in her voice.

The woman glanced around. "I saw your family here a moment ago, didn't I?"

Did she mean the other Amish people? Abby clutched at that straw. "They've gone outside."

"We do make rare exceptions for the Amish, but you really should get a no-picture ID if you are going to travel."

Relief made Abby's knees weak. "I will. *Danki.* I mean, thank you."

She paid for her ticket with the cash she had taken from Logan's pockets over the past weeks. He was careless with his money and never noticed, but she had only taken what she needed to get away. She tucked her last three dollars into her pocketbook and picked up her ticket.

After that she took a seat and kept one eye on the door as people came and went. She stiffened when a police officer walked through, but he barely glanced her way. She kept her gaze down and noticed a copy of a newspaper the Amish family had left behind. It was *The Budget*, an Amish periodical read nationwide by the plain folk. She picked it up and pretended to read as the officer completed his rounds and walked past her again.

When he left, she used the paper to fan her hot face. Had he been looking for her this far from the city? Had her escape been discovered already? Her father wasn't likely to have called in the police. Not when he had a small army of men working for his security company at his disposal, but it was possible. She couldn't trust anyone.

Waiting for her boarding call turned into the longest thirty minutes of her life. When it finally came without the officer's return, she boarded the bus going back to Kansas City, still clutching the newspaper. The bus would stop briefly in KC. She could only pray her absence hadn't been discovered but if it had, her father's men would be looking for her to board a bus heading out of town. She was banking on the fact that they wouldn't check inside a bus that had just arrived. To be safe she never looked up from the newspaper.

A want ad caught her eye. *Amish maid needed full-time. Apply at Harts Haven Inn.* Harts Haven was a little over five miles from her grandmother's house. It would be perfect if she could get the job. Otherwise she would be begging charity from the local Amish bishop until she found employment. She knew he would help, even if reluctantly.

The Amish took care of one another, but she needed to be able to take care of herself and her baby.

An elderly couple took the seat in front of Abby. She chanced a look back. Two men in dark suits stood off to the side of the building watching the passengers boarding another bus. She knew them. A third man came out of the building and stopped beside them. It was Logan. Her escape had been discovered.

Her father would have men checking the airports and car rental companies, but the hints that she had dropped to Logan had brought him here exactly as she had hoped they would. Only she didn't expect him to get here so quickly. She needed more time.

Please, God, don't let him check this bus.

Her mouth went dry with fear as her pulse pounded in her ears. After several agonizing minutes the bus pulled slowly out of the station. Logan didn't look in her direction. The bus turned the corner, and she lost sight of him.

Logan Brewer, her baby's father. A man who pretended to love her but had only used her to move up in her father's firm. Tears sprang to her eyes. He was every bit as ruthless as her father. What a fool she had been to believe his whispered words of love. She had wanted so badly to be loved. Once she gave in to him, he quickly became controlling and then abusive, emotionally and physically. Just like her father.

She let her head fall back against the seat. Never again would she allow a man to touch her heart. From now on she could only depend on herself.

Once the bus was on the open highway, Abby closed her eyes and drew a deep breath of free air. She had done it. Then for the first time in twenty-four hours, she gave in to the luxury of sleep.

* * *

Ten hours later, Abigail Martin started to knock on the door of an unfamiliar two-story house in Harts Haven, Kansas, but the sound of raised voices inside made her pause. She looked for some indication that she was in the right place. There weren't any electric lines coming to the property. That meant it had to be an Amish home, but there wasn't a sign out front to prove it was the Harts Haven Inn she was looking for.

The directions she had gotten from the young Amish boy riding his bike past the bus stop where she stumbled off the nauseating bus twenty minutes outside of Hutchinson, Kansas, had seemed simple enough. The inn was at Rose Yoder's home. The place was only a stone's throw east at the second intersection in Harts Haven.

As the town had only four streets, she didn't think she could have taken a wrong turn, but the boy clearly threw rocks farther than she could. She had walked more than a quarter of a mile east before spotting this place tucked off the road on a tree-lined lane.

With nowhere else to go and only three dollars in her pocketbook, Abby took a deep breath and knocked. If this was the place looking to hire an Amish maid, she had to get the job.

Be modest. Keep your eyes downcast. Be humble. Never draw attention to yourself. She could hear her grandmother coaching her on how a proper Amish girl behaved. It was good advice for a woman wishing to hide her identity, too.

The voices grew louder, but no one answered the door. Abby's mother had once told her that any Amish home would welcome an Amish traveler. Their doors were never locked. She tried the knob. It opened, and she stepped inside.

Please let this be the place.

She followed the voices to a kitchen that appeared to be in the middle of a renovation. There was no stove and no refrigerator that she could see. Half the kitchen cupboards were hung, but they didn't match the lower cabinets. Several large crates were lined up waiting to be opened.

Three women sat at a square gray card table off to one side with cups of coffee in front of them. Two of them were Amish by their clothing. The third woman appeared to be an Old Order Mennonite. Her modest dress was a light blue print with tiny white flowers. Amish women wore only solid colors. All three of the women were older with gray hair beneath white *kapps.*

The Mennonite woman crossed her arms over her chest and glared at the younger Amish woman facing her. "I still think we should have a bar. All the best places do."

The Amish woman slapped a hand to her forehead. "Are you joking? The bishop would have a heart attack if we suggested such a thing."

"Did I have strawberry jam for breakfast or was that boysenberry?" The most elderly of the trio absentmindedly chewed on the ribbon of her *kapp.* "Grape jelly gives me indigestion, and I have a touch of it now."

"Excuse me." Abby took a step into the room. No one noticed. "I've come about the ad in the paper."

The Mennonite woman raised her hands in the air. "Susanna King, I have no idea why you think your bishop would object to us having a breakfast bar."

"You expect to serve alcohol first thing in the morning? And you think Bishop Wyse would be okay with that?" the one called Susanna asked, aghast.

"People serve themselves food at a breakfast bar, Susanna. Not alcoholic beverages," the Mennonite woman said calmly. "That way we won't have to hire waitstaff for the morning meal."

"Oh." Susanna looked mollified.

The small elderly woman nodded as she mumbled, "I believe it was peach preserves. Definitely apricot jam."

Abby took a step back. Maybe this wasn't the best time to ask for a job.

The movement caught the jam woman's attention. She smiled brightly at Abby. "Oh, look. Our new maid has arrived."

The other two women stopped glaring at each other and turned their frowning faces toward Abby.

She took another step back. "If this is a bad time I can come back later." Not that she had anyplace to go.

"Nonsense." The little woman jumped spryly off her chair and rushed to take Abby by the hand. "Come in, my dear. You must be tired after your long journey."

Abby sighed. "I am."

The woman tipped her head to the side for a long moment as she gazed at Abby. She smiled and squeezed Abby's fingers gently. "You're home now. We'll discuss your other problem when you're settled in."

Abby wondered what the woman was referring to. She couldn't possibly know about the trouble Abby was in.

The tall woman's frown deepened. "Mamm, what are you talking about?"

The small woman winked at Abby. "Don't mind my daughter. Susanna likes to believe she's on top of things. We're three widows trying to run a business, but it seems to be running us into the ground. We're remodeling the kitchen in case you didn't notice. I'm Rose Yoder."

"I'm Abigail Martin. Are you offering me the job?" Her hopes rose for the first time in weeks.

"Absolutely." Rose patted Abby's hand again.

That earned a stern glance from Susanna. "We should discuss this, Mamm."

"All right, dear, in a minute. This is Grace Sutter. A fine woman but not Amish." Rose gestured toward the Mennonite lady then leaned close to Abby and whispered, "Which is a shame because Bishop Wyse is a widower now. They were close before she broke his heart by choosing not to join the Amish faith and marrying a Mennonite farmer."

Grace shook her head. "Rose, I wish you would stop repeating that story. There isn't a grain of truth in it. I only moved to this area three years ago."

"And you have made a wonderful addition to our community. As will Abigail. Come along and I will show you to your room."

That took Abby aback. "My room?"

"It's a live-in position. Didn't I make that clear in my advertisement?"

"What advertisement?" Susanna asked. "This is the first we've heard about hiring a maid. When did you come to this decision without consulting us?"

Rose shook her head sadly. "Honestly, Susanna. Sometimes I think you don't listen to me. I told you last month that I was going to put an ad in *The Budget*."

"I thought you were talking about an ad for the inn. Letting people know that we will be open in time for the state fair at the end of the summer."

"Is that what you thought? Has anyone seen my cat? Her food bowl hasn't been touched."

"My dear," Grace said gently. "Your cat died six months ago."

Rose nodded slowly. "That would explain why she isn't eating."

Susanna got to her feet. "I need to leave for my shift at the lumberyard, I'm already running late. When I get home this evening, we'll discuss this, Mamm."

"As you wish. Come along, Abigail. Tell me all about yourself. You're the first person I've ever met from New Mexico."

"I'm not from New Mexico. I came from Missouri." Abby followed her with a puzzled glance back at the two women in the kitchen, who were listening with interest.

"Do you know anyone who is from New Mexico?" Rose asked.

"I'm afraid I don't."

"We have something in common, then." Rose headed down a hall toward the back of the house. "When is your baby due?"

Shock brought Abby up short. How could this woman possibly tell she was pregnant? She was only three months along and not showing in her loose-fitting Amish dress. "What makes you think I'm expecting?"

Rose cackled. "I've been a midwife for fifty years. I knew the minute I saw your face. Pregnant women have an inner beauty that just shines."

Abby had hoped to conceal her condition for a few months yet, until she was free of her father's control, but she couldn't lie or deny her child. "I wish you wouldn't mention it to the others." She stared at her feet. "I don't have a husband."

Rose dismissed Abby's confession with a wave of her hand. "I gathered as much. Young Amish girl travels far from New Mexico seeking a job in an out-of-the-way place in Kansas. Don't worry. I promise I won't say anything until you're ready to share your blessed news. Rest and take care of yourself. Everything will be fine."

"You can call me Abby." Tears pricked the back of Abby's eyes. She quickly blinked them away. Of all the things she expected when her pregnancy became known, unconditional acceptance was not near the top of her list.

Rose opened the next to last door in the hall and went in. "This will be your room. The bathroom is across the hall. It's a bit stuffy in here. I'll open a window."

The whine of a power saw, and the smell of fresh-cut wood came in with a warm May breeze. Rose faced Abby. "That's better. Supper is at seven. We'll talk about your duties in the morning. Why don't you take a nap? This evening I'll give you a tour of the place. Now I really must find my cat."

It was a shame such a sweet woman wasn't quite with it. Abby laid a hand on Rose's shoulder. "Grace said your cat passed away."

Rose chuckled, looked about and then dropped to her knees to peer under the bed. She withdrew a smoky gray feline and stood up with the purring cat in her arms. "Phebe died. Wilma tends to get shut in the rooms by our guests or when someone is cleaning."

Abby frowned. "Don't your daughter and Grace know you have another cat?"

"Wilma doesn't like them. She stays out of their way. Grace doesn't care for cats. She's a bird-watcher, you know. I'm too old to hide under the bed, but there are days I consider doing it anyway." Rose walked out and closed the door behind her.

What a strange little woman.

Abby sat on the edge of the bed, gripping her backpack as she looked around. This was her room now. The bed was covered with a soft cream-and-blue quilt. A walnut chest of drawers stood against one wall with a small mirror above it. A matching bedside table held a kerosene lamp and several books. The walls were painted a pastel blue. Sheer white curtains drifted in and out with the breeze. It was a room much like the one she had stayed in as a child when she spent summers with her Amish grandparents. It felt welcoming. The sound of the saw cutting wood stopped, and a sense of peace filled her heart.

She pressed a hand to her stomach and rubbed softly. "This morning we had nothing but a few clothes and a newspaper ad. Now I have a job and a place for us to stay. I told you I was going to take care of you."

Her far-fetched plan to blend into the Amish community and eventually join the faith of her beloved grandparents was working. Provided her father or Logan didn't find her.

She closed her eyes. "I'm going to work hard and save my money. In a few months I'll have enough to hire an attorney. Then he will help me find a doctor to prove I'm not mentally unbalanced as my father insists. I'm not sick anymore. I'll show the court that I'm competent, that I don't need a guardian controlling my life. When the courts agree, the house and land my grandfather left me will be mine free and clear no matter what my father says."

She crossed her arms over her tummy. "We'll have a home of our own, and I'll have you to love. I'll keep you safe always."

Please, God. That's all I want.

It would not be easy to get out from under her father's thumb. Victor Worthington had money and lawyers who twisted the law to suit him. Lawyers like Logan. No one took what belonged to Victor. She would have to be very sure she had everything in place before she filed a motion with the courts.

A yawn caught Abby unaware. Rose's suggestion of a nap was an excellent idea. She hadn't managed more than catnaps on the bus. The whine of the saw started again. Sleep with that kind of noise wasn't going to happen.

She got up to close the window and caught sight of the man operating the power tools in the yard beside the inn. He must be the one doing the kitchen remodel. She thought he was Amish or Mennonite because of his clothing. He wore a blue shirt with the sleeves rolled up, dark blue trousers and suspenders over his wide shoulders. A straw hat was pushed back on his head. Chestnut brown hair clung to his forehead and temples in sweat-soaked ringlets peppered with sawdust. His face was strong, chiseled, with a leanness in his suntanned cheeks that spoke of hard work and time spent outdoors. He didn't have a beard. That meant he was single.

Two young Amish women approached the split-rail fence that enclosed the yard where he was working. "Good afternoon to you, Joseph Troyer," the dark-haired one called out. Her blonde companion elbowed her and giggled. They were fresh-faced and friendly. Abby thought they must be near her age if not a little younger.

The man they called Joseph kept working.

"We said hello," the blonde shouted over the sound of the saw. She set a foil-covered plate on the fence.

He shut off his equipment and faced them. "I heard you."

"We came to invite you to a barn party," the dark-haired one said boldly.

"Not interested. I've got work to do." He turned away.

"It isn't until Sunday evening. You can't work on Sunday," she said with a faint frown of uncertainty on her young face.

"It's my day of rest." He switched the saw on and ignored them.

"We're just trying to be friendly to someone new. We brought you some brownies," the second girl shouted.

"You're wasting your time. I'm not interested in courting you or anyone else. Tell your friends not to bother stopping by to be nice to the new guy. I won't be here that long."

Abby saw the hurt and humiliation on their faces before they turned away. She knew exactly how it felt to be made to feel small. To be dismissed as if she didn't matter. She had endured it every day she was with her father. Sudden anger welled up inside her. It wasn't right to treat people that way.

The man finished his cut and shut off the saw. He happened to glance up and caught sight of her. "Did you want something?" he snapped.

She did. She wanted to tell him exactly what she thought of him. "I'm curious. Are you naturally so rude or do you have to keep practicing?" she asked, her words laden with as much sarcasm as she could muster.

His eyes widened, and his mouth dropped open in shock.

"You should be ashamed of yourself," she added, angry that he had treated the women so dismissively.

The shock on his face turned to a fierce scowl. "Are you finished? Who are you?"

Abby realized her mistake when he spoke. This was not how an Amish woman behaved. She pressed both hands to her lips. She'd never spoken like that to anyone in her life. Now had been a very poor time to start. She slammed the window shut and backed away.

Fifteen minutes inside an Amish home, and she had already given herself away.

She peered through the curtains. He was still looking at her room. She sat down on the bed and clenched her hands together. She might as well wear a sign that said she was a fake. No one would believe she was Amish after speaking so rudely to an Amish fellow she didn't even know. He was sure to tell others about her behavior. Would she lose the job she desperately needed? What had she done?

Two

Joe Troyer stared at the window of the room where the young woman had retreated from sight after delivering her scathing rebuke. Who was she? He hadn't seen her at the inn or around town.

"That's a first for me, Joe."

He turned to see his boss standing a few feet away. Oliver Hershberger was the owner of Mennonite Builders, the firm Joe had worked for since he was seventeen. If it hadn't been for Oliver giving him a place to stay after the fire, Joe didn't know what he would have done. Oliver's offer had been his deliverance at the darkest moment of his life.

Joe arched one eyebrow. "What's a first for you, boss?"

Oliver nodded toward the window overlooking the side yard. "I've never heard an Amish woman speak to anyone in that sarcastic tone. Who is she?"

Joe began cleaning around his saw. "I have no idea, but she clearly had no problem speaking her mind. I haven't been scolded like that since I was eight years old and my *mamm* caught me trying to cut my sister's hair."

He deserved the reprimand then and now. He owed an apology to the two young women who were only being kind. When had he become so jaded? He avoided people as much as possible, but he had never deliberately hurt someone's feelings, had he?

"Does she work here?" Oliver asked.

Joe shrugged. "No idea. Never laid eyes on her before."

Oliver punched Joe playfully on the shoulder. "Well, I don't think you made a good first impression."

"That isn't such a bad thing." Joe normally dismissed young women out of hand. He never intended to marry so there was no point in getting friendly, but the sharp-tongued woman had caught his interest. "I'm sure Rose Yoder will supply me with the details of who the mystery woman is, whether I ask or not."

Oliver chuckled. "Rose is quite a character."

"She is. I haven't known her long, but I like her."

Rose reminded Joe of his grandmother Ada with her gentle ways and wry sense of humor. He missed her and all the members of his family. His parents, his three brothers, his sister, and sweet Kara, the girl he had planned to marry, had all been taken from him in one night in a fire that destroyed his home.

Kara had been staying over at the farm to help his mother with the baking that had to be done before the wedding dinner. On his last night as a single fellow he had slipped out to go to a party with some of his *Englisch* coworkers. A "bachelor party" the guys had called it. Foolishness. Joe had taken his baptismal vows. He knew he should have declined. He hadn't joined in the drinking, but simply attending such a party went against the church's teachings. He'd broken his vow of obedience.

Joe closed his eyes and saw in vivid detail the blazing inferno that had greeted him when he arrived home before dawn. It was a scene that still filled his nightmares. Every member of his family gone except for him. He should have been there to save them. He should have perished with them. Why had God allowed him to survive when everyone he loved was gone?

Nothing could change the way he had failed them. He shut away the painful memories and looked at his boss. "What can I do for you?"

"I just stopped in to see how you're getting along. Any problems?"

"None so far, but I've only finished the demolition of the outside wall. Once I get the framing in place and a tarp up to keep the elements out, I'll be good to start inside."

"Any chance that you'll need another man?"

"I don't see why. It's a straightforward job. A couple more weeks at the most."

"I thought you would say that. You're the only man I've got that likes to work all by his lonesome. I just got the bid on a big machine shed build over by Kingman. The fellow wants a rush job so I'm gonna put the rest of the crew out there. Oh, and I brought the propane tank you asked for. I'll unload it by your trailer."

"Let me give you a hand. Do you mind taking back my empty?"

"Not at all. I've got to stop at the lumberyard on my way out of town anyway."

The two men began walking toward Joseph's camping trailer that had been set up in the shade of a tree beside the

barn. A white pickup truck with the Mennonite Builders
logo in red letters on the doors was parked in front of it.
Three brown horses stood watching them over the corral
fence. One mare with a white blaze on her face laid back
her ears and nipped her neighbor on his neck. He beat a
quick retreat. A young colt came galloping up to see what
was going on.

Joe and Oliver installed the forty-pound propane tank
on the rack at the rear of the trailer. Joe carried the empty
tank around and lifted it into the bed of Oliver's truck. "I'll
get word to you if I need anything. You have the number,
right?"

"I do."

Like most Amish, Rose shared a community phone with
her neighbors. The small building that housed it was a quarter mile south of her lane. Oliver could leave a message for
Joe on the answering machine there.

Oliver nodded toward the house. "Get it done on time
and on budget. This could bring more work our way if the
widows like it. Don't let me down."

Joe crossed his arms over his chest. "I won't. I promise."

Abby lay on the bed staring at the ceiling. Her need for
sleep had vanished. She expected a knock on the door at
any moment with one of the widows telling her to pack her
bag. She hadn't bothered unpacking following her sudden
outburst of righteous indignation. What had the stranger
made of her behavior? She had shocked him. She'd seen
that plain enough.

Amish women were meek and humble. They never drew
attention to themselves. Oh, but she had drawn his attention. Shame rounded her shoulders. Her behavior hadn't
been any better than his.

She covered her face with her hands. How could she have messed up so badly? Escaping her father would only work if she disappeared by blending into the Amish world and becoming one of them. Eventually he was sure to check if she had gone to her grandmother Miriam's house. She couldn't go there. Not yet. Her father had control of the estate that was rightfully hers. Anyone living there would likely know him and report her presence.

She needed this job and a place to stay until she was ready to make her move. Begging charity from the local Amish bishop until she found employment was still an option if all else failed, but she didn't like the idea. She needed to start earning money as soon as possible.

If you are there, God, please don't let Rose fire me.

After fifteen minutes ticked away, Abby got up. She couldn't take waiting any longer to find out if she was going to lose her job.

She walked to the mirror to make sure her *kapp* was on straight. The still-unfamiliar face looking back resembled death warmed over. There were dark circles under her eyes. Abby pinched some color into her pale cheeks and smoothed what little of her hair was visible.

She missed her wild, wavy mane that reached to the middle of her back. Hiding behind her hair to shield her emotions and thoughts was second nature. This stern Amish hairstyle left her face completely exposed. It was unnerving, but in a way it was the perfect disguise. She was hiding in plain sight. How many people who knew her or her father had really seen her?

Only one. Logan.

She frowned at the reflection of a gullible fool. "Logan said he loved me, but he lied." *Why couldn't he love me? Why doesn't Father love me? What's wrong with me?*

Abby straightened her shoulders. Such thinking would only lead her back to that dark time in her past. She left her room and went downstairs prepared to beg Rose to let her keep the job.

She walked into the kitchen, expecting to see the women. Instead, he was standing at the kitchen table pouring coffee from a thermos into a white mug. The smell made her stomach rumble. She hadn't eaten since yesterday morning.

He glanced her way. She dropped her gaze to her feet and clasped her hands in front of her. "Where is Rose?"

"No idea. I haven't seen her since this morning."

Abby looked up. "You haven't spoken to her?"

"Nope." He tilted the thermos in her direction. "Want some?"

Was he extending an olive branch? "I guess."

He crossed to the cupboard and pulled out a matching white mug. He filled it with coffee and set it on the counter. He leaned casually against one of the crates and crossed one booted foot over the other. She picked up the mug then took a step away from him.

A wry grin lifted one corner of his mouth. "I don't bite. You don't have to be scared of me."

She raised her chin. "What makes you think I'm afraid of you?"

"My mistake, then. What did you want to see Rose about?"

"I thought she might have second thoughts about hiring me now."

"Because?"

Was he toying with her? He knew exactly why. She stared at him intently. He seemed genuinely curious. Had she blown the incident out of proportion in her own mind? "Because I spoke rudely to you."

He shrugged. "You had cause."

That surprised her. "I did?" She quickly cleared her throat. "I mean, I did. You were very rude to those young women."

"I don't spend much time around people. I'm easily irritated." He took a sip of his coffee.

"You should work on that."

He sputtered out his drink and coughed a couple of times. She resisted the urge to pound his back. When he recovered, he stared at her with wide eyes. "Do you always say what you think?"

"It's a newly acquired skill." She wasn't blurting out everything that crossed her mind, or she would have mentioned that he was a handsome fellow when he wasn't scowling. She liked the sound of his voice, too. It was low and smooth with the characteristic lilting German accent so prevalent among the Amish.

She set her coffee mug down. "Somewhere in this conversation I'm supposed to apologize for the way I spoke to you earlier."

"Apology accepted. I'm Joseph Troyer. Folks call me Joe. You said that Rose hired you. What are you going to do here?"

That was it? Apology accepted? No other digs at her? Did the Amish really forgive those who offended them so readily?

"I'm Abigail Martin. Abby. The ad I answered was for a maid. Rose said she would give me a tour of the place this evening and go over my duties tomorrow."

"I don't expect you'll be busy. The inn isn't officially open." He took another sip of coffee, but his eyes were on her—as if he truly saw her. It was unsettling.

"Das goot." She played up her knowledge of Pennsylva-

nia Dutch. "This is my first job. I'd hate to be overwhelmed right off the bat."

He cocked his head to one side. "Your first job? How old are you?"

Now what mistake had she made? "What does my age have to do with anything?"

"Most young women get some kind of job to help out their families as soon as they finish school."

"My *daed* didn't allow it." It was best to keep as close to the truth as possible. She had learned that lesson well when dealing with her father's temper.

"Lucky family if you didn't need the extra money. I'm sure you'll do fine here although Rose can be forgetful. If you have any questions, you should ask Grace. She ran a bed-and-breakfast in Shipshewana."

"Is that near here?"

His mouth dropped open. "Shipshewana? Ship-she? It's a big Amish and Mennonite settlement in Indiana. A popular tourist spot."

"Oh, right. I knew that." She tried to laugh it off. "I guess I'm still a little foggy after my long bus ride."

"Where did you come from?"

Her smile froze on her face while her mind raced. How should she answer that? Why hadn't she come up with a story. People were bound to ask. "Missouri."

His grin widened. "I've worked out that way. Maybe I know some of your people."

She had to get out of the kitchen before he asked for more details. "I doubt it. Thanks for the coffee. I've got to find Rose."

"Okay." His frown came back.

She forced herself to walk out of the kitchen when every cell in her body was screaming for her to run. She didn't look for Rose. Instead she hurried to her room, shut the door and leaned against it. She pressed a hand to her chest, feeling her heart hammering against her ribs.

Becoming Abigail Martin was harder than she had imagined.

Abby was definitely an odd woman. Joe couldn't quite put his finger on it, but he got the sense that she was hiding something.

He shrugged. Whatever it was, it had nothing to do with him. He had a job to do in Harts Haven. In a couple of weeks he would hook his trailer behind Oliver's truck, and his boss would take him to his next job. It didn't matter where.

And that was the way he liked it.

Joe measured the opening he would need for the new doorway and went out to cut the two-by-fours. He had the framing finished when Rose came into the kitchen a half hour later. "You've gotten a lot done today, Joe. It's time to wash up for supper."

"I'd rather eat in my trailer tonight if it's all the same to you."

She spun around and planted her hands on her hips with all the indignation of an angry biddy hen. "What's wrong with eating at my table? Has the company of three old women become too boring to bear?"

He tucked his tape measure in his tool belt and held up both hands. "Don't take my head off. That's already been done today."

"Did you deserve it?"

"Maybe. Okay, yeah. I did."

"*Goot*. It is a reminder to be humble. You will eat with us this evening and that is the end of it. I want you to meet someone." Her eyes narrowed. "Unless you are having company tonight."

He stepped over to her and draped his arm around her shoulder. Her head barely reached the top button of his shirt. "Rose, you know you are the only woman for me in this town."

She playfully pushed him away. "Bah! There are plenty of women who might interest you if you bothered to look their way. Take my new maid, Abigail, for instance."

"You can't be matchmaking for her already. She only stepped off the bus this morning."

Rose's eyes narrowed. "And how do you know that?"

"We've met," he said, not wanting to share the details of their first exchange.

"What do you think of her?"

"She's not as demure as most Amish girls her age."

Rose waved aside his comment. "That's because she's from New Mexico. The Amish are different in the West."

He smothered a laugh. "Are they? I didn't know there *was* an Amish community in New Mexico. Abby said she was from Missouri."

"Did she? You seem to have learned quite a bit about her."

"We visited over a cup of coffee, that's all."

"Don't ask about her past. It's a sad subject. I reckon the same could be said for you."

He didn't want to talk about himself. "What makes Abby's past sad?"

Rose gave a quick wave of her hand. "Oh, here I am gossiping away. Shame on me. Go wash up. Supper will be ready in ten minutes. It's a blessing Karen Garth next door is letting us use her kitchen. I'll sure be glad when you can hook up my new stove."

"It'll be here tomorrow. I'll connect it to your propane line then you can cook to your heart's content. Tonight, I'll take supper in my trailer. I've had enough visitors today."

He started to leave the room but turned back to look at her. "Rose, did you put out the word that a single Amish man was working for you?"

She pulled her *kapp* ribbon to her mouth and nibbled on it. "I might have."

"I thought so. I imagine you said baked goods were high on the list of things I enjoy?"

"You can't deny you like *goot* cooking. How were the brownies?"

"How did you know—never mind. I enjoy your cooking, but I don't care for your matchmaking efforts."

She grinned. "You will when the right *maydel* comes along. I'll bring your supper out tonight, but I won't make it a habit."

"Danki."

He went outside and made sure the tarp over the open wall was secure before heading to his camper. He opened the door and saw a pie sitting on his step. Another gift. From a shy hopeful *maydel* this time?

Oliver had warned Joe that Rose fancied herself a matchmaker. Joe figured his temporary presence in the community would make him a poor candidate. Apparently, he'd been mistaken. Rose would just have to put out the word that he wasn't interested in settling down.

He set the dish in the last clear spot on his counter beside the stack of unwashed plates, flatware and glasses, then collapsed onto his worn brown-plaid easy chair and pulled off his work boots. He wiggled his toes in relief. One sock had a small hole in the toe. He'd fix that some other time.

Sewing wasn't one of his favorite domestic skills. He pulled his socks off and tossed them on the dinette.

Laundry day wasn't until Friday. It was only Monday, and his hamper was already overflowing onto the floor by the mini propane-powered washer just outside his bedroom door. He'd wear the socks a few more days yet.

He considered getting out of his chair to get something cold to drink from his little fridge but decided it was too much effort. Instead he pulled the book he'd been reading out of the side pocket of his chair and opened it to the page with the folded corner and resumed the story of a couple's experience living in the wilds of Alaska. It was one place he hadn't been to.

A little later there was a quiet rap on his door. Expecting Rose with his supper, he called out, "Come in."

The door opened and Abby came up the single step with a covered plate in her hand. "Grace sent me with your meal."

He shot to his feet, suddenly embarrassed about the condition of his place. "Set it anywhere." He snatched up the overflowing laundry hamper and shoved it into the tiny bedroom on his unmade bed. He closed the door with an unintended bang and turned to face her with his hands in his pockets.

She was holding his socks. The dinette was the only spot left to put a plate. He grabbed them from her, tossed them into the bedroom and shut the door again. She was looking around with interest. "This is cozy. I've always wondered what the inside of a camper looked like."

"They come a lot fancier, but I don't need much. This suits me."

"I see. Well, I should get back."

"What did Rose say about your job?"

She quickly looked at her feet. "I haven't had the chance to speak to her."

The silence stretched for several minutes. He couldn't think of a single thing to say.

"Does your boss supply his workers with campers?" she asked at last.

"He doesn't. I own this one. Most fellas will work within driving distance of their homes. The men usually catch rides with their non-Amish coworkers to the site. I prefer this arrangement."

"How do you get it to your next job?"

"Oliver hauls me where I need to go. He owns a construction business out of Hutchinson."

"You mentioned you had worked in Missouri. That's a long way from Hutchinson."

"Oliver is a member of the Mennonite Disaster Service."

"My *daadi* told me about them when I was little. They helped after a tornado struck the next town over one summer."

"Volunteers like Oliver provide the skilled labor and materials needed to rebuild in the wake of a disaster anywhere in the United States and Canada. I've worked from the Mexican border into Canada and from Colorado to Florida."

Her eyes roved over his trailer. "Don't you sometimes wish for a real house?"

"Nope. My camper is my home wherever it is parked. I attend Amish services in whatever community I'm staying in." That was how he liked it.

She tipped her head slightly as she stared at him. "You don't have a real home? What about friends and your family? Don't you miss them?"

"I get along with the guys on Oliver's crew. Oliver is my family."

"That is so sad. I'm sorry."

Her words touched a nerve he didn't know was raw. "Don't waste your pity on me," he snapped. "Save it for someone who needs it. Weren't you just leaving?"

Her eyes narrowed and then flashed with anger as her chin came up. "Still practicing rudeness, I see. You're getting quite good at it."

"And you should learn to mind your own business instead of sticking your nose where it doesn't belong."

"I was simply trying to be nice." She stormed out, slamming the trailer door behind her before he could say he was sorry. Only maybe he wasn't. The woman had a way of getting under his skin. He didn't need or want her sympathy. He'd put this town behind him in a couple of weeks and forget all about her.

He picked up the plate she had left and returned to his chair. His life wasn't sad. What gave her the right to judge him? His life was an adventure. Always a new place filled with new people.

Not everyone wanted to settle down in one place, see the same people day after day, hear the same voices. He put his untouched food aside and stared at the door. Why did he care what she thought?

Maybe he did miss the closeness and the laughter that had filled his family's home, but he tried not to think about it. God took that away from him once. God could do it again. It wasn't worth the risk.

Joe knew in his heart that he hadn't paid for his sin yet.

No, it was best that he keep moving on. And better still that he ignore Rose's new maid while he was stuck in Harts Haven.

Three

Abby returned to the inn fuming and hurt by Joe's brusque dismissal. She shouldn't have bothered trying to be nice to him. In the future she would simply ignore his rude ways. She had more important things to worry about than his feelings. Like blending into the community and learning to become Amish.

The widows were sitting down at the card table in the kitchen for supper. Abby joined them. They folded their hands and bowed their heads to pray silently. It was the way her grandparents had started each meal. Always in silence for a minute or so until Grandpa signaled the prayer was over by picking up his fork. She had been taught to silently recite the *Gebet vor dem Essen*, the prayer before meals, followed by the Lord's Prayer.

The silence at the card table allowed Abby to quiet her mind and in doing so she was able to forgive Joe for his rude words. That's what her grandmother would have expected her to do. Abby had to start thinking Amish if she was to become one of them.

Rose cleared her throat, and everyone began eating. There was little talk. When the meal was finished, Rose and Susanna waited until Grace cleared the table. Rose smiled at Abby. "I was going to show you around, wasn't I?"

That didn't sound like she was ready to dismiss her new maid. Abby's spirits rose.

"Before you do, I'd like to say something." Susanna was looking at Abby.

"Yes, ma'am." Abby waited, wondering what Susanna had on her mind.

"It was brought to my attention that you were outspoken and harsh with Joseph today."

So he *had* tattled on her. Abby pressed her lips together to keep from saying something about his behavior.

"It won't do," Susanna stressed. "Especially if we have guests about. Understood?"

"Ja." Abby nodded once. "I did apologize. It won't happen again."

She wanted to keep this job. No matter what Joseph Troyer did or said in the future she would bite her tongue and ignore him. She'd had plenty of practice swallowing her words over the years.

"Goot. Now we will forget it and not mention it again," Rose declared.

Susanna looked as if she wanted to say more, but she stayed quiet. Abby realized she had come close to being sent on her way. She breathed a silent prayer of thanks for her good fortune.

After the dishes were done, Rose led the way through the house giving Abby a peek into each room. It was a large and rambling place. Propane lamps suspended from the ceiling provided light in every room. Beside the kitchen there was a breakfast room with four round tables covered with red-and-white-checked tablecloths. A pair of French doors led to a colorful flower garden. At the front of the home was a living room for the family's use. Beside it was a cozy sitting room with overstuffed chairs and a sofa for the guests.

There were four guest bedrooms on the ground floor and four upstairs. Abby realized her room and the family's living quarters were actually in the *daadi haus* or "grandpa house," a small separate home connected by a hall to the main building. Rose outlined Abby's duties as they went along. Daily cleaning of all the guest rooms, bathrooms, common areas along with laundry from the inn. The laundry space was on the back porch where a ringer washer sat beside a galvanized rinse tub. The washer was propane powered. It looked daunting, but Abby was determined to learn to use it.

Rose turned to her. "I reckon that's all there is to the place. Do you have any questions?"

Abby looked around. "Is there a dryer?"

Rose laughed. "You're a funny one."

Abby flushed. How foolish of her. The Amish didn't use dryers when God provided sunshine and wind to do the job for free. "I thought perhaps you had one that ran on propane. Where is the clothesline?"

"Through that door." Rose opened it. Outside a pair of clotheslines stretched across a grassy yard. Grace was gathering sheets and folding them into her laundry basket as she went.

"We also have a couple of lines strung in the basement

for when it's too wet to hang things out. I'll leave you now to explore on your own. Don't stay up too late. You've had a long day."

Rose started to walk away but paused and looked back. "I want you to know that I'm very happy you found us. I hope you'll stay for a long time."

Her sincere words touched Abby's heart. It was wonderful to be wanted. "*Danki*, Rose."

Abby went to bed a short time later but had trouble getting to sleep. After the events of the past few days her mind wouldn't shut off. She kept replaying her exit from her father's house, wondering if she had left behind anything that would give her plans away. She had only used Logan's laptop to purchase her bus ticket. The rest of her planning had been done in her head. Her father should be looking for her in Miami by now.

Victor Worthington III was no fool. He ran an international private security firm with clients in every corner of the globe. It didn't matter if they were sheiks, politicians or criminals. If they had the money to pay for his services, he had the manpower to protect them. When he worked outside the law, he was careful to cover those dealings with a veneer of legitimacy. He employed well-paid lawyers like Logan who knew how to bend the law to their advantage.

Her father would try to track her down. She didn't doubt that. He didn't tolerate defiance. Not from his dogs, his men or his daughter. He controlled everyone and everything in his orbit with an iron hand.

She had always wondered why he'd married her meek ex-Amish mother. Or rather why her mother had married such a tyrant. If it had been for love, that emotion was long gone from their lives by the time her mother died when Abby was fourteen.

Her poor mother. Shunned by her Amish family for marrying outside the faith and trapped in an abusive marriage, she felt she had nowhere to go. Her only act of defiance had been her insistence that Abby spend the summers with her Amish grandparents. Abby suspected her father enjoyed sending her away to live in "squalor" as he called it. If he thought it would give her an appreciation for the life of luxury he provided, he was sadly mistaken. It was more likely he hadn't even noticed she was gone.

She cupped her hands over the tiny bulge in her tummy. It would be different for her child. Her son or daughter would know only love, never fear, neglect or abuse. It was the one promise she had to keep.

After a fitful night, Abby went downstairs ready to take up her new position. Rose was in the kitchen and so was Joe. Abby paused in the doorway. She was hungry but not hungry enough to sit beside him.

Rose caught sight of Abby before she could retreat. "Come in. There is fresh *kaffi* on my new stove, and I have fresh-baked rolls on the table. I believe you have met Joe."

"I have." The smell of the coffee and fresh-baked bread drew Abby into the room. She fixed a cup for herself and sat at the table across from him. Joe ignored her except to push the plate of cinnamon rolls closer. She self-consciously helped herself to one and took a bite. The crust was just crispy enough while the inside was wonderfully moist. Cinnamon, sugar and spices exploded in a burst of sweetness in her mouth. Someone was an excellent baker. Rose probably.

"Do you like it?" Rose asked, taking a seat at the table.

"This is so good," she muttered around her mouthful.

Rose smiled. "I'm glad. Now down to business. Joseph,

Abigail needs a husband, and you are an answer to her prayers."

"What? No!" Abby almost choked on her mouthful.

"Nee!" Joe all but shouted. They stared at each other in horror.

Rose looked disappointed as she shrugged. "Well, I thought it was worth a try. I'm something of a matchmaker hereabouts."

"I don't need or want a husband," Abby said to make sure he and Rose understood.

"And I'm not the marrying kind. I like my freedom," he said.

"If living in a cluttered little trailer is your idea of freedom, please save me from that," Abby snapped.

"Don't worry. You're safe, believe me."

"Kinder, kinder, the breakfast table is not the place to argue," Rose said, giving each a stern look.

They both fell silent. Abby concentrated on her coffee. A single glance at Joe's face told her he had taken Rose's point.

Kinder meant "children." Abby wasn't a child, and Joe wasn't the answer to hers or any other woman's prayer unless they wanted a gruff, bad-tempered, surly spouse who liked to carry tales.

Rose smiled. "That's better. Now I must go feed my cat." She got up, took a can of cat food from the cupboard and left the kitchen.

The uncomfortable silence lasted until Abby choked down the last of her roll with a sip of black coffee.

"Rose may be getting a little senile in her old age," Joe said.

Abby rolled her eyes. "That's pretty clear if she thinks we go together."

"She does get confused easily so please keep an eye on her while you are working here."

He sounded as if he cared about Rose. Abby's irritation with him faded. "I will. Did you tell Susanna I was impolite to you yesterday?"

"I did not."

"Someone did. There wasn't anyone else around."

"There was. My boss overheard you. He was shocked that an Amish person would speak in that manner. Maybe he repeated the tale. He said he planned to stop at the lumberyard. Susanna works there."

"Then I'm sorry I accused you."

"About Rose. Grace told me her cat died a few months ago but she still feeds it every morning."

Abby tried to hold back a laugh but failed.

He scowled at her. "What's so funny about that?"

Abby couldn't keep the grin off her face. "She has another cat. Phebe died. Wilma is alive and well. I've seen her, but she apparently avoids Grace, Susanna and you."

"Are you serious?"

"She's gray as smoke and prefers to hide under the beds."

His mouth tipped up at the corner in a half grin. "Maybe Rose isn't as confused as I thought." He sobered. "Except about us."

"Oh, right. She's way off base there." Abby swept her hand through the air. "Way off base."

He frowned but nodded. "Completely."

Abby relaxed but wondered why his assertion rankled when she felt the same way.

He needed to get to work, but Joe wasn't in a hurry to leave the table. Abby was pleasant to look at when she was smiling. She amused and surprised him when she wasn't annoying him. He didn't know what she would say next. He'd never met an Amish woman like her. She'd said Rose was "way off base." He'd never heard an Amish woman use that expression. It was something the *Englisch* would say.

"You must come from a progressive Amish community," he said, wondering where there was such a group in Missouri. The only Amish he'd met there were ultraconservative.

She stared at her plate. "What makes you say that?"

"I don't know. You talk like an *Englisch* girl. Do you have *Englisch* friends?" That would explain a lot.

"Some. I'll have to mend my ways here, won't I?"

"It's sort of refreshing."

"I don't want to stick out. That isn't right."

"Then maybe you shouldn't speak."

Her eyes widened. He thought he saw a flash of pain before she looked down. "I'll keep your advice in mind."

She pushed back from the table and left the room. Surely she didn't think he was serious about her keeping quiet. He'd been teasing.

It had been so long since he'd dealt with any young woman that he may have lost his ability to have an ordinary conversation. He was the one who should learn to keep his mouth shut. If he didn't say anything to Abby, he couldn't be called rude.

He got back to work outside cutting lumber to use for the studs in the new wall. Then he cut the plywood panels he needed for sheathing the outside. It was only the middle of May, but the day quickly grew from warm to hot. Halfway through the morning, Abby came out of the house with a tall glass of lemonade.

"Rose thought you might be thirsty," Abby said without looking at him.

"Danki." He took the glass and drained it in a few seconds. He handed it to her. "I'm sorry about this morning."

She glanced up and then kept her eyes downcast. "You didn't do anything wrong. Would you like more?"

"Nee, I'm fine now. It was *goot."*

She turned away without another word and went back in the house. He stood staring after her.

"She's a pretty girl, isn't she?" Rose said as she came up behind him.

"Well enough, I guess." He waited for one of her matchmaking suggestions.

"I think she's looking for peace and a place to call home. I hope she finds it here. Home isn't a place. It's the people we love and who love us in return that makes a place a true home." Rose turned her sharp gaze on him. "You're looking for a home, too."

He glanced away. "I had one once. It doesn't exist anymore." There was nothing for him there but a pile of ashes and the charred remains of his former life.

"Harts Haven is a fine place filled with *goot* people. You would be welcome here if you decide to put down roots again."

"Danki, Rose. Did you give Abby the same speech?"

"Not yet. She is too afraid to trust us."

"Afraid? Of what?"

Rose gazed into the distance. "I'm not sure. I pray she finds the peace she seeks." Rose looked at him. "Until she does, she won't be ready to find her home. We must do what we can to help her."

She walked away, leaving Joe to ponder her words. What help could he give Abby? He hadn't found peace. He was in no position to aid her in her search for it, but Rose had piqued his curiosity. Just what was Abigail Martin afraid of?

The following day Rose sent Abby out to Joe with coffee and crumb cake at midmorning and then cookies in the afternoon with lemonade. The old woman wasn't subtle in her matchmaking attempts, but Abby wasn't subtle about her feelings, either. She didn't say a word to him. Just put down the tray and left.

He joined the women for supper that evening. He tried not to look at Abby but found his gaze drifting to her frequently. She never looked up from her plate but there were spots of color in her cheeks by the time the meal was ended.

The Harts Haven Birdies were meeting at the inn tonight. The bird-watching group only had three members. Grace and two of her *Englisch* friends. Rose happily introduced Abby.

"This is our new maid, Abby Martin. She's only recently come to Harts Haven. Abby, this is our friend Herbert Young."

"Major, US Army JAG Corp, retired." Herbert bowed slightly in Abby's direction. He was a tall fellow with erect bearing, snow-white hair and fearsome bushy white eyebrows.

"I'm pleased to meet you," Abby said.

"And this is Dr. Bertha Rock," Grace said, gesturing to the tiny woman at her side.

Abby suddenly looked interested. "You're a physician?"

"I am."

"And now practicing in the town where she was born," Rose added. "Bertie and I went to school together until the eighth grade. Then she went off to study doctoring and forgot all about us."

Bertie smiled. "You are unforgettable, Rose. I opened a small clinic here in town about twenty years ago when I retired from my practice in Wichita. I do mostly minor stuff really. The majority of people go to the newer clinic over in Hutchinson since it's only a short drive. You may call me Bertie or Doc. I'm eighty-three, and I don't ever intend to retire," she said with a wink for the major.

"Don't let her fool you. Stitching folks up, delivering babies, setting broken bones, she does it all for our Amish families," Grace said with a warm smile for her friend.

Herbert rubbed his hands together as he grinned eagerly. "Ladies, I hope I can count on your company tomorrow for our outing."

"Oh, yes," Grace said. "Where are we going? We saw so many species down by the river last time. I'd love to go back there."

"You guessed it," Herbert said, beaming. "I went there early this morning. I was able to capture three minutes of the song of a two-barred crossbill. Would you like to hear it?"

Bertie gave an impressed nod of her head. "A white-winged crossbill? How wonderful. They're very rare in this area. Did you post it to our online friends?"

Herbert looked pleased with himself. "Not yet. I wanted you ladies to hear it first."

The birding group eagerly retired to the front living room, where Herbert opened his laptop as the women gathered around him. Almost immediately a distinctive cheeping sound filled the room.

"The clarity is amazing, Herbert," Grace said.

Herbert grinned. "The new parabolic microphone I have captures the sound perfectly. It was money well spent."

"I agree," Bertha said, leaning closer. "Let's hear it again."

Abby listened briefly and then moved away from the

group. Joe watched to see where she went, instead of going back to his trailer. She left through the side door that led to the flower garden. He followed. She walked among the blooms before stopping to smell the red roses climbing a trellis by the garden wall.

He approached her without knowing what he would say. As he stood looking at her slender figure, he realized he was being foolish. If she didn't want to talk to him, that was fine. He started to turn away.

"I love the smell of roses in the evening, don't you?" she asked.

He looked around to see whom she might be talking to. They were alone. He cleared his throat. "I'm fonder of lilacs."

She turned to face him with her head tilted to the side. "I never would have taken you for a lilac man."

"What's that supposed to mean?"

"Lilacs are so delicate and short-lived. I see you as a sunflower guy. Always following the sun. A practical flower. Filled with eatable seeds."

"But not an overly pleasing fragrance," he said.

"True. This is pleasant."

He cocked his head. "What is?"

"Being nice to each other."

"I'm always nice."

"Of course you are," she said meekly.

"A *goot* Amish woman doesn't lie."

A smile tugged at the corner of her mouth. "Do we bend the truth to save someone's feelings?"

"Often."

"That's a relief."

He stepped closer to her. "I'm sorry I told you not to talk. I didn't mean it. I was only teasing you."

"I guess I took it the wrong way. When I was growing up my father never wanted to hear what I had to say."

He could see it was a sad memory. "Why do you like roses the best?"

She turned to study the arching sprays of blooms. "Because they are beautiful and because they have their own thorns for protection."

"Why do you need thorns?"

She glanced at him. "I didn't say that I did."

"Then call it my impression. Do you need them?"

She raised her chin. "I've grown a few, and I intend to keep them."

"Goot."

She looked surprised. "Really?"

"We question why God gave rosebushes thorns, when we should be grateful He gave the thornbush such beautiful flowers. I think He must have a soft spot for thorny things."

"Like me?" She smiled softly. "That's *goot* of you to say."

She was pretty when she smiled. His grin widened. "See. I'm not always rude."

"I'll try to remember that the next time you are."

He arched both brows. "You're sure there will be a next time?"

"Positive. But not tonight."

"Why not?"

She took a deep breath. "Because it's a beautiful evening, and you don't want to spoil it."

"Fair enough. Would you care to take a walk?" He held his breath waiting for her answer.

She scrunched up her face. "Will we have to talk?"

"Not if you don't want to."

"Then let's not so we can stay in this pleasant frame of mind."

"Okay." He held open the garden gate and she went out ahead of him.

"Which way?" she asked.

"What would you like to see? Wheat fields, unplanted soybean fields or wheat fields?"

"Wow. Tough choice. Wheat fields, I guess."

"This way." He started walking down the lane, and she fell into step beside him. Her hand accidently brushed against his. He resisted the impulse to take hold of it and was glad he did. She took a quick step away from him.

She wasn't looking for romance and neither was he. She was only interested in a quiet walk on a cool summer evening. He was a fool if he let himself think otherwise.

Abby wanted to rub the hand that had brushed against Joe. A strange sensation seemed to linger there. It wasn't unpleasant but brought her a heightened awareness of him. He had shortened his long-legged stride to match hers as they ambled along. She was thrilled to be walking barefoot again as most Amish did in the summer. The earth was warm and firm under her feet. The breeze that undulated through the knee-high green wheat brought her the smells of summer and the rugged scent of the man beside her. Sawdust and sweat and a unique earthiness. Something in her was drawn to him. Something she had to ignore. Too much was riding on the success of her plan. She couldn't afford a distraction.

She had already met the town's doctor. Would the woman be able to help her? It was hard to imagine someone so small and elderly going up against the doctors her father paid to say Abby was mentally incompetent so he could continue to control her life. It was too soon to confide in anyone. She needed an attorney first, and that took money. She had to be patient. A rash mistake could cost her everything.

"The wheat is pretty at this stage when it's still green but tall enough to wave in the wind," he said.

"You're talking."

"Oh, sorry."

"But it is very pretty," she admitted.

He bent slightly to see her face. "Are you still in a pleasant state of mind?"

"If you stop talking."

He didn't say another word, and she was sorry. Sparring with him was more enjoyable than she cared to admit. Walking with him was, too. She stopped in her tracks. Her attraction to him was trouble in the making. She wasn't safe. She couldn't let her guard down again. Not yet.

"What's wrong?" he asked.

"I'm tired. I'd like to go back."

"Sure."

They began to retrace their steps along the dirt road. Around them the wheat fields stretched to the horizon where they met the blue sky overhead with nothing to come between them but an occasional bird. Because the land was so flat, she spotted the car coming toward them almost a mile away. A black SUV like the ones owned by her father's firm.

Her heart started hammering in her chest. She pressed a hand to her suddenly queasy stomach. It might not be them, but she knew it was. They were coming to check if she had gone to her grandmother's house. She hadn't expected them so soon. Why weren't they looking for her in Miami? What mistake had she made to bring them here so quickly?

She battled the urge to turn and run. Any action on her part would only draw their attention. Standing still as the car approached was nerve-racking. They slowed down, and she gripped her hands tightly together to hide their shaking.

Joe moved to step between her and the vehicle. Amish men did the talking. Amish women waited quietly and let the men deal with outsiders. She hung back with her eyes glued to the ground and her bare feet as any modest Amish woman would do.

Her father would be furious with her for going without shoes like a beggar. She wished she didn't care what he thought, but she did.

The man in the passenger seat rolled down his window. He appeared to be in his mid-thirties with short cropped black hair. "Buddy, can you give me a little help?"

"If I'm able," Joe said cautiously.

"We're looking for a girl that might be in this area." He handed Joe a photograph. Joe studied it a moment and then handed it to Abby. Her fingers shook as she took it. It was a grainy image from a security camera. Probably from the bus station. She was standing with her bag over her shoulder. Her pink shirt and long blond hair made her stand out from the crowd, but her hair hung over her face obscuring much of it.

Was this the only image her father had of her? How sad was that and how much did it say about him as a parent that he didn't have a single photograph of her in his possession? Her mother had been raised Amish. She had held to her belief that photos were graven images and shunned them, but Abigail's father had no such objections. He simply hadn't cared enough about his daughter to keep a picture of her. Apparently, Logan felt the same.

Abigail realized the men were watching her. She shook her head and handed the photo back without speaking. Joe gave it to the man in the car. "Sorry we couldn't help."

The driver, a younger fellow with sandy-blond hair leaned toward the open window. "We plan to stay around town for a few days. We were told there's an inn nearby. Can you give us directions?"

"The inn is being renovated and isn't accepting guests. I can give you the address of a couple of people who have rooms to rent if that would help," Joe suggested.

"One inn? Is that it?" The dark-haired man rolled his eyes. "Hicksville."

"We should go back to Hutchinson and get a motel room, Phil. We can come back tomorrow," the driver said.

"Okay. Let's do that."

"What is the girl wanted for?" Joe asked. "I assume you are the police."

"Private investigators," Phil said after a moment of hesitation. "She's a runaway with a history of mental illness. Her father wants her found before she has a chance to hurt herself or someone else."

It was a twisted version of the truth, which made it all the more painful to hear. Abby kept silent and didn't look up. Her father's men were thorough and dangerous. Not that they would harm a hair on her head, but the same didn't apply to anyone helping her.

She watched as they drove off. The tension drained from her body, leaving her weak and shaking. They hadn't recognized her, but tomorrow they would be back asking questions of everyone in town. She'd only met the widows, Joe, the bird-watchers and the boy on the bicycle, but by now most people in the community would know Rose had a new maid at the inn. That was the way small towns worked, and it could be Abby's undoing.

She placed a protective hand over her stomach. Should she run or should she brazen it out?

Four

Joe stared at the dust cloud the car raised as it drove away. Normally he didn't pay much attention to outsiders, but something about those men didn't feel right. They seemed more concerned about where they would stay than the ill woman they were searching for. Her family must be frantic wondering what had happened to her. Why did they think she might be in Harts Haven?

It didn't matter. There was nothing Joe could do to help them except keep his eyes and ears open. Only the men hadn't bothered leaving a way to contact them. The whole thing was strange. He was prepared to dismiss them from his mind until he glanced at Abby.

All the color was gone from her cheeks. She swayed slightly as she pressed both hands to her midsection.

"Are you okay?" he asked, quickly reaching toward her.

She flinched away from his outstretched hand as she stared at the car disappearing in the distance. He looked closer at her face and saw fear in the depths of her eyes. Raw fear. He lowered his hand.

"Abby, do you know those men?" he asked softly.

She blinked rapidly as if to clear her vision and cocked her head slightly. "What did you say?"

"I asked if you knew those men."

She shook her head. "I've never seen them before."

"But they upset you. I can see that. What is it? What's wrong?"

Her gaze shifted to his face but quickly slid away. "I was thinking about the poor woman they're looking for."

"So was I. I hope they find her soon."

Her gaze flashed to him. She took a step back. "Why would you say that?"

He moved closer. "You heard them. She's ill, and her father is searching for her. He must be out of his mind with worry."

She shook her head. "Think how alone and frightened she is if running away from him is the course she chose. I pray they never find her."

Something in her voice made him study her closely. "Abby, do you know her?"

She looked down at her feet. "We should get back. The others will be wondering what happened to us." She gave him a half smile and began walking rapidly toward the inn.

He let the subject drop. That she ignored his question told him she knew more than she was letting on. Rose had mentioned that Abby was afraid of something. What did it have to do with the missing *Englisch* woman?

He hurried to keep up and pretended to ignore her

strange reaction to the two outsiders, but it wasn't easily dismissed. The sight of her eyes so wide with fear had touched something inside him. He wanted to comfort her. Protect her.

And that was a foolish notion. He had failed to protect the people he cared about most. He never wanted to be in that position again. Not caring was far easier than enduring the guilt of failure and the pain of loss.

They walked toward the inn without speaking. The wind sighed through the wheat and kicked up tiny swirls of dirt on the road. Crickets and other insects began their evening drone as the sun slowly sank below the horizon in a blaze of red and gold. He glanced often at Abby's face. There was still enough light to show the worried crease between her brows.

She gave a muffled cry and hobbled to a stop. He caught her arm to steady her. "What's wrong?"

She jerked away from him. "I stepped on a sharp rock. I'm not used to going barefoot."

"You don't go barefoot at home?"

She stared at him for a long moment. "Of course I do, but not in the winter. We had a cold spring, so I haven't had a chance to toughen up."

"That's understandable. Watch for goat head stickers when you're out walking like this. They can puncture a bike tire."

"I'd forgotten about them. I'll be careful. *Danki.*" She kept her eyes glued to the ground as they walked on, but her pace was slower.

Joe noticed the bird-watching group's cars were gone from the parking lot when he and Abby reached the inn. The meeting must be over. At the door to the kitchen Abigail turned to face him. He gazed at her worried face and wished for the first time that he wasn't moving on when the job was done. "It was almost a pleasant evening," he said. "We'll have to try again. Maybe tomorrow?"

That wasn't what he'd intended to say but he realized it was what he wanted. Abigail Martin was an intriguing woman unlike anyone he'd met before. She was a contradiction, a puzzle he wanted to solve. He wanted to see that worried frown banished and replaced with her pretty smile.

She glanced around nervously. "I don't think so."

He sighed heavily. This was more than a simple brush-off. "Do you want to tell me the truth about why meeting those men upset you?"

Her face registered her surprise. "I don't know what you mean?"

"*Ja*, you do."

She crossed her arms and looked down. "All right. I don't want to tell you."

That took him aback. "Not what I had hoped to hear but an honest answer." It was enough for now. He wouldn't press her. She was already upset and on edge.

He should forget the whole thing but something about her wouldn't let him. "I'll help if I can. I hope you know that, Abigail."

She stared into his eyes as she bit the corner of her lower lip. "*Danki*, but I don't need help."

Two things were clear. She did, but she didn't want it from him. He got the message. "Okay. If you feel like talking, you know where to find me. Good night."

"*Guten nacht*, Joseph." There was a hint of puzzlement in her voice. As if she wasn't sure what to make of his comment.

He touched the brim of his hat and walked toward his trailer. He wanted to look back and see if she was watching him, but he didn't. He'd be leaving in a couple of weeks. It was better if he put some distance between them and kept it.

Abby hurried inside and rushed down the hall to her room without meeting anyone. She closed the door and leaned against it, trying to control the panic that wanted to overwhelm her. She closed her eyes and deliberately slowed her breathing.

How had her father's men discovered where she went so quickly? She had laid her plans carefully. Where had she gone wrong? Had they followed her? It didn't seem possible. Yet it shouldn't have come as a surprise that her father had guessed her ultimate destination. Staying one jump ahead of his adversaries was how Victor made and kept his fortune. Apparently, her elaborate plan to send him scouring Miami hadn't fooled anyone.

She had told Joe the truth. She hadn't seen those men before, but that didn't mean they hadn't seen her. Someone had always manned the desk in the surveillance room where cameras monitored every part of her father's estate, including the small walled patio where she had been allowed outdoors and the hallway outside her apartments. The light had been fading this evening and she had kept her face averted, but in the bright daylight they were much more likely to recognize her.

Run or stay? What should she do?

The answer was simple. How could she brazen it out if Joseph, a man she had only known two days, could see how upset she was? She wasn't skilled at deception in spite of her recent practice with Logan.

She pressed the heels of her hands to her temples. Her whole plan was in tatters. Maybe her father was right.

Maybe she was mentally ill, and this glimpse of freedom was a delusion. How could she know?

Wrapping her arms tightly across her middle, she fought back tears. No. She was well now. She was—and she would prove it.

After several deep breaths, Abby's racing heart slowed. The panic receded. Delusion or not, her freedom wasn't something she would willingly surrender. There was someone else to think about. Her baby. Her child didn't deserve to grow up under her father's domineering influence. He couldn't know about the child until she was free of his control. Logan didn't know. Only Rose had guessed her condition, but she had promised she wouldn't divulge Abby's secret. *If* she remembered she had given her word.

Abby put her head back and rubbed her tense neck muscles. Why wouldn't Victor just let her leave? It wasn't from an abundance of affection. He could barely stand the sight of her. Why convince people she was mentally imbalanced and needed to be kept locked up? What did he gain by it? Victor Worthington never did anything without an angle that benefited him.

When her mother died and then both her beloved Amish grandparents passed away only a month later, Abby had fallen into a deep depression. At fourteen it had seemed like the end of the world. She endured a hopeless existence and her father's scorn for two more unbearable years until she finally lost her will to live. All she wanted was her pain and grief to end. On her sixteenth birthday she took an overdose.

Deeply ashamed of what she had tried to do, Abby hated to think about those horrible days. She had been hospitalized for a time, but with treatment and the kindness of the hospital staff, she began to recover. That was when her real nightmare began.

Her father swooped in and against her doctor's advice he had taken her home and placed her under the care of a new physician. A woman who prescribed meds that kept Abby groggy and unable to function for months. When she finally realized what was happening, she stopped swallowing the pills, spitting them out later instead. Once the fog lifted from her mind, she realized she was a prisoner in her own lavish cage. She also discovered convincing the people around her that she was sane was impossible. They had all been told by the doctor that she was delusional and manipulative.

Would the people at the inn think the same thing? Would Joe or Rose look at her differently? Pity her? Avoid her? Would they believe she wasn't fit to be a mother? She couldn't chance it. No one could find out.

She crossed to the bed, dropped to her knees and pulled her backpack from beneath it. Carrying it to her bureau, she pulled open the drawers and began stuffing her few belongings into it. She needed to find out when the next bus was leaving. It didn't matter what direction it was going. She had to be on it before those men returned. She needed to disappear. Maybe if she didn't know where she was going, her father couldn't outguess her.

A knock at her door made her gasp. Were they back? Had they figured out who she was?

The door opened and Rose peeked in. "Oh, there you are. Are you settling in?"

Abby turned away and pulled her backpack closed. "I've changed my mind. I don't think this is the job for me."

"Oh, my dear. Is it something I said?" Rose came to

stand beside Abby and peer at her face. Her eyes behind her spectacles were clear and sharp. Too sharp.

"No, you've been very kind."

Rose's eyes narrowed. "Did Joseph upset you? I'll have a talk with him. Courting can't be rushed. A girl wants to be wooed. I know I did. I had half a dozen suitors asking to marry me." Rose twirled her *kapp* ribbon around her finger and batted her eyes. "I don't mean to brag, but I was quite a catch in my day. In fact, I still am if any of the old men around here would open their eyes."

Abby couldn't help but smile. "I'm sure that's true."

"I'll speak to Joe. I don't want him upsetting my best maid."

Best maid? She had only worked a couple of days. "It wasn't anything Joe did. I can't explain. It's just better if I left."

"How is it better to leave a job and new friends in your condition?"

"Trust me. It's what I have to do."

"*Liebling*, running away never solves the problem."

Abby bit her lip. Her grandmother used to call her *liebling*. It meant "darling." For a moment she hesitated but then hardened her resolve. "It will this time."

"I was sure you and Joe would hit it off. I do hate to be wrong."

"Where can I get a bus ticket?"

"You'll need to go to Hutchinson for that. The line lets passengers off here, but you'll have to go into the city to board it."

"How far is it to Hutchinson?"

"About thirty miles."

That was too far to walk. "I'll need a ride. Could someone take me?"

"Herbert will be here in the morning at eight o'clock. I heard him say he's taking Bertha and Grace on one of their bird-watching outings. I'm sure he'll be happy to run you into the city first. He always has his computer with him. You can have him purchase your ticket. He does it for the Amish around here when we need to travel for weddings or funerals and such. You'll have to put up with his endless questions, of course. He's something of a busybody but he has a good heart."

Abby's spirit sank as the reality of her situation hit. Tickets cost money. She had three dollars. "Do you think you could give me a small loan? Just enough to get a ticket."

"To where?"

"Shipshewana?" According to Joe it was a big Amish community. She could disappear there. "I'll pay you back as soon as I can."

"Oh, I think so. I owe you two days' wages anyway."

Abby sagged with relief. "I'd be so grateful."

Rose took Abby's hand and squeezed it. "There now, you don't have to fret anymore. But please pray about your decision and sleep on it. Remember you have friends here who will help if you decide to stay. Nothing will seem as bad when the sun comes up in the morning."

Abby didn't realize until that moment how much she had come to care for the funny little woman. "I wish I could stay."

"Wishes are prayers looking for a place to go. Send them to *Gott*. He has all the answers you seek. Now, I was going to have a cup of herbal tea. It soothes me and helps me sleep. Come join me. It will do you good, I promise."

Abby needed something to soothe her rattled nerves but doubted herbal tea would do the trick. Still, she gave in and followed Rose to the kitchen. There wasn't anything else she could do tonight.

The elderly woman opened a cabinet and pointed to the top shelf. "Could you reach that jar of tea for me?"

"Sure." Abby got it down and handed it to Rose.

She opened it and took a sniff. "This is my grannie's special bedtime recipe. She was a gifted herbalist. She was always collecting and studying plants. The water in the kettle is still hot. Pour us a couple of mugs, dear."

Abby filled the mugs and watched Rose spoon some of the loose leaves into a mesh tea infuser. She put it in the mug closest to Abby and dunked it gently. After a minute she pulled it out. "This will help you rest. Try it and tell me what you think. Oh, no wait. It needs honey first. Everything goes better with a touch of honey."

She opened the cabinet again and pulled down a jar of the golden liquid. She drizzled a generous portion into the mug of tea, stirred it and then pushed it toward Abby. "Be careful. It's hot."

Abby blew on the steaming liquid and then took a sip. The honey didn't quite disguise an odd aftertaste, but it wasn't bad. She took another drink. Rose kept up a steady flow of chatter about her plans for the kitchen and the inn. Abby didn't have to do more than nod. By the time she finished her tea she was nodding for real.

"Are you done? *Goot.* Off to bed with you, then," Rose said, moving the cup out of the way.

Abby noticed Rose hadn't fixed herself any tea. "Weren't you going to have some?"

"I've decided to stay up for a bit. *Guten nacht.*"

Abby returned to her room and sat on the edge of her bed. She clasped her backpack to her chest. Leaving was the best decision. The light of day wouldn't change anything. She yawned, surprised she was so tired. She un-pinned her *kapp* and lay on her side on top of the quilt to wait out the long night.

When she opened her eyes, sunlight was streaming through her window. Startled, she sat up. How late was it? Had Herbert arrived? Had she missed him?

She scrambled off the bed and hurried downstairs with her backpack in her hand. Only Grace was in the kitchen. She grinned at Abby. "I think you forgot something." Grace patted her own head. "You don't have your *kapp* on."

Abby touched her hair. Some of it had worked free of her hairpins and the curly frizz was sticking out every which way. She smoothed it with both hands. "I was afraid I would miss seeing the major."

"You haven't missed him. He's in the breakfast room with our other guests. Go get put together and then help me serve the coffee while I heat up some rolls."

Abby turned toward the back hall. She nearly bumped into Joe as he came in from the outside. His eyes widened. "Tough night?"

What was that supposed to mean?

"Excuse me." She brushed past him without meeting his eyes. She had hoped to be gone before he came in. Now she would have to explain why she was leaving. Would he accept that the job just wasn't for her? Somehow she doubted it.

She rushed into her room, snatched up her *kapp* and turned to the mirror. Her hair looked like it belonged on a scarecrow. No wonder Joe had asked her if she'd had a tough night. She looked like she had come through a wind-storm. No, she looked more like the woman in the photo. Taking her hair down, she brushed it into submission and secured it again before she put her prayer covering on.

Once she was sure she looked the part of a serene Amish woman, she left the room and returned to the kitchen. Joe wasn't in sight.

Grace handed her a tray with six cups and saucers on it. "Take these in. The coffee is almost ready."

Abby started for the swinging door that led into the breakfast room from the kitchen. Before she reached it, Joe came through. He stopped in front of her. "Those men are here."

She didn't drop the tray. She was proud of that, but the cups rattled badly.

"Let me get this for you," he said, meeting her eyes with a pointed look.

She nodded, not trusting her voice. He took the tray and backed through the door. She caught sight of Rose just beyond, seated at one of the three round tables covered with red-and-white-checked tablecloths in the cheery east-facing room overlooking the flower garden.

"I haven't seen any strangers," Rose said, looking toward the kitchen door. She leaned sideways to peek around Joe. "Come in, Abby. This is Phil, and what did you say your name was?"

"I didn't say," the blond man replied.

"Oh, well, these men are looking for a girl who has run away from home. The poor dear child. I do hope she is safe."

Abby had no choice except to follow Joe into the room, but she stayed by the door in case she had to run. Foolish notion. Where could she run to?

"I believe you met everyone else yesterday. Bertha and Herbert." Rose gestured toward an empty chair. "Oh, he was here."

"He stepped out to make a phone call, but he'll be back in a minute," Bertha said.

Joe put down the tray and returned to her side. She was grateful for his solid presence between her and the men in dark blue suits standing beyond the tables with their backs to the wall and their hands clasped in front of them. They looked so out of place it was almost funny. She didn't laugh. It was hard enough to breathe.

"We've been asking around town. A boy said he gave directions to this place to a woman who got off the bus three days ago," the one called Phil said.

"Oh, that was Abby," Rose said cheerfully.

Abby wanted to sink through the floor. The dear woman was exposing her without realizing it.

"She isn't the girl you're looking for, of course," Rose said quickly with a dismissive wave of her hand. "Abby is the great-granddaughter of a friend of mine. You remember Sappy from school, don't you, Bertha? We called her that because…" A vague look came over Rose's features. "Why did we call her that?"

Bertha chuckled. "Because she helped her father cut hedge trees for fence posts and she always had tree sap stains on her dresses. Sappy Sarah. I haven't thought of her in years. Abby is her great-granddaughter, you say. I can see the resemblance now that you mentioned it. I don't know how I missed it before. Where did Sarah go when she moved away?"

"It could have been New Mexico," Rose said vaguely.

Bertha shook her head. "That doesn't sound right. Wasn't it Missouri? Abby, where did you say you were from?"

"Missouri," she answered softly. Her fingernails dug into the palms of her hands as she clenched them to stop their shaking. Her nerves were stretched to the breaking point.

She needed some excuse to leave the room, but her mind refused to work when her father's men had their eyes on her.

"I believe you are right, Bertha. That's where she went first," Rose said brightly, "but I'm sure she moved again in 1987 or was it 1988? *Nee*, I'm sure it was '87."

Phil gave Rose an exasperated look. "The girl we're searching for isn't Amish, but we are sure she took a bus out of Kansas City. Could she have been on the bus with you, miss?"

Abby cleared the lump in her throat. "I didn't see anyone who looked like your picture," she answered meekly without looking up. She prayed her Amish accent was convincing.

The outside door opened. Herbert came in. He slipped his cell phone into his shirt pocket and took a seat at the table beside Bertha but never took his eyes off the men.

"Did you get hold of Franklin?" the doctor asked quietly.

"I did. He'll be here in a few minutes."

"Wunderbar," Rose said. "Frankie is a man who knows everything that's going on in our town. He's just the fellow you should speak to. Until he gets here, gentlemen, you have enough time to enjoy some of our famous breakfast rolls. Cinnamon rolls the size of your plate. That's our motto. Grace thought of it. She's quite good when it comes to marketing strategies. I believe that's what she calls them. Of course, Susanna thinks that it's wasteful because very few people finish the whole thing but as they can take the rest home with them, I don't feel it is. I make the rolls myself every morning. Do try some. You can split one if you aren't up to eating the whole thing by yourself. Abby, *hohla zvay rulls.*"

Abby stood frozen as she struggled to translate the phrase in her mind. She had heard it before.

"Shnell." Rose shooed her away.

Hohla was "fetch."

"Ja." Abby bobbed her head and spun around. *Fetch the rolls. Two. Quick.* She entered the kitchen and grabbed the back of the nearest chair to keep from falling as her knees threatened to buckle.

"Are you all right?" Grace asked in concern. "You're white as a sheet."

"I'm a little dizzy." Abby sat and put her head down. She couldn't run if she had to. The room was spinning.

"Let me get you some water." Grace's voice came from far away. A few seconds later a cool cloth was laid on the back of Abby's neck. "This should help. Take deep breaths."

Abby did. The blackness at the edge of her vision receded and the room stopped spinning. She felt a glass pressed into her hand. "Drink it all," Grace said.

Abby finished the water and handed the glass to Grace. "Rose wants two cinnamon rolls for the guests."

"All right. Are you feeling better?"

"Ja."

"You just rest for a few minutes. I'll take the rolls in."

As much as Abby wanted to dash out the back door, she knew she had to return to the breakfast room. She was an Amish maid—not a mentally ill woman on the run. Her father's men had already had time enough to recognize her. They wouldn't have let her leave the room if they suspected who she was.

"I'm fine now, Grace. I'll take them." She needed to finish the charade. All she had to do was carry in the cinnamon rolls and then leave without drawing attention to herself. They would conclude Victoria Abigail Worthington wasn't in Harts Haven when they finished questioning the people of the town. She could do it.

For her baby's sake she could do anything.

She took a plate in each hand and pushed open the swinging door with her elbow. Joe held it open for her. She caught his worried look and managed a tight smile to reassure him. She set the plates on the table in front of the men and moved to the back of the room by the kitchen door.

"We'd like to be notified if this girl shows up here," Phil said, handing the picture to Herbert. "We'll make sure she gets home safely."

Herbert took it and frowned. "You've led us to believe you're looking for a runaway teenager. This isn't a child. How old is the woman?"

"She's twenty-two."

Herbert snorted. "The age of majority in the state of Kansas is eighteen. She can't be compelled to return home if she doesn't wish to go."

"Sadly, Victoria isn't competent to make her own decisions. She's emotionally unstable. Her father is her legal guardian. Here's a 1-800 number for you to call if she is seen. There is also a substantial reward for information leading to her return." He held out a business card.

"Emotionally unstable is not a diagnosis," Bertha said. "Is she schizophrenic, bipolar? Is she depressed, is she suicidal?"

"We're not at liberty to say," the blond-haired man replied with a smug smile. "She isn't in touch with reality, and she is dangerous. She attacked one of her care workers. Don't try to approach her."

Abby wanted to rush forward and shout a denial of their accusations. It wasn't true. Not a word of it. They weren't just portraying her as delusional, but as someone willing to hurt people. How could she convince anyone she was sane if people were afraid of her?

She couldn't. If her father's men didn't expose her, that part of her past would stay hidden forever.

The outside door opened. Everyone looked toward it as a man in a blue police uniform walked in. He stopped to remove his sunglasses and then scanned the room with piercing gray eyes.

Five

Rose moved to Abby's side, took her hand and squeezed gently. "It's going to be all right," she whispered.

Abby didn't believe her for a second, yet a strange calm settled over her as the policeman's intense gaze landed on her and hung there. She closed her eyes and clenched her fists to stop their shaking. Was he here for her? Despair hit her like one of Logan's punches.

Had Susanna or Joe's boss reported a woman pretending to be Amish at the inn? Was that a crime? Maybe not, but using a stolen credit card was. She had taken Logan's credit card without his knowledge. She'd used it only once to buy her bus ticket. Then she'd left it in the bathroom of the bus hoping someone would turn it in to prove to her father that she had been on her way to Miami. The circumstances didn't matter. She was a thief.

Her fingerprints were on that bit of plastic. She hadn't wiped it clean because she didn't expect her father to involve the police. Had she guessed wrong? Her prints were all over the inn now. No Amish dress or *kapp* could disguise them.

The weight of her guilt bowed her head. When she was arrested, they wouldn't believe her story. Her history of mental illness perpetrated by the doctor on her father's payroll would show she was delusional.

At least she wouldn't be in jail long. Her father was too influential. She would be back in her locked rooms facing Logan's and her father's wrath. The urge to get it over with was overwhelming. She took a small step forward. Rose pulled her back.

"All right, I'm here. What's so important, Major?" the officer asked.

Abby glanced up. The policeman's gaze had settled on Herbert. Hope slowly unfurled inside her. She unclenched her fingers and started to breathe again. Had she been too quick to assume he was here for her? Had she nearly revealed herself for nothing?

"Thank you for coming, Sheriff." Herbert gestured toward the outsiders. "These men are searching for a missing person. Gentlemen, this is Sheriff Franklin Hart."

"The town is named after his family, who settled here at the end of the civil war," Rose added brightly. "Frankie has been our sheriff for fifteen years."

Sheriff Hart gave her a half smile. "It's Franklin, and I'm sure they don't want a history lesson, Rose."

She chuckled loudly. "I delivered you, young man, and

I gave your bare bottom its very first whack. You'll always be Frankie to me."

He shook his head in resignation, pulled a notebook from his pocket and addressed the two men standing by the wall. "Can you give me the particulars? The name and age of the person you're looking for, a description, and how long he or she has been missing?"

Joe glanced from Abby's pale face to the outsiders as they exchanged a speaking look. They weren't happy to have the sheriff involved. The dark-haired fellow managed a condescending smile. "I'm afraid I can't give you that information, Officer. The family wants this unfortunate incident kept quiet."

"I don't like the look of them," Herbert declared, glaring at the men.

Joe agreed with him. There was something off about the pair. He thought so yesterday, too, and their attitude today confirmed his feelings. He glanced at Abby again. Some of the color had come back into her cheeks. When the sheriff walked in, she had gone deathly pale. He'd never seen anyone look as frightened and as desperate as she had at that moment. She was afraid of these people, but he had no idea why.

Nor was it any of his business.

What was he doing standing here watching? He shouldn't care that some Amish girl he barely knew was in trouble with the law. He had work waiting, a job to do for his boss and then he'd be moving on.

"I was suspicious from the get-go when they wouldn't give her full name." Herbert handed the photograph to the sheriff. "The whole story smells fishy. That's why I called you. This is the only picture they have. As you can see, she looks like a grown woman, not a teenager. They claim she has mental problems, but they won't supply pertinent information about that, either."

Joe headed toward the kitchen. The *Englisch* would solve their problems without his help. He was two steps away from the door when he glanced at Abby again. She looked dazed. It touched something deep inside him. Something he wanted to ignore but couldn't. He stopped by her side instead of leaving the room. She gave him a weak, grateful smile proving he made the right choice.

"Herbert is suspicious by nature," Rose whispered, but Joe heard her plain enough. So did the rest of the room. Everyone looked in her direction.

She held up one hand. "What? It's not gossip. It's a fact. Isn't it, Herbert? Always tell the truth. That's the way I was raised."

He looked the strangers up and down. "I wouldn't say suspicious. I'd say I'm cautious. I don't share the Amish belief in the goodness of all men. My experience in the courtroom has taught me otherwise."

"That's why he likes birds," Rose said. "They don't break the law."

The sheriff stared at the photo he held for a long moment then scowled at the strangers. "Care to explain what's going on?"

"It's really none of your affair. We're just asking around town if anyone has seen her. Someone we questioned mentioned that a woman got off the bus and came here a few days ago."

"That was our little Abby," Rose said loudly.

Joe felt Abby stiffen. He wanted to put his arm around her shoulders, but he had no right to act with such familiarity.

"Abby is Sappy Sarah's great-granddaughter, Frankie," Rose said. "Sarah was before your time, but she went to school with Bertha and me. Then she moved to New Mexico."

"Missouri," Bertha corrected her.

"Are you sure it wasn't New Mexico?" Rose scowled and held one finger to her cheek. "Maybe it was Missouri. Or Indiana. There are lots of Amish in Ohio."

The dark-haired man rolled his eyes. "Okay, lady, enough. Look, Sheriff, our client wishes to locate his missing daughter, but he wants to keep her disappearance out of the media."

The sheriff laid the photograph down. "I'm not the media, I'm law enforcement. A missing person is serious business. The more information you can give us the better your chances are of locating her."

The blond fellow elbowed his partner. "I think we're done here. This yokel doesn't need to know anything."

The sheriff moved his hand to rest on the butt of the gun he wore. "What I need is to see some ID and the concealed carry permits for those guns you've got tucked in your shoulder holsters."

Joe felt Abby tense. She started forward, but he caught her arm to stop her. What was she doing? If they had guns, he didn't want her in harm's way. He tried to pull her toward the kitchen door, but she shook off his hold.

The blond man sneered. "The family resides in Kansas City, Missouri. That's outside your quaint little jurisdiction, Sheriff."

"And yet here you are, asking questions in my county. ID and permits or you'll get to see the inside of our quaint little jail." The sheriff clicked the radio mic on his shirt-front. "This is Franklin. I need backup at the Harts Haven Inn. Be aware the suspects are armed."

"We're not looking to cause trouble, Sheriff," the dark-haired one said quickly, holding up both hands.

Sheriff Hart's smile turned cold. "No trouble. It's been a slow day. My deputies will be happy to have something to do."

"You should check if they really are private investigators, Sheriff," Herbert said. "Kansas and Missouri both require PIs to be licensed."

"See, suspicious by nature," Rose whispered again.

The men exchanged looks and then reluctantly complied with the sheriff's order. Abby sank onto a chair at the table nearest the kitchen door.

Joe gave her an encouraging smile. The fear in her eyes had begun to fade. She bit the corner of her lip before she looked down at her hands clasped on the red-and-white-checked tablecloth. He wanted to know what she was hiding behind those troubled eyes. Maybe it was foolishness on his part, but he wanted to help.

He heard a faint buzzing sound. The blond fellow pulled a cell phone from his pocket and answered it. He spoke quietly, nodded, then slipped the phone inside his jacket. He turned to his partner. "That was Sims. The credit card she stole has been used in St. Louis. Looks like Mr. V's hunch was wrong. We're to head back as soon as we've checked the house."

The dark-haired one looked at Sheriff Hart. "We've just received a new lead. Do we have your permission to leave this backwater town?"

The sheriff snapped a picture of each open wallet with his phone and then handed them back. "Are you filing an official missing person report, Mr. Dalton?"

"We are not." He frowned as he tucked his wallet inside his jacket.

"Then I reckon you don't have any more business here. Good day, Mr. Dalton and Mr. Wyatt. Have a pleasant trip home." The way the sheriff emphasized their names made Joe think he wanted the pair to know he wasn't about to forget them.

Two more men in blue police uniforms came into the breakfast room. One from the kitchen and the other from the door to the garden. Sheriff Hart held up his hand. "These fellas are just leaving, men. See them out of town."

Abby giggled nervously and then pressed a hand to her mouth as her father's men headed out the door followed by the two deputies. They were leaving! She was safe.

They were going to search for her in St. Louis. Her plan was working thanks to the person who had found Logan's credit card and used it instead of turning it in. Hopefully, he or she had run up a hefty amount on Logan's account. He would be furious.

Abby grinned at the thought and then chided herself for taking un-Amish-like pleasure in another person's misfortune. Even if he deserved it.

She wanted to forgive Logan for taking advantage of her innocence, but she couldn't find it in her heart yet. Her naive need to be loved had made it easy for him to manipulate and seduce her. She had been foolishly thrilled to think a handsome, worldly man like Logan cared for her. As one of her father's attorneys, Logan was always dressed in the finest suits and wore a signature black cowboy hat. He wasn't a tall man, but he carried himself with a swagger that made him seem bigger.

The wonderful scenario she imagined where he would

stand up to her father and take her away had crumbled to dust the moment she voiced her dream to him.

Logan had laughed. Said he had hoped to curry her father's favor by courting her, the poor, sad nutcase daughter, but once he learned her father couldn't care less about her, Logan had dropped his pretense of being a loving partner and proved over the following weeks how cruel he could be.

He told her point-blank that they would marry. She wouldn't object if she knew what was good for her. She was her father's only child and heir. Once they were wed, Logan would be in line for a piece of her father's business empire as her husband and the family's main attorney. Logan took a strange delight in telling her about her father's business ventures and how he would do things differently. According to him, the illegal side of her father's business paid much better than the legal cover operations and Logan wanted to expand them.

When Abby discovered she was pregnant, she knew that wedding could never take place.

It was Logan's arrogance that had allowed her to get away. He thought she was stupid and suitably cowed by his threats of retaliation if she disobeyed him. She had been afraid, but for her baby, not for herself.

He often left his wallet on the dresser and his laptop in his briefcase on the coffee table in her rooms when he visited. Thankfully he was a heavy sleeper. When she was finally ready to make her break, she took his credit card, bought a bus ticket online and then took his key card to open her locked door. Wearing his coat and hat, she had walked down the hall and out a side door. Without his unknowing help she would never have been able to leave her father's estate.

But she had gotten away. She was free. Her father's

henchmen said they were going to check the house before they left the area. She knew they meant her grandmother's home. She had been right to wait before going there.

Herbert, who had been in quiet conversation with the sheriff, picked up a plate with an untouched cinnamon roll and held it toward the officer. "We can't let Rose's delectable delights go to waste, can we? Coffee?"

"No thanks, Major. I want to do a little checking into our visitors. I'd sure like to know who they work for, who they're looking for and why."

"You don't believe their story?" Bertha asked.

Sheriff Hart shrugged. "Let's say I'm keeping an open mind."

"You'll find they're up to no good," Herbert stated firmly.

The sheriff chuckled. "Did you want me to arrest them on the spot?"

Herbert shook his head. "No probable cause since their paperwork was in order. Pity. But they weren't straightforward. I saw enough like them in my career to know they're ex-military. Who sends a pair like that to look for his runaway daughter?"

"That's what I intend to find out." Sheriff Hart touched the brim of his hat with one finger and left.

Herbert turned to Bertha. "Well, are you up for some bird-watching now that the excitement is over?"

"Of course I am."

"That's my gal. Grace?"

"I'll be right with you." She stacked the cups and carried them into the kitchen.

"Are you going to let us use your new microphone?" Bertha asked eagerly.

He frowned. "It's a delicate and expensive piece of equipment."

She propped her hands on her hips. "Is that a no, Herbie?"

"I didn't say no. I'll show you how it is used. Then we'll see."

Grace joined them, and the bird-watching trio went out together.

"I told you it would be fine," Rose said. She looked over her shoulder at Joe, then leaned toward Abby and whispered, "You don't really want to leave us, do you?"

As Abby's pent-up tension drained away, she managed to smile and shake her head. "*Nee*, I don't."

"I'm glad." Rose patted Abby's shoulder and went into the kitchen.

Abby sighed deeply. Her identity was safe. She didn't have to find somewhere new to hide or another job. She could stay in Harts Haven and work toward her goal of reclaiming her life and her freedom for good. All she needed was a doctor to say she was mentally competent and an attorney willing to go against the best that her father's money could buy. One of them would surely be Logan. She swallowed hard at the idea of facing him in a courtroom.

Joe slid into the chair across from her. "You know her, don't you? The woman they're looking for."

Startled, Abby was tempted to lie but she couldn't. For some reason she wanted Joe to think well of her once the truth came out. It was a forlorn hope. She was a thief, unwed and pregnant, with a history of mental illness. How could he think well of her? She couldn't tell him everything, but she needed to tell him something. She nodded. "I do know her."

"Why didn't you say anything?"

"Because she deserves to live a life free of fear."

"You heard them. She's mentally unstable and dangerous."

Abby leaned toward him, trying to hold in her anger. "It's all lies. Do you hear me? She isn't insane, she isn't dangerous. She's all alone but determined to escape the cruelty of others, including her father."

Joe gazed into her eyes for a long moment. "You sound like you know her well."

"Very well," she admitted quietly and sat back.

"Where is she?"

Abby looked away from his inquisitive gaze. It would be easy to pour out the truth to him. On the surface Joe seemed like a good man. She was drawn to him, but she had learned the hard way that a handsome face and a ready smile could hide a treacherous heart. "I can't say more."

He reached across the table and laid his hand on hers. "Then I won't ask you anything else."

Despite his heartfelt reassurance, Joe noticed Abby's guarded expression didn't change. Now he understood why she had been so upset by the arrival of those men. It was concern for the woman she knew. He admired her desire to protect her missing friend's identity and whereabouts. She was loyal and he respected that. He would keep his curiosity in check until she was ready to confide in him.

If that day came before he left town.

He pulled his hand away from hers. What was he doing getting involved with a single woman who had secrets? This wasn't the way to keep distance between them. He started to rise. "I've got to get back to work."

"You have time for a cup of *kaffi* and a cinnamon roll," Rose said as she plunked both items in front of him and took a seat at their table. "I've been thinking about the kitchen remodel, Joseph. I believe I would like to make some tiny changes. Would that be a problem?"

Joe scowled. The plans had been finalized. All the materials were on order or sitting outside. He sank back onto his chair in resignation. "What kind of changes?"

"That depends on how much of a delay it would cause. We do need to be open before the first of September to take advantage of the tourists who come for the state fair. How soon do you think you'll be finished if I don't change anything?"

"I can easily be finished in two weeks, but I want you to be happy with the project. What would you like changed?"

"Well, I'm not certain I like the countertop that Grace and I chose."

That was an easy fix. "If you pick something the supplier has in stock, it shouldn't delay me at all. It's one of the last things to go in."

Rose wrapped her *kapp* ribbon around her finger. "That's good to know. I'll look at some countertop samples soon. Abigail, would you like some hot tea?"

"Not if it's the same stuff you gave me last night."

Rose laughed. "It did help you sleep though, didn't it? I thought perhaps some Earl Grey might be more to your liking this morning."

"That sounds wonderful. And a roll," Abby added quickly. "I'm starving."

Rose picked up a butter knife and cut the roll she had brought Joe in half. "Joe will split his with you. He needs to get used to sharing."

"Why?" he asked, knowing he wasn't going to like her answer.

"Because that's what courting couples do. They share things."

"Rose, we are not courting," Abby said forcefully.

"That's right. We aren't," he added, stressing the point.

Rose folded her hands in front of her and shook her head sadly. "That's what you say now, but I've found that once an idea is planted in a person's mind it can stick. I'll be right back with your tea, Abby dear."

Joe waited until the kitchen door closed behind her. "Why is she obsessed with getting us together?"

"You're asking me? It's not my doing. I've only been here a few days."

"And I've only been in town two weeks." He rubbed his jaw slowly. "Something tells me she's not going to give up on the idea."

Abby frowned at him. "What makes you say that?"

"Apparently she has a reputation as a matchmaker to uphold in the community."

"I can already see she isn't a very good one. We don't belong together. I mean, I'm sure you're a nice fellow when you aren't being rude."

He drew back. "That's high praise coming from someone who hangs out windows to scold complete strangers."

She frowned. "I wasn't hanging out the window."

"As good as."

"Well—well, you deserved to be scolded. You were rude." She folded her arms and glared at him.

"You're not exactly sweetness and light. Pointing out the faults of others does not rid you of your own."

He stared in amazement as tears gathered in her eyes. She sniffed once and her lower lip began to quiver.

Not tears. He couldn't bear to see a woman cry. "Abby, don't do that."

"You're mean." She pushed her half of the roll toward him. "I don't want to share anything with you."

He pushed it back toward her. "Oh, come on. Think of it as a peace offering. You said you were hungry."

Rose came in with Abby's tea. She set the cup on the table. Her eyes narrowed as she glanced between them. "Have you been quarreling again? It is better to give others a piece of your heart than a piece of your mind." She crossed her arms and waited with one foot tapping impatiently.

"We were having a minor disagreement," Joe said, stepping into the pointed silence. "I'm sorry if I hurt your feelings, Abby."

"Are you?"

His mouth dropped open. "I said I was. Are you calling me a liar now?"

Rose held up one hand. "Abby, Joe has said he is sorry. I'm sure you are, as well."

"Maybe. Maybe not." She sniffed and wiped her cheeks with both hands.

"Abigail Martin, I'm ashamed of you. This is not our way." Rose's sharp tone caused Joe to look up. Her face was set in stern lines. She was serious.

Abby seemed to grasp that she had stepped over the line. "I'm sorry, Rose. I apologize for my surly tongue, Joe."

"That's okay. I have been rude at times. I'll do better."

"And I won't hang out my window to scold strangers," Abby said with a shaky grin. She looked at Rose. "Am I forgiven?"

Rose smiled at them both. "*Ja. Das ist goot.* Drink your tea and eat. Some folks get cranky when they're hungry. Always make sure she has eaten before you disagree with her, Joe."

As Rose left the room, he chanced a glance at Abby. A smile trembled on her lips. It widened when she met his gaze. He chuckled. "My grandfather always kept hard candy in his coat pockets. I thought it was for us grandkids but maybe it was for my grandmother. They disagreed sometimes."

"I like lemon drops if you want to keep some handy."

"I'll pick some up at the store today. Are we being nice to each other again?"

She nodded shyly. "I think so."

"Still no talking though?"

That brought a real smile to her lips. "I don't mind if you talk."

"Glad to hear it." He took a bite of his half of the cinnamon bun. "This is really *goot.*" He gestured toward her half. "Try it."

She did. Her face lit up with enjoyment. "Oh, *ja, das ist goot.* Very *goot.*"

Rose came in a few moments later with a plate of bacon and sausage. They helped themselves to some of each and finished their breakfast in companionable silence. Joe was reluctant to leave the table.

Abby could be good company when she wasn't scolding him, but he knew her mind was on something else. Most likely her runaway friend. Would she ever tell him the whole story?

Rose came in drying her hands on a dish towel. "Joseph, about the kitchen. The new doorway you're putting in isn't big enough. Can you make it wider?"

Did she realize that meant tearing out all the framing he'd already finished? "Rose, are you sure you want that?"

"I am."

Joe sighed. He wanted to stay with Abby and make sure she was okay. He glanced at her delicate face, surprised by how beautiful she was when she wasn't terrified out of her wits. He wished he could sit with her longer.

And that was exactly why he got up from the table. "How wide do you want it, Rose?"

Six

Abby woke the next morning to the purring sound of Joe's saw. She yawned and stretched, then sat up and clasped her arms around her bent knees.

She had done it. She had pulled off her escape.

A small bubble of excitement formed inside her, but she didn't allow it to grow bigger. Too many things could still go wrong. At least now she could go see her grandmother's house. Until a month ago she thought she would never see it again.

Logan was the one who told her that her grandparents had left their farm to her. She had been stunned. She always assumed the property had been inherited by her father since her mother was gone and her grandparents had no other children. She had imagined it had been sold long ago. When she asked Logan why she hadn't been told, he laughed and said that as a minor and then as a mentally incompetent person her father retained control of her trust. There was no need for her to know.

Until that day she had no idea there was a place she could go.

Swallowing her fear and disgust of Logan, she had carefully pumped him for snippets of information about the trust. He soon caught on and realized he had a way other than fear to control her. Her property became the carrot he dangled in front of her. Once they were married, he said he would petition the court to declare her competent and the property would be hers. She didn't believe him, but she agreed to marry him, telling him once the farm belonged to her he could sell it for her. Then she'd have her own money to buy clothes and jewelry and even a car.

She amused him by making lists of the things she wanted. Logan understood greed. He never suspected that she loved the farm for the memories it evoked and couldn't bear the thought of selling it. And so she began planning her escape.

She had begged Logan to take her to St. Louis on their honeymoon. She told him it was a place she had always dreamed of visiting. She wanted to go up in The Arch and see a Cardinals baseball game at their home field. And then she wanted to go to Miami and spend a week on the beach. She talked about it frequently in the following days hoping he would recall those conversations when she disappeared.

Her scheme to return to her grandparents' home had taken a lot of patience and planning, but it was paying off. Knowing that she might one day own that beloved home was almost too much to grasp.

She closed her eyes, remembering the smell of roses in

her grandmother's flower garden beside the front porch and the smell of fresh-baked bread in the mornings. She fondly recalled going with her grandfather to milk the cow. She never helped care for the horses, they were so big, but the cow had lovely soft brown eyes. Simply gathering the eggs had seemed like an adventure to a girl who'd spent most of her life inside her father's walled estate in the city. Her only sadness had been that her mother never joined her at the farm. She didn't understand until she was older that her mother had been shunned by her Amish community for marrying outside of her faith and wasn't allowed to come home.

Abby took a deep breath. After so many years she was going to the farm again. Not today, of course. She had to be sure her father's men had left the area before venturing out to the property. But soon.

She sat on the side of the bed and peeked through her curtains. It was barely past dawn, but Joe was already hard at work. The play of the golden morning light across his rugged face and lean muscular body mesmerized her as he moved with precision, cutting and stacking the wood without wasted motion. She enjoyed watching him work.

Joe's clothes were well-worn. There was a patch on one knee of his pants. His rolled-up sleeves were covered in sawdust. The straw hat he wore was pushed back on his head, and he had a pencil tucked behind his ear. A look of intense concentration showed on his face. He was so different from Logan's handsome, tailored perfection. Better really. Much better.

Yesterday Joe had proved he could be a friend, too.

Maybe.

It was hard to be certain. It wasn't like she excelled at judging people's characters or motives.

She pulled her robe on over her nightgown and settled her *kapp* on her head without putting up her long braid. Raising the window sash, she leaned out. "You're at it early today."

"Sorry if I disturbed you," he muttered and cut another piece of wood.

"It's time for me to get up anyway. What are you working on?"

"Rose has changed her mind about the size of the outside door."

"I know. I heard her say she wanted a bigger one, but didn't you do that yesterday afternoon?"

"I did. First thing this morning she told me she liked the smaller doorway better. So I ripped out that work, and I'm starting over."

Abby heard the disgust in his voice and felt sorry for him. "Rose can be a bit odd, but she is such a dear."

He nodded. "Yep, she is. If she wants a bigger door again tomorrow, I reckon I'll do it. As long as she is busy planning changes to the kitchen, she isn't matchmaking for us." He paused and looked up at her. "I thought you were going to give up hanging out windows to scold people."

"I'm not scolding anyone. I was curious to see what you were doing."

"When your curiosity is satisfied, maybe you could find me a cup of *kaffi* and bring it out here?"

She was oddly happy that he had asked for a small favor. "Sure. I'll be right down."

Abby dressed quickly, taking special care to tie her apron loosely. She wasn't showing much, but in a few months she would need to switch to an apron without ties. She unbraided her hair, brushed it smooth and folded it in flat layers against the back of her head, then pinned it in place.

After securing her *kapp*, she glanced in the small mirror. It was still strange to see an Amish woman looking back, but she was beginning to feel more comfortable with the change.

There were so many things she needed to learn about being Amish. She had to overcome her childhood fear of horses because she would need her own horse and buggy someday. She would have to learn to drive a tractor and learn how to plant and harvest crops on her farm. She had baked with her grandmother, but it had been years since she'd made bread. She knew how to hoe weeds and pick produce. She had learned to can vegetables, but she hadn't been on the farm in the spring when the garden was planted. She didn't know how to prepare the soil or what to plant first. She had a lot to learn, but she would take it one step at a time.

In the kitchen she found Grace and Susanna at the table. She nodded to them. "Good morning. Joe said he would like a cup of *kaffi*. I'll be happy to take it out to him if there is any ready."

"I just made a fresh pot," Susanna said. "If there is one thing I can't abide, it is old tasting coffee. Mamm told me about all the excitement yesterday. Were they really gangsters?"

"I don't think so," Abby said, holding back a smile as she got a mug from the cupboard. "Rose does know how to spice up a story."

Grace gave a dismissive wave of her hand. "That's what I said. Of course, I was in the kitchen most of the time but all I saw was two *Englisch* men in business suits."

"They probably didn't even have guns." Susanna took a sip of her coffee. "Sometimes I wonder about Mamm. The Lord knows I love her, but the way she forgets things.

She opened another can of cat food this morning for her dead cat."

"It wasn't for Phebe. It's for Wilma," Abby said. "And the sheriff was the one who saw the men were carrying guns."

Grace frowned. "Who is Wilma and why does she want cat food?"

Abby grinned. "Wilma is Rose's gray cat that likes to hide under furniture."

Both Susanna's eyebrows shot up. "Mamm has another cat? Why haven't I seen it?"

"Wilma knows you dislike cats, so she hides when you're around," Rose said, coming up behind Abby. "And I'm not as forgetful as you think." She glared at her daughter.

"I didn't say it to be mean, Mamm. I said it because I worry about you. I wish I could be home more."

"Ha! You need your job to keep me from getting on your nerves."

Susanna looked hurt. "That's not true."

Rose smiled at her. "I know. When we reopen the inn, I think it will bring in enough money so you can leave the lumberyard before the end of the year. In fact, I've decided to reopen today."

"What?" Susanna sat up straight.

"I went down to the phone shack and checked our messages. We had a request for rooms from a party of six adults for the weekend. I called them back and confirmed. They will be here tomorrow morning."

"You're going to run a bed-and-breakfast inn without a kitchen?" Grace asked in astonishment.

"I will have Joe stop work on the addition and get our new fridge hooked up. I'll stock up on the perishables that we'll need. We don't have countertops, but we can get a couple of folding tables to use as our workspace in here. The woman I talked to said they wanted to see Amish country and have an Amish experience."

"I hope she knows we don't do tricks," Susanna said sourly.

Rose shot her a reproachful look. "That is not kind. You know better. I've asked Dwayne Lapp to give them a ride in his buggy and he has agreed. I think that is the kind of thing they're after. Oh, and they want to see Amish quilts."

"That shouldn't be a problem," Grace said. "Lisa Bieler has some nice ones for sale at her fabric shop. But, Rose, are you sure about taking in guests before the kitchen is done?"

"It will be fine." Rose dismissed Grace's concern with a wave of her hand.

"I hope this remodel will be worth it," Susanna said. "It's going to take forever at this rate. We might have to get another contractor if Joe keeps making mistakes. He's built that doorway twice, and now he's tearing it out again." She pointed to the opening covered by a blue tarp.

"A slight misunderstanding between Joe and myself." Rose winked at Abby. "I'm sure Joe is the perfect fellow for the job no matter how long it takes. Don't you think so, Abby?"

Abby filled the mug she held. It suddenly dawned on her exactly what Rose was doing with her changes. She turned to face the older woman. "I reckon that depends."

Rose tipped her head slightly. "Depends on what?"

"On if he quits or not before the job is done."

"What would make him quit?" Rose tried to appear innocent. The other women weren't buying it. Susanna and Grace were looking at her with narrowed eyes.

Abby tipped her head toward Rose. "You might make him quit. If he finds out you are changing the kitchen plans just to keep him around longer because you want us to make a match, he won't be happy. Besides, it isn't going to happen. Joe and I are not meant for each other."

"Is that what you're doing, Rose?" Grace sounded aghast.

"Mamm, is she right?" Susanna demanded.

Abby chuckled and walked away with the familiar sound of raised voices growing behind her. It was satisfying to be the spoon that stirred the pot for a change.

Joe had been keeping one eye on the door, waiting for Abby to appear. Was she feeling better today now that the outsiders had left? Was her friend safe? She had looked rested and at peace when she spoke to him from her window earlier. He didn't know when he first saw her if he should bring up yesterday's episode or ignore it. He chose not to mention it. He didn't want her to think he was prying, because he had promised not to.

He hadn't been able to shake the image of her stricken face from the day before. He had dreamed about her last night. Even when he was asleep, he couldn't escape her.

In his dream he saw Abby leaning out a window begging for his help, but it wasn't strange men threatening her. He saw the flicker of flames growing brighter behind her. He couldn't reach her. His feet wouldn't move. He could only watch as she disappeared backward into the fire. It was a new and unsettling version of the recurring nightmares that plagued him.

When Abby walked out of the inn he was stunned at the sight of her wide grin. She looked happy and amazingly beautiful in the early-morning light. She giggled as she handed him a white mug filled with steaming coffee. Every trace of fear was gone from her face.

"What's so funny?" he asked.

"The widows. They're so charming. Even the way they argue is sweet."

He glanced at the house. "Are they arguing now?"

"Uh-huh. I'm afraid I started it."

"This I need to hear."

"Susanna suggested they might need another contractor since you keep redoing the same door."

He frowned. "She knows Rose asked me to do that, right?"

"She didn't, but I told her Rose is making these changes because she's trying to keep you around longer and improve her chances of making a match between us."

He folded his arms over his chest and leaned back against his worktable. "Are you joking? That's why I'm rebuilding the doorframe for the third time and why I'm behind on getting the cabinets in and why I'm waiting on a countertop she hasn't picked out yet?"

"Isn't it funny?" She giggled.

He wasn't inclined to laugh. "To you maybe. I'm the one who is going to have to explain to my boss why this job didn't get done on time and why I'm over budget." He swept a hand toward the cut lumber. "These boards aren't free."

"I'm sure now that Susanna and Grace know what Rose is up to, they'll put a stop to it. Oh, and Rose wants you to quit working on the addition and bring in the new refrigerator. She's taking guests starting tomorrow."

"I was assured the kitchen wouldn't be in use until I was finished. Working around women who are cooking and serving meals will slow me down even more. My boss is expecting me to be finished here sometime next week."

Some of the laughter left her eyes. "So soon. Do you know where your next job will be?"

"I haven't heard. Oliver is on a rush project in Kingman right now. He'll let me know when he comes by next week."

"Could it be here in Harts Haven?"

"I reckon it could, but it could just as easily be in another state."

She wrinkled her nose. "Doesn't it get old moving all the time?"

"*Nee*, I like it. New places, new people." Maybe if he said that often enough it would become true.

"Not me. I want a place to put down roots. Deep roots that will last for generations." A faraway look came into her eyes. As if that sense of connection had been missing in her life.

He nodded. "Most Amish feel that way."

"But not you? Why not?"

He was tempted to share the pain of his past. To lay bare his faults and reveal the deadly consequences of the decision that had driven him to become a drifter.

She waited, her eyes filled with curiosity, a slight smile parting her lips. Would she understand and forgive him? Or would she be repulsed?

He couldn't do it. He wasn't going to burden her with his sins when she was finally happy. "It's a long story, and I've got work to do." He finished his coffee and handed her the mug. *"Danki."*

He turned his back on her and started the saw again. From the corner of his eyes he caught her going into the inn. She paused in the doorway and looked back before heading inside. What was she thinking? That he was being rude again?

He grabbed a board, marked it and wished he could dismiss Abby from his mind as easily as he cut the next piece of lumber.

What he needed to do was concentrate on his work, take his meals in his trailer and avoid seeing her. He glanced over at her window. Was she watching him? He waited but the curtain didn't move. Abruptly, he turned off his saw and began gathering up his tools. The first thing he needed to do was move his workstation away from her window.

The arrival of the Barrett family the next day filled the inn with activity. It wasn't until after four o'clock that Abby was finally able to get away. She told Grace she was going for a walk and left by the side door. She was certain she could locate her grandparents' property from memory. All she had to do was find the river.

She stopped first at the corral, determined to work on overcoming her fear of the animals so important to the Amish. Horses. A young colt came up to the fence. Abby took a step back and chided herself for being a coward. This wasn't a big animal. She moved closer and held out her hand. The colt sniffed it. Then it simply stood looking at her with large brown eyes. "Okay, you aren't so scary."

Abby reached out and drew her fingers down the horse's cheek. It shook its head and snorted. She quickly jumped back. "I guess that's enough for now. I've got to go."

She turned and rushed down the lane to the highway. There wasn't much traffic on the paved road leading north out of town. Two pickups passed her, both going much too fast. She met a farmer on a green tractor coming her way pulling a feed wagon. The man inside the enclosed cab gave a friendly wave. She waved back, relishing the feeling of belonging to a rural community like the one she had known as a child and having the freedom to go where she wanted without constraints for the first time in years. Laughing, she kicked a stone along the road until it bounced off into the ditch. It was easy to imagine a little boy or girl walking at her side, enjoying the fun, holding her hand. Being a good mother was the most important thing in the world to Abby.

When she saw a dark car coming toward her, she put her head down and clenched her hands into fists as it went past.

She chanced a glance over her shoulder. It was still going. No red taillights signaled it was stopping. Reality followed close behind her relief. She wasn't free yet. She still had to be watchful.

Like almost all the local roads, this one ran straight as an arrow into the vast farmland. It was bordered with strands of barbed wire on old wooden fence posts. Long stretches had gnarled, thorny hedges of Osage orange trees on one side or the other. She had learned from her grandfather that the hedgerows were planted to protect the soil from blowing away like it had during the Dust Bowl.

She followed the highway until the Arkansas River meandering across the plains abruptly stopped it. There wasn't a bridge. She stared at the tree-lined stretch of water that was little more than sandbars hooked together by trickles in the summer. It looked placid now, but she had seen it grow to a raging torrent a quarter of a mile wide after one of the violent thunderstorms had swept across the land. She had to find the bridge and cross over. The road turned west. She followed it for another mile and finally found what she was looking for. A long bridge with low concrete guardrails spanned the muddy brown water flowing slowly under it. Abby knew she was going the right way now.

She rested for a while, sitting on the bridge watching the eddies and swirls that emerged from between the pilings below and massaging her aching left calf. She hadn't walked so far in ages and didn't realize she was so out of shape. Her feet were starting to sting where her shoes rubbed. It was a long walk back to Harts Haven and she hadn't even reached the farm. It would be dark in a couple of hours. She was tempted to turn back but she couldn't give up now. She had risked so much to get this far. Rising, she crossed the bridge and kept walking.

At the next intersection she turned north again. It was a sand road, not paved. It crunched softly under her shoes as she walked past now-familiar landmarks. There was the rock house that had belonged to the Trent family. Their neglected barn had fallen further into disrepair. It didn't look as if anyone lived at the house anymore.

A wooded creek ran parallel to the road for a few hundred yards and then curved away. Abby stopped in the spot where the creek came closest to the road. Picking up a pebble, she tossed it into the water and watched the ripples spread in ever widening circles. The tall cottonwood trees along the stream were shimmering in the late-afternoon breeze, their heart-shaped leaves flashing silver and green. There was a woodpecker somewhere hammering away for his supper, but she couldn't see him.

She used to fish at this spot with her *daadi*. If they caught enough catfish, Grossmammi would fry them to a delicious golden brown for supper. Abby smiled at the memories that bombarded her. She would teach her son or daughter how to fish here someday.

Her grandparents' lane was just up ahead. What kind of people lived on the farm now? She couldn't imagine her father would rent the place to an Amish family. Whoever they were, she hoped they were taking good care of the house.

She wouldn't stop today. She'd only walk past. Seeing it would be enough. Having the people who lived there report a female Amish visitor was a sure way to bring unwanted attention to the place.

She began walking more slowly as she realized she didn't have a reason to be in the area if someone stopped her. What would she say? That she was lost or that she was on her way to someone else's farm? No one lived east of her grandfather's place. The road ended in a marsh.

The landscape became more overgrown the closer she got to the house. No-trespassing signs adorned several fence posts. Looking around, she saw the fields her grandfather had tended so carefully were nothing but weeds. No crops had been planted. He had owned over six hundred acres of fertile bottomland. Why wasn't it being farmed?

At the lane she saw the mailbox lying rusted and bent in the ditch. No one had collected mail from it in months if not years. She walked up the overgrown lane in disbelief and stopped in front of the house.

There were no flowers in front of the porch on the two-story white farmhouse with a green metal roof. Weeds and small trees grew up to the foundation. The same was true of the barn and all the outbuildings. She walked closer in dismay.

The wooden front gate stood crookedly open, held up by one rusty hinge. It, too, bore a no-trespassing sign. It was hard to even see the flagstone walkway in the overgrown grass. The trellis with her grandmother's prized roses had fallen away from the house. The scraggly rosebush was fighting the weeds for a place to bloom and losing. Her grandfather's wicker chair on the front porch had fallen over in front of the door. The windows were covered in grime. The paint on the house was starting to peel. It was nothing like the pristine farm her grandparents had worked so hard to keep up.

Abby pressed a hand to her mouth to hold back a sob. This was not what she expected. The place was abandoned.

It looked as if no one had been here since her grandparents died. Clearly her father hadn't spent a penny on upkeep in the last eight years. Not on the farmland nor on the buildings.

When Logan told her that her father managed the property in her trust, she assumed he was milking the profits for his personal gain. That was Victor's style. This farm wasn't profiting anyone. Why keep it from her? It made no sense. He might have despised his wife's parents and their pious lifestyle, but he wouldn't leave the place abandoned out of contempt. Victor Worthington III never did anything unless it benefited him. Whatever reason he had for keeping control of the farm it wasn't because it generated income.

At least she wouldn't have to evict a family when she was granted legal rights to the place. That was good. She took a step back and surveyed the house. It would take hard work, but she could fix it up. Pull the weeds, clear the flower beds, clean the windows. She bent to lift the trellis, but let it drop as a new realization hit her.

As soon as she did anything to clear the yard or repair the house it would be apparent someone was fixing it up. Her father's men were gone, but they might check back periodically. Her father was a thorough man. He could even have one of the locals watching the house if he suspected she would come here.

She glanced around, looking for any sign of movement. A rustling sound in the bushes near the house made her jump. A rabbit darted out of the brush and disappeared into the long grass across the lane. Wrapping her arms across her middle, she shivered in the warm evening air. She shouldn't be here. It was too soon. Yet she had come so far. She couldn't leave without at least looking inside.

Was the furniture still here? The books her grandmother

had loved, the family Bible, the dishes and sewing machine, the handmade quilts? Abby had to know. This was where she would make a home for herself and her baby.

Rather than move the overturned chair on the porch blocking the entrance, she went around to the back. Stepping up to the small, enclosed porch, she grasped the knob of the back door with a trembling hand. She glanced down and she saw a muddy footprint on the threshold. Her fingers turned icy cold with fear. She heard a man's voice inside. She jumped back from the door as panic clutched her heart. Looking around, she saw a dense clump of lilacs and scurried behind them. She threw herself down in the long grass, curled into a ball and prayed.

Seven

Joe sat down in a lawn chair outside his trailer. He put his head back against the side of his little home and closed his eyes. It had been a long day, but he had made good progress in getting back on schedule. Abby hadn't bothered him once today. Rose hadn't changed a single thing in the kitchen plans. Two more uninterrupted workdays and he'd be back where he needed to be, but he would have to wait a day longer.

Tomorrow was Sunday. It wasn't *Gemeesunndaag*, the Sunday with a church service the Amish attended every other week. It was the off Sunday. Unlike most Amish who spent the day visiting or entertaining friends and relatives, he had no plans except to catch up on his rest.

The cicadas' whirring songs rose and fell on the early-evening air in the trees around him. A cool breeze dried the sweat on his brow. His life was returning to normal.

"Joseph, I need you to take a buggy and look for Abby."

He opened one eye. Rose stood in front of him with her hands on her hips. He shut his eye. "Nope. I'm not falling for it."

"What?"

She could play coy all she wanted. "I'm not falling for whatever scheme you've cooked up to get Abby and me alone together."

"Oh, never mind that. I've given up on the pair of you. I'll find someone better for Abby, but right now I need you to go look for her. She went for a walk hours ago, and she hasn't come back."

He opened both eyes. "What do you mean someone better?"

"A man who isn't stuck in the past and can appreciate what a treasure she is."

"I'm not stuck in the past."

One eyebrow rose above the wire rim of her glasses. "Aren't you?"

He closed his eyes to avoid her sharp gaze. "I'm glad you've come to your senses. Abby and I are not a good fit."

"Joseph, please, I'm worried about her."

He ignored the twinge of concern her words brought on. "I'm sure she's fine. The exercise will do her good. It'll put some color in her pale cheeks."

"Those men may still be in the area."

He opened his eyes and looked at Rose closely. She was worried. He sat up. "I thought the sheriff's men escorted them out of town."

"There's nothing to stop them from returning once the

sheriff's back is turned. Abby was frightened half to death by them."

She had been. Joe frowned and shook his head. "I'm sure they're gone."

"Are you going to look for her or not? Honestly, Joseph, I thought better of you. I never took you for a man who would willingly turn his back on a woman in trouble."

"I'm not turning my back on anyone. You don't know that she's in trouble."

"I feel it in my bones."

Was this some new tactic by Rose? She almost had him convinced. "Are you sure it isn't just your arthritis kicking up?"

"I should wash your mouth out with soap for speaking to an elder with such disrespect."

He sighed, pushed out of his chair and started toward the barn with Rose following close behind him. "If this is one of your matchmaking stunts, Rose, you can find a new contractor tomorrow."

"It isn't. How could I plan for her to get lost or hurt? I have guests I must look after, or I would go myself. Please find her."

He rolled open the wide door of the barn where the family buggies were housed. "Do you know which way she went?"

"*Ja*, toward the river. Cross the bridge and then take the first left and go a mile east."

"Okay," he said slowly. Such a detailed answer was out of character for Rose. At least he knew where to look but the bridge was five miles away. "What is she doing way out there?"

"How should I know. It will be dark in an hour or so. Please hurry."

"Okay. Which horse do you want me to take?"

"Bendy is the fastest. Take her. She's the one with the white blaze and sour temper. The two of you should get along fine." Rose turned on her heels and strode toward the inn.

"I don't have a sour temper," he mumbled to the horse in the first stall. She laid back her ears.

Rose hadn't exaggerated. Bendy balked at the stall door, then tried to bite him when he snapped on the lead rope. A stern word and a forceful tug were all it took to correct her attitude.

He slung the harness over the mare's back. "What did Rose mean by someone better, anyway? Was she saying I'm not good enough for Abby?"

The horse snorted. He wasn't sure if she was agreeing or not. "Rose doesn't know anything about me. I'm not poor. I've got enough money saved to start my own construction business someday. She doesn't know anything about Abby, for that matter, and neither do I. Maybe she isn't good enough for me."

It was contrary to his faith to judge someone without cause, but he was sure the horse wouldn't mention this conversation to the bishop. Bendy stamped her hoof impatiently. He finished buckling the harness in place. "That was wrong of me. Abby's a nice woman, and she deserves to be happy with whatever poor fellow Rose picks next."

In a few minutes he had Bendy harnessed and hitched to the open buggy the widows used for local shopping trips. It had a single bench seat with a box on the back for hauling goods. It was lighter than the enclosed buggy, which meant Bendy could pull it easily and faster.

Climbing on board, Joe switched on the battery-powered outside lights that would alert other vehicles to his presence on the road. There were also reflective tape strips and a slow-moving vehicle triangle on the rear of the box. Most *Englisch* locals knew to watch for horse-drawn buggies even at night, but not everyone was careful in sharing the road.

He headed Bendy out of town at a fast walk. When he found Abby, should he warn her that Rose was looking to pair her with a new match? He chuckled to himself. No, he'd let it be a surprise. It would be interesting to see who this better man might be.

Afraid to move, Abby waited and listened for what seemed like an hour but must have only been ten minutes until she heard the door open.

"That was a good game."

"I knew the Lakers would win it."

She recognized the voices. They belonged to the men who'd come to the inn searching for her.

"I hate watching sports on my phone when I've got a fifty-inch plasma screen in my apartment. Nobody has been near this place in years. Call Mr. V and see if we can head back."

Abby raised her head a fraction. She could see them through the thick branches. The dark-haired one had his phone to his ear. "Yes, sir, it's Phil. No sign of anyone at the place... He's not going to like that... Yes, sir. I will."

The other man pulled the door shut. "What did he say?"

"He wants Gilly to check the place periodically."

Gilly? She knew the name but couldn't put a face to it. One of her father's men for sure.

Phil touched his phone again and held it to his ear. "I've got instructions. The boss wants you to keep an eye on this place... No, you won't have to confront her. She could probably take you in a fair fight, you wimp. Call Mr. V if you see anything suspicious… Fine… Look, I'll send you a couple of pics of the place. If anything changes. If you see lights at night… Figure it out!"

Phil ended the call with a grunt of disgust. "He says he'll drive by in a few days, but he doesn't want to be seen poking around here. He's afraid it will attract attention."

"He could be right."

"I'll be surprised if the wimp comes by more than once. He says the sheriff isn't the fool we pegged him for."

Abby heard them walking away. She sat up cautiously. A few moments later she heard a car drive off. They must have had it hidden in one of the outbuildings.

She didn't know why they hadn't seen her when she had been out front, but she thanked God for her deliverance. It sounded as if they were leaving the area for good this time. Stepping out from behind the lilacs, she brushed off her dress. Her impatience to see the place had almost been her undoing.

She opened the back door. The rear hallway separated the two ground-floor bedrooms. There was dust on the plank floor and cobwebs hanging from the ceiling. Instead of the scent of the pine cleaner her grandmother had used, she was met with the musty smell of decay. On one side of the hall was the bedroom that had been used by her grandparents. The other one had been kept ready for visitors. Abby had slept in one of the upstairs bedrooms when she stayed during the summer.

The door to her grandparents' room stood open a crack. She hesitated then pushed it wide. The fading light through the grimy windows showed a handmade blue-and-white quilt still covering the double bed. Her grandmother's dresses were hanging limply on the pegs on the wall along with her grandfather's straw hat and his shirts. Everything was covered in a thick layer of dust and cobwebs. Abby wrapped her arms across her middle. Her heart ached at the signs of neglect. It would have broken her grandmother's heart to see the place in this condition.

At the foot of the bed stood a cedar blanket chest. Abby lifted the lid and was relieved to see the quilts inside looked as good as the day her grandmother had packed them away. She ran a hand lovingly over the material as she admired the delicate, tiny stitches that had turned scraps of material into beautiful and useful works of art.

Abby left the room and went toward the kitchen. She paused in the doorway. Tears gathered in her eyes. Debris littered the floor beneath a broken window on the side of the house, proving birds and animals had found their way inside. The floorboards were rotted where the rain had blown in and mildew coated the wall. Evidence of mice and a pack rat nest in the corner sent a shiver down her spine. The cushion from her grandmother's rocker had fallen on the floor. Rodents were using the stuffing for nesting material, leaving it scattered across the floor. Abby turned away from the sight and her gaze landed on the cookstove.

She skirted the oak table that looked dusty but untouched and laid one hand on the old black wood-burning stove. It sat cold and devoid of the life it had seemed to give to the kitchen when she was young. There had always been the most amazing smells coming from it. Fresh-baked bread, sticky buns and cinnamon rolls, hot coffee or hot cocoa, rich stews and roasting chicken, cookies and homemade candy. Tears slipped unheeded down Abby's cheeks. Her clearest memory was of her grandmother standing in front of the stove humming as she cooked, then smiling at Abby and beckoning her closer. *Come*, liebchen, *help me make your* daadi*'s breakfast.*

Abby turned away. One day she would make wonderful meals for her son or daughter just as her grandmother had.

A quick look through the rest of the house showed the mice had made their homes in the sofa in the living room, too. The cushions couldn't be saved, but the wooden frame was intact. She would be able to make new cushions and re-cover the arms. It was clear this was where her father's men had spent much of the past two days. Empty soda cans, snack wrappers and take-out cartons from a café in Hutchinson littered the floor.

The upstairs bedroom where Abby had slept was unchanged except for the dust everywhere and a few mouse droppings. She would certainly have to invest in some cats for the farm. Making her way back downstairs to the kitchen again, she surveyed the mess and her shoulders slumped. She sat down in her grandmother's rocker and faced her disappointment.

Turning the house into a home for herself and her child would be a daunting task. How could she do everything that needed to be done before her baby was born? She couldn't bring a child into this. She closed her eyes and began rocking as tears threatened.

Amish folks were never alone, her grandmother used to say. God and their neighbors were always there for them. Abby needed and wanted to be a part of that kind of community, but doing so meant trusting others, an ability her father and Logan had stripped away over the past months and years. It would be hard, but she would have to manage alone until she was free of her father's control.

She got up and left the house by the back door, checking around carefully before stepping out. Near the front gate, she stopped and gave the house one last look. Someday it would be a home again. Her home. A place of refuge for her and her child.

Could she somehow start tidying up inside without touching the outside? Even sweeping away the dust and cobwebs from the kitchen would make her feel better. She didn't want to leave her grandmother's home as it was. Now that she had seen it, she wanted to do something.

Her common sense quickly put that dream in its place. Cleaning and repairs would have to wait if one of her father's men was coming by to check it. Her impatience had almost ruined everything today. Even if she wasn't recognized, she had no business being in this area. That alone might rouse suspicion. The road out front ended a quarter of a mile farther east at a large marsh. Unless something had changed, only a few farmers used the road to access their fields to the north of Grandfather's land.

With a sinking heart she realized returning wouldn't be worth the risk. She started back to town, limping as her feet became more painful with each step.

By the time Joe reached the bridge he started to wonder if Rose had given him bad directions. Or maybe her bones were right. Maybe Abby had met up with those men. Bendy balked at the edge of the bridge, refusing to step onto it. Annoyed, he started to get down and lead the stubborn mare across when a flash of blue and white caught his eye down by the river.

He backed Bendy away from the bridge and moved her off the roadway, then scrambled down the steep embankment. Abby sat at the water's edge with her feet in the river.

"Abby, are you okay?" he asked, moving to her side.

She looked up in surprise. It took him a second to realize she had been crying. She wiped her cheeks with both hands. "What are you doing here?"

"Rose sent me to look for you."

"Why?"

"She was worried that you weren't back yet. Are you okay?"

"Not really. I stopped to soak my feet because I have blisters on my heels. It hurt too much to keep walking." She stifled a sob.

The poor kid. "I don't think muddy river water is the best treatment."

"That shows what you know. Native Americans used to use mud packs to draw out infections."

"Did they?"

She sniffled and wiped her nose on her sleeve. "I read that somewhere. I'm not sure it's true."

He sat down beside her. "I stepped on a rusty nail once, and my *mamm* made a poultice of bread soaked in milk and wrapped it on my foot."

"Wasn't that soggy?"

"Very."

"Did it help?"

"I didn't get lockjaw, and I still have my foot."

She lifted her left leg out of the water. The back of her heel had a blister the size of a silver dollar. "I don't want to put my shoes on."

"Then don't. Stand up and lean on me."

"I'll be okay." She rose and balanced on the balls of her feet.

"I know you will be because I'm going to carry you up to the buggy."

Her eyes widened. "Oh, no, *nee* you can't do that."

"Who's going to stop me?" He swept her up into his arms. She closed her eyes and held herself rigid as a board.

"Relax, I won't drop you."

"Put me down. Put me down!" Her panic was real. She started trembling violently.

"Okay. Take it easy." He lowered her feet to the ground. "I'm sorry. I didn't mean to frighten you."

She pushed him away. "I'm not frightened."

He didn't believe her. She was panting like a dog on a hot day. "Okay, you aren't scared."

"I don't like to be manhandled."

"I noticed," he said, taking a step back to give her some breathing room. "How can we get you to the road?"

She looked up the steep slope. "I can crawl."

"Won't that be awkward in a dress?"

"I'll manage."

"I have a better idea. When was the last time you had a piggyback ride?" he asked.

"A what?"

"You know. Piggyback. You get behind me, put your arms around my neck, and I'll carry you up. That way you can let go whenever you want. No manhandling involved. What do you say?"

"Maybe."

"It will take a load off those poor feet."

She grimaced as she took a step. "Okay, we can try it."

"Great." He turned around, squatted in front of her and waited. She tentatively laid her hands on his shoulders.

"Get a good grip around my neck and then lean on me. You won't hurt me."

"Are you sure?"

"The longer we stand here talking, the more worried Rose is becoming."

"Okay." She wrapped her arms tightly around his neck. He stood and bent forward at the waist to take her weight and keep her feet off the ground. Struggling up the incline with her choke hold on his neck and her weight hanging behind him was harder than he thought. He was seeing spots by the time he reached the buggy. He leaned back to put her down beside it. She let go and he sucked in several deep breaths.

"Danki," she said shyly.

He coughed twice. "Don't mention it."

"Are you okay?"

"I will be as soon as the blood gets back to my brain."

"I'm so sorry."

"Don't be. I got you up here. Can you get in the buggy?"

"Of course." She hobbled to the front and climbed in.

He took his time going round to the other side. When his vision was clear, he got in and picked up the lines. "What were you doing all the way out here, anyway?"

She looked off into the distance. "Exploring."

Something about the way she said it made him look at her more closely. Her guard was up the way it had been when they first encountered the outsiders. "That's about the lamest explanation I've heard in a while."

She stiffened but didn't look at him. "Are you calling me a liar?"

"Nee, but you like to leave out a lot of the truth."

"I don't know what you're talking about."

"See, that right there. You do know what I'm talking about. You didn't explain that those men were looking for someone you knew until I guessed it. Now you don't seem inclined to explain why you're exploring miles from town, so I'm going to assume the two parts of the unspoken truth are somehow related."

She cast him a sidelong glance. "That's a big assumption."

"But not incorrect or you would have pointed that out."

"You said you weren't going to ask me anything else about her."

"I'm not. It wouldn't do me any good anyway." He clamped his mouth shut. Let her keep her secrets. He turned Bendy toward Harts Haven. The mare sprang into a trot without his urging. She knew she was headed home.

"I am thankful you found me," Abby said softly. The gratitude in her voice lessened his annoyance.

"Du bischt wilkumm," he said grudgingly. Saying she was welcome was common courtesy, but it would be the last thing he said to her until he returned her to Rose's care.

The seat on the wagon was small and narrow. There was barely room for both of them. Her shoulder bumped lightly against his as the buggy swayed, making him acutely aware of her. She moved over as far as possible. Another inch and she might topple off the side if he hit a bump. Why didn't she trust him?

Because she barely knew him and that was the way it should stay. Rose would find her a better match. Hopefully, a man who didn't care that she had secrets. He urged Bendy to a faster pace. The fence posts began flying past. The sooner they got back to the inn, the sooner he could retire to his trailer and forget all about how Abby felt in his arms.

Abby glanced at Joe's set face. The sinking sun turned the thin clouds on the western horizon to tattered flags of red and orange fading to pinks and golds. The light shone on one side of his face with a golden glow, the other was in shadow, making it hard to tell what he was thinking.

He was angry with her. She couldn't help her reaction

to being grabbed without warning, but he didn't know that. She couldn't tell him why she had come so far from Harts Haven without jeopardizing her identity. If she had only herself to consider she might trust him, but the fate of her unborn child wasn't something she could gamble with. Trusting any man was risky. Even one as appealing as Joe, a hardworking Amish fellow.

Sitting in the dust-covered rocking chair that had belonged to her grandmother in the familiar kitchen had brought home to Abby just how much she wanted to belong to the faith her grandmother had cherished. What would her grandmother tell her to do? What would a devout Amish woman do?

She would trust God. God had brought Joe into Abby's life for a reason. The Amish depended on each other. They never faced trials alone. The community was ready and willing to help one another. If she was going to practice the faith she had admired since she was a child, she had to start somewhere. Maybe she was supposed to start by trusting Joe. He was only going to be in town for a short time. He was as much a stranger here as she was. They had that in common.

"Were you looking for me a long time?" she asked.

He stayed silent for so long she gave up hope of having a conversation. She looked out over the darkening countryside. Only a few lights marked the farms along the way.

"Rose knew right where you'd gone."

Surprised, Abby half turned toward him. "How could she know that? I didn't tell anyone. I mean, I told Grace I was going for a walk, but I didn't say where."

"How does Rose know anything? Maybe the cat told her."

"I'm sure I didn't mention it to the cat." Abby tipped her head slightly to see if he caught her joke.

He glanced her way but didn't smile. She looked down at her hands. She had no idea how to offer Joe her friendship. It had been too long since she'd had a friend.

"Cats are sneaky. She might have heard you talking in your sleep and squealed on you," he said.

Her hopes for some sort of truce were rekindled. "That's a possibility. My trip today has been on my mind for a long time."

"Has it?"

She took a deep breath. "*Ja*, and I know you are wondering why."

"Me? *Nee*, I'm not wondering anything," he said flatly.

She gripped her fingers tightly together. "A long time ago I used to visit an elderly couple who lived on the other side of the river. They were relatives of mine."

"Is that so." He didn't sound the least interested.

It had taken all her courage to utter that much about her past. He wasn't making this easy. She wasn't sure she should have shared that much.

"They're both gone now, but I remember them fondly. I wanted to see the old place, but I was worried that the new owners wouldn't appreciate my dropping in. There was a split in the family." That was putting it mildly, but it was the truth.

He looked at her. "And did they mind?"

"No one was home. It wasn't the same as I remembered from my childhood."

"Things seldom are."

She sighed deeply. "I don't know why I expected it to be unchanged. That was foolish of me. I also didn't realize how far it was from town."

"The widows would have let you use a buggy if you had asked."

Her grandfather had taught her how to drive a buggy, but she'd never found the courage to learn how to harness a horse and he'd never insisted that she learn. Probably because he knew she wouldn't need that skill in the *Englisch* world. She would need it soon but how did she ask someone to teach her? It was sure to make them suspicious of her background. She shrugged. "I guess I'm not good at asking for favors."

"I can understand that. I'm sort of that way myself."

"Do we have something in common? Oh, no." She pressed her hands to her cheeks in mock horror. "Don't tell Rose. She'll be sure her matchmaking is working."

"Rose said she's given up on us."

"Are you serious? When did she say that?"

"When she asked me to find you. I told her I wasn't going to fall for another one of her matchmaking schemes."

"But you came anyway."

"Rose has a way of making you feel guilty if you don't do what she wants."

"Emotional blackmail. I'm familiar with that tactic."

"How so?"

She flinched. That careless remark was the kind that would easily trip her up. She glanced at Joe. It was getting dark. She couldn't see his face clearly. Somehow that made it easier to talk to him.

"I could never gain my father's approval no matter how hard I tried. I always felt I wasn't enough for him. He used to say I needed to try harder to be the best. I did try but it was never enough. I stopped trying after my mother died."

"How old were you then?"

"Fourteen."

"Your *daed* sounds like a hard man."

"Hard. That's exactly what he is. What about your father? Do the two of you get along?"

"We got along when I was young, but when I turned fifteen or so we started butting heads."

She heard a catch in his voice. "Are you still at odds?"

He looked down. "Daed died before I came to my senses."

She laid her hand on his arm, wanting to offer him comfort. She knew what it was to lose someone close. "I'm sorry, Joe."

"*Gott* allowed it."

"That doesn't ease the grief."

He looked at her and nodded slightly. "You're right. It doesn't."

Abby moved her hand away from his arm. "My grandmother would have said it makes acceptance easier."

"She was a wise woman."

Abby smiled at her memories. "She was. Rose reminds me of her."

Joe turned to look at her. "Was your *grossmammi* a matchmaker with a spying cat?"

Abby chuckled. "No. So why did Rose decide we didn't suit?"

He shrugged. "It doesn't matter. I for one am glad to stop worrying about it."

"So am I." She had more pressing things on her mind. Her pregnancy was one of them. She wasn't about to get into a new relationship when her last one had ended so badly.

His smile widened. "Oh, *you're* not off the hook."

She scowled. "What do you mean?"

"Rose is on the lookout for a better man for you."

"She said that?" Abby was shocked.

He stared ahead. "She did. To my face."

It was hard to imagine a nicer man than Joe. Abby shook her head to clear that thought. "I don't want a husband. I know she thinks I need one, but I don't."

"All Amish women want to be married. Why don't you?"

Abby rubbed her hands up and down her arms. "I don't need another complication in my life. I don't want someone telling me what to do, making decisions for me, holding me back."

"That's a harsh outlook on marriage."

She glanced his way. "Maybe it is, but you don't want to get married, either. Why don't you?"

He rubbed one hand across his lips. "I was almost married once. She died."

"Oh, Joe. I'm so sorry. I didn't mean to bring up bad memories." Her heart ached for his losses. First his father and then the girl he loved. It wasn't surprising that he didn't want another romantic relationship. Logan hadn't died, but he had killed the image of love she'd had with him. She grieved that loss, too.

Joe clicked his tongue to get the horse moving faster. "It was a long time ago. *Gott* allowed it."

They had the pain of loss in common. It made Abby feel closer to him. Not knowing what else to say, she kept silent until he turned the horse into the driveway of the inn and pulled up in front of the house.

"Sit still," he said abruptly.

He got out and came around to her side. "You shouldn't get dirt in those blisters. I'm going to carry you to the porch. Okay?"

Abby swallowed hard. "That's very kind."

He held up his arms. She slid close enough that he could

slip one arm beneath her knees and the other behind her back. He lifted her easily. She wrapped her arms around his neck while holding her shoes in one hand. A tremor coursed through her and she bit her bottom lip.

"Are you okay?" he asked softly, gazing into her eyes. She wasn't.

Eight

Abby nodded slightly because she couldn't speak. It wasn't fear that stole her voice, it was amazement. She wasn't frightened this time. Somehow it felt right to be in Joe's arms.

The light shining through the window on the front door highlighted the angles and planes of his face. His mouth was bracketed with deep lines. Not from laughing. Joe had known tragedy. It was etched on his features.

He was a ruggedly handsome man with an unspoken toughness that was at odds with the gentle way he held her. It wasn't easy to read the emotions in his dark brown eyes. He kept his feelings in check even now as if hiding them was second nature. She understood what kind of control that took.

His gaze roved across her face and settled on her mouth. She licked her suddenly dry lips. His eyes darkened. She looked away from the desire she saw there. He didn't know anything about her. He wouldn't find her attractive if he did. She was a fraud. A desperate, unwed pregnant woman with a history of mental illness. Who could care for someone like that?

It was wrong to read Joe's kindness as something more. If only her foolish heart would stop pounding. He was a good man, but she had to ignore the pull he somehow exerted on her. She needed her wits about her. Joe managed to scatter them with a simple touch.

"Ready?" he asked.

She nodded. He hitched her higher and carried her up the steps. The door opened before they reached it.

Susanna frowned at them. "What has happened?"

"She has managed to get blisters on both her feet," Joe said, turning Abby so Susanna could see the injuries.

"Well, don't just stand there. Bring her in. Put her on the sofa. I'll get something to clean and bandage them. What on earth possessed you to walk so far, Abby?"

"She was exploring," Joe said, giving Abby a wink. She smiled but knew she was blushing. His arms were strong, but he held her with great tenderness, as if she were a child.

Susanna left the room as Joe put Abby on the sofa. Rose walked in as he straightened. "Ah, I see you found a way to put some color in her cheeks, Joseph."

He just shook his head and walked out without speaking. Rose turned to Abby. "He's a sweet boy. I may give him another chance."

Abby frowned. "To do what?"

Rose chuckled. "Finish the kitchen, of course. You seem to have gotten yourself in a bit of a fix."

"It was such a pretty day I didn't realize I had walked so far until my feet started hurting. By then it was too late."

"You must take more care in the future. I have an old bicycle around somewhere that you can use if you want to go exploring again. I'll have Joe look for it. Or you may use the buggy anytime you like." She went into the kitchen.

Susanna returned with a large basin of warm water, towels, ointment and bandages for Abby's feet. Although Abby protested that she could manage, Susanna brushed aside her objections. "You'll be sore for a few days, but there's no real harm done as long as they don't become infected. Do you have some thick socks to wear around the house? You should avoid putting those shoes back on for a few days."

It felt odd having someone fuss over her. "I don't own any thicker socks. I'll launder these when I wash out my dress." She brushed at the grass stains and dirt. "It's the only one I have."

"You only have one dress?" Susanna looked shocked.

Abby nodded sheepishly. Most Amish women had two or three everyday work dresses and one good one for Sundays or special occasions. Abby hadn't been able to make more than one garment without the sheets being missed. "I was planning to sew one for church, but I haven't had—a chance to buy material."

Susanna's expression softened. "Or the money?"

Abby nodded.

"I've been poor, too. There's no shame in it. I'm sure we have enough material in the sewing room to make a dress or two for you. We can't have our maid looking stained and threadbare."

"I couldn't take your material."

"Nonsense. It's not doing any good in a box. You might as well have the use of it." Susanna raised one finger. "Don't object again. Charity is easy to give and hard to accept, but it is prideful to refuse help when it's needed."

Susanna's generosity surprised Abby. She didn't think Rose's daughter liked her. "*Danki.* That's very kind."

Susanna's scowl returned. "We'll look and see what might work on Monday. In the meantime, I will get a pair of my socks for you to use. You must avoid getting these bandages dirty. Wait here. I'll be right back."

Abby bent to examine her feet. Susanna had done a fine job wrapping them. They still hurt but not as much. When she went back to the farm, she would need some kind of transportation.

Now that she knew the condition of her grandparents' home, she wished she could start fixing it up. It was a shame to leave it in shambles, but she didn't want anyone checking the place to see there was work being done. It was disheartening, but it would be best if the place continued to look undisturbed and abandoned.

She only had a short window of time to make the place habitable before the baby came. She had a job, but she needed a place to live that wasn't simply a maid's room at the inn. A home of her own where she and her baby were safe—that was what she wanted more than anything.

When Abby looked up, she saw Joe standing in the doorway. "I thought you had gone."

He held a hammer and a square in one hand. "It seems I left a couple of my tools in the kitchen although I don't recall doing so. Thought I'd better round them up and put them away. Tools that are left out have a way of wandering off around here. This is the second hammer I've had to buy since I started working on this project. How are the feet?"

"They would've been a lot worse if I'd had to walk all the way home from the river bridge. I appreciate the ride."

"Thank Rose. She was the one who made me go look for you."

"She is turning out to be a much better friend than I expected."

"Remember you said that when she presents the next suitor for your approval."

"I can handle Rose. I withstood having *you* thrown at me, didn't I?"

"So you did."

Was there a note of regret in his voice? Surely not. She changed the subject. "Susanna has been considerate tonight. I didn't expect that."

"I don't know her well. From what I've seen she's gruff but kindhearted. I think she's worried about the business and about Rose's absentmindedness."

"Rose is sharper than she lets on," Abby said, determined to defend the woman who had taken her in.

Joe stood at the doorway for a long moment. "Tomorrow is the off Sunday. Do you have plans?"

"I don't plan to walk far. Other than that, no."

"Since you were eager to explore the area, I thought I might show you around. If Rose will loan me the buggy again."

Joe was asking her out? Abby hid her astonishment and tamped down the tiny thrill his words sparked, not trusting her reaction. Why? What did he hope to gain? Was he attracted to her?

She did want to learn her way around the community, but she didn't want to expose herself again. Today had been a close call. It would be better if she stayed inside the inn for a while. "*Danki*, but I don't think so."

"Okay, another time maybe," he said brightly. Too brightly.

Was he disappointed? A stab of guilt made her reach out to him. She didn't want to hurt his feelings. "I'm sorry, Joe."

He took a step back. "Nothing to be sorry about."

"I appreciate the offer. I do."

"Sure." He nodded once and went out the door.

She bit the corner of her lip. What if he hadn't offered to take her around because he was hoping to spark a romance? It was silly to think he might be. He was only being friendly. She had to remember that not all men had ulterior motives for their kindness.

Abby sighed. She liked Joe a lot—more than she should—but a romantic relationship wasn't in her plans no matter how attractive she found the young carpenter.

Joe stopped on the steps of the inn and pressed his hammer against his head. "*Dummkopf*, stupid, stupid." He was tempted to pound some sense into his brain. What had possessed him to ask Abby to go for a buggy ride?

He blew out a deep breath. He knew what had prompted the offer. The feel of her in his arms when he lifted her from the buggy earlier. It had been years since he'd known such an attraction to a woman.

Abby wasn't indifferent to him. He was sure of that. The expression in her eyes hadn't been fear the second time he held her. It had been something akin to wonder. No one had ever looked at him in quite that way. He had been so tempted to kiss her.

What a mistake that would have been. He wasn't the settling-down sort, and he sure didn't want to give Abby the idea that he was. A Sunday buggy ride was the kind of thing courting couples did. He didn't intend to court Abby Martin. Far from it.

He hadn't intended to see her again tonight but when he

discovered two of his tools were missing, he'd gone into the kitchen to see if he'd left them there. He was sure he hadn't, but to his surprise they were sitting on the counter where he'd been working last. He'd heard her voice in the living room and decided to see how she was doing. When he saw her sitting alone on the sofa, he couldn't pass by without speaking. Then she had smiled at him, and the whole evening became brighter.

Fortunately, she declined his invitation to go for a Sunday drive. He wouldn't have to spend the night worrying about what to say to her or how to act. It had been a narrow escape, and he would make the most of it. He jogged down the steps and headed for his trailer. There was movement in the shadows at the rear of the camper where he kept his toolbox. He stopped. "Who's there?"

A little squeak preceded a moment of silence. Rose stepped into the moonlight. "It's just me."

Baffled, he started toward her. "What are you doing?"

She had both hands behind her back. "I was borrowing something."

"Borrowing what?"

She stared at the ground, brought one hand around and showed him a crowbar. "This."

He tipped his head to see her face better. "Rose, why do you need a crowbar?"

She rose on her tiptoes and rocked back on her heels. "It occurred to me that I don't have one."

"And?" He waited.

"That's all." She smiled and gave it to him. *"Danki."*

She walked to the inn and stepped inside, leaving him utterly confused. What was she up to now? Was she the one who had been taking his tools? Was she still trying to prolong his stay? Abby might think Rose was sharp, but he wasn't so sure.

Maybe he should tell Susanna about this. What if Rose was taking other things, too, without even realizing it? Oliver's mother had developed dementia in her final years. It took the whole family to keep track of her because she became prone to wandering away.

If he saw Rose doing something like this again, he'd mention it to Grace or Susanna, but for now he'd make sure he kept his tools locked in his trailer.

He opened his door but decided against going in yet. Instead, he turned his lawn chair so he could see the inn. The lights in the living room were still on, as were the lights in the kitchen. The guest rooms upstairs were all dark. He could hear occasional voices and laughter from the garden so they must be sitting out enjoying the mild evening.

He kept watch until the light in Abby's room came on. What was it about her that made him want to know her better? She wasn't like Kara, the girl he had planned to marry until the night of the tragic fire. Kara had been shy and meek. Sweet and caring, she had been an open book. Every emotion had been written plainly on her face unlike Abby, whose eyes held shadows, secrets and fear. Maybe he was attracted to Abby because he wanted to erase the sadness she tried to hide. It mirrored something inside of himself.

After a while her light went out. Only then did he get up from his chair and go inside.

Abby's feet were sore the next morning but with the addition of Susanna's large slippers over the thick socks and bandages, she was able to get around with barely a limp. She helped serve breakfast to the guests and then cleaned up the dining area while the group checked out. She was wiping down the last table when Rose and Susanna came in.

Rose was tying the ribbons of her black traveling bonnet under her chin. "Susanna, will you ask Joe to bring the buggy around."

"Of course." She went out the front door.

Rose turned to Abby. "We're going visiting."

"Enjoy yourselves," Abby said, putting the napkin holder in the center of the table.

"You're coming, too."

"Oh." Abby glanced at her feet. "I'm not sure that's a good idea."

Rose gave a dismissive wave with one hand. "You'll be fine. We'll see at least two families today and there is no telling how many people will drop in this evening to meet you."

Abby knew folks would be curious when word of her arrival got around, but she wasn't ready to go on display. "I don't think it's proper to go about in slippers."

"Maybe not proper but certainly acceptable considering your injuries. Are you ready?"

"I'd rather stay here, Rose."

"If you don't come, folks will wonder what you're hiding from."

Abby swept some imaginary crumbs from the tabletop. "I'm not hiding."

"Then there's no excuse not to join us."

"I don't think I'm up to meeting more new people yet."

Rose came back, slipped her fingers under Abby's chin and lifted her face. "You want to put down roots here, don't you? You want to become one of us. You can't do that by staying inside the inn."

Abby chewed the corner of her lip. She did want to become part of this Amish community. It was what she had dreamed about during those long years inside her small apartment at her father's house. To live among people who didn't care about money or prestige, who worshiped God and took care of each other. Meeting the other Amish who lived in Harts Haven would be the first step. The first hard step.

What if she did or said something that gave herself away?

"We're going?" Rose grasped Abby's hand and led her out onto the porch.

Outside Abby saw Joe walking toward them, leading a brown horse, with two white socks and a white snip on his nose, hitched to a black enclosed buggy. Joe stopped in front of the steps. He tipped his hat slightly toward Abby but didn't speak. He avoided looking at her.

"Do you want to drive or shall I?" Susanna asked Rose.

"We'll let Joe drive," Rose said, opening the back door.

Abby turned her startled gaze on him. "Joe is coming with us?"

"I'm not." He looked as surprised as she was.

"You are," Rose said. "It's time you met more of the people in this community. You do want other customers interested in your work, don't you?"

"How does visiting the neighbors get them interested in my work?"

"It doesn't. It gets them interested in you. Then they'll come to see your work. The reason I need you today is to help Abby."

"He's not going to carry me anywhere," Abby said flatly.

"*Nee*, that wouldn't be proper, but he knows you, a single woman, and other young men will want to know if you are married, seeing anyone, or if you might consider going out with them. They will be more comfortable asking Joe than they would be asking Susanna or myself."

Abby couldn't believe what she was hearing. "I'm not interested in going out with anyone."

"You will be when the right fellow comes along. Sit up front with Joe. Susanna prefers to ride in the back."

"No, I don't," Susanna said, but she walked around to the other side and got in.

That left Abby and Joe staring at each other on the steps with Rose looking on out the open buggy door. "We're not going," Joe said.

"That's right. We aren't," Abby added for good measure.

Rose pressed her hands together over her heart. "Oh, I understand perfectly if the two of you would rather spend the day together here. I had quite given up on making a match between the two of you. I'm delighted to hear you are getting on so well. You make a sweet couple. Don't they, Susanna?"

"We aren't a couple," Abby said with growing irritation.

"Well, if you say so." Rose sounded disappointed. "In that case, Abby, you can tell the local girls that Joe is free and perhaps give them some ideas on how to attract his attention. Assure them you'll pass on any messages."

Abby tipped her head slightly as she looked Joe up and down. "I guess I could list his better qualities, tell them what a hard worker he is. Assure them he'll make some woman a fine husband so long as she is a good cook. What's your favorite dish, Joe?"

"Whose side are you on?" he asked, scowling at her.

Teasing him was fun. "It's all true."

His eyes narrowed. "And I can tell the fellas what a sweet disposition you have, that you aren't seeing anyone and they should come calling at the first opportunity."

"That's the spirit, *kinder*. Hurry up, we want to catch the Hostettler family at home. They have three sons and two daughters to marry off." Rose closed the buggy door.

Joe stepped close to Abby. "If we stay here, she'll keep thinking she's made a match between us," he whispered. "If we go, it will prove her wrong and give us the chance to fend off interested parties for each other."

Abby looked over his shoulder. "She'll catch on."

"Then maybe she'll finally get the idea that we aren't interested in dating. At least I'm not."

"Neither am I."

"Okay, then. We'll go."

She squinted at him. "You won't try to set me up with some weird guy, will you?"

"*Nee*, I'll tell them the truth about how you hang out windows to scold people, and they'll run in the other direction."

"Once. I scolded you out the window once."

"Let's just say it made a big impression on me. Ready?"

"As long as you stick to your side of the bargain and tell any would-be suitors I'm not in the market for a husband."

"I will as long as you return the favor." He held her elbow as she climbed in the buggy.

They arrived at the Hostettler farm twenty minutes later. Abby was introduced to Josiah Hostettler and his wife, Lydia, and their children. The boys, all redheads with freckle-covered faces, were in their early twenties and late teens. They took after their ginger-haired father. The girls had darker auburn hair but freckles aplenty. Lydia was a blonde with a flawless complexion and a ready smile who seemed genuinely pleased to meet Abby and Joe.

Abby was quickly and comfortably settled in a chair in the living room with a plate of sandwiches and cookies on her lap and a cold glass of milk on a small table beside her. Joe disappeared outside with the men, who were getting up a game of horseshoes, leaving the women to chat in the house.

The Hostettler daughters, Kathy and Becky, were twins although not identical. Abby discovered they were prone to giggling and gossiping as they sat beside her while the older women visited at the other end of the room.

From the twins Abby learned which girls in the community were walking out with which young men and who might be getting married in the fall. Although Abby couldn't yet put faces to the names, it was fun to hear the girls talk about local boys they liked and what the newest color was for dresses among the younger women. Pale lavender was popular as was a new dark pink that had recently arrived at the Plain Colors Fabric Shop run by Lisa Bieler, a cousin of Mrs. Hostettler. It was a daring color, but the unbaptized girls were hopeful it would be allowed.

Becky grinned. "Now tell us about Joseph. He's so handsome. Is he seeing someone?"

Abby laughed. "He isn't, but he claims he's not the marrying kind. He'll be moving on to another job soon, anyway."

Becky's grin turned to a frown. "That's a shame."

"He'll settle when he meets the right woman," Rose said, proving she had been listening in on their conversation. "Are you wanting to make a match, Becky?"

"She's much too young," Lydia said.

"You started dating Daed when you were sixteen," Kathy pointed out. "Becky is dying to know if you have someone in mind for her, Granny Rose."

"Let me think." Rose twisted the ribbon of her *kapp* around her finger. Both girls leaned forward eagerly. Susanna rolled her eyes. Abby smothered a giggle.

"Carl Wyse," Rose said solemnly and nodded once.

"The bishop's son?" Becky asked in astonishment.

"The very same. Are you opposed to him?" Rose asked.

"Opposed? I guess not," Becky said, slowly sharing a puzzled glance with her sister. "I've just never thought of him in that way. We've grown up together."

Rose unwound her *kapp* ribbon. "You're already friends?"

"We are."

"You should avoid speaking to him for a few weeks," Rose said.

Becky frowned. "Why?"

Rose chuckled. "To see if the absence of your friendship makes an impression on him."

Becky glanced at her sister. "What do you think?"

"I think Granny Rose is usually right."

Becky sank back in her chair. "Carl Wyse. I never would have thought about going out with him."

"And now you are thinking about what it might be like. *Das es goot.*" Rose smiled and winked at Abby. "Sometimes all a person needs is a suggestion, and then the idea sticks."

"And sometimes you're wrong," Abby said.

Rose grinned. "Not often, my dear. Not often."

"Abby, you should come to the quilting bee next month," Becky said.

Abby had watched her grandmother quilt, but she hadn't done much herself and that had been years ago. "I'm afraid I won't know anyone there."

"You'll meet all our friends at the church service next Sunday and you already know us. Say you'll come," Becky begged.

Abby glanced at the twins' earnest faces. They truly wanted her to say yes.

This was what Abby had dreamed about. Making friends. Enjoying ordinary things like girl talk and cookies with milk. Belonging to a community where she could work and live a simple life. Now that her father was looking for her elsewhere, she didn't need to hide while she was in Harts Haven. She had a chance to build bonds with young people like the Hostettler twins and become a part of the community.

She grinned and nodded. "Okay, I'll come."

"*Wunderbar!* We're making a quilt for Mary King. She married a boy from Castleton last fall, but they're going to live near Harts Haven so we're making it as a housewarming gift."

Abby tensed. Castleton was the church district her grandparents had belonged to. She had attended church services and community gatherings with them as a child. It was only fifteen miles from Harts Haven. The river was the dividing line between the two districts. Would anyone from there recognize her after so many years? "Will the groom's family be at the bee?"

"Nee, it will just be Mary's friends. We'll have loads of fun."

"Are you baptized?" Kathy asked.

"Not yet." Abby smiled at the inquisitive girl.

"You're still in your *rumspringa*? We can't wait for ours." Becky grinned at her sister.

Lydia pressed her hand to her heart. "They turn sixteen in a few months."

"Two months and one week," Kathy said.

Her mother gave her a stern look. "The running around time isn't all about fun and games. It's about discovering if you can give up the ways of the world and live separate from the world as God has commanded."

"We know, Mamm," the girls said together.

"Have you made your choice, Abby?" Kathy asked.

Abby didn't hesitate. "I've always wanted to be Amish."

"Then you should talk to the bishop," Lydia said. "*Die Gma noch geh* will be starting in a few weeks."

Abby frowned. "'To follow the church,' what is that?"

Lydia turned her shocked gaze from Abby to Rose. "How can she not know this?"

Rose got up to get another cookie. "They call it something else in New Mexico. I must have your recipe for these coconut macaroons, Lydia. *Dawf* classes for the youth, Abby."

"'Baptism classes,' of course." Abby kept her smile in place, but she knew she had made a terrible blunder.

Nine

Joe helped Abby into the front seat of the buggy as they were getting ready to leave the Hostettler farm. It was a simple thing to take her hand, but he was stunned by how reluctant he was to let go of her. He heard her quick intake of breath, then she slowly pulled away from him.

He gazed at her face. Her eyes were wide with surprise. A faint blush touched her cheeks. Did she feel the same attraction he did? Forcing himself to look away, he hoped no one noticed that he'd held her fingers a few seconds longer than necessary. He didn't dare look at her again for fear she would see the effect she had on him. Why did she leave him feeling like a tongue-tied teenage boy when he was with her?

Joe waved to the family lined up along the porch and

headed Rose's buggy horse out onto the roadway. They were on their way to the Shetler farm, the second family Rose had decided to visit that day. He glanced at Abby when the horse didn't require his full attention. She looked subdued.

"Did you enjoy yourself?" he asked, hoping to put their relationship on a more casual path.

"I guess. You?" There wasn't a trace of enthusiasm in her voice.

"It was a good visit. The sons are a likable bunch." He glanced over his shoulder at Rose and Susanna in the back seat. They had their heads together discussing something.

He leaned close to Abby. "You would do worse than be matched with one of them." It almost hurt to say that. He couldn't imagine her going out with any of the brothers but if someone better could make her happy, as Rose had suggested, then he wanted that for her.

She expression turned sour. "I hope you didn't encourage anyone."

"The two eldest already have girls, and the youngest is more interested in engines. He wants to set up a small engine repair shop."

"Are you joking? What kind of engines would the Amish need repaired?"

He tipped his head to see her face better. "That sounds like something a tourist would ask."

She looked startled. "Does it?"

"Every Amish home has a washing machine that's run with a gas or propane engine. My tools are powered by a gas generator. Rose has a lawn mower, a garden cultivator, a chain saw. It's not just the Amish that own these things. There are lots of small engines that require maintenance."

"Oh, small engines. I thought you were talking about automobile engine repairs."

"The Amish in this community don't drive cars, but they farm with tractors so large engine repair shops are needed, too."

"I didn't think of that."

"Where you're from they use horses to farm?"

"That's right. Are we almost there?" She sat up straighter to look down the road.

"Another quarter of a mile."

"Do you know the Shetler family?"

"I met David Shetler at the church service last Sunday, but not his wife."

"The Shetlers are a young married couple with a new baby," Rose said, sitting forward to look ahead and proving she had been listening. "I'm responsible for getting them together."

Susanna snorted. "The good Lord is the one who brings two hearts together. I don't think you should take credit for His work, Mamm."

"I would never take credit away from *Gott*. I'm merely a tool He uses to fulfill His purposes. Such as getting folks married and bringing their babies into the world. He and I work well together."

"Have you left your humility at home?" Susanna asked in exasperation.

"*Nee*, I'm sure I have it somewhere. I'll check my bag," Rose said.

Joe saw Abby struggling to smother a laugh. He liked the way her eyes sparkled when she smiled. He liked a lot of things about Abby Martin.

"You will make one too many jokes like that and the

bishop will hear of it," Susanna said. "You are not too old to be chastised."

"You're right, *dochtah*. Please forgive this foolish old woman," Rose said seriously.

"Danki." Susanna sounded mollified.

Rose didn't stay subdued for long. "Joseph, were any of the Hostettler boys interested in asking Abby out?"

"Nope. Not a one. It seems there are plenty of local girls for the fellows here to choose from." He winked at Abby.

"That's a shame but understandable." Rose fell silent.

Abby nudged Joe's shoulder with her own. *"Danki,"* she whispered.

"That's what friends are for." He wanted her to think of him as her friend since that was all he could offer.

"This is the place, Joe," Susanna said.

He turned into a small, neat farmstead just west of the Harts Haven grain elevator. The house was a single-story cream-colored ranch with a porch along the front. The barn was small and painted bright red with white trim. Three horses were eating at a hay feeder in the corral until they noticed the buggy approaching. They hurried to the corral fence to whinny at the unfamiliar horse pulling it. A half dozen chickens clucked and scratched in the dirt in front of a henhouse on the other side of the barn.

Joe stopped the horse by the white rail fence surrounding the lawn and flower gardens at the front of the house.

"I'm anxious to see how much little Micah has grown," Rose said. Abby got out of the buggy without waiting for his help as he assisted Rose and Susanna. The women walked toward the house. Joe tethered the horse and patted the animal's neck.

David walked up to him. "I'm surprised to see you today,

but it's a pleasant change. Since the baby arrived it has been a steady stream of women visitors."

"Rose asked me to drive them."

"How do you like working for the widows?"

"It has been…" Joe searched for the best word "…challenging."

David laughed. "Knowing Rose, I can imagine that's true. Has she been matchmaking for you?"

"She's been trying, but she won't have any success with me."

"I used to say that. She introduced me to my wife and, before I knew it, I was setting a wedding date. Then she delivered my son, so I have a soft spot for her."

"She did mention that."

David grinned. "Let me show you around the place."

Following a tour of the farm buildings and some time spent poring over David's newest acquisition, a well-used International 1086 tractor, the men returned to the house. Stepping inside, Joe saw a spacious kitchen with a black-and-white linoleum floor and finely crafted oak cabinetry. A petite woman with dark hair stood at the kitchen sink. She smiled at Joe and walked toward him, drying her hands on her apron. "The others are in the living room."

"This is my wife, Barbara. Babs, this is Joe Troyer. He's the contractor remodeling the kitchen at the inn."

"Rose has been telling us all about you. Go in and sit down. I'll have coffee ready in a few minutes."

Joseph followed David into the adjoining room. Rose and Susanna were seated on the sofa. Abby was in a rocker by the window. Sunlight spilled around her. She held the baby in her arms. A strange tug pulled at his heart and stopped his breath. She gazed at the infant with the softest smile he'd ever seen.

David walked over and crouched beside Abby. He lifted one tiny hand from the blanket folds and looked at Joe. "This is my son, Micah. He'll be six months old in a week."

Joseph wasn't sure what to say. He cleared his throat. "He's a nice boy."

"Nee," Abby said softly as she stroked the infant's head with one finger. "He is a beautiful baby. I've never seen a *bobbli* with so much hair." There was a serene, faraway expression in her eyes.

"He gave me weeks of heartburn," Barbara said, smiling at her son. She placed a tray with filled coffee cups on a low table in front of the sofa. Joe took a cup and retreated to the other side of the room where he sat in a straight-backed chair, but he found it hard to take his eyes off Abby. She seemed perfectly at ease with the baby in her arms. He could imagine her as a mother with children of her own.

Realizing where his mind was taking him, he concentrated on his coffee. Barbara came in with slices of chocolate cake for everyone. Talk turned to other members of the community Joe hadn't met, so he listened with only half an ear. His gaze was drawn again and again to Abby. She looked so relaxed and happy. Happier than he'd seen her since they met.

David walked over to Joe. "I've got a mare in labor. I'm just going to run out and check on her."

"I'll come with you." Joe started to get up.

"Nee, relax and enjoy your cake. Barbara will be upset with me if I drag you away. I won't be a minute." David left the room.

Joe sank back into his chair, finished his cake, and put the plate and his empty cup aside.

Rose got up from the sofa and moved to stand in front of Abby. "You've had him long enough, dear. It's my turn to hold him." Abby looked disappointed but she allowed Rose to take the baby from her arms.

Rose walked over to Joe's side of the room. She began cooing and making faces at Micah as she bounced him gently. He seemed enthralled, making little squeaks and pumping his arms. "No one can resist the sweetness of a *bobbli*. What do you think, Joe? Are you ready for one of these?"

"I don't think David would let me have him."

Barbara chuckled. "You're right about that. David loves his boy. Would you ladies like to see the new quilting frame David made for me? It can be extended two extra feet, and it tilts. The good Lord gave me a very clever fellow for a husband."

Abby and Susanna got up and followed Barbara down the hallway. Rose smiled at Joe. "My arms are getting tired. Take him, please. I'd like to see this new frame myself."

Shocked, Joe shook his head. "Take him? *Nee*."

Rose simply put the child in his arms and walked away. Joe froze. The babe was so little. He couldn't weigh more than his bundle of blankets. What if he accidently hurt him? Micah stared at him for a few seconds and then his little chin started to quiver.

"Whoa, hey now, don't cry. Rose? Barbara?" Joe looked toward the hallway. Where were they?

Micah arched his back and started to whimper. Joe began to bounce the child as he had seen Rose do. "It's okay. Your *mamm* will be right back."

The motion seemed to soothe the little boy. He stopped whimpering and managed to get his fist to his mouth.

"That's right. You're fine." Joe shifted the babe to the crook of his arm. Micah continued to stare at him. He really was an appealing little fellow.

Joe leaned a little closer to him. "Don't think I don't

know what Rose is up to. She's a sly old gal. She wants me to start thinking about having my own family."

He'd managed not to think about that for years. Rose couldn't understand that he didn't deserve a family. Not after the way he had failed to protect all of them. The thought of loving someone and losing them was more than he could bear. He was fine on his own.

Most of the time.

Some days he did long for the closeness he'd once shared with his family. He missed the sense of security and belonging he hadn't even recognized until it was gone. The evenings were the worst when he was alone in his trailer. And the nights when his nightmares woke him.

Joe slipped one arm out from under the baby and adjusted the blanket beneath his little chin. Micah gave a fleeting smile before trying to capture his fist in his mouth again. Joe tapped the baby's nose softly. "I saw that. You grinned at me. Guess I'm not so scary after all."

It had been a long time since he'd held a baby. Not since his littlest brother had been born. The memory of holding Henry should have been a painful one, but surprisingly it wasn't. The ache of missing his baby brother was still in Joe's heart, but he could look back on that time with his brother fondly. It was something he didn't think was possible until now.

He glanced up and saw Abby watching him from the hallway.

Abby crossed her arms and grinned at Joe. "You might be scary at first glance, but you grow on a person pretty quickly."

"Is that so? Come over here and take this baby before I drop it."

She leaned her shoulder against the wall and shook her head. "You're doing fine, and Micah seems happy."

"There's no telling how long his good mood will last, is there, little man?" Joe sat back in the chair and started to relax. It wasn't so bad.

Abby crossed the room and knelt beside Joe. She took Micah's hand in hers. "I never knew babies were so amazing."

"They are as long as they aren't crying."

"That's cynical. Even when they're crying they're adorable. Then sadly little boys grow up."

He tipped his head toward her. "Are you saying a grown man can't be adorable?"

"Oh, I'm sure there are some, but I haven't met one."

He scrunched his face in mock pain. "Ouch. See if I give you a ride back to town when you've walked blisters on both your feet again."

"That was very nice of you but not really adorable."

"What would a fellow need to do to meet your definition of *adorable*?" His eyes sparkled with mischief.

She grinned and rubbed her chin with one hand. "I'm not certain. I'll have to think about that."

"That's the trouble with some women," he whispered to Micah. "You can never be sure what they really want."

"I object to that statement."

"Okay, then give me an example of adorable behavior for a grown man."

"Well, hugging a puppy."

He chuckled and scanned the room. "What if there aren't any puppies around?"

She took Micah's tiny hand. "Then I guess holding a baby would qualify."

"So now she thinks I'm adorable. Did you hear that,

Micah? Don't tell Rose or she'll be sending out our wedding invitations."

"We wouldn't want that," Abby said firmly. "He is kidding, of course."

His grin faded. "*Nee*, we wouldn't want that. You should take him."

"You seem comfortable and so does he. I am a bit surprised by just how comfortable you do look."

"Holding a baby is like riding a bicycle. Once you've done it you never really forget how."

"Have you held lots of babies?"

"A few."

"When was the last time?"

He grew sad. "Not long after my baby brother was born. His name was Henry. For some reason he liked the sound of my voice. I could get him to go to sleep when no one else could. He was fussy so Mamm had me hold him a lot."

"Where is he now?"

"He died when he was four."

"I'm sorry. I can't imagine what that must be like. I never had siblings, but I always wanted a brother."

Sadness filled his eyes. "I had three brothers and a sister. I was the oldest."

"You said 'had'?" she asked softly.

"They are all with our Lord. I'm the only one left. You should take this little guy. David hasn't come in from checking on his mare. I should go see if there's a problem."

Stunned by Joe's revelation, Abby accepted the baby and watched him leave the house. His father, his siblings, even the girl he had planned to marry—he'd lost them all. How did he bear it? It was unimaginable.

The world was filled with so much sadness and tragedy. Why did God allow it?

She hugged Micah close and laid her cheek against his head. She could feel his warm breath against her face. His wonderful baby-lotion smell eased the tightness in her chest. The weight of him in her arms gave her a deep sense of comfort. One day she would hold her own baby. The tiny child growing inside her who had been conceived in deceit and cruelty but who carried none of that stain. Abby vowed to never see her child as anything but a blessing.

She kissed baby Micah's head. God had also filled the world with wondrous things. She would do her best to remember that and cherish the gifts the Lord gave her, be they great or small.

The other women came into the room. Rose stopped beside Abby. "I see Joe ran off as soon as my back was turned."

"He went out to help David with a horse."

"Men always find things to do in the barn when there's a baby in the room," Barbara said as she took Micah from Abby. "Unless it's their own baby. David is a great help to me. He even changes diapers."

"That was one thing my husband would never do," Susanna said with a little chuckle. "Feed them, bathe them, dress them, not a problem, but a dirty diaper always required my attention."

"Just like your father," Rose said poignantly. "Barbara, are you coming to the quilting bee for Mary King?"

"Absolutely. If I had known David was making a new quilt frame, I would have offered to host it here." Micah began to fuss. Barbara tried to soothe him, but he started crying.

"There will be other opportunities," Susanna said. "It's

getting late. We should get along home. It sounds like Micah is ready for his nap."

"I know I am ready for mine," Rose said.

Abby followed the two older women outside. David and Joe were just coming out of the barn.

David looked disappointed. "Leaving so soon? I thought you might want to see our new filly."

Joe smiled at Abby and nodded toward the barn. "Come on. She's a pretty one."

David led the way to a wide box stall at the rear of the barn filled with fresh golden straw. In the center lay a tiny brown-and-white-spotted foal. Her mother stood over her licking and nosing her gently.

"She wants her baby to get up," Joe said.

"Already? Wasn't she just born?" Abby asked in amazement.

"Most foals can stand within a few minutes," David said.

"She's beautiful. She's a pinto horse, right?" Abby asked.

David nodded. "She's an American paint horse, but *pinto* is the right term for the spotted coloring, too. Her markings are called overo. See how none of the white crosses her spine. Her mother has the more common markings called tobiano. Her father was a black-and-white overo. I'm glad she takes after him. I raise them to sell. It makes a little money on the side. They're a popular breed with the *Englisch* in this area and I've always liked them."

Abby gripped the stall door. "Oh, look. She's getting up."

The foal unfolded her gangly legs and lunged to her feet where she wobbled and staggered until she spread her legs far enough apart to keep from falling over. Her mother moved between her baby and the watching people.

"We should leave them to get acquainted," David said.

"I'm glad you let me see them." The mare had been very

gentle with her baby. Seeing them together made Abby feel less fearful of grown horses.

Outside at the buggy David held out his hand to Joe. "Come by anytime."

Joe shook his hand. "I may do that. If you decide you want that room addition on the house, I can give you an estimate."

"I'll talk it over with Barbara."

Abby and Joe got into the buggy. Rose leaned forward as Joe headed home. "What did I tell you. They get to know you and then they will become interested in your work."

"Okay, Rose, you were right this once."

"That's very kind of you to say so." She sat back laughing softly to herself.

He turned the horse into the lane leading to the inn and pulled to a stop in front of the porch. Susanna got out. He stepped down to help Rose. "Don't forget I need your decision on countertops tomorrow," he reminded her.

"Countertops? We have already picked the countertops," Susanna said, scowling at him.

"Rose changed her mind," he said quickly.

"Did I?" She tried to look innocent.

He stared at her intently. "You did. We aren't playing this game again, Rose."

"Oh, fine. I'll give you a decision tomorrow. Come along, Susanna. I could use a rest."

"I have a few things I want to discuss with you first, Mamm." Susanna took her mother's arm to help her up the steps.

Joe smiled as the mother–daughter duo went inside. Abby stayed in her seat.

"Are you going in?" Joe asked.

"Not yet. Can I help you put the horse away?"

"Sure." He got in and drove to the barn and stopped. She hopped out and went to stand by the horse's head without getting close to it. She tentatively patted the animal's nose and talked softly to him. Joe watched her closely. Something was up. She looked ill at ease. He unhooked the harness from the shafts. "You can lead him into the barn now."

Abby gathered her courage and cautiously grabbed the bridle. It was important not to show her fear. To animals or to humans. It was something she needed to work on. Holding the bridle awkwardly at arm's length, she led the horse into the barn. He stopped when she did and stood quietly. This horse wasn't so bad. "What's your name, fella?"

"I think I heard Rose call him Cooper." Joe came inside the barn, and she looked at him, wondering how to ask about the things she wanted to know.

"Do I need to cool him down before I let him have some water?" she asked, stalling to gather her courage.

"*Nee*, let him drink what he wants. I'll get the harness off." He undid the buckles and lifted the leather tack from the animal, then set about cleaning it.

"This comes off next, right?" she asked, holding the side of the bridle. Thankfully her voice didn't tremble like her fingers. She had to learn to do this. All Amish knew how to care for their horses. And she was Amish now. A horse and buggy would be essential to her new way of life. For her baby's sake she would be brave.

Abby undid the neck strap, pulled the headstall over the horse's ears and let the bit drop out of the horse's mouth as she had seen her grandfather do. The metal bit was covered with slobber. She wrinkled her nose and handed it to Joe. He gave her a lead rope. "Take him out to the tank."

It took all her remaining courage to snap the lead to the

halter and walk the horse out of the barn into a small corral with a large water tank. Cooper walked quietly beside her. If she stopped, he did, too. He was almost like a big dog. That was a good way to think of him. As a big friendly dog.

When the horse was finished drinking, Abby began walking him around inside the corral. She was still limping a little. Joe hung up the cleaned equipment, gathered a currycomb, a brush and a cloth then walked out to her. "Is he cooled down?"

"I'm not sure. I think he's a little warm yet," she said with her hand on the animal's neck.

"I'll get a couple of rags and we can wipe him down. That should help."

Together they sponged off the horse and made sure he wasn't sweating. Abby discovered the task was much less frightening with Joe beside her as she tried to copy his confident movements. When the horse was cool, Joe led him into his stall and gave him some hay.

Abby stopped by Bendy's stall. With the sturdy door between them, Abby felt safe enough to rub the mare's forehead.

"Be careful," Joe said. "She bites."

Feeling foolishly confident, Abby tentatively scratched the mare under her chin. "She doesn't want to bite me."

Joe walked up beside Abby. Bendy laid back her ears and nipped at him. Abby laughed. "Maybe she just doesn't like men."

"This man doesn't like her," he said. Rose's nanny goat bleated for her share of the attention. Joe walked down to her stall and rubbed her head. She was due to have her kid any day. Abby followed him.

She glanced at Joe from the corner of her eye as she patted the goat's neck. Joe was a stranger to this community the same as she was. Was it much different from the church group he'd grown up in? She knew there were many differences among the Amish. Each congregation decided their own rules. How did a person from one group join another? She didn't want to make another mistake like she had at the Hostettler farm.

She took a deep breath. "Can I ask you a question, Joe?"

"Sure."

"You may think it's an odd question and I'd rather you didn't tell anyone that I asked."

He chuckled and crossed his arms. "I can't wait to hear this."

She turned to face him. "It's not a laughing matter."

"Sorry. Ask your question."

"How does someone learn about the Amish faith?"

"I reckon you get born into an Amish family and then you find out everything you need to know while you're growing up."

She turned back to Bendy. "If someone wanted to become a member of a different community, how would they go about it?"

"You're thinking about staying on here, then?"

"I am. How do I learn the rules here?"

"I reckon you should talk to the bishop or the church elders."

"Like Rose?"

"Rose isn't a church elder. Those are men."

"Of course, but she is an older member of this church." Abby pressed her lips together. Another blunder.

"She would know all there is to know about this community's *Ordnung* even if she does like to bend the rules."

"You weren't raised here. How do you keep from making mistakes?"

"No one in this community expects me to know their ways. If I do something that isn't considered proper to them, they turn a blind eye unless I am influencing church members to do likewise. If that were to happen, I'm sure I would get a visit from the bishop. In some communities my power tools would not be acceptable. I can still use them because they are acceptable in the community where I was baptized."

"So if I make mistakes no one will really care?"

"I wouldn't go that far. There are always disapproving people anywhere you go, but you haven't been baptized. You aren't bound by any *Ordnung*. You know that, right?"

"I just don't want to appear too different. I want to fit in."

"You will. It takes time for people to get to know the real you."

"I suppose." That was exactly what she was afraid of, that people would learn who she really was and not who she wanted to be.

"What brought this on?"

"Something Mrs. Hostettler said. It's not important."

He tipped his head slightly. "It is if it troubles you."

She gave him a little smile. "I appreciate that. I expect that you're right and it will just take time for me to feel comfortable here."

"If it turns out that you don't like it here, you can always move on."

"*Nee*, this is where I want to stay. I'm certain of that. What about you? Is there anywhere you have wanted to stay?"

"I've seen a lot of nice country and met a lot of fine people, but I've never been tempted to settle down."

"What would it take to get you to settle in one place?"

Abby wasn't even sure why she was asking but she wanted to know.

The goat nudged his hand for more attention. He looked down and scratched her forehead. "I guess I would have to meet the right people."

"If you decided to stay put, what would you do then?"

"Not that it's going to happen, but I'd start my own business instead of working for someone else. Don't get me wrong, I like working for Oliver. He's a *goot* employer. He takes care of his people, and he's been a true friend to me."

"Was your father a carpenter?"

Joe shook his head. "He was a farmer. We had a small place near Fort Scott. Like most Amish families the youngest son was expected to inherit the farm. Buying more farmland for his older sons wasn't something my father could afford, so my brothers and I learned a trade as teenagers. I started working for Oliver as well as farming with Daed and my brothers."

"Would you like to go back to farming?"

"Sure, but buying farmland and equipment takes money. A lot of money. I have savings but not that much. How can you be sure you want to settle in Harts Haven? You don't have family here, do you?"

"*Nee*, I don't."

"I go where my boss sends me. You bought a bus ticket and traveled hundreds of miles to stop in a place where you don't know a soul. Why here?"

"I had my reasons."

"Was it because of your runaway friend? Is she here?"

"I'd rather not talk about her."

"I think it's time for some honest answers, Abby."

Ten

Joe watched an array of emotions cross Abby's face. Her struggle was painfully clear. Whatever troubled her, he wanted to help. He hoped to earn her trust. They had only known each other a short time, but it felt as if he'd known her for years. How could he prove that she could rely on him?

She looked away and his hopes sank. Then, to his surprise, she turned to face him squarely. "She *was* the reason I came here, but I said goodbye to her in Missouri and the truth is, I hope I never see her again. I want to build a new life here." She clutched her hands to her chest. "I want to belong."

Her eyes searched his face. "Maybe that's difficult for you to understand because you like moving on, but I want to sink my heart and soul into a place and never leave."

She looked down, crossed her arms and hunched her shoulders as if expecting a rebuke or scorn. What kind of life had she lived that she needed so badly to escape? He stepped closer and lifted her chin so she had to look at him. Tears glistened in her eyes. It was as if some giant hand reached in and squeezed his heart.

"I do understand, Abby. Whatever you need to make that happen I'd like to help."

"Truly?"

The hopefulness in that one word made him think she hadn't been shown much kindness in the past. "Yeah."

He would do his best to see her smiling and happy in her new life here.

"Danki." A hint of a smile trembled on her lips.

He was tempted to draw his thumb across them. Were they as soft as they looked? Would he frighten her if he kissed her? He dropped his hand so he wouldn't cup her face and find out. She wasn't looking to be kissed, and he wouldn't take advantage of her emotional state.

"Joe, could you—?"

"Could I what?"

"Could you maybe teach me how to harness a horse to a buggy? I do know how to drive one."

He tried not to let his surprise show. He'd learned to harness a team when he was seven or eight. Every Amish person he knew had learned as a child. Why hadn't she? "Sure. I'll give you a few lessons after work this week."

She wiped her eyes with both hands. "That would be great. Well, I should go in. We don't want Rose thinking we're courting or something."

"Right."

She started to walk away but stopped after a few steps and looked back. "I haven't had a real friend in a long time."

He stood up straighter. "You have one now."

She smiled and pointed at him. "That right there makes you adorable. Bless you, Joe."

He stood watching her until she went inside the house, then took a deep breath. "What am I getting myself into?"

She wanted and needed a friend. He could be that friend. All he had to do was stop thinking about kissing her.

Early the next morning, Herbert burst through the front door of the inn, startling Abby. "It's here. Where's Grace?"

Abby patted her chest with one hand. "Oh, you scared me. She's in the kitchen. What's wrong?" He rushed past her without answering. She followed.

He barged into the room. "Grace, where are you? It's here. I saw it with my own eyes."

Grace was chopping carrots by the stove. She put down her knife and clasped her hands together in excitement. "The cerulean blue? Oh, how amazing!"

He nodded. "I came to get you as soon as I could."

"Where did you see it?" She ripped off her apron and threw it on the counter. "I need my camera and my binoculars."

"Hurry, woman. There's no telling how long he'll stay."

"I won't be a minute." Grace hurried out of the room.

"Mr. Young, what's going on?" Abby asked, not sure if she should be worried.

"A fellow birder reported a cerulean warbler at his property south of here yesterday. He was sure it was heading this way, and he was right. I saw it at the marsh this morning. What is taking her so long? I need to get out there and get some sound."

Grace came back into the room. "This is so exciting. I've

only seen pictures in books. Abby, you must come with us. You may never see this bird again."

Herbert tossed up his hands. "*I* may never see it again unless you hurry, Grace. We still have to pick up Bertha."

"I'm out the door." She grabbed Abby's hand and pulled her along. "Rose? I'm taking Abby bird-watching," she shouted. She didn't wait for a reply.

Abby found herself bundled into the back seat of Herbert's car. "Where are we going?"

"Bertha's house," Herbert said and tore out of the parking lot spraying gravel from his tires.

"Herbert, slow down. We want to get there alive," Grace said sternly.

"You're right. I'm being impulsive and that isn't good for someone behind the wheel." He slowed down a smidgen. A block later he screeched to a stop and the front passenger door opened. Bertha got in. "Are you sure you saw a cerulean warbler?"

"Of course I'm sure," he said sharply. "You think I don't know the difference between a cerulean and a blue jay?"

"I'm sorry. I don't doubt your word, Herbert, I'm just excited."

"Buckle up, Bertha. We have to go."

"Right." She pulled down the shoulder harness. Abby heard it click and Herbert hit the gas again.

Abby turned to Grace in the back seat beside her. "Why are we in such a hurry?"

"Spring is the time of year for the warbler's seasonal migrations. The birds are only passing through. An individual bird won't stay here long. But there are many thousands of them that come through this part of the state. We're fortunate to have a marshland area just north of town where large numbers of birds can be seen. The cerulean warbler is a rare species here. When word gets out that one has been spotted, people will drive here from all over the state and from other states as well just to see it."

"To see a blue bird?"

Grace laughed. "A rare one."

Bertha turned in her seat to look at Abby. "Warblers are among the prettiest in my opinion. So many bright colors. The fall migration is more haphazard but during the spring migration the birds flock together. When they migrate through here it's like seeing flying candy."

"Flying candy? Are they really that different from cardinals or meadowlarks?" Abby was skeptical.

"Cardinals and larks are beautiful birds, but warblers are something special. Wait until you see the colors. There are bright yellow ones, white ones with rust markings, then there's the black-and-white warbler. I think of them as the zebras of the bird world."

"Don't forget the blackburnian. I saw one once when I was visiting family in Ohio. So beautiful." Grace closed her eyes and smiled.

"And so rare in this part of the state. She isn't likely to see one of those," Herbert said.

Bertha shook her finger at him. "Ah, but that is the wonder and magic of birding. Sometimes we do get a glimpse of the rare and the beautiful as well as the common."

They sped north out of town along the road that Abby had recently walked. They turned west at the river and then crossed the bridge. When Herbert turned at the first road going east, Abby tensed. This was the way to her grandparents' farm.

When the property came into view, Herbert didn't slow down but sped past. Abby looked back. Nothing looked different but it was hard to tell because they were going so fast. Herbert slowed down a quarter of a mile past the farm. A narrow dirt road led north again but Herbert crossed a culvert into a field. He followed a narrow track through the tall grass that ended at a clump of trees. There was a gray Jeep parked off to one side. A young couple leaned against the hood as they scanned the area with binoculars. A camera on a tripod stood next to them.

Grace handed Abby a pair of binoculars when they got out of the car. "Do you know how to use these?"

Abby took them. "Not really." Grace showed her how to adjust and focus them.

Herbert opened the trunk of the car and removed a clear dish-shaped piece of equipment with a handle from a padded container. He put on a pair of headphones and headed toward the trees. "I left some chairs here earlier for you ladies. Follow me. I'm afraid I don't have one for Abby. I didn't know she was coming with us. Of course, I'm glad she's here. Everyone should have a chance to enjoy birdwatching."

Bertha stopped beside the young couple. "Are you here for the cerulean warbler?"

"We are. A birding friend emailed us that one had been spotted near here. We drove out from Wichita. Have you seen it?" the man asked.

"Our friend saw it this morning. Good luck," Bertha said with a wave.

"Same to you." The woman smiled then put her binoculars to her eyes again.

When they reached the spot Herbert had chosen, Grace and Bertha sat down and began to scan the marsh beyond the trees. Abby was vaguely familiar with the area. Her grandfather's land included part of the marsh that lay south toward the river. He had talked about draining it once to farm the land, but her grandmother had been against the idea. She said if God put a marsh in the middle of dry dusty Kansas, then they should leave it alone for the wildlife to enjoy. Abby didn't think they were actually on her grandfather's land.

"We aren't trespassing, are we?" she asked.

"No, this is public land," Herbert said. "About fifty acres are privately owned, the rest, around four hundred acres, has been purchased or donated to the Kansas Department of Wildlife, Parks and Tourism. We have tried unsuccessfully to purchase the remaining acres."

"Who owns it?" Abby asked. Was there something here that her father found valuable? It didn't seem likely. An expanse of small ponds surrounded by cattails, trees and scrub brush was all she saw.

"It's part of a trust fund for a woman who lives in Kansas City. I've dealt with her attorney very briefly. I was told she has no intention of selling any part of the property. We can be thankful for that. At least we know it won't be developed or drained."

When everyone was looking out across the marsh, Abby turned her binoculars toward the farmhouse. She could just make out the metal roof of the house and part of the barn. So close and yet so far away. Her fingers itched to start clearing away the neglect, but it was still too risky. Something bright flashed in front of her. She lowered the glasses and saw a lemon-yellow bird sitting fifty feet away on a tall weed. "That's a pretty one," she said.

"Where?" the others asked together.

"Behind us." She pointed.

They all turned in their chairs. "That's a yellow warbler," Herbert said, aiming his microphone in the bird's direction. "Quiet, please."

Abby stood still and listened to the colorful bird's cheerful song. As she watched, three more bright yellow birds flew into the branches of a nearby willow tree. She tapped Grace's shoulder. "I see more over there," she whispered and pointed.

Grace nodded and turned her binoculars in that direction. Another flutter of movement caught Abby's eye. It was a smaller bird without as much yellow on its body.

Herbert had put down his microphone and lifted his headphone off one ear. "One can pick out a yellow warbler song by its brevity compared to others."

"Is that a female of the species, Mr. Young?" Abby pointed out the plainer bird to him.

"No, that's just another butter butt. We see them all the time." He walked away toward the nearest pond.

Bertha and Grace exchanged amused looks and chuckled. "That is actually a yellow-rumped warbler," Bertha said. "Herbert just likes to call them butter butts."

Grace chuckled. "He isn't the only one. I've heard several birders call them that. You have a good eye, Abby."

Within half an hour Abby had seen a dozen different types of warblers, ducks, thrushes and larks. The snowy-white egrets standing immobile in the ponds were the birds she liked best. To her amazement she was thoroughly enjoying the morning. God made many beautiful creatures, but He had outdone himself with birds. She would never ignore or dismiss them again.

Another vehicle pulled in beside theirs and a middle-aged gentleman got out with his binoculars and a camera around his neck and a book in his hand. He walked up to them. "I had a report of a cerulean warbler in this area. Have you seen it?"

"Our friend saw it here this morning, but we haven't yet," Bertha said.

Just then a flash of blue zipped past and landed in a small bush twenty yards away. "Is that one?" Abby asked.

"It is!" The man switched his binoculars for the camera that hung from his neck and began to take pictures. Abby, Bertha and Grace simply watched the beautiful little bird until it flew off.

The man lowered his camera. "That was worth the drive."

"Where are you from?" Bertha asked.

"Dodge City. You?"

"Harts Haven."

"You're fortunate to have these wetlands in your backyard. If I lived closer, I would be out here every day. Is that a rose-breasted grossbeak?" He walked toward a dead tree fifty yards away.

Abby looked toward her farmhouse. A reason to be out here every day that no one would question. Bird-watching? Could it be that simple?

Herbert came walking back. "I'm sorry but I have to get back to town. I have a client coming to my office in half an hour. I'm sorry you didn't get to see the blue."

"We saw it," Bertha said, folding her chair.

"You did? When?"

"Just a few minutes ago," Grace said. "What do you think of us birders, Abby?"

"I had no idea it could be so interesting. Thank you for bringing me."

"Well, perhaps we have made a new convert," Herbert said, puffing up a little.

"I'd certainly like to learn more about it."

"Ornithology is the study of birds," Herbert said. "It's also been a lifelong passion for me."

"Oh, no," Bertha said. "Don't get him started on the study of ornithology or we will be here all day. Loan her a book, something for a beginner, Herbert, give her a pair of binoculars and let her discover if it's something she will enjoy before you start lecturing her."

A pair of binoculars and a book about birds was all she would need to look the part of a birder. When the coast was clear she could slip into the house. She couldn't clean up the outside but if she were careful, she could start working on the inside. It was a long walk from town but if she had a bicycle, she could park it here or perhaps hide it near the barn.

It would be chancy but the thought of setting the house to rights almost seemed worth the risk. No, it was definitely worth the risk. She would do it.

Just then a small green airplane buzzed overhead barely above the treetops. The birds scattered in panic. Herbert shook his fist in the air. "He did that deliberately. There's no reason to fly that low when he isn't crop-dusting. He just does it to drive the birds away and annoy me."

"Herbert, take it easy. Remember your blood pressure," Bertha said. "He could've been spraying the wheat on the other side of the river for all you know."

"Who was that?" Abby asked.

"Roger Gilman. He owns a crop-dusting service. His airfield is just over the rise."

"Herbert and Roger have had a running disagreement for years," Grace said, making a sad face.

"He and I have had words about the way he disturbs the birds with his low-altitude flying over the wetlands. He is not a wildlife lover. Unfortunately, he isn't breaking any laws. Let's go. I have some books for you at my home, Abby. We can pick them up on our way into town."

Abby got in the car, excited to learn more about birds and put her new plan into action.

Joe was carrying a sheet of plywood across the yard when Herbert Young pulled in. The back door of the car opened. Abby got out. She hurried toward him, holding several books in her hands. "I had the most wonderful morning."

"Wish I could say the same. Rose is still hemming and hawing about the countertops. The lumberyard sent the wrong grade of plywood, and I can't find my level. I had it not thirty minutes ago. What were you up to?" He kept walking and she fell into step beside him.

"I went bird-watching with Herbert, Bertha and Grace."

She sure looked happy. He loved it when she was smiling. "I take it you enjoyed yourself."

"I really did. I mean, I thought it would be boring, but it wasn't. Did you know there is a wetlands bird sanctuary just north of the river?"

"I did not. Do they need someone to build birdhouses for them? I could take on a side job."

She frowned slightly. "I didn't see any birdhouses."

"I was kidding."

"Oh." She giggled. "I guess I'm too gullible."

"Could you get the door for me?"

"Sure." She jumped ahead and pulled open the new door he had hung that morning. "Anyway, I'm going to go again but first I have to learn a little about ornithology and the different kinds of birds. Grace said I had a good eye for spotting them."

He went inside. "Were any of them as big as a door?"

She followed him in. "Oh, no. The warblers are tiny."

He set the plywood against the wall, closed the door and patted it. "So, if any of them were as big as this, you would have noticed them right away?"

"I think only an ostrich is as big as a door." Suddenly she caught on. "Oh, you put up the new door! That looks nice."

"Better than the tarp?"

"Much better. What did Rose say?"

He opened and closed the door to show how well it had been hung. "She liked it. Now she has to decide on the color."

"I like white."

"So do I, but she can't decide between white or light blue."

"Blue would be pretty."

"And it would keep the wasps away."

"Blue paint keeps bees away?" She looked skeptical. "I'm not that gullible. You're kidding me again, right?"

"*Nee.* Haven't you noticed the ceiling of the porch is painted pale blue?"

"I guess not."

"It stops wasps and mud daubers from building nests under there."

"Really? I've been stung before. I do not like wasps. I'll have to do that at my place."

"Your place?" Was she moving out of the inn?

Her eyes widened. "When I get a place of my own," she said quickly. She started backing away. "I'd better get to work. I'm sure the laundry is still waiting for me. I didn't intend to take the morning off. I'll see you later."

"Five o'clock okay?"

"Five is fine." She spun around, nearly tripping in Susanna's large slippers, and almost ran into Rose as she came in from the breakfast room.

"There you are, Abby. Susanna wants you in the sewing room," Rose said. "She found some material for you."

"Oh, well, I haven't finished the laundry."

"It's going to rain this afternoon so leave it until tomorrow."

Abby tilted her head slightly. "How do you know it's going to rain?"

Rose grimaced and rubbed her left shoulder. "I could tell you it's because my joints are aching, but the truth is I heard it on the radio when I was at the lumberyard earlier."

Joe pushed up the brim of his hat with one finger. "When you were at the lumberyard, did you happen to change my order for plywood?"

"That would've been a silly thing to do. I'm glad we settled on this size for the door. You did a nice job hanging it." She smiled, walked past him and went outside.

Joe crossed his arms and looked at Abby, who was still standing by the door to the hall. "Did you notice anything unusual about Rose's answer?"

Abby nodded. "She didn't deny changing your order."

"*Nee*, she did not. Is she back to her old tricks trying to keep me around longer?"

"I suppose it's possible. Do you want me to talk to her?"

"I have a feeling she'll skirt the issue no matter who talks to her. But you can ask her what she did with my level."

"You think Rose took it?"

"I caught her taking a crowbar from my tool chest the other night."

"Why would Rose take a crowbar?"

Joe shrugged. "That's what I asked her. In true Rose fashion she said because she didn't own one."

Abby grinned. "At least now you know what you can get her for her birthday."

He smiled back. "Go on. Susanna is waiting for you."

"Okay. The door does look nice."

"There's an art to properly hanging one."

"I'm sure there is. See you later. Five, right?" She gave a small wave and left the kitchen.

Five o'clock couldn't come soon enough as far as Joe was concerned.

Abby found the sewing room when she passed the open door across from Susanna's bedroom. Susanna was bent over a folding table cutting fabric. The room had a large north-facing window that provided plenty of light. There was also a propane lamp affixed to a small cabinet with wheels that could be moved to wherever additional brightness was needed. A treadle-operated sewing machine sat in front of the window. Off to the side a small quilting frame held a partially completed star-patterned quilt in beautiful colors of blue, maroon, gold and forest green on a cream background.

Abby stepped in and stood awkwardly waiting for Susanna to notice her. Finally, she cleared her throat. "Did you want to see me?"

Susanna glanced over her shoulder. "There you are. I have several bolts of fabric for you to choose from. How are your feet today?"

"Sore but better. Thank you for the loan of the slippers."

"Don't mention it. Which of these fabrics appeal to you?" She had laid out several samples. One was a lovely royal blue, another a deep mossy green. She had her hand on a maroon bolt the same color as in the quilt, and a plain brown.

Abby's eye was drawn to the blue. "Are you sure you can spare them?"

Susanna smiled. "I'm afraid I'm guilty of buying more fabric than I need because I'm always thinking what a nice color it would make in a quilt." She picked up the blue fabric and draped it over Abby's shoulder. "Definitely the royal blue for you. It makes your pretty eyes look even bluer."

"I don't want people to think I'm vain."

"*Gott* gave you bright blue eyes. There's no shame in wearing a dress that brings out their color."

Abby fingered the material. "I like this a lot."

"*Goot*. For a Sunday dress, I think. Now for a workday dress."

"The brown."

Susanna draped that fabric over Abby's other shoulder. She tipped her head one way and then the other. "*Nee*, I don't think so. It doesn't suit you. Let's try the green broadcloth. Rose and I both have everyday dresses made from this fabric. It's lightweight for summer. It breathes easier than polyester and still doesn't wrinkle much. I think there's enough to make a dress and a matching cape."

She held the material up beside Abby's face. "It will do. There are scissors over on the table. Once we have it cut out it won't take any time at all to sew it up." Susanna's eyes narrowed as she leaned closer to Abby and fingered the edge of her cape. "Is this all hand stitched?"

"The sewing machine wasn't available when I made it." She had worked in secret in her father's house, hiding her work between the mattress and the box springs of her bed. Several times Logan had almost caught her with it when he came in. She pushed aside the bitter memories of their time together.

Susanna frowned but didn't say anything else.

Abby and Susanna worked together to lay the material out and pin a homemade pattern to it. Abby supplied the needed measurements. She didn't want Susanna taking them for fear she would notice Abby's small baby bump. When they had the pieces cut out, Abby carried them to the sewing machine. She sat down in the chair and worked the treadle a few times with her foot. There were a half dozen pieces of red-and-white-checked material sitting beside the machine and one half-completed square still in it.

She looked at Susanna and smiled. "I learned on a machine just like this at my grandmother's home."

"*Goot.* Why don't you finish hemming that napkin for me while I cut out the second dress."

Abby quickly got to work. When she was done, she held it up. The seams weren't as straight and neat as her grandmother had sewn. "I'm done with this one."

Susanna came over and examined the napkin without comment. She went back to the cutting table. "I will finish sewing your dresses. You can run along."

Susanna wasn't impressed with her effort. Failing at such a simple task brought tears to Abby's eyes. "My sewing leaves something to be desired, doesn't it? I'm afraid I haven't done much in a while."

"A little practice will help you improve. You're welcome to use the machine anytime."

"I don't have anything to make." She would need curtains and the like for her home when it was finally hers, but she didn't know when that would happen.

Susanna glanced over her shoulder. Her gaze softened. "We need new napkins to match the tablecloths in the breakfast room. Would you mind cutting and hemming a dozen more tomorrow? Now that Mamm has decided to start accepting reservations, we'll need them sooner rather than later."

Abby sniffed once and managed a smile. "I'll be happy to do that for you. You've all been so good to me."

Susanna cleared her throat and lifted her chin. "The living room needs dusting. If you do that for me, I'll have your dress done by the time you finish."

Abby left the sewing room with lagging steps. All Amish women knew how to sew. It was something they learned at their mother's knee and did all their lives. She had learned from her grandmother, but she had lost much of her skill over the past years while she was locked away. It was another in a list of growing deficiencies she would have to overcome to live Amish, but she would relearn old skills and master new ones. She cupped her hand over her tummy. One day she would teach her child what he or she needed to know, too.

When she was done cleaning, she returned to the sewing room. Susanna held up the dress she had finished. It was expertly constructed and made the dress Abby had on look shabby by comparison. After thanking Susanna, Abby took the dress to her room and laid it on her bed. It was supposed to be a work dress, but it was so clean and crisp she hated the idea of getting it dirty.

Should she wear it when she went down to the barn to see Joe? Would he notice? Would he like it? It shouldn't matter what he thought, but it did. She quickly changed out of her old dress and pulled on the new one.

Joe managed to stay busy and keep his mind off seeing Abby at five o'clock until thunder rumbled in the distance about four, putting an end to his work. He moved his table saw and the lumber he was cutting into the barn just as the wind switched bringing the fresh scent of rain to the dry dusty air. He loved that smell.

He stood in the open doorway of the barn, watching as the trees bent in a sudden gust of cold wind. A thunderstorm was nothing to take lightly. Hail and high winds could flatten wheat fields, injure livestock and damage homes. The torrential rains they sometimes unleashed could cause flooding locally and even miles away. It was best he stay out of his little home until the worst of it had passed. He'd seen trailers much larger than his rolled like toys in windstorms and twisted into unrecognizable wreckage by a tornado. He watched the rain coming across the prairie as the trees and buildings in the distance disappeared behind a blue-gray curtain.

So much for giving Abby a lesson in harnessing a horse this afternoon.

The first splatters of rain hit the barn roof. He glanced toward the house and saw one of the women running in his direction with an umbrella held in front of her face.

Another gust of wind pulled it from her hand and sent it skittering across the yard. It was Abby. She stood for a moment as if debating whether she should go after the umbrella or not. She held something long in one hand. What was she doing?

A brilliant flash of lightning followed immediately by a deafening crack of thunder blinded him. When his vision cleared, he saw Abby hunched over with her arms covering her head. Why was she just standing there?

"Abby, get over here!"

She looked in his direction but didn't move.

Eleven

Joe raced out and grabbed Abby's arm, pulling her along until they reached the cover of the barn.

"I lost Rose's umbrella," she mumbled, wiping the rain from her face with one hand.

"You can find it later. You're crazy to come out in a storm like this."

She rounded on him. "Don't use that word. I hate it."

"Sorry. It's ill-advised to step out into a thunderstorm. I wouldn't like watching you get struck by lightning." A blinding flash and simultaneous crash made him flinch. He pulled her farther into the barn.

"It came up so fast," she said and shivered.

"It should blow past just as quickly, unless there's a line of storms behind it."

"I've always been frightened by the thunder, but rain makes everything smell wonderful."

"I was just thinking that. What possessed you to come out with a storm blowing up?"

"Rose sent me. She found your level in the refrigerator." She held it out to him.

This had to be another one of Rose's addlebrained schemes to get them together. It could have ended badly. He would have a talk with the woman. "I did not leave it in the fridge. I didn't even open the icebox today."

Abby shrugged as he took the tool from her. "She said it was important that you have it. I should go back."

"Not until the storm moves past. It will let up in a little while. You don't want to get your new dress soaked."

Abby smiled. "You noticed. Susanna helped me make it. Well, I cut it out and she sewed it together. She tries to be gruff, but she's really a sweetheart. She's finishing a second one for me. That will be my Sunday dress. It's a pretty shade of royal blue, but I like this green."

"You look very plain in it."

"Rose and Susanna both have dresses made out of this fabric so I will fit right in."

"That's important to you, isn't it?"

She stared at the ground. "I don't want people to look at me like I'm different."

He tipped his head slightly. "You are different."

She looked up and frowned. "What do you mean?"

"Different but in a good way. You can be outspoken. That's unusual. You have determination. You're afraid of something, but you won't give in to that fear."

She moved closer to the door and stared outside. "Everyone has things that make them afraid. I'm sure even you have been frightened sometimes."

It was true. He was afraid of getting involved with this woman. Afraid of caring too much. She was chipping away at the wall he kept between himself and others. "You're right. I can't stand snakes. They give me the willies."

She turned her gaze on him. "Somehow I don't quite believe that."

"All right. I'll tell you my secret if you'll tell me yours."

Abby turned away from Joe's questioning gaze. If she told him all her secrets, she would lose his friendship. That meant more to her than she could ever explain. Not telling him could drive him away, too. Perhaps she could share something he was already guessing at. Did she dare?

It was still raining outside, but the patter of it on the roof wasn't as loud. The sounds of the storm were moving away. The wind was dying down. The trees drooped under the weight of their soaked branches. Leaves and twigs littered the ground everywhere. There was something comforting about being with Joe in the dim light of the barn surrounded by the smells of old wood, fresh hay and low sounds of the animals. She felt safe. She looked back at him. Her feelings had more to do with Joe's presence than the place where they were taking shelter.

He was still watching her. Waiting, not pressing for answers. That gave her the courage to admit something of her past. She wanted to tell him everything, but she didn't dare. There was more at stake than her friendship. Her child's future might depend on her silence.

"All right, Joe. I wasn't raised in an Amish family."

His eyes widened. He didn't say anything for a long moment. Finally, he drew a quick breath and blew it out slowly. "Whoa. I reckon that explains a lot."

"Does it?"

"Except, how do you know Pennsylvania Dutch?"

"My mother was ex-Amish. She and I spoke it at home when we were alone. I'm fluent because I spent every summer until I was fourteen with my Amish grandparents. I loved every day on their farm. Every minute of it. I knew it was the life I was meant to live. Sadly, my grandparents passed away before I was old enough to live on my own."

"Your parents wouldn't allow you to stay with other Amish family members?"

"My mother was an only child. She had passed away from leukemia a few weeks before my grandparents died in a buggy accident."

"That must have been a rough time."

"It was terrible. I had no one left. You understand what it's like to lose people you love."

"Yeah, I do. What about your father?"

"He has only contempt for the Amish. He's a very controlling man. He wouldn't consider letting me choose my own path. I lived unhappily in his *Englisch* home until I got up enough courage to leave, and I came here." That was as close as she could come to admitting she had been locked away. Even to Joe. She was too ashamed to tell him about her suicide attempt. It went against everything their faith stood for, everything her grandparents had believed in. She had been weak instead of strong in the face of her trials. She had failed God's test of her faith.

Joe wouldn't understand her mental breakdown. What was he thinking now?

"I'm not someone pretending to be Amish," she said to fill the awkward silence. "It may seem that way, but I will never go back to the *Englisch* world. It holds nothing for me. I intend to be baptized as soon as I can."

He shook his head slightly. "That's some secret. If you

spent all your summers on an Amish farm, why don't you know how to harness a horse?"

She bowed her head. "Because I've always been afraid of them. I was badly frightened by my father's stallion when I was three or four years old. My fear was another reason I failed to live up to his standards."

"But I saw you leading Cooper yesterday. You were petting Bendy, and she has a mean streak."

"I realize I must get over my fear. Seeing David's precious foal with her gentle mother helped. I know there won't be anyone to harness or care for my horse when I get a place of my own. It might not have looked like it, but it took a lot of courage to take Cooper's bridle off yesterday. Grandfather taught me how to drive, but he never insisted I harness a horse. He didn't expect me to join the Amish. His daughter, my mother, was shunned for marrying an outsider after she had taken her vows. I was the only common ground they had left. Grandfather knew my father wouldn't allow me to stay with them."

"Now I'm starting to understand."

"Maybe I should've told everyone this, but I thought if I did—they would treat me differently. Look at me differently."

He stared at her as if seeing her for the first time. Had she ruined things between them? "Does it change how you feel about me?" She held her breath.

Joe lifted his hat from his head, ran his fingers through his hair, took a deep breath and settled his hat back on. How should he answer her? It was a shock.

She wasn't what she seemed, but he'd sensed there was something different about her from the start. He'd assumed it was because she had grown up with *Englisch* friends who thought little of being loud and outspoken. She hadn't. She was one of them. Or she had been. He did believe her when she said she'd made her decision and would take her vows when she could. There was conviction in her voice when she said it.

In many ways she was like other young Amish women still in their *rumspringa* experiencing the outside world. While they had the advantage of growing up in an Amish family and learning everything an Amish woman needed to know, Abby was still filling in the blanks. He gazed into her bright blue eyes filled with uncertainty. It had taken courage to share her deception. Was she wrong to have kept it secret? Maybe, but he didn't share his past with people.

It was easier to say nothing than to explain why he was the only member of his family who had survived the fire. She didn't want to be seen as different. He didn't want pity. So they both stayed silent about the past.

She was still waiting for him to answer her question. He read the concern in her eyes. The truth was that he remained drawn to her in ways he didn't understand in spite of her confession. Perhaps even more so because he recognized the courage it took. "Does it change how I feel about you? Honestly, I don't think it does."

She gave him the sweetest smile he'd ever seen. "*Danki.* I'm glad. I don't have another friend. I'd hate to lose you."

"You won't." It was a promise he intended to keep. He would be her friend above all else.

Abby wanted to hug Joe but that wasn't how Amish women behaved. "I suppose you think that being afraid of horses is just plain silly."

"Not when you're making an effort to overcome that fear."

"Your help is making it easier. Are you going to tell

the widows about me?" Her secret was bound to come out eventually.

"Only if I'm asked."

That was a relief. She wouldn't want him to lie for her. "*Goot.* Okay, that was my secret. What's one of yours?"

"I'm not really afraid of snakes."

She folded her arms over her chest. "What? That's not a secret."

"Is it something you knew about me already?"

She frowned a little. "I guess not."

"Then it was a secret and now it's not. Are you ready for a harnessing lesson?"

She stood up straighter and closed her eyes. "I reckon I am."

He didn't say anything. When she opened her eyes, he was grinning at her with a funny, knowing smile. "What?"

"Your determination is showing again."

"You said that was okay, right?"

"*Ja. Das ist goot.* We'll use Cooper to practice on. He's a gentle soul."

Joe led the way to the tack room beyond the stalls. "Each horse has his own harness. They are kept here after they're cleaned."

Abby looked at three sets of harnesses hanging from racks. "How do you know which one goes to which horse?"

"I can tell by their size. Cooper's is the largest. Bendy's is next. The last one belongs to Buttercup, the smaller mare that Grace uses." He grabbed a brush and comb from the bench. "First you have to make sure the horse is clean. Get the dirt and dust out of his coat so the harness doesn't rub a sore on him." He turned around and handed her the comb and brush.

"You want me to brush him?"

"The best way to learn is to do."

"Right." She walked toward the stall where Cooper was watching her. "Bear with me. I'm new at this." The horse snorted.

"Take his halter and lead him to the crosstie posts. Clip both of the ropes to his halter and that way he will stand quietly."

She looked over her shoulder at Joe. "Promise?"

He chuckled. "Horses are rarely unpredictable because this is what they do all the time. They're comfortable with a routine." He opened the stall gate. Abby had no choice but to grasp the halter because Cooper was already on his way out.

The horse led her to the posts instead of the other way around and stopped. Her heart was hammering as she clipped each rope to his halter and stepped back. "Now what?"

"Go ahead and comb out his mane."

Abby reached up and pulled the comb through the long hair tentatively. She had to work out a tangle and then gained a little confidence. Cooper shook his head violently. She jumped back. "Did I do something wrong?"

"*Nee*, you're fine. He just had a fly on his ear. Wouldn't you shake your head if you had an insect land on your head?"

"I would swat it with my hand."

"That's what his mane and tail are for. They're his fly-swatters."

"I know that." She finished combing his mane then held the brush up. "Where do I start with this?"

"Start on his withers and work backward."

"Like this?" Abby drew the brush lightly along the side

of Cooper's body. He shivered and she jerked her hand away. "Why did he do that?"

"Because you tickled him. Use firmer strokes. Like this, in the direction his hair grows." Joe covered Abby's hand with his own and ran the brush along the horse's back. He repeated the motion going lower on the horse's side and Abby lost track of what she was doing.

She became acutely aware of Joe's body close beside her, of his hand holding hers. The scent of the warm horse, hay and old barnwood mixed with the smell of rain. The sound of the raindrops dripping off the roof and the dim light formed a cocoon around them. She glanced up and found Joe was watching her. Her heart tripped over itself as it sped up. She shouldn't feel this way about a friend.

"I've got it," she said breathlessly.

He released her hand, stepped back and cleared his throat. "That's fine. Do both sides, his belly and his chest. Everywhere the harness touches. Always speak to him when you walk behind him. Horses can't see directly behind themselves and they may kick if you startle them."

"Good to know. I think."

Abby quickly finished brushing the horse and then watched as Joe applied the harness. She tried to remember where each leather strap was buckled and the names of each of the pieces. Finally, she shook her head. "I'll never get it."

"Sure you will. Like anything else it takes practice. I think that's enough for today." He lifted the harness off Cooper.

"I'm sorry if I'm keeping you from working."

He carried the harness to the tack room and hung it up. "I had to break down my work area because of the storm anyway. It won't set me behind much."

"Do you still think you'll be done by the end of this week?"

"Close to it."

It made her sad to think about him leaving. She would miss him dreadfully. She'd grown fond of him and cherished his friendship, but perhaps it was for the best. He'd never have to learn she was an unwed mother with a history of mental illness. Still, she wished he could stay a little longer.

"I might have another job in the area," he said, and her hopes rose.

"Really?"

"The chances are *goot*. If I get it and Rose doesn't mind, I might keep my camper here awhile longer."

"I don't think she'll mind." Abby suddenly laughed. "What am I saying? She'll be thrilled. She's been trying to keep you around longer ever since you arrived."

"I don't believe she's given up on us making a match of it."

"Why do you say that?"

"Something tells me she hid my level and then used it as an excuse to send you out here so we would be stuck in the barn together until the rain let up."

"You don't need your level this evening? She told me it was important."

"It's an important tool, but I don't need it until tomorrow when I set the cabinets in."

"I can't believe her. Should we talk to her again?"

"I think we'd just be wasting our breath. We know what she's up to. If she thinks we are getting along, she won't be looking to make us matches elsewhere."

"That's true. I do hate to get her hopes up and then disappoint her."

"I'm sure we're not the first match that didn't work out for her."

"You're probably right." If things had been different, Abby would have seriously considered going out with Joe. He was everything that a woman could want. Kind, funny and handsome although she knew looks meant little to the Amish. An attractive man was one who was hardworking and faithful to God. Joe fit that description, too. But things weren't different, she reminded herself sternly. She was pregnant and hiding an even more shameful secret that she couldn't bear to have him learn. If God was kind, Joe would be long gone before her situation came to light. She was fortunate to have him as a friend for as long as he was here. She wouldn't ask for more.

He moved to the barn door. "It looks like the rain has stopped."

She joined him in the doorway, wishing she had a reason to stay. "I should get back to the house. Thank you for the lesson."

"I appreciate you sharing your secret with me. I'm honored to have earned your trust."

Standing close beside him, she was overwhelmed with the urge to lay her head against his chest and let him hold her. Just for a little while. Before he was gone from her life forever.

What she was feeling must have shown on her face because he reached out and drew his knuckles along her cheek. "It will be okay. You'll find what you're looking for here. Harts Haven is full of caring people."

"People like you?" she asked softly.

A shadow filled his eyes. He took a step away. The closeness she'd felt evaporated. "Better people," he said. "You should run along."

Embarrassed that she had let too much of her feelings show, Abby left the barn and ran toward the house.

Joe gave a deep sigh as he watched until she was inside. He was falling for that woman, and it was a huge mistake. He didn't know how to reverse course. She was vulnerable, alone and troubled. She had lost most of her family the way he had but none of that had been her fault. He couldn't say the same. His guilt lay like a lead weight in his heart.

Abby needed someone she could depend on, not someone who let other people down. She didn't need him. It was a good thing he was almost done with Rose's renovations. If David decided he wanted the addition on his house, Joe would let Oliver give the job to someone else. It was time he moved on.

Sometime later that evening he heard a knock at his trailer door. He laid aside his book and got up to answer it, praying it wasn't Abby. Instead it was Rose. She held the covered casserole dish. "You didn't come in for supper, so I brought you some leftovers."

"Danki." He took the plate from her and set it on the counter. When he turned back, she was still standing in front of his door. "Is there something else?"

"I've been thinking about putting in a bigger window above the kitchen sink. The one we have just seems so tiny now that the kitchen is bigger. May I come in?"

"Nope. I'm not going to do it. The minute the work you hired me for is finished I'll be leaving. If you want a bigger window, hire another contractor. Is there anything else?"

"Oh, dear, you're angry with me."

He folded his arms over his chest. "How observant."

She winked at him. "It's a gift. Another one of my gifts is that people can never stay upset with me for long."

"You're right. I won't be mad at you for long because I won't be here."

"Not exactly what I was thinking. I did want to apologize for hiding your level."

"And for sending Abby out into an electrical storm for no good reason? There was a lot of hot lightning in that storm. She could've been killed."

"I'm getting a crick in my neck looking up at you. Would you please let me in?"

"Fine." He returned to his recliner. Rose came in and sat on his only kitchen chair.

"I'm worried about you, Joseph," she said, surprising him.

"About me? Why?"

"*Gott* gives all His children a chance to find happiness in this life. Is the world filled with sorrow? It is, but we can overcome our sadness and find joy again. Only I don't think you want to be happy."

"You don't know what you're talking about."

She braced both hands on her knees and leaned toward him. "Do you deserve to be happy, Joseph? Answer me truthfully."

Why was she doing this? He wanted to be left alone. He didn't want to examine his life. He just wanted to get through each day with as few painful memories as possible. He wanted to get through one night without a nightmare.

"I'm waiting?"

"I have accepted God's plan for me."

"To live alone? To shut yourself away from others who could easily learn to respect and love you?"

"What do you want, Rose? You want me to say that I'm happy? Okay, I'm a happy man."

"And a very poor liar," she said dryly. "What I want is

for you to accept that being happy isn't a sin. We all experience grief and loss. Holding on to that grief and using it to hide from happiness, that is the sin."

Her words hit too close to home. He had been holding on to his grief. It was a shield to keep others away.

"I've grown fond of you, Joseph. I hope you know that. Now I will leave you to think about what I've said. If we are to love our neighbors as ourselves, doesn't that mean we must love ourselves first?"

"I appreciate your concern, Rose," he said softly.

"You're a good man, Joseph. And think about the window." She got up and left his trailer.

Joe sat in his chair staring at nothing in particular. Was he holding on to his grief to hide from the joy of life? It had been so long since he had been happy he wasn't sure he knew what that felt like.

Then again, that wasn't true. When he held Abby's hand beneath his while she brushed Cooper, he'd seen a fleeting glimpse of happiness. In that quiet moment with the woman he cared about, he had cherished the feeling of having her close beside him. He had been content.

If he accepted that God wanted him to be happy, then he had to accept that his past sins had been forgiven. Forgiveness was the cornerstone of his faith and yet he had never been able to forgive himself.

He was more of an Amish pretender than Abby.

If he could forgive himself, then maybe he could think about a future with someone special. Someone like Abby.

By Wednesday, Abby was anxious to return to her farm, but she wasn't in any condition to walk that far again. Her feet were improving but a five-mile hike was beyond her. What she needed was transportation. Free transportation.

She was hanging up the laundry when Rose came out to give her a hand. "It's easier to do the sheets if you have someone to help," Rose said, lifting the corner of one from the basket.

Abby lifted the other corner. "*Danki.* I should be angry with you."

"Whatever for?" They folded the sheet in half and hung it over the line.

"You sent me out into the rain yesterday for no good reason. Joe did not need his level, and you are the one who hid it in the refrigerator in the first place."

"Forgetful elderly people do strange things sometimes."

"I don't think you are forgetful, but I wish you would stop pushing me and Joe together."

"Don't you like the young man?"

"I like him as a friend. He feels the same way."

"Friendship can turn into love over time. I've seen it happen."

"Maybe if things were different. But they aren't." Abby shook out a pillowcase with unnecessary vigor.

"Well, you can't blame this old *frau* for trying. You just seem right for each other. I know you think the baby will make a difference in Joe's feelings toward you, but I'm sure it won't. He is going to find out eventually."

"No, he won't. He'll move on to another job in another town, maybe even another state, and he won't think about me again."

Rose shook her head sadly. "Child, you are not forget-table."

Abby wanted to be. She wanted to blend in and never stand out again.

"Rose, you mentioned once that you had a bicycle I could use. Is that offer still open?"

"Changing the subject? Very well. *Ja*, you can use it. I believe it's in the small shed at the side of the barn. I don't know what shape it's in. Grace's grandsons were here last summer, and they were off somewhere every day. I remember one of them saying the chain slipped loose. Ask Joe to take a look at it. That fella can fix just about anything. Maybe even a broken heart if someone would give him the chance." She wagged her eyebrows.

Abby rolled her eyes. "I never said I had a broken heart."

"You don't strike me as the kind of woman who would have a casual encounter with a young man. You may not love him anymore because he hurt you terribly, but I think you cared deeply for your baby's father. My guess is that he betrayed you. Am I right?"

Abby nodded.

"I thought so," Rose said. "That kind of pain lasts longer than a couple of blisters on your feet, but the cure isn't to stop walking. The remedy is to find a better pair of shoes."

"And you think Joe is a better fit for me?" If only that was possible.

"Maybe. I can finish hanging out this laundry. Go see if the bike is in decent shape. I'm glad you have a new undertaking."

"What do you mean?" Abby frowned.

"Bird-watching. That is the reason you want the bike, isn't it? I think it's a wonderful hobby. Grace is ecstatic that you enjoyed your first outing."

"I did enjoy myself, and I'm eager to go back. The wetlands sanctuary is an amazing place." Abby pinned a pillowcase to the line.

"It is, and so close to the old Martin farm, too."

Abby slowly lowered her arms and turned to look at Rose. What did she know about the Martins?

Twelve

Abby tried for a casual tone, but she was quaking inside. "Is that the abandoned farm out by the marshes?"

Rose's smile faded. "You know it is. Isn't it a shame that your grandparents' home is falling into ruin?"

Abby's mind reeled. Rose knew her grandparents had owned that farm. That meant Rose knew who she was? How was that possible? How long had she known? How many other people knew? Martin was such a common Amish name that she didn't think using it would give her away. Had she made a terrible mistake?

Abby wished she could sit down. She swallowed hard and tried to bluff. "I don't know what you're talking about."

"You went to your grandmother Miriam's house on Saturday. It would have been a long walk. Your blisters gave you away. I've been there a few times since *Gott* called her and her husband home. It makes me sad and angry to see such a fine farm lying abandoned. I always hoped you would come back and take it over. We met when you were little. You don't remember me, do you?"

Abby shook her head, dumbfounded by Rose's comment.

The elderly woman smiled softly. "I visited your grandmother Miriam a few times when you were there. Her mother, Sarah, and I were great friends at school, so I liked to keep in touch with Sarah's only daughter after she moved away. Miriam belonged to a different church group, so I didn't see her often, but I remember you. You're very much like Sarah was when she was your age. Dearest, you do make me feel old."

Abby hadn't paid much attention to the women who came to see her grandmother. There had always been people stopping in to visit, especially on the off Sundays. Mostly she had liked the families who came with their children, bringing someone for her to play with. Because she had met members of her grandparents' church district, she had planned to avoid going to Castleton in case anyone might recognize her.

Abby pressed a hand to her forehead as she tried to grasp the implications of what Rose was telling her. "Who knows?"

"If you mean who knows you're Victor and Jennifer's child, only me."

"What are you going to do?"

"I thought I'd have a cup of tea and then I'm going to check on little Micah Shetler and his *mamm*." Rose picked up the empty laundry basket and headed for the door but paused and looked back. "Did you know that you were born in Taos, New Mexico?"

Abby shook her head. "I wasn't."

Rose giggled. "You were. Victor worked there for a year after he married your mother. Then they moved to Kansas City. I still have the birth announcement your mother sent me along with your newborn picture. You were a homely babe. Bald as a marble."

"If you knew I was Victoria when I arrived, why did you let me keep up the pretense?"

"Sarah, Miriam and I exchanged circle letters for many years after Sarah moved away. When your mother left the faith, all our hearts were broken. Your grandmother's most of all. She prayed Jennifer would come back to us but of course she didn't. When you were born, and Jennifer allowed you to stay with your grandparents during the summers, Miriam was overjoyed. It was her fondest wish that you might embrace our ways. When you walked into my kitchen that first day, I thought her prayers had been answered at last. After I guessed you were pregnant, and you confirmed you weren't married, I assumed that was why you were concealing your real identity. My desire to see the fondest wish of my two departed friends come to pass led me to aid you in your deception. Now I'm not sure it was the right thing to do."

Abby struggled to take it all in. "No one can know about me, Rose. Please. You can't tell anyone I'm Jennifer's daughter."

"I don't see why I would have to mention it. Your grandfather had two brothers who moved to Ohio. They are both married with large families. A woman my age can't be expected to remember which of those Martin families you came from if anyone should ask, but they won't. Bertha and I are the last of Sarah's friends. Place your trust in *Gott* and don't be afraid."

"You don't understand. My father wants me back, and he isn't a fool. I can't risk being discovered."

"Miriam always refused to talk about him. Why do you fear him? What hold does he have over you?"

Shame kept Abby silent. She couldn't bring herself to tell Rose about her mental breakdown or the aftermath of her illness under her father's manipulative care. It was painful to even think about those dark days.

Rose nodded slowly. "I understand if you'd rather not say. He is your father after all. Tell me something, Abigail. Are you here to hide among us? Or are you here to become one of us?"

"Both."

Rose shook her head. "It can't be both. Our faith is not a cloak to be thrown over your head and then cast aside when it isn't needed."

"That's not what I'm doing. I want to be Amish. I loved my grandparents and I want to live as they did, worship as they did, belong as they did."

"Then you will have to stop pretending to be Amish and embrace what it means. Honesty, faith in *Gott*'s mercy and protection, unconditional forgiveness for those who have harmed you. Can you do that? You must pray about this. Is this truly *Gott*'s plan for you? It may be what you want, but it may not be His will."

"It has to be, Rose. For my baby's sake. I can't be found out. Not yet. Won't you help me learn what I need to know?"

Rose grew pensive. "I may have been too eager to see my old friend's granddaughter settled here. I might have risked the happiness of someone else I care about, too. I won't speak of your identity, but I must pray about this."

After Rose left, Abby tried to figure out her next move.

If Rose kept quiet, it wouldn't change Abby's plans, but could Rose be trusted to keep a secret?

Apparently, she had known immediately who Abby was. A young woman from New Mexico. Abby had assumed Rose was a bit addled, but it seemed she was sharper than Abby gave her credit for.

If Rose had known from the start, then she had kept Abby's secret thus far. Abby had no choice but to continue to trust her.

This was God's plan for her and her child. Abby believed that with all her heart. There was so much to do before her baby arrived. Today she needed to find Rose's bicycle and then go back to the farm to make it habitable. It was all she could do until she had enough money to hire a lawyer.

"Joe, are you busy?"

He looked up from the base cabinet he was working on to see Abby pushing a beat-up blue bicycle toward him. He smiled and remembered Rose's words. Seeing Abby made him happy. He didn't have to run from that feeling. "I've got a few minutes. What seems to be the trouble?"

"The chain keeps coming off. I can't get it to stay on. Would you mind looking at it?"

He put his hands on his hips and bent closer. "Okay, I'm looking."

She chuckled. "What I meant was, can you fix it?"

He liked it when he could make her laugh. He took the bike from her and turned it upside down. "I see what needs to be done. Let me take it down to my trailer." He turned the bike right side up.

She gestured toward the cabinet. "What are you doing here?"

"I'm using a hand planer to take off some wood on one

side of the bottom so it will sit level. Old houses rarely have even floors or walls for that matter." He began pushing the bike across the drive and she fell into step beside him.

"I appreciate this," she said.

"It's no problem." He didn't mind doing something that helped her. He glanced her way. She seemed pensive.

"Is something wrong?" he asked.

She shook her head. "It's just that sometimes I don't know what to make of Rose."

"I know the feeling. She's far more astute than I gave her credit for."

"Exactly. So why does she act scatterbrained some-times?"

"I think only Rose could tell you that. *If* you could get a straight answer out of her. Has she been pushing our match again?"

"Not today. You?"

They stopped in the shade of the trees at the rear of his camper. "Maybe a little. Don't let her upset you."

"I'm not upset."

"*Goot*, then smile."

She managed a half-hearted one. "Sorry. I've been wrapped up in my own troubles."

"Anything I can do to help?"

"You're doing enough."

He opened his toolbox and found the size of socket wrench he needed. "The rear wheel has to go farther back to pull the chain tighter. I'll loosen the nuts on the bolt and then I'll have you pull on the tire while I retighten them."

Together they managed to affect the repair in short order. He held it out to her. "The seat looks a little low. Shall I adjust it for you?"

"That would be great seeing as how I don't own any tools," she said, giving him a little smile.

"That's what I was hoping to see."

She tipped her head. "What?"

"You, smiling. I like your smile." He liked the way her eyes sparkled when she was happy, too. How did she feel about him? Was there a chance for more than friendship between them? He wasn't brave enough to ask.

She blushed and took the bike out of his hands. "Let me see if I remember how to ride."

She got on and took off down the driveway. At the end she made a wobbling turn, came back and stopped beside him.

"How does the seat feel?" he asked.

"It's a little low. Rose said one of the grandchildren used it last. They must've had shorter legs than I do."

"Hop off." She did and he adjusted the height for her. "There. You should be set. Would you like something to drink? I have a couple of 7UPs in the fridge."

"That sounds nice. *Danki.*"

"Have a seat and I'll get them." He indicated the lawn chair at the side of the trailer then stepped inside to get the cans. When he came out, she was watching him with an odd look on her face. "What?"

"There's something different about you today."

That surprised him. "Something *goot* or something bad?"

"I'd say *goot.*"

He could hardly admit that he was allowing himself to think about a future for the first time in years. "It must be your imagination. I'm the same rude guy." He sat on his steps.

"Maybe that's it. I haven't seen you be rude to anyone in over a week. I think your rudeness has worn off."

He grinned. "You didn't see me trying to level those cabinets earlier. If the guy who laid the floor had been in the room, he would've gotten an earful."

"That I can believe."

After that he ran out of things to say. They sat together sipping their drinks and enjoying the cool breeze that slipped through the branches of the trees overhead on a warm spring day. He didn't mind that she wasn't talking. He just allowed himself to enjoy her company without any expectations.

She finished her soda and handed him the can. "I'd better get back to work. We have three new guests checking in tonight."

"Then I should get the cabinets in. See you at supper?"

She smiled shyly and nodded. "Sure."

Joe wanted to say more but decided against it. For now, it was enough that they could be in each other's company without any awkwardness between them.

As soon as Abby was finished with her work that afternoon, she took a bottle of pine cleaner from the broom closet and put it in her shoulder bag along with several of her books on birds. She hung her binoculars around her neck, got on the bicycle that Joe had fixed and pedaled away from the inn.

At the end of the lane she met Joe coming in with Rose's horse and wagon. Although she was in a hurry, she didn't want to pass up a chance to chat with him for a little while. There was something about talking to Joe that made her feel good.

"Off to go bird-watching?" he asked.

"That plus I have a few errands to run. Is that the countertop Rose picked out?"

He turned in his seat to look into the wagon bed. "Actually, this is the countertop that Susanna picked out. She is tired of using the folding tables as substitutes and she is annoyed with her mother for taking so long to make a decision."

"Aren't you afraid that Rose will make you take it back?"

"I don't think she will. This is the style she originally picked out. I'm going to get them installed today before she gets home from visiting the Shetlers, and then I'm going to refuse to remove them."

"Perhaps you should hide your crowbar. I wouldn't put it past Rose to take them out herself if she didn't want them."

He laughed, making Abby smile. "That's an excellent suggestion. Enjoy your bird-watching. Are you looking for anything special?"

"Not really. I'm just learning to identify the ones I see. Herbert suggested I jot down some notes about each bird and he will help me identify them if I'm having trouble. He said I should get a camera but I'm not sure that would be permitted."

"Ask Rose or Susanna. I know Grace has one, but she's Mennonite."

"I will." Abby couldn't think of anything else to say, but she was reluctant to bid him goodbye.

He stared at her for several long moments then sat up straighter. "I better get to work or I won't finish before Rose gets home."

"All right. I'll see you later." She rode out onto the street and headed out of town. As she pedaled along she couldn't stop thinking about Joe and how much she enjoyed his company. He always made her smile. She cared for him a lot.

What she felt for Joe was growing into something more

than friendship. He was nearly done with Rose's kitchen and that meant he would be leaving soon. The thought of him drifting out of her life brought a stab of pain to her heart. Somehow she had to stop falling for him before it was too late.

Joe was surprised that Abby had taken to bird-watching so quickly. It seemed an odd hobby, but he was glad she could enjoy herself. Who knows, maybe he would take it up if it meant spending a little more time with her.

He parked the wagon by the side of the house and was unloading the countertops when he saw his boss's pickup turn in the drive.

Oliver stopped beside the wagon and got out of his truck. "You don't have the countertops in yet? I thought you would be further along with this project by now. What's been the holdup?"

"You name it, and I've had to deal with it. Tools disappearing. The wrong lumber being delivered. Rose changing her mind about the size of door she wanted three times and dragging her feet about picking countertops. Now she wants a bigger window over the kitchen sink. I may be an old man before I finish here."

Joe expected Oliver to chuckle at his joke. He didn't. Oliver took off his ball cap and ran a hand through his thinning hair. "I need you with me in Kingman to get that project done on time. Well, I guess I'm going to have to pull you off this job for a couple of days. I sure hope the widows will be understanding."

"Rose will be thrilled."

"Why would she be happy that her kitchen isn't getting done?"

"She seems to think that the longer I stay here the better the chance she has of matchmaking for me. She's been behind every stall maneuver that I've encountered including hiding my tools."

"Harts Haven is a nice town, but I can't see you settling down here."

The idea was beginning to appeal to him. "There are worse places."

Oliver stared at Joe intently and then cracked a smile. "Well, I'll be. What's her name?"

Joe wasn't ready to share that information. "It's not serious."

"I'm glad to hear that. I'd hate to think Rose's reputation for being a matchmaker is more than local gossip. Besides, I can't afford to lose you now."

Joe frowned. "What's up?"

"I have to take that banker from Andover to court to get paid for the work we did on his house. He claims it isn't up to code, and he won't pay. It could take months to sort it out."

"That's ridiculous. We did a fine job for him and under budget."

"I know, but I've got to stay and handle this. Which means I can't oversee the build in Oklahoma City we're due to start at the end of June. That's a multi-unit building for a company that can send a lot more work our way. I need a foreman on the job I can trust. That's why I'm putting you in charge. Congratulations on your promotion. It comes with a nice raise that won't offset the headaches, but it may make them bearable."

It was a flattering offer, but it would mean months away from Abby. "Oliver, I'm not sure I'm the man for the job."

"You've got the most experience and I can trust you to do it right."

"The thing is, I've been thinking about sticking around Harts Haven for a while."

Oliver took a step back. "You're joking, right? I need you, Joe. My reputation is already on the line with this lawsuit. The Oklahoma build must be done right and on time. I'm counting on you. We've been together for years. I don't want to say that you owe me, but I have done a lot for you."

It was true. Oliver had taken a scared, pitiful, homeless kid under his wing and saw to it that Joe had a place to live and money in the bank. He owed everything to Oliver. How could he refuse to help the man who'd been like a father to him?

Oliver stepped close and laid a hand on Joe's shoulder. "I still need you over in Kingman for the next three days. I've got to order some supplies and make a few calls. I'll pick you up about nine tonight. I should have you back by late Saturday."

"Okay. See you later."

Joe headed to the house. At least he hadn't said anything to Abby about his growing feelings for her. Now he wouldn't. Rose had made him believe he deserved to be happy. He thought his future might be with Abby, but how could he disappoint Oliver? No matter what decision he made, it wasn't going to leave him feeling good.

Abby covered the distance to the river bridge in under half an hour. The flat landscape made cycling easy. When she crossed the bridge and turned onto the sand road leading to the wetlands, she grew increasingly watchful. There were only a few tire tracks in the sand proving there had been little traffic since the rain. When she reached the farm, she saw where a vehicle had pulled into the driveway and then turned around to go back the way it had come.

Had the tire marks been left by her father's man in the area? She wished she knew what kind of car or pickup had made the impressions. It could have been someone who realized they were on the wrong road and simply turned around to get back to the highway. There was no way of knowing. She rode slowly past the farm, looking for any signs of activity but saw none. Realizing her bicycle was leaving tracks in the damp sand, too, she kept going until she reached the entrance to the marshland. There was no one at the parking spot today.

She left her bike against a tree and went back to the road. By keeping to the grass at the edge of the ditch she was able to walk back to the farm without leaving footprints on the road. When she got closer, she slipped through the corral fence and reached the side of the barn. No one in the house could see her from here and the thick trees hid her from the roadway. She hoped her green dress would help her blend in. She had left her white apron at the inn, but she couldn't bring herself to remove her *kapp*. She needed to make a black one or wear a dark scarf over her hair. Why hadn't she thought of that sooner?

Abby carefully made her way around to the back of the house. It looked undisturbed.

She opened the door. A thin layer of dust had settled onto the footprints she and her father's men had left in the hallway. She was risking everything if she was discovered, but with no sign that anyone had been inside since her father's men left, she started feeling more confident about her plan. She stepped inside. The same feeling of pain and loss hit her again as she took in the dust and neglect. Only today she could do something about it.

She went into the kitchen and checked under the kitchen sink. Her grandmother's cleaning supplies were still there although covered in dust and cobwebs. Abby pulled out a pail and worked the handle of the pump at the sink, but no water came out. After all this time the pump probably needed to be primed and she had no way to do that. Another setback.

Undeterred, she found her grandmother's broom and dustpan and took them upstairs. The first room she wanted to clean was her old bedroom. This was where she and the baby would sleep. She swept the cobwebs from the ceiling, dusted the furniture and then swept the floor. She looked at the bed and wondered how she could get the linens and bedding out to be washed. She decided to leave them for another time. It was satisfying enough to have made this much of an improvement.

She went downstairs and stood in the kitchen. She needed a way to know if someone had come into the house while she was gone. Her gaze settled on the flour canister on the kitchen cabinet. She lifted the lid. There was still flour inside. From a drawer of the china cabinet, she took out a yellowed linen napkin. She wrapped a small amount of flour in it and then walked backward down the hall tapping her hand against the pouch of flour.

A light coat settled to the floor, looking almost indistinguishable from the dust in the dark hallway. It covered her recent footprints. At the door she stopped and grinned. Maybe she had inherited some of her father's talent at subterfuge.

She listened carefully, then opened the door and slipped out. She put the napkin with the remaining flour in her bag and made her way to the barn, taking care not to trample a path by walking the same way twice.

There was no traffic on the road, but she stayed in the grassy ditch until she reached the entrance to the marsh. It was getting late, but she sat down and took several deep breaths as the strain she had been under subsided. It wouldn't matter if she was seen here now. She was bird-watching. No one would care.

She listened closely for birdsong and then focused her binoculars in that direction. Within half an hour she was able to spot American goldfinches, a catbird, more yellow warblers and butter butts, plus several black-and-white warblers that she identified using Herbert's book. Each new species she saw was like finding an unexpected gift. She soon realized she didn't have to pretend to be bird-watching. She thoroughly enjoyed it.

It also left her time to plan her next step. She would wait several days before returning. She would have to practice something she wasn't good at. Patience.

Getting on her bicycle, she started toward town and didn't encounter anyone until she was at the bridge, and that was only a farmer on his tractor. When she reached the inn, she parked her bicycle by the kitchen door and went inside. Joe was bent over applying a bead of caulk to the backsplash on the countertop. He looked over his shoulder at her and smiled. The sight sent a thrill through her. It was becoming harder to hide her attraction to him.

"How was the bird-watching? Did you see lots of new feathered friends?" he asked.

Why did he sound so odd? Like he was trying to be cheerful but wasn't. She gripped the strap of her bag, hating that she had to hide her true purpose from him. "I did. I saw goldfinches and several different species of warblers. There were a couple I couldn't identify. I'm going to have to study my book more closely."

Grace came into the kitchen. "Abby, you look like you've been crawling through the weeds."

Abby brushed at the front of her dress. "I am a mess."

"Run and get changed, then come give us a hand in the dining room. Our guests are here."

"Of course. I'll be right there."

Joe straightened. "I thought you might like to go for a walk after supper."

"Honestly, I'm a little tired. I'll take a rain check on it though," she added, hoping he would understand.

"Never mind. My boss stopped in. He wasn't happy that I'm not finished here. He needs another worker on the rush project he's got going, so I'm off to Kingman until late Saturday."

"Oh, I'll miss you."

"I doubt that," he said abruptly. "Have a nice evening and don't let the guests work you too hard." He walked out the door, leaving Abby to wonder what was bothering him.

She didn't have time to dwell on it. She hurried to her room and found her new royal blue dress and a freshly starched new white *kapp* hanging on a hanger. Susanna had finished them today. Abby admired the workmanship. She would have to find a way to repay Susanna for her kindness.

After changing out of her soiled green dress and into the blue one she had arrived in, Abby put on the new *kapp* and went downstairs to help serve the evening meal and clean up afterward. The guests, Mr. and Mrs. North and their grown daughter, Jean, turned out to be bird-watchers who intended to spend several days out at the wetlands. Abby was able to give them directions and enjoyed visiting with them about the different species they hoped to see.

"I'm surprised that an Amish woman is also a bird-watcher," Mr. North said. "It isn't a hobby I expected the

Amish to enjoy. Isn't it rather frivolous for such solemn people?"

Abby wasn't sure how to answer him. Fortunately, Grace came by at that moment. "The Amish enjoy many hobbies just like other folks, Mr. North. Admiring God's beautiful, feathered creations is quite acceptable."

Mrs. North smiled at Abby. "You must forgive my husband. He tends to judge a book by its cover."

Abby didn't mind. For the first time, it felt like she was an ordinary Amish woman. She was, at least in the eyes of these outsiders.

Two days later Grace was grinning from ear to ear as she entered the kitchen with a funny gleam in her eyes. "Do you know what today is, Abby?"

"It's Friday." Abby leaned on her mop in the middle of the kitchen floor.

"It's the Friday before your *Gemeesunndaag*."

"I'm looking forward to the prayer meeting." It was true. She was eager to worship in devout company the way she had as a child.

"The reason the Friday morning before *Gemeesunndaag* is important is because it's payday." Grace held out an envelope with a flourish. "Your first paycheck. Spend it wisely."

She had earned her own money. The knowledge was exhilarating. Abby took the envelope and stared in amazement at its contents. "I think this is too much."

"Nope. I do the books around here and this is what you've earned. I didn't withhold for your federal and state income taxes this time. The Amish are exempt from Social Security and Medicare taxes, of course, but you'll have to report this income when you do your taxes next year. I'll need your social security card to start withholding for-mally."

Abby kept a smile on her face. She had a Social Security number, but it was in Victoria Worthington's name. "Do I have to have one?"

Grace looked surprised. "Oh, yes. You can't do any banking business without a social security number and ID. That's the law, even for the Amish. You'll need to get one."

"How do I get an ID?"

"That's simple. All you need is your birth certificate and a letter from your bishop back home stating that you are who you say you are."

Another roadblock. How was she going to get around it? "That's good to know. I'll take care of it, but it may take a while."

"There isn't a big rush. We can pay you in cash for a few more weeks. Now, go get your purse."

"Why?"

"Because Herbert is taking us into the city so we can do some shopping. Is there anything you need?"

Abby looked at her feet. "Shoes. And stockings."

"Then the shoe store will be our first stop."

"Oh, I also need a basket for the bicycle so I can carry things." A large enclosed one with the lid so that she could bring the sheets and quilts back to launder. She would let a few more days pass before she went back to the farm. If the house hadn't been visited by then, she would step up her work inside.

Now that she had money, she could start looking for a lawyer. She was sure it would cost more than she had earned so far, but knowing it would soon be possible made her want to sing for joy.

Rose came in the kitchen. "Abby, there is someone here to see you."

One glimpse of Rose's serious expression sent a shiver of unease up Abby's spine. "To see me. Who?"

"Bishop Wyse."

Abby's happiness dropped away in a heartbeat. What had Rose done?

Thirteen

Abby walked slowly to the living room and opened the door with a trembling hand. Had Rose betrayed her confidence? What other reason could the bishop have for wanting to see her?

"You must be Abigail Martin." A tall man with bright blue eyes, a tanned face and a white beard rose to his feet from a chair by the window. He was an imposing figure. "I am Bishop Wyse."

"I'm pleased to meet you." She took a seat on the sofa and waited for him to come to the point with her hands clenched tightly together to still their trembling.

He sat back down in the chair. "Rose tells me you plan to stay in our community."

So Rose had talked to him. "I do. At least, I hope I can. Did Rose ask you to speak with me?"

"She invited me to come by and meet you. She did promise one of her cinnamon rolls so I couldn't refuse. Who was your bishop in Missouri? I know several of them in the southern part of the state."

Whatever Rose had said, she hadn't revealed Abby's identity. Abby had an inkling of what Rose was up to. She was forcing Abby's hand. This man had to know the truth if he was to become her spiritual counselor. The time for hiding her *Englisch* upbringing was over. She rubbed both hands on her thighs. "I didn't belong to an Amish community in Missouri."

He looked surprised. "I thought that's where Rose said you are from?"

"I am from Missouri. Kansas City, Missouri. I didn't grow up in an Amish home. My mother was ex-Amish. She married outside of the faith, but I spent many wonderful summers with my grandparents who were Amish. They are both gone now but they instilled in me a love for God and for the Amish way of life. I made the decision to leave everything I have known to come here and live as one of you. You are the person who can help me learn what I need to know about the Amish faith. I'm not rushing into this decision. It's what I've wanted for years."

"If that's true, what has prevented you from coming to us sooner?"

"My father objected." Abby didn't want to go into those details unless the bishop insisted on knowing more.

"I see. You speak the language very well."

"I was rusty when I first came but speaking it every day has brought back much of what I learned as a child. It is my desire to be baptized, Bishop Wyse, but I have realized that there are many things about the Amish faith that I don't know. I was fourteen when my grandparents passed away."

"Then how can you be sure that our faith is right for you?"

"I believe this is where God wants me to be. In my heart I feel He has led me here, to you. I ask for your prayers and your counsel."

He rubbed his beard thoughtfully. "Yours is a most unusual situation. I have heard of the occasional outsider who wishes to become Amish. I don't know of any instance where they have succeeded. Our way is a difficult one."

Abby smiled and shook her head. "The way I lived before was difficult. Living with Rose, Susanna and Grace has not been difficult. I feel I belong here. I hope you can understand."

"I appreciate your candor."

"There is one more thing you should know about me." She braced herself for his reaction. "I'm pregnant."

His eyebrows rose, but he didn't say anything.

Abby found the courage to continue. "I don't have a husband. The child's father no longer has a place in my life nor I in his. I want my son or daughter to know the same happiness I did when I lived with my grandparents. Their Amish home was a place of hard work, unshakable faith and incredible joy in the goodness of God."

"I see. You say that you want instruction in the faith?"

"I do. As soon as possible. I had hoped to become a member of the church before my child is born in November."

"There can be no rush into baptism. All the baptized members of our congregation must agree to accept you into our church. Most don't yet know you. Rose speaks highly of you but hers is only one opinion."

Abby frowned. This wasn't what she wanted to hear. "What should I do?"

"Stay with us. Live as we do. Take instructions when classes start in the fall or next spring and get to know our people. In time it will become clear whether this is *Gott*'s will or not. In the meantime, consider carefully and pray for His guidance."

His smile widened. He wasn't nearly as imposing as she first thought. "I will be happy to answer your questions and instruct you in our *Ordnung*. We can meet after the prayer service on Sunday and set up a schedule if that is acceptable."

"It is and I'm truly grateful for your understanding. However, I'm not eager to be known as an outsider trying to be Amish. I fear telling others that I was raised in an *Englisch* home will make them doubt my convictions and question my motives."

He was silent for so long that Abby thought she had made another blunder. At last, he nodded slowly. "I won't mention it, but you must reveal the truth at some point before I ask the church to accept you as a member."

"I will. I simply want people to get to know me first."

"I hope you find what you seek among us." He picked up his hat and went out the door. Rose came in from the kitchen the second the outside door closed.

Abby scowled at her. "You were listening at the keyhole."

"I wasn't. The door doesn't have a keyhole. It does have a very thin wooden panel in the center. I'm pleased with you, Abby. You did the right thing."

Abby smiled at the little woman. "I didn't have much choice. Are you coming with us into the city?"

"Of course. I never pass up an opportunity to go shopping."

It was a little after ten o'clock Saturday night when Oliver dropped Joe off at his camper. Oliver leaned out the window of his truck. "Think over my offer, Joe. I hope you accept it. I do need you. If you want more money."

"*Nee*, it isn't the money."

"Okay. Finish up here and then take a couple of weeks to think it over. You deserve a break, and you've got vacation time coming. I can pull your trailer over to Cheney lake. I know you like to fish, just say the word, but I'll need you in OKC by the end of June if you accept. You know how to get in touch." He nodded and then drove away.

Joe stood outside his trailer, wishing he knew what to do. He was tired but he didn't want to go in. He glanced toward the inn. It was too much to hope that Abby would still be up. He wanted to see her again. He needed to see her. Three days away hadn't changed his feelings for her. If anything they had grown stronger. If only he knew how she felt about him.

He walked around to the side yard below her window and was surprised to see the light on. Looking around at the ground, he spied up a few small pebbles and picked them up. He tossed a couple against the window glass.

Abby opened her window and leaned out. "Who's there? Joe, is that you? What are you doing?"

The sound of her voice made him smile. "Waiting for you to lean out the window and scold me."

"All right. You've got what you wanted, now go to bed. It's late."

"I can't sleep. It looks like you can't, either. Let's take that walk you promised me."

"Now? In the dark?"

"There is enough moonlight to see by."

"See what? It's nighttime."

"You like bird-watching. Well, I like stargazing."

"Stargazing?" She sounded skeptical.

"Right. That's where you find a comfortable spot and just look up at the night sky. It's quite amazing. I can point out most of the major constellations."

"The man likes lilacs and stargazing. You continue to amaze me, Joseph."

It pleased him that she remembered which flowers he liked. He remembered her love of roses because they had thorns. "So are you coming?"

"I shouldn't."

"Okay."

"That's it? Just okay? Go away."

He sat down on the ground and lay back with his arms behind his head. "I think I'll just lie here and watch the stars. Go ahead and put out your light so my eyes can adjust to the darkness. You wouldn't happen to have a pillow to spare, would you?"

She didn't say anything but a few moments later a pillow landed beside him. Then her light went out. He stretched out on the grass. It was ridiculous to think this silly conversation could make his day, but it had.

"I don't see many stars."

He tipped his head back to see her leaning on the windowsill. "It takes about fifteen minutes for your eyes to adjust to the dark. Just close your eyes and relax."

"I could do that on my bed and then I would be asleep."

She wasn't really annoyed even though she was trying to sound that way. Maybe she did like him. "I'm not stopping you."

"You're lying in the grass right outside my window. How am I supposed to go to sleep with you here?"

"You could come out and keep me company?"

"You know there are probably chiggers in the grass. You'll have red itchy spots all over you tomorrow."

"It's a chance I'm willing to take. Also, I know Susanna had the lawn sprayed earlier this year so the guests wouldn't get insect bites. Throw down another pillow and a blanket if that worries you."

"I'm not going to get grass stains on Rose's nice bedspread."

"Suit yourself. I see Ursa Major."

"What's that?"

"The Great Bear or the Big Dipper as it is commonly called." He pointed toward the constellation. "Can you see how it looks like a pan?"

"I don't think I see it."

He tipped his head back. She was leaning out the window.

"I reckon the side of the building is blocking your view. If you draw a line from the two outermost stars in the pan of the Big Dipper, it points to Polaris. The North Star. Polaris is the tip of the handle of the Little Dipper."

"I still can't see it."

"Okay, I'll stop talking. *Guten nacht.*"

She didn't say anything. He looked toward her window, but she wasn't there. He thought about getting up but decided he was comfortable where he was. More and more stars became visible as his eyes adjusted. Suddenly a flashlight blinded him. He squinted his eyes against the painful glare. He heard a soft thud and then felt someone sit beside him. When he was able to focus, he saw Abby with a quilt wrapped around her. She positioned her pillow and then clicked off her light.

"I see even less stars out here," she muttered.

"You can always go back inside." He didn't want her to leave. It was comforting to have her beside him even though they weren't touching.

"Now that I'm out here, I'm going to stay to see what you find so fascinating. You realize this means you're going to have to come bird-watching with me one day. Fair is fair."

It reminded him of his dilemma. How to be fair to himself and to Oliver. "It'll have to be one day soon."

"I keep forgetting that you have to leave," she said softly. "Can't you find more local work?"

"My boss wants to make me the foreman on his next job. It's in Oklahoma City."

"I see. That's a good thing, right?"

She didn't sound happy. He turned his head to gaze at her. She was lovely in the moonlight. "If I accept, I'll have to be there six months at least."

"So you might not take it?" Did she sound hopeful? He wasn't sure.

"I have a couple of weeks to think it over."

"What do you want to do?"

He didn't know how to answer that. "Can you see the Big Dipper now?" He pointed to the northwest. "Four bright stars form a rectangle and then three stars form the handle."

"I do see it."

"Now draw an imaginary line up through the two stars that form the bowl and follow it up to the next bright star. That's Polaris. It's the only star that never changes its position in the sky. Oliver has been my best friend for years. I owe him a lot. He needs me to take over the job because he's not going to be able to be there."

"And you don't want to let your friend down. I understand that. I admire you for it. Friends should be there for each other when things get tough."

"You're right. I can't let him down." He would do the right thing by his friend and take the job. That would mean leaving Harts Haven and the sweet girl he was starting to care for far more than he should.

"You're a good man, Joe. I'm blessed to have you as a friend. I'll miss you when you leave."

He turned to look at her. She met his gaze. "Will you?" he asked.

She looked away and pointed to the sky "Are those five bright stars a constellation? They kind of make an *M* on its side."

"That's Cassiopeia."

"What a pretty name."

"She was a vain queen in Greek mythology who boasted endlessly about her own great beauty."

"So not Amish?"

He chuckled. "*Nee*, she was not Amish."

"She doesn't sound like someone I would want to know."

"She wasn't a real person."

Abby elbowed him. "I may not be a stargazer, but I know what *mythology* means."

"Glad to hear that. Do you see that hazy band across the sky that looks like tattered gauze? That's called the Milky Way. It's our galaxy. It contains millions and millions of stars. *'And God said, Let there be lights in the firmament of the heaven to divide the day from the night; and let them be for signs, and for seasons, and for days, and years: And let them be for lights in the firmament of the heaven to give light upon the earth: and it was so.'*"

"Genesis," she said softly.

"Yes, 1:14–15," he said. "Can you believe *Gott* made this beautiful night sky just for us? It really is wondrous."

"How is it that you know so much about the stars?" There was a touch of amazement in her voice. Did she think of him as a simple carpenter and not much else? He chose not to tell her about the nightmares that drove him from his bed most nights.

"I liked to read. I liked to lie out and watch the way the night sky changes. I saw the beautiful patterns that God created, and I wanted to learn more about them. So, I checked out a book from the library back home and got hooked on stargazing." He found comfort looking at the heavens when he couldn't get back to sleep after one of his night terrors.

"Back home was Fort Scott, right? Is it far from here?"

As far away as the stars because home didn't exist anymore. "About a hundred miles east. We had a small farm on a winding creek with lots of places to explore for us kids."

"You must miss it."

Sometimes, but there was too much sorrow in his memories of home. "I don't."

She took hold of his hand. "I'm sorry, Joe."

He didn't look at her. "For what?"

She gave his fingers a gentle squeeze. "For the unhappiness you endured. For the loss of the ones you loved."

He pulled his hand away. "It was a long time ago. It's getting late. You should go in."

He didn't deserve her sympathy.

Abby scrambled to her feet and picked up her pillow, sorry that she had ruined the moment between them. "Thank you for showing me the constellations. Wherever you go I will know that we will be looking at the same stars."

He raised up on one elbow. "I'm glad you came out."

She hugged her pillow tightly. "So am I."

"I didn't ask how your week went," he said quickly.

Did that mean he didn't want her to go yet? A second ago he had sounded angry when he said it was late. She was confused by his abrupt change of mood, but she wasn't ready for the night to end. "Rose sicced the bishop on me."

"She did what?"

Abby sank to her knees and sat back on her heels. "She invited the bishop to meet me. Rose knows that I wasn't raised in an Amish home and that I'm pretending to be Amish."

He lay back with his hands behind his head. "You aren't pretending. You're waiting to become a baptized member of the Amish faith just like a lot of young folks are."

"You're right. I'll try to think of myself that way."

"Did she tell the bishop about you?"

"*Nee*, she wanted me to do that."

He looked over at her. "And did you?"

"Yes."

"I'm glad. What did he say?"

"He was surprised but understanding. He says I must live in the community and pray about my decision to join the faith. If that's still what I want, I can join the baptism preparation classes in the fall. I will have to tell everyone that I wasn't raised Amish, but he agreed that people should get to know me first."

"So they don't prejudge you."

"Exactly."

"And because you don't want to be treated differently."

"You understand me pretty well, don't you?"

"I'm beginning to. Are you ready for church in the morning?"

"I'm a little nervous. I'm not sure I'll remember the hymns. I'll have to meet a lot of new people. It's scary."

"You'll do fine."

"Do you really think so?"

"I do. I have faith in your determination."

She was grateful for Joe's confidence, but what if she made an even bigger blunder than the ones she had already made?

She looked up at the stars and prayed God would guide her. She glanced over at Joe. He was watching her intently. When he left, she would have so few memories of him to cherish. Maybe she was selfish, but she wanted more. "Tell me about some other constellations."

"Sure." He smiled and pointed to the southern sky. "Those three bright stars in a line are called Orion's Belt."

"Where are his pants?"

He choked back a laugh. "That's one thing I like about you, Abby Martin. I never know what you are going to say."

Abby got ready for church the next morning with an equal measure of excitement and dread. She would be sitting with the unmarried women and not with Rose or Susanna. They had been her security blanket during her meetings with other members of the community. Today she would be on her own. She tried to recall all the services she had attended with her grandparents. Could she still remember the songs, or would she stumble through them?

What would she talk about when the younger women were waiting their turn to be served the meal? How would she answer their questions? She knew people would be curious about her.

She put on her new Sunday dress, slipped her still-tender feet into her new shoes, and put on her freshly washed and starched *kapp*. Staring at herself in the small mirror, she knew she looked the part.

"That's wrong. Looking the part implies you're not what you appear to be. You are an Amish woman waiting to be baptized just as Joe said. You have to stop thinking otherwise, Abigail Martin."

Thoughts of her evening with Joe made her smile. He would support her today. She knew that without a doubt and that gave her courage. She smoothed the front of her dress. If she told him about the baby, how would he react? She might be brave enough to tackle harnessing a horse but she wasn't brave enough to tell Joe that secret.

She went downstairs and into the kitchen. Susanna was wearing a dress made from the same material as Abby's. She handed Abby a basket packed with food for the noontime meal. "Take these out to the buggy. Mamm and I will be out in a minute."

"All right." She carried the heavy wicker container out the front door. Joe had already brought the buggy around. He was standing by the horse's head. He looked amazingly handsome in his black *mutza* suit. He had left off the collarless coat and wore a simple black vest over his white shirt. His black pants were neatly pressed. She did wonder if he was wearing the socks with holes in them. She smiled. Probably not for church. His black felt hat was set low on his brow.

He left the horse and came toward her. "Let me get that for you."

"Danki." She handed him the basket and he stowed it in the box at the rear of the buggy. She got in the back seat.

"Not gonna sit with me?" he asked. Was he disappointed?

"Susanna doesn't like to ride in the back so I thought I would park myself in here before Rose can figure out a way to make me sit with you."

"You just watch, Rose will offer to drive so we can sit together."

"I think that would be a little too obvious even for Rose. Did you get enough sleep?" He looked tired.

"Enough. I went in just after you did."

"I had a nice time last night."

"No chigger bites?" A little smile played across his lips.

"Not a single one." She scratched her left shoulder and scrunched her face.

Joe laughed. Abby realized she had never teased Logan, never joked with him. She couldn't imagine now what she had seen in him. Thoughts of their time together took some of the enjoyment out of her morning.

"What's wrong?" Joe asked, tipping his head slightly to gaze at her face.

"Nothing." She pasted a happy smile on her face.

Fortunately, Rose and Susanna came out of the inn at that moment. Rose was wearing a dress identical to Abby's, too. It gave Abby a feeling of belonging to the family that she hadn't experienced before.

Rose stopped on the step and frowned at Abby. "I thought Susanna and I would ride in the back."

Susanna went straight to the front seat and got in. She glanced back at Abby. *"Danki."* She turned to look at her mother. "Get in, Mamm. Your matchmaking can take Sunday off."

Rose appeared miffed. "I have no idea what you're talking about." She climbed in with Abby without another word. To Abby's surprise, Grace came out and joined them.

"Are you coming to the Amish service?" Abby asked.

"I like to attend once in a while. It's refreshing."

"She enjoys the bishop's sermons more than his own people do," Rose said.

"He's a fine preacher," Grace said primly.

"And a fine-looking fellow," Rose said almost under her breath. "A widower, too."

"Don't make it into something it isn't, Rose," Grace warned her.

"Oh, never." Rose looked at Abby. "It's spring and love is in the air everywhere. It's the time of year when young people get stars in their eyes just looking at each other. Isn't that right, Joe?"

Abby's jaw dropped. Joe mumbled something under his breath. Rose must have seen them together last night. Abby didn't say anything. She stared straight ahead but she knew she was blushing.

Joe drove out to the highway leading south of town. There were two buggies on the road in front of them. The horse pulling the first buggy was ambling slowly along. Joe had trouble keeping Cooper to an equally slow pace. It would be improper for him to pass another buggy while on the way to church.

"Elmer Lapp needs to get a faster horse," Rose grumbled. "At this rate we'll be late."

"They won't start before we get there," Susanna replied.

"What makes you so sure?" Rose asked.

"Because the bishop is behind us." Susanna chuckled smugly.

Grace promptly turned around and gave him a little wave. Rose nudged Abby with her elbow and winked.

They arrived at the home of the Zook family twenty minutes later. The house was a large two-story white building. The barn and outbuildings had been painted red with white trim. A white picket fence enclosed a colorful flower garden at the side of the house. Abby got out and helped Rose down. Susanna retrieved the food basket from the back of the buggy. Joe drove over to the line of buggies parked beside the barn. A semicircle of men stood nearby visiting. One of them went to help unhitch Cooper and lead him into the corral with the other buggy horses.

Abby followed the widows into the house. The kitchen was a whirl of activity as women were unpacking lunch baskets, setting out cookies and cutting pies. Everyone was visiting and chatting happily. Some of the older girls were in charge of the younger children, keeping them occupied until it was time for the service to start. Abby stayed near Susanna, feeling out of place and unsure of what she was expected to do.

Susanna gave her a kindly smile. "Go outside and visit."

"Are you sure I can't help?"

Susanna nodded toward the roomful of women. "We have enough hands."

Abby walked out onto the porch. She looked for Joe and saw he had joined the semicircle of men by the barn. A large buggy pulled up and the Hostettler family piled out. The twins made a beeline for Abby. "Come and meet our friends," Kathy said, grabbing Abby's hand and pulling her along to a shady spot beneath the spreading branches of an old silver maple tree. A group of young women were gathered there. "Everyone, this is Abby Martin," Kathy said. "She's newly come from New Mexico."

"Missouri," Abby said quickly. "Rose gets a bit mixed up sometimes."

"You're staying at the inn. Have you met Joseph Troyer? What's he like?" one of the girls asked.

"Rude," another girl said. Abby recognized her as the blonde Joe had given the brush-off the first day she arrived. Her dark-haired friend stood beside her.

"He was," Abby admitted. "But he regrets it. I'll ask him to apologize."

"No need," he said from behind her. "I came over to say I'm sorry to both of you girls. I was inexcusably rude that day. I hope you forgive me. The brownies were great, by the way."

The girls shared a speaking look and then smiled at him. "Apology accepted," they said in unison.

Joe nodded once and walked away. Abby's heart swelled with happiness. Joe could be counted on to do the right thing. She liked that about him.

"It's time to take our places," Kathy said. She headed inside and Abby followed with the others as all the women moved down to a large basement room.

Backless wooden benches were lined up either side of the center aisle down the middle of the room. Men and boys would sit on one side while women and girls sat on the other side facing each other. The preachers would stand in the middle.

Married women sat in front rows while the unmarried women and girls sat behind them. The women in their Sunday dresses and white aprons were more colorful than the men though most women wore blue. A few mauve and dark green dresses were sprinkled in. Women and girls of the same family had dresses made from identical material.

Some of the elderly members were seated beside the benches in more comfortable chairs, including Rose. Susanna sat on a bench up front with a ramrod-stiff back. Grace sat beside her.

The bishop and two other preachers filed in with the married men followed by the single men and boys. As soon as the men entered, they removed their hats and hung them from rows of pegs on the back wall in a quiet and orderly fashion. The room filled with a tide of black on the men's side. Black *mutza* coats and pants were standard Sunday dress for men. A few, like Joe, had left off the coat and wore black vests over white shirts. The youngest boys took up the last row nearest the door so they could make a quick escape when the preaching ended.

The *Volsinger*, the song leader, announced the page of the first hymn. There was a wave of rustling as people opened their copies of the *Ausbund*. The thick black songbook contained the words of all the hymns the Amish used in their services but no musical scores. Songs were sung from memory with melodies passed down through dozens of generations, slowly and in unison without musical instruments. Abby picked up her copy of the *Ausbund* and found the song and joined in the beautiful chant-like opening hymn. This one she remembered.

During this song, Bishop Wyse and two ministers who would help him preach filed out to have prayer and counsel. Abby knew they would retire to a room in the house and discuss what the sermons would be about that day. All of them preached as the spirit moved them. None of them had prepared sermons. They stayed out for an hour while the rest of the church sang songs. Abby found she recalled many of the melodies and she didn't have to follow the book. Instead, her gaze wandered to where Joe was sitting. Several times she caught him looking at her.

When the bishop and preachers returned, the sermons started. The men spoke mostly in Pennsylvania Dutch. The Bible readings were in High German, but each preacher stopped and translated it into Dutch so the young children could understand. Pennsylvania Dutch was spoken in all Amish homes. Children didn't learn English and German until they started school. Like the younger children, Abby needed the translation, too.

She was amazed at the quality and sincerity of the sermons. Bishop Wyse was a gifted speaker. As a youngster Abby had learned the office of the bishop came with plenty of responsibilities but no pay. The same went for his ministers. The appointments were lifelong.

Amish ministers were chosen by lot. Every baptized man agreed to serve if he was chosen. Most, like her grandfather, prayed they would be passed over. Her grandmother had told her that the wives of some newly chosen preachers would break down wailing and sobbing because of the stress that came with the lifelong unpaid job for their husbands. Ultimately every congregation was led by one man, their bishop, who had the final word in all spiritual and community matters.

The service lasted over three hours. Many times, young children would sit with one parent for a while and then get up and walk over to sit with the other one. A small table had been set up by the hostess where the children could take turns going to fill a baggy with animal crackers or cookies. Someday she would allow her son or daughter to go get a treat. The thought of her child sitting beside her, learning the hymns and prayers, filled her with a deep sense of peace. This was what she wanted.

Abby was prepared to spend three hours enduring the service. What she wasn't prepared for was the swell of emotion that engulfed her as the familiar hymns brought back memory after memory of her grandparents. The slow and mournful chanting rose in volume as voices blended in the ancient songs. Most of the hymns had been composed by early martyrs of the faith during their persecution and imprisonment. Listening to the words of sorrow, hope and God's promise of salvation, Abby became aware of a stirring deep within her soul. This was where she belonged.

* * *

Joe joined in the singing half-heartedly. It was hard to feel joyous when his time in Harts Haven was drawing quickly to an end. No matter how hard he tried to convince himself that his evening with Abby last night had simply been two friends enjoying a harmless pastime, it wasn't working.

What he felt for Abby was more than friendship.

He looked across the aisle and caught her eye. She smiled at him, and his heart turned over. He looked away in case she could read his feelings on his face. He was leaving and she was staying. He would take the new position Oliver had offered him because he owed his friend more than he could ever repay.

He tried to concentrate on the message of the sermons, but it did little good. He needed to get his feelings for Abby under control. He didn't need more heartache and regrets. He was used to being alone. That was the way he liked it.

Only he'd never felt this lonely before. She was the cause, and he didn't know what to do about it.

Fourteen

Joe filed out of the building with the men when the service was over. The benches in the basement would be rearranged and stacked together to make tables for people to eat the noon meal. The older men had that well in hand and didn't need his help. He stood on the sidewalk wondering if he could just leave. It wasn't too far to walk, and he knew Susanna could handle the buggy to take the women home.

Caleb, the oldest Hostettler brother, came up to him. "We're getting up a volleyball game, Joe. We could use one more player. Are you any good?"

"It's been a while."

"Great. You're on my team."

"What if I said I'm no good?"

"Then I'll offer you to the other team."

Joseph chuckled. "I hope I don't disappoint you."

"*Nee*, just get the ball to my *brudder* Jedidiah. He's the best spiker in this part of the state."

Two volleyball nets were being set up by a half dozen young men while ten more stood around waiting for the game to begin. Coats and hats had been laid in a pile on a quilt at the sideline.

Caleb introduced Joe to the other members of his team. Besides Jedidiah and Wallace Hostettler, he met their cousins John and Wayne Bieler. David Shetler agreed to be the referee. As soon as the net was in place and the tautness was satisfactory to David, the men faced off against their opponents. One young man on the other team stood head and shoulders above the rest. Joe turned to Caleb. "Should I try to keep the ball away from the tall fellow?"

Caleb laughed. "Get the ball to him as often as you can. Tiny Mast is a terrible player."

The game got underway. It was soon apparent the teams were evenly matched in spite of Tiny's lack of ability. Joe found he still knew how to play and made several diving saves that earned him praise from his team members but put grass stains on his shirtsleeves. He would have to do laundry tonight.

He didn't realize the game had drawn a crowd on the sidelines until it was his turn to serve. Caleb handed him the ball. Joe glanced about self-consciously and caught sight of Abby standing with a group of girls. She cupped her hands around her mouth and shouted encouragement.

He hammered the ball straight into the net giving the other team the point they needed to move ahead. His teammates groaned but still clapped him on the back when it was over and told him it had been a good game.

Caleb handed the ball to one of the girls with Abby. "It

looks like the married men are finished eating. It's our turn." Joe's team walked off without him as the girls took their places on the makeshift court. Abby stayed on the sidelines.

Joe dried the sweat on his brow with the back of his sleeve. "Aren't you going to play?"

"Not this time. I'll just watch." She turned to the girl beside her. "Joe, this is Mary King."

He nodded to her. "Pleased to meet you."

She was a plump girl with rosy cheeks and a wide smile that showed her slightly crooked teeth. "Abby tells me that she's going to stay in Harts Haven. What about you?"

"Joe doesn't like to stay in one place," Abby said cheerfully.

Why did she sound so happy? Did she want him to leave? He hadn't considered that before. Maybe she had grown tired of his company.

"He's been offered a promotion to foreman at Mennonite Builders. He's thinking it over, but I believe he'll take the job. His boss is fortunate to have such a skilled fellow working for him."

"You work for Oliver Hershberger?" Mary's smile widened. "My cousin James Schultz worked for him before he married. He was a foreman for a few years. He liked the travel, too, but once he met the girl he wanted to marry, he quit right quick."

Joe smiled. "I remember James. He was a hard worker. Oliver was sad to lose him."

"I think James is sorry now that he left. He became a hog farmer with his father-in-law and he's not happy there. The business is struggling. So, are you going to take the promotion?"

"I am." He tried to gauge Abby's feelings. He caught a

flash of something like sadness in her eyes, but she quickly managed a smile. A smile that looked too bright and didn't quite reach her eyes. He was her friend. He understood she might be sad because he was leaving. He hoped it wasn't more than that. The last thing he wanted to do was hurt her.

"You should go eat," she said, then clapped her hands as she looked back at the game. "Good play, Kathy. Way to go after the ball."

He wasn't sure what to say so he walked away feeling that he had somehow let Abby down.

Mary leaned closer to Abby after Joe had retreated. "I'm going to take a wild guess and say you're very fond of that young man."

Abby gave Mary a look of astonishment. "He's a dear friend."

Mary tilted her head. "Perhaps more than a friend?"

Abby looked away. She wasn't ready to admit her affection for Joseph was growing stronger. Three months ago she thought she was in love with Logan. How could she trust what she was feeling now? "Why would you say that?"

"Because it looked like you were going to cry when he said he was taking his promotion."

"You must be mistaken. I'm happy for him."

"Oscar and I started out as friends." Mary ran her hand over the front of her dress. "Now we're married."

"I'm happy for you both. Kathy and Becky invited me to your quilting bee. I hope you don't mind."

"Of course not. They're good friends. Soon we'll be stitching up a quilt for them."

"Not too soon," Abby said. "They aren't yet sixteen."

"It seems like yesterday that I was sixteen. Now I'm twenty-one."

"So am I."

"Really? When is your birthday?"

"September 27."

"Are you joking? My birthday is September 26. We must have a birthday celebration together."

Abby grinned at Mary. "With cake and ice cream?" She hadn't had a birthday party since her mother died.

"Absolutely. We'll have it at the inn and invite all our friends."

"I don't know many people here, just Katie and Becky, Mr. and Mrs. Shetler. I think Micah is too young to be considered a friend."

"Definitely too young for cake." Mary chuckled. "By then he might like a few licks of ice cream. Let's go see if the men are done eating. I'm starved. Then again, I'm always hungry these days 'cause I'm eating for two."

A flush of embarrassment turned Mary's cheeks pink. "I don't know why I said that. It isn't common knowledge, but the truth is I'm really happy that I'm going to be a mother."

Abby smiled at her. "I'm glad you're excited about it. A new life is something to celebrate."

"That's exactly what Dr. Bertha told me."

Abby should see a doctor soon, too. She felt healthy, but prenatal care was important. "When is your baby due?"

"The first week of October. I can hardly wait. Will it be a girl or boy? Will it look like Oscar? I hope he or she has his eyes. He has the most beautiful brown eyes. He wants a boy, of course, but I'm hoping for a little girl. That's not exactly true. What I pray for is a healthy *bobbli*."

"I know."

"It's nice of you to listen to me rambling. My other friends don't really understand."

"I do understand. Better than you think." Abby crossed

her arms over her chest and looked around to make sure no one could overhear them. "Can you keep a secret?"

"I'm the best secret keeper in all of Harts Haven. Ask anyone." Mary leaned close. "So tell me."

"I'm expecting a baby, too."

Mary's eyes widened in astonishment and then crinkled at the corners as she grinned. "That's *wunderbar*. Truly. You're married, then?"

Abby looked down, wishing she hadn't said anything. *"Nee."*

"Ah. Is it Joseph's?"

"Oh, no." Abby shook her head vehemently. "We've only just met. I'm not with the baby's father anymore. Our relationship was a mistake in more ways than one."

"And that's why you have moved here. To have your baby in secret. I understand. Are you keeping it?"

"Ja, I want this child."

"It's hard to imagine you can love someone so very much when you've never met them, isn't it?"

"It's an amazing kind of love. I never knew I could feel this way."

"Do you get weepy for no reason?"

"Sometimes."

"I cry buckets at the least little upset. Did you have much morning sickness?"

"Almost none. You?"

"Oh, it was terrible. Every morning for a month I threw up my breakfast. We were staying with my parents while our house was being built. There was no keeping it a secret from my mother. She knew almost before I did. How did your mother take it when she found out?"

Abby couldn't be sure how her mother would have reacted, but she hoped her mother would have accepted her and the baby. "She died when I was fourteen."

Mary threw her arms around Abby, startling her. "I'm so sorry. I don't think I could do this without my mother's support. Come. You should meet her."

"I'd rather no one else know just yet. You understand?"

"Completely. No one will hear it from me." Mary drew a line across her lips. "When are you due?"

"Early November, I think. I'm worried about what the community will think of me when they find out." It was a relief to put her fear into words.

Mary patted Abby's shoulder. "Not everyone will be understanding, but most of them will be. Your friends will stand by you. I'm your friend now. You can count on me to support you. We all believe a child is a gift from God. Once you are baptized all sin is forgiven and it will never be mentioned again. Your child will be accepted here."

"Are you sure?" That is what she prayed would happen.

"Positive."

"Thanks, Mary."

"Let's get something to eat first and then I'll introduce you to my *mamm*. Are you hungry all the time?"

"Not so much."

"I'm farther along than you are. Don't be surprised if in a month you're ready to eat everything including the plates."

Abby followed her new friend to the house, where they discovered the men were finishing up. The tables were being cleared as soon as the men rose, and clean plates, silverware, cups and glasses replaced the ones being carried into the kitchen. The married women would eat next, but there were enough empty seats for Abby and the twins to join Mary. Susanna came by to fill the clean glasses with water and the cups with hot black coffee.

Abby stared at the array of food set out on the tables. Slices of homemade bread were stacked on the clean white tablecloths at both ends of the table. Bowls of jam, butter and church spread, a sweet mixture of peanut butter, marshmallow cream and syrup, were all within reach. A platter with slices of cold cuts and two different kinds of cheese were passed along as well as homemade pickles and bowls of red pickled beets. Cookies and slices of pies were available for dessert. Abby chose a piece of apple pie that Rose had made. Mary added a second piece of bread with church spread and two slices of pie to her plate. Abby had to hide a smile.

Mary caught Abby's eye and grinned. "I told you I'm eating for two. Plus, Oscar says he likes a plump woman."

"No wonder you love him," Abby said with a wink.

Mary burst out laughing. "I like you, Abby Martin. I'm mighty glad you came to Harts Haven."

Abby was glad, too. Mary could easily become a dear friend.

After that there wasn't much conversation at the table. When they finished, Kathy and Becky led the way outside to the same shade tree they had been standing under before the service. Abby quickly realized it was in plain view of the young men who were back to playing volleyball. A short time later the older men began loading the benches into the church wagon signaling that everyone had finished eating.

The hostess, Mrs. Zook, came outside on the porch. "Girls, the basement is cleared. I have set out some board games if you would like to come in."

"I hope it's Pictionary," Becky said. "We had such fun playing it the last time our singing was held here."

Mrs. Zook smiled at her fondly. "I have that one and I have Sorry!. Or you may play charades if you like."

"What would you like to play, Abby?" Mary asked.

"I've never played Pictionary. I'd like to learn if someone can teach me."

"Great," Becky said. "We can show you. It's simple. Do you like to draw?"

"I sketch sometimes but I'm not really good."

"Then you should have Becky as your partner," Kathy said. "She loves to draw."

Abby followed the other young women inside and was soon engaged in a game where everyone was having fun. She laughed at her own crude attempts to draw and even managed to guess the word correctly twice. She glanced around in awe at how quickly she had been included in this circle of friends with girls who had known each other their entire lives.

She could be happy here.

Joe finished his last game of volleyball with a win. He looked to where he had last seen Abby, but all the girls were out of sight. "I expect they have gone inside to play board games," Caleb said after he noticed where Joe was looking. "Come on. Mrs. Zook will have cookies or brownies set out along with something to drink."

Joe tagged along after the brothers. They led the way into the house and down into the basement. The room seemed much more spacious without the benches and all the people. A group of young women, including Abby, were seated around a chalkboard calling out words or instructions as Mary drew something on the board.

Abby stood up and shouted, "School."

"That's right," Mary said. "Another point for us. You're good at this, Abby."

She handed her chalk to another player and took a seat

in the empty chair beside Abby. All the women were smiling and laughing. Abby looked at home among them. She needn't have worried about fitting in. He collected a napkin and a brownie and stood back against the far wall, watching the game in progress.

"She seems to be having a good time," Rose said. "There's *kaffi* if you want some or fruit punch."

"Punch sounds good."

"I heard that you are getting a promotion. I reckon that means you will be leaving Harts Haven soon."

"In spite of your best efforts, I will."

"You can't blame me for trying to make two people see that they belong together. Some people realize it right off the bat, while others need more time and encouragement."

"Sorry to spoil your record, but I tried to tell you we wouldn't suit."

"It won't take me long to find another fellow in need of my services."

"A better man for Abby?"

"Maybe in time but it's going to take her a while to get over you."

He scowled at her. "Abby and I are friends, Rose. Sure, we will miss each other, but it's not like I'm going to break her heart when I leave."

She patted his arm. "You can tell yourself that if it makes you feel better, Joseph. I'll go get your drink."

Rose was wrong. Abby didn't think of him in that way. And if she was starting to have romantic feelings for him, then it was best that he leave soon. He wasn't going to settle here. The idea might've crossed his mind, but he had discarded it. Oliver needed him. He couldn't let his friend down. He'd let enough people in his life down.

He glanced across the room when he heard Abby's lilting laugher. She looked his way and smiled. It was funny how her smile could brighten his day the way no one else could. As he watched her, he saw the bishop come in and speak quietly to her. The two of them walked toward the stairs. At the doorway she looked back. He nodded his encouragement. She was going to learn what she needed to know about the community. She would soon be surrounded by many friends. She counted him among those. Was he letting her down by leaving?

"You are quiet this afternoon," Joe said.

Abby sat beside him in the buggy on the way home from the church service. He was looking straight ahead. The three widows were in the back seat. Rose was dozing between Grace and Susanna.

"I reckon I just have a lot to think about today," she said.

"Like what?"

Like the fact that you're leaving soon.

She didn't say it, but she wanted to. His announcement that he was taking the job had come as a surprise. Why hadn't he told her first?

She folded her hands in her lap and laced her fingers together. "Stuff."

"You looked like you were enjoying yourself after the service. You seem to have made some new friends."

"I did enjoy the day. Everyone was kind to me. Mary and I seem to have a lot in common."

She couldn't share what that was, either. "I think we'll be good friends. I remembered the songs. The bishop gave me some books to read and talked about the *Ordnung*. We'll meet again on Sunday to go over the material he gave me. It's hard to believe that it's actually happening. I've wanted this for so long."

"I'm happy for you."

"I appreciate that. I hope you'll find time to write to me when you get to Oklahoma City."

"I'm not good at keeping up correspondences. Don't look for a letter every day."

"I won't. Just drop me a line now and then to let me know how you're getting along."

"You'll write, won't you?" he asked.

"Sure. You'll want to know what the widows are up to. Your life may seem dull without Rose in it."

He glanced over his shoulder at the women in the back seat then leaned toward Abby. "It might be boring, but I'll be able to keep track of my tools."

She giggled softly. "She tried so hard to push us together."

He gave her a strange look. "But it didn't work."

"Nee." She looked away. "It didn't work."

It wasn't long before they arrived back at the inn. Rose woke up when the buggy stopped. "What did I miss?"

"Nothing, Mamm," Susanna said. "We're home."

She helped her mother out of the buggy and the three women went inside. Abby stayed on the seat beside Joe, reluctant to end the day.

"You might as well learn how to unhitch Cooper and take care of the harnesses," he said.

Abby cheered up. "That's an excellent idea. Drive on."

He handed her the lines. "Let's see how well you drive."

"I may not like horses, but I do remember how to do this." She took the driving lines from his hands and slapped them against Cooper's rump. "Cooper, walk on."

Joe half turned in his seat to watch her. "Take him out to the end of the lane and then back him up."

She sat up straighter, determined to show him she remembered everything her grandfather had taught her about driving horses. Joe had her take Cooper out onto the street and then back him about twenty feet before turning him in a half circle and coming back. Cooper tossed his head a little as if he could sense her nervousness, but he did everything she asked.

She stopped him in front of the barn. Joe got out and opened the wide doors where the cart and wagon were. "Now back the buggy into here."

"I'm not sure about that. There isn't much space on either side. I don't want to damage Rose's buggy."

"Then don't hit anything with it."

She turned Cooper and lined up with the opening. As she got him to back up, he veered off to the side a little and the buggy jacked in the opposite direction.

She looked back at Joe. He was standing with his hands on his hips watching her. "Start over."

She tried again with the same results. Frustrated she sent Cooper forward again.

"Can I make a suggestion?" Joe asked.

"I'll get it," she snapped.

"Determination is a good thing. Sometimes. At other times it can be a hindrance."

She would show him. She tried again. When the back wheel hit the barn door, her shoulders drooped. "I can't do it."

"Do you want me to tell you an easy way?"

"Yes," she admitted reluctantly.

"Step down."

"You don't have to do it for me," she said as tears pricked her eyes.

"I'm not going to do it for you. Go to the horse's head and take his bridle."

She got out and went to stand in front of Cooper. She hesitantly took hold of his bridle with one hand. He shook his head. She jerked her hand away.

"He isn't going to hurt you if you respect that he's a big animal and you don't do something foolish."

She glared at Joe. "That wasn't helpful. Is this kind of work allowed on Sundays?"

"Caring for our animals is essential. You're not going to get out of it that easily. Let's see some of that determination at work."

"Sometimes I think you enjoy being mean."

He chuckled. "Take hold of the bridle beneath the bit and back him from there. You can see exactly where the buggy is going, and you can correct him before he gets too far out of line."

She spoke softly to Cooper and he backed the buggy into the barn as if he had been doing it forever. Which he had. She was the one who didn't know what she was doing.

She scowled at Joe. "Why didn't you tell me this was the way to do it sooner?"

"Sometimes failure is the best teacher. Now come back here and unhitch him."

Fuming, she stomped to Joe's side and he showed her how to unhook Cooper from the buggy. It was less complicated than she had expected. Then he stood by as she unbuckled the harness and took the pieces off.

Pleased with herself, she turned to him with the heavy leather gear and chains in her arms. "Here you go."

"Goot." A mischievous gleam flashed in his eyes. "Now put it back on and hitch him to the buggy."

"What?"

"You wanted to learn."

He was right. But stronger than her desire to learn about horses was her longing to spend more time with Joe. They didn't have many more days together and she wouldn't waste them. She tucked that thought away and lifted the harness to Cooper's back. "Is this right?" she asked just to hear the sound of his voice again.

"It needs to sit farther forward. Let me show you." He stepped close beside her and adjusted the harness. Their hands touched. He met her gaze for a long second then he turned away. "You've got it now."

"Danki." She should have been happy to accomplish the dreaded task, but all she wanted to do was cry.

"Have you made an appointment to see Bertha yet?" Rose asked.

She and Abby were tidying up the patio area in the garden outside the breakfast room early Monday morning.

Abby glanced around to see if anyone else could overhear them. "I can't afford to see a doctor yet, Rose."

"Bertha charges on a sliding scale. If someone's flat broke she'll see them for free. Pay what you can. It's important that you and your baby stay healthy."

"I know that." Rose was right. Abby hadn't yet seen a doctor about her pregnancy. Somehow that step made it seem too real. The fantasy of having a baby to love was easier than facing the nitty-gritty details. "I'll make an appointment tomorrow."

"The clinic is open today. Go down to the phone shack and call right now."

Abby finished sweeping the patio and handed Rose her broom. "You will just keep nagging me until I do."

"I'm not nagging. I'm strongly suggesting, and I will continue until you take care of yourself. Check our messages while you're there."

Abby impulsively hugged the woman. "I'm glad that God led me here. I don't know what I would do without you."

Rose patted Abby's back. "I will stand in for your grandmother because I know that is what she would have wanted. Now go."

"Would you be able to come to the appointment with me? I don't know what to expect."

"Just try to keep me away. Now run along. I have work to do. We have five guests coming the day after tomorrow."

"I'll be back as quick as I can."

"There's no need to rush. Perhaps you could take Joe's crowbar back to him for me. I forgot to return it yesterday."

Abby folded her arms over her chest. "What were you doing with a crowbar?"

"I was looking for Wilma late last night. She hadn't touched her food all day. I heard her crying in the basement and went to see what was wrong. She managed to get stuck behind some crates of potatoes. I couldn't move them. I didn't want to rouse the house, so I went down to Joe's trailer and got his crowbar from his tool chest. I used it to move the crates and get her out. I was going to take it back later. You're thinking I took it deliberately as an excuse to have you return it to him."

"That's exactly what I'm thinking."

"I'm sure if I put my mind to it I could come up with a better reason to send you to see him. Borrowing a crowbar to encourage a romance is a little strange even for me."

Abby couldn't tell if Rose was being truthful or not. It was only later when she knocked on Joe's door that she realized Rose hadn't actually denied Abby's accusation. When he opened the door, Abby forgave Rose for any white lie. It didn't matter what excuse she was given. Abby was just happy to see him.

"What are you grinning about?" he asked.

Abby held up the crowbar. "Rose asked me to return this."

They looked at each other and laughed. "Did she spin you a *goot* yarn?"

"It was quite involved with her poor cat trapped in the basement late last night and not wanting to wake anyone up to help."

He opened the door wider. Wilma slid past his legs, padded down the steps and dashed off. "That cat? The one that slept in here with me all last night?"

"Maybe Wilma has a twin," Abby suggested, trying to keep a straight face.

"Two gray cats that nobody sees roaming the inn?"

"Unlikely, right?"

"I would think so. What are you up to this morning?"

Abby opened her mouth and snapped it shut. She had almost admitted she was going to make a doctor's appointment. She was so comfortable around Joe that she sometimes forgot he didn't know she was expecting.

"What's the matter?" he asked.

"Nothing. I'm just on my way to the phone hut to check the messages."

"Want some company?"

She took a quick step back. "That's okay. I know you're busy. I'll see you later." She turned around and forced herself to walk away quickly when what she really wanted was to run. He was leaving soon. There was no reason to tell him about her pregnancy.

At the phone shack she found a directory hanging from

a chain. She looked up the number to Bertha's clinic and called. The receptionist told her she could be seen Friday morning at ten o'clock. Abby hung up the phone slowly. Her pregnancy was about to get very real very soon.

Was she ready?

Fifteen

Abby left the inn on Monday afternoon as soon as she could and headed to the farm on her bicycle. She didn't meet a single vehicle. After checking that no one was behind her, she slowed to a stop at the lane leading to the house. There were no new tire tracks or footprints on the driveway that she could see. She started forward. A rustling in the brush stopped her in her tracks. She stifled a yelp when a deer jumped in front of her, scaring her half to death. The doe bounded out of the trees beside the barn, crossed the road in a single leap and vanished into the overgrown weedy field on the other side of the roadway. Abby pressed a hand to her chest to calm her wildly beating heart.

She waited a long minute. No other animals and no human appeared. Looking at the place where the doe had entered the field, she saw a well-worn trail leading into the brush. She checked the ground and saw dozens of hoof-prints in the road. It was clear the deer came through this spot often.

She pedaled to the bird sanctuary and got off her bike. As she leaned it against her usual tree, the same doe jumped the fence that was the boundary between the wetlands and the field and ran into the marshes.

Abby looked in the direction the deer had come from. Was there a way she could approach the farm without having to walk along the road and risk being seen?

Taking her basket from the back of her bike, she walked to the fence where she had watched the deer cross. There were bits of hair on the barbed wire fence. Beyond was a narrow game trail leading into the field.

She slipped through the loose wires and waded into the tall weeds. The path meandered through the field. Occasional trails led in other directions, but Abby stayed as parallel to the road as she could until she was back across from the barn. She checked the road in both directions and hurried across.

The overturned chair lay in the same position on the porch blocking the front door. No one had gone in that way. Going to the rear of the house, she listened carefully at the back door but heard nothing. She opened it slowly. Her sprinkling of flour in the hallway lay undisturbed. Smiling, she stepped inside knowing it was safe.

She went into the kitchen and put her basket on the counter, unlatched it and pulled out a plastic gallon jug of water. Taking the lid off, she slowly poured the water into the top of the red pitcher pump at the sink while she worked the handle. Soon she could feel a change in the resistance and then water poured out with each stroke of the lever.

Abby grinned. Now she could begin cleaning in earnest. Turning around, she looked over the kitchen and decided it would have to wait. The front door opened directly into the room. Anyone who opened it would see the work she had done without stepping inside. The kitchen and the windows would be the last things she cleaned.

She pumped a pail of water and carried it upstairs. Using her grandmother's mop, she scrubbed the ceiling, walls and floor of her bedroom. The other bedroom would have to wait for another day. It would take her at least twenty minutes to ride home and she wanted to spend a good half hour bird-watching. That meant she couldn't work in the house for much more than an hour if she wanted to avoid pedaling home in the dark.

She carefully folded up the chenille bedspread and sheets from her bed, pressing them as flat as she could to make them fit into her basket. Then she opened the window that overlooked her grandmother's flower bed a crack to allow the room to dry in the warm breeze and for the scent of her pine cleaner to dissipate. From her vantage point she could see the driveway and the road beyond through the grimy glass. Nothing moved except a squirrel and the birds in the trees.

She carried her pail of dirty water downstairs and emptied it in the kitchen sink. She dried the sink, put the cleaning supplies away and packed up her things. Dashing upstairs, she closed the window and then powdered the hallway as she backed out. At the road, she crossed quickly and went into the field. Following the game trail, she came out where she had parked her bike.

She secured her basket over the rear wheel and glanced around. She was alone. She relaxed and began looking for birds. Methodically she scanned the area, then used her binoculars when she spotted movement, making notes about the birds she saw. She was getting ready to leave when a small green plane buzzed overhead just above the tree line as it had when she and the others had been looking for the cerulean warbler. Like that day, the birds scattered wildly in all directions. She was glad Herbert wasn't along to witness it.

Joe went to the inn looking for Abby. One last harnessing lesson for hitching two horses to a wagon was in order. Grace was coming out as he was going in. "Hello, Grace. Is Abby busy?"

"She isn't here, Joe. She left to go bird-watching for a while."

"Again? By herself?"

"I'm afraid she has the bug. I'm glad to see her enjoying something. When she first came here, she seemed so sad."

"Leaving her friends and family behind had to be tough."

"I agree. Making such a big change is never easy. I understand you will be leaving us soon."

"I'm almost done with the kitchen. A little paint touch-up and the new window are all I have left."

He had been eager to get finished. Now he wished he had taken more time.

The sound of a horse and buggy approaching at a fast clip made them both look toward the lane. David Shetler pulled his sweaty horse to a stop in front of the house and jumped out. "Is Rose here?" he asked breathlessly.

"Yes. She's in the kitchen," Grace said. "Is something wrong?"

"Micah has spiked a fever. We're real worried about him."

"I'll get her." Grace hurried into the house.

THE INN AT HARTS HAVEN

Joe had rarely seen a man look so scared. He took hold of the horse's bridle. "It'll be okay. Rose will know what to do."

"My wife is beside herself. I hated leaving her alone but what else could I do?"

"Why don't you go back. I'll bring Rose out to your place."

"Would you? That would be a blessing."

Just then Rose came out of the house. "How high is his fever, David?"

"Barbara says it's 103. That's mighty high for a little *bobbli*, ain't so?"

"It is. I need to get some things. I'll only be a few minutes."

"David wants to get back to his wife," Joe said. "I'll take you out to his place and bring you home."

"*Goot.* Has Barbara given Micah any fever medicine?"

David shook his head. "She wasn't sure if he was too little to have it. She's been sponging him is all. Have we done wrong?"

Rose laid a hand on David's shoulder. "*Nee*, you've done exactly right. Go home. We'll be there quick as we can."

David jumped back into his buggy and urged his horse to a fast trot down the lane.

Joe was already running toward the barn when he saw Abby come in on her bike. She changed directions to meet him at the barn door. "I just saw David Shetler rushing out of here. What's going on?"

"Micah is sick. I'm taking Rose out there. You might see if you can give her a hand."

"Of course." She leaned her bike against the barn and ran to the house.

Joe had Bendy harnessed in record time. For once she

didn't try to bite him and he gave thanks for that. He drove her to the house just as Rose and Abby came out together. Rose opened the back door of the buggy. "Abby is coming with us. I might need some help."

"I don't know how much help I can be," Abby said, her eyes wide with concern. She carried a large basket over her arm.

"A calm, reassuring voice and someone to make tea can make all the difference to a worried mother."

"I can do that." Abby helped Rose in and climbed in after her. Joe pushed Bendy to a fast trot as soon as they reached the highway.

He drove as fast as he dared. The sun had set, and they were losing the light. A pickup flew around them, making Joe cringe. Bendy swerved toward the ditch. He moved her back to the center of the lane. Why did the *Englisch* have to go everywhere so fast?

He didn't take an easy breath until the Shetler farm came into view. Turning off the highway, he drove up to the front door. David was waiting for them. His horse and buggy were still standing by the gate.

Rose and Abby got out and hurried into the house. Joe's adrenaline rush slowly ebbed away. He got out and clipped the buggy weight to Bendy's halter so she wouldn't wander off. She reached around and nipped his elbow. He jerked away and rubbed the smarting spot. "I knew it was too *goot* to last."

A frantic wail came from the house. Joe rushed inside.

He saw everyone gathered around Barbara, who was holding Micah. The baby's arms and legs were jerking as he arched his back.

"Rose, what's wrong with him?" Barbara's frightened cry sent chills up Joe's spine.

Rose calmly took the baby from his mother's arms. "It's a febrile seizure. I know it looks scary but he's going to be okay. Abby, start timing it. I'll tell you when to stop." Rose placed the baby on his side on the sofa cushion and used a pillow to prop him up.

David and Barbara clutched each other. "Should we give him the fever medicine?" David asked.

"In a little while. After he comes out of this," Rose said as she knelt beside the baby. "These usually only last a minute or two."

Joe had never felt more useless in his life. He could see that Abby was frightened, too.

David looked at Rose. "Does this mean my son will have fits like this all his life?"

"Epilepsy?" Rose shook her head. "Unlikely. This is due to the fever. It doesn't mean there's something wrong with his little brain."

"Are you sure?" Barbara asked.

"Only our Lord has all the answers," David said.

Micah gave a feeble cry and went limp. "There, it's over," Rose said. "How long was that, Abby?"

"Two and a half minutes."

Rose picked up the baby and handed him to his mother, who took him tenderly. "Ah, my *liebchen*, Mamm is here," Barbara said tenderly.

"You can wipe him down with a cool cloth as you were doing before. Abby, get the fever medicine from my basket."

Abby opened the lid of the wicker container and withdrew a small bottle with a dropper attached. She handed it to Rose, who read the label. "It's important when you give medication like this that you make sure it can be given to babies, because they make it for older children, too, but the dosage is different." She measured out a small amount in the dropper and placed it in the corner of the baby's mouth.

"They usually sleep after a seizure." Rose handed the medicine to Barbara. "Keep this in case his fever goes up again."

"Will it stop another one from happening?" Barbara asked.

"*Nee*, but it's rare to have more than one febrile seizure in a day. Abby, there is some herbal tea in my kit. Why don't you make some for all of us? I think the worst is over, but we will stay for a few hours to make sure the fever comes down. You should let Dr. Bertha know about this first thing tomorrow, Barbara. She may want to see Micah."

"We will." David drew a relieved breath. "*Danki*, Rose, you are a true blessing from *Gott*. I guess I should get on with my chores."

"I'll take care of that," Joe said, happy to do something useful. "What needs to be done?"

"Put the buggy away and take care of Homer. I pushed him pretty hard. Hay and grain for him and the other horses. Make sure they have water and shut up the chickens."

Joe followed Abby into the kitchen before he went out. She still looked shaken. "Are you okay?"

"I had no idea what to do. Rose was so calm. I never realized caring for one small baby could be so complicated or frightening. I've just thought of them as sweet darlings."

"I can take you back to the inn after I've done the chores."

She gave him a half-hearted smile. "I'll stay as long as Rose does. I'm fine."

He took her hand and squeezed her fingers. "Are you sure? Because you don't look fine."

Abby wanted to throw her arms around Joe's neck and

blurt out all her secrets and fears. She wanted Joe to tell her she and her baby would be fine even though she knew he couldn't guarantee that. No one could. She forced herself to pull her hand from his. "Go do the chores. I'll have some hot tea for you when you're ready unless you would rather have coffee."

"Herbal tea is okay this late. I'll be back as soon as I can."

Abby busied herself in the kitchen and tried not to think about what it would've been like to see her own child suffering the way Micah had. She had started praying for the baby and his parents as soon as she saw how sick he was. She had prayed God would spare him and it seemed that her prayers were heard.

She carried a mug of tea into the living room. Micah was quiet. Rose was sponging him and humming softly. David paced back and forth across the floor before opening the outside door. "I'm just going to see if Joe needs any help."

Abby sat down beside Barbara on the sofa and handed her the mug. Barbara took it with a grateful smile. "Thank you for coming."

"I didn't do anything."

"You were here. I think you were praying as I was. That means a lot."

"I was. I wish I could do more."

Barbara looked toward her baby. "I wish I could do more, too. *Gott* sends us trials to strengthen our faith. He did not fail me. He is my shelter in times of trouble."

They were words Abby hadn't truly understood until that moment. God had sent her a test of faith when her mother and grandparents died. She had failed Him miserably. Shame weighed her down.

She longed for the same kind of faith her grandparents

had lived every day. Her time among the Amish of Harts Haven was teaching her more about herself than she had realized. Belief that God had a personal and loving relationship with each of his children was at the forefront of everything. The clothes, the rules and the language were trappings, outward signs of their beliefs and adherence to God's laws, but faith in His love and mercy was the core. No matter how many rules of the *Ordnung* Abby memorized, she would still be pretending until she believed as completely as Barbara did.

"Rose says the fever will have to run its course." Barbara took a sip of her tea and then smiled at Abby. "This is delicious. I hope you can stay awhile."

She reached over to pat Barbara's hand. "Of course."

Barbara gripped Abby's fingers. "I'm glad."

The outside door opened sometime later. Joe stepped inside. "Barbara, your folks are here."

The young mother gave a glad cry and raced into the arms of a small plump middle-aged woman. Her husband stood looking at Rose. "How is my grandbaby?"

"Better," Rose said. "His fever is down."

Rose wrapped the boy in a light blanket and handed him to his grandmother. She kissed the baby. "My prayers are answered."

"And mine," her husband said, cupping the baby's head in his large hand as he slipped his other arm around his daughter's waist.

Abby picked up Barbara's empty mug and carried it to the kitchen. She fixed another cup to give to Joe. He wasn't in the living room. She opened the door and saw David sitting on the steps. Joe was kneeling beside him with his arm over the sobbing young father's shoulders.

"You heard Rose. His fever has gone down. He's going to be fine," Joe said.

"I'm just so grateful." David's voice broke. "I've never been so scared in my life. I thought he was going to die in front of my eyes."

"It's okay. I understand."

"I'm not being very manly."

"Hey. Tough guys are overrated."

"Danki." David wiped his face on his sleeve and took several deep breaths. "I'm fine now."

Joe looked up and caught sight of Abby. "I think a cup of Rose's tea might help before you go in."

"Yeah, that sounds *goot*."

Abby handed the mug to Joe and went back inside. He was a man of constant surprises. A gruff, rude man who hid a deep well of compassion and kindness. How was she going to keep from falling in love with him? She had to find a way.

"Abby, I need you to make breakfast this morning," Grace said as she gathered her bonnet and purse three days after their trip to help little Micah. "I've got to run over to the neighbors'. I'll be back in ten minutes."

"Me? Cook breakfast? I'm just the maid." Abby swallowed hard. How did she get out of this? She hadn't cooked anything since she was fourteen, and then she'd only helped her grandmother.

"Not for the guests. Just the family and Joe, of course. They'll be in soon."

Abby had spent the last two days trying not to think about Joe and avoiding him while he added trim and moldings to the kitchen walls. Her feelings for him were getting out of control. If only he would leave sooner and not hang around.

"Grace, I'm not a good cook."

"Don't be silly." Grace headed for the door.

"What should I make?" Abby asked before she left. Amish women were known for their excellent cooking. It was a skill Abby thought she would learn once she was in her own home.

"Anything. Scrambled eggs and pancakes are easy. Oatmeal. Toast if anyone wants it. I've got to run." Grace went out the French doors in the breakfast room, leaving Abby thunderstruck.

"Okay, don't panic." Scrambled eggs. That wouldn't be difficult. Oatmeal. How hard could that be? Pancakes might be tougher. Her grandmother had made them from scratch. Abby tried to recall what her *mammi* had used. Flour, oil, what else? Why hadn't she paid more attention?

She turned in a circle in the kitchen, looking for inspiration. Maybe there was a box of mix somewhere or a cookbook. Yes, she needed a cookbook.

She began opening cabinets and drawers until she located several spiral-bound books in a drawer by the stove. The first one she picked up was in German. Not any help. The next was in English but it was for sugar-free desserts. Finally, the last one she pulled out was what she needed. *Easy Everyday Meals for Children to Make*. It was well-worn and the pages were sticky in places, but it contained a section on breakfasts.

Abby scoured it eagerly. Oatmeal and pancakes jumped out at her. "Bless whichever child or grandchild used this."

She began to gather her pans and utensils. "You can do this, Abby girl."

Fifteen minutes later she was stirring the eggs when the

lid on the oatmeal began to rattle. She put down her spatula and reached for the pan that was boiling over onto the stovetop. She moved the pan off the heat and stirred the contents. It seemed thin for oatmeal but maybe it would thicken up when it cooled.

Something was scorching, she could smell it. Her eggs. She pulled the pan off the heat and set it aside. At least they were done. The book said to test the griddle heat by sprinkling a few drops of water on it. The drops just lay there. She wasn't sure what they were supposed to do.

She heard the outside door open. "Breakfast will be ready in a minute. Have a seat." She poured some of the pancake batter onto the griddle.

"Something's burning," Joe said.

Abby looked at him over her shoulder. "The oatmeal boiled over."

"It smells like burnt eggs." He stepped up to her side at the stove and lifted the lid from the scrambled eggs. They were definitely scorched.

"Do you have a plate for them?" he asked.

"Of course." She grabbed one from the cabinet and handed it to him. He emptied the skillet onto the plate. There was more that stayed stuck to the pan. He carried it to the sink and filled it with water.

"*Danki.*" It wasn't going well. Why couldn't she do something as simple as make breakfast?

Rose and Susanna came into the room. Abby forced herself to smile. "Have a seat. It's almost ready."

The widows exchanged confused looks. "Do you need some help?" Rose asked.

"*Nee*, I'm fine."

Joe hung up his hat by the door. "I'll just have a pancake and some *kaffi*."

The coffee! She hadn't started it. "Would you put some on to perk, Rose?"

Abby carried the platter of eggs to the table and handed them to Susanna, then went back to the stove and flipped the pancake on the griddle. It didn't look brown enough, but she didn't want to burn something else.

She lifted the lid from the oatmeal. That at least looked normal. She spooned into a large bowl and set it on the table.

"Anyone besides Joe want a pancake?" she asked brightly.

Everyone declined. Abby could feel her throat tightening. She had made a mess of a simple task that a ten-year-old Amish child could have managed. Grace came in the back door and stopped. "What's that smell?"

"Breakfast," Susanna said dryly.

Grace sat at the table. Abby slid the pale pancake onto a plate and carried it to Joe then stepped back nervously. He looked at her. "Aren't you eating?"

She didn't think anything would go down past the lump in her throat. "I'm not hungry today."

"The *kaffi* will be a few more minutes," Rose said. "We might as well eat while it perks."

They all bowed their heads to pray. Abby could feel tears pricking the backs of her eyes. She wasn't going to cry. She wasn't.

When the prayer was over, Joe poured syrup over his pancake and cut his first bite. Raw batter oozed out of the center. He looked at Abby and tried to turn his laugh into a cough. She wasn't fooled. He was laughing at her. Why did she ever think she liked him?

Tears spilled down her cheeks. "I'm sorry," she mumbled and fled from the room.

* * *

Joe pushed his plate away. Grace stirred her burnt scrambled eggs with her fork. "The child can't cook. What woman her age can't make a pancake or scramble eggs?"

"She can't sew a straight seam, either," Susanna said. "Her mother did a poor job of teaching her."

"She'll learn," Joe said, wondering if he should share Abby's story.

"She lost her mother at a young age," Rose said. "We must be patient with her."

Grace looked at Joe. "I thought I saw you showing her how to put a harness on Cooper the other day. Was I mistaken?"

"You weren't. Abby admitted she's always been scared of horses and never learned to harness one."

"She has never harnessed a horse?" Susanna asked in astonishment. "That's unbelievable. I could do that by the time I was eight."

"Abby wasn't raised in an Amish home," Joe said finally. "Her grandparents were Amish. She spent her summers with them until they passed away when she was a teenager."

"She told you this?" Rose gazed at him with a speculative light in her eyes.

"Do you mean she has only been pretending to be Amish?" Susanna asked in bewilderment.

"She's not pretending." Joe had to defend Abby. "She wants to be baptized. She has lived in the outside world and in the Amish world with her grandparents. She has made her choice to become one of the faithful. She just hasn't had a chance to live Amish for a long time because her father objected."

"Why didn't she tell us this?" Grace asked.

He sighed. "She didn't want to be treated differently. She thought if people knew they wouldn't accept her."

Rose gave him a knowing smile. "You have gotten to know her well, haven't you, Joseph?"

"It's not what you're thinking, Rose. We're friends. Nothing more."

Susanna sat back and crossed her arms over her chest. "I'm not sure how I feel about this."

"I know how I feel about it," Grace said. "If her true desire is to become Amish, then we should help her."

"She could just as easily become a Mennonite," Susanna said.

Grace scowled at her. "Why? Because it's easier? I believe the bishop cautioned your community to beware of spiritual arrogance in his sermon just last month." Grace waited for Susanna's answer.

"He did," Susanna admitted reluctantly.

"Abby believes in her heart that this is the path God has chosen for her," Joe said. "She deserves our help. Maybe her mother couldn't teach her what she needs to know but there's no reason why you women can't remedy that."

Rose nodded slowly. "Joseph has a point, but how do we do it without hurting her feelings? She doesn't want to be treated differently."

"The same way our mothers taught us when we were children," Grace said. "By example. I can show her how to cook by asking her to help in the kitchen. Rose, surely you can teach one more child how to bake bread. Even the best of us need to follow a recipe when we're making something new. I have some cookbooks in my room. I can say I want to try out some new items to put on our menus."

"I'll help her with her sewing," Susanna said grudgingly. "I don't imagine she quilts any better than she cooks."

"Joe, you can continue to help her with learning how to care for the horses and buggies."

He could be finished with the kitchen renovation today, but he didn't have to leave yet. He would stay a few more days to make sure Abby learned what she needed to know about caring for a horse and buggy. It was what a friend should do. Staying longer than that would only make it harder to leave.

"We shouldn't think of Abby as an outsider," Rose said. "We should think of her as an Amish child who was taken away from the faith through no fault of her own and has now returned." She looked at all of them.

Everyone nodded in agreement.

Joe left the house and went down to the barn to get a can of leftover paint to touch up the baseboards. He was surprised to hear a muffled sob coming from one of the stalls.

Abby was huddled in the corner with one of the baby goats in her lap. "I hate it when women cry," he said.

"Then go away."

"So you burned the eggs. It's not a disaster. The chickens will lay more."

"You're not funny and you shouldn't laugh at someone because they made a little mistake."

He walked in and sat in the straw beside her. "Honestly, Abby. It's not worth crying over."

She wiped her eyes on the back of her sleeve. "Now you'll tell me I'm being stupid."

He draped his arm over her shoulder and pulled her close. "You're not being stupid. Everyone gets upset and cries sometimes. Okay, maybe not Susanna. I can't see her dissolving into tears, but I'm sure Rose and Grace have cried over little things before."

"You're probably right," she admitted grudgingly.

"Of course I am," he said firmly.

She cast him a sidelong glance. "What makes you so sure?"

"Because we all get emotional at times. It's not a bad thing."

Abby wiped her face with both hands. "I can't afford to fall apart over something as stupid as runny pancakes."

"Right. It's not a big deal. Everyone messes up once in a while. Even me."

She put the little goat aside and got to her feet. He scrambled to his mother. Abby glared at Joe. "You don't understand. I have to be strong. I don't have anyone to lean on."

"You have friends here, Abby. They'll help you."

"You're my friend. Are you going to be here to help me when I need it?"

He looked down. "I can't. You know why."

"That's what I thought. Have a nice life, Joseph Troyer. I hope your dinky little house gets four flat tires on the road."

He got to his feet and went after her. "Abby, wait. Where are you going?"

"I'm going bird-watching so I can practice being alone," she shouted.

She stormed into the inn, came out a few minutes later with her binoculars and tote bag, got on her bicycle and rode past him without a backward glance.

He stacked his hands on his head. What was wrong with her?

"Don't pay any attention to Abby's mood swings right now," Rose said. "It will pass."

He turned to her. "I hope so because you are the ones who'll have to deal with her. I'm done here today and I'm leaving as soon as Oliver can haul me away."

Sixteen

It was for the best. Abby tried to convince herself of that as she rode out to the wetlands. She didn't need Joe's friendship, anyway. He was leaving, and she had to get on with her life. He was never going to be a part of it.

She hadn't intended to be so distraught when she ended the relationship or so mean, but she couldn't seem to help herself today. All she wanted to do was cry. And it had nothing to do with pancakes. She wasn't even sure why she was so upset. She should've laughed it off. Made a joke out of it. Maybe it was just being pregnant. Mary had said she cried buckets for no reason. That was exactly what Abby wanted to do. Cry buckets. She sniffled and wiped her nose on her sleeve.

She looked toward her grandmother's house as she rode

past the lane and nearly wrecked her bike. A white flatbed truck was parked a dozen yards away. She caught a glimpse of a man in a dark shirt and jeans walking up to the front of the house. She couldn't see his face, but it had to be one of her father's men.

She put her head down and pedaled away. A minute later she heard the truck start up. She glanced back. The driver had backed out of the lane and was coming in her direction. Had the man recognized her?

She rode as fast as she could into the marsh entrance, bouncing over the rough tracks as she headed for the trees. Maybe she could hide in the tall reeds. She glanced back once more. The truck turned north and drove into her grandfather's field. Abby stopped. The truck disappeared over a slight rise.

Why would he be going that way? There was nothing in the field except a hay shed. She got out her binoculars and scanned the area. After about ten minutes the truck came back and sped toward the highway but now it was loaded with large round bales of yellow straw. Almost immediately a green plane came over the rise nearly skimming the ground before it flew south toward Harts Haven.

Abby turned her binoculars toward the house. Nothing moved there. Was it safe to go in? Would the truck driver be back? The more she thought about it, the more unlikely it seemed. But what had he been doing at the back of her grandfather's field? Was someone using the shed to store their hay? Her grandfather had never baled wheat straw. She was sure that was what the bales had been on the back of the truck. Their bright yellow color was unmistakable.

Perhaps Herbert or Dr. Bertha could tell her who might be using the shed. Whoever it was, they were trespassing if they weren't working for her father. Abby didn't know what straw might be used for besides mulching the garden and bedding down animals. It was poor-quality feed. The whole thing didn't make sense. If the man hadn't been checking on the house, she might have thought it was just someone expanding their hay storage into what looked like an abandoned farm.

She made her way along the game trail to the road. She knelt to look at the tire tracks in the sand. She couldn't be sure, but she thought they were the same size treads she had seen before.

She carefully entered the house and saw nothing had been disturbed. Feeling more confident, she got out her cleaning supplies and started on the second upstairs room. As she washed the wall around the window, she noticed she had a good view of the hay shed through a break in the trees. She leaned closer to the window. The grass beside the building had been mowed recently. It was a little wider than a road. Then an idea struck her. It was wide enough to be a runway.

Was that where the plane had come from? There was something going on at the farm and for some reason her father didn't want her to know what it was.

When she finished cleaning the room, she stuffed a pair of bedroom curtains that looked like they could be washed and reused into her bag, and made her way back to her bicycle. She was tempted to ride out to the hay shed but decided it wasn't worth the risk. She'd have no reason to be in the vicinity if she was seen. She could profess to be bird-watching when she was walking along the game trail, but it was better not to arouse suspicion by venturing where she didn't belong.

Joe wiped down the last baseboard and stepped back to look at the finished project. It was passable, considering all the changes Rose had tried to make. He could leave here knowing they had a kitchen they could enjoy for years to come. Abby might even learn to cook here.

He didn't want to think about her, but she kept creeping into his thoughts. He had hurt her feelings. He'd laughed at her when she had been trying hard to succeed and had failed miserably. He couldn't blame her for getting angry.

"It looks *wunderbar*, Joseph," Rose said.

He turned and saw Rose, Grace and Susanna watching him. Grace had tears in her eyes. "Are you really leaving us?"

"I'm done."

"We need a new garden shed," Rose declared.

"We don't, Mamm." Susanna rolled her eyes at her mother. She came over to Joe and shook his hand. "You've been very kind to three old women. We will miss you, but we can't afford a new garden shed."

"Just a small one," Rose suggested.

Grace rushed over and enveloped Joe in a hug. "You're a fine fellow. I'll tell everyone what a good job you did in case you come back this way."

"Mennonite Builders will be grateful for the recommendation."

Rose crossed her arms. "All right. When is your boss taking you away?"

"I've got to go call him."

"I think the phone is out of order," Rose said quickly.

"Rose!" He shook his head and scowled at her.

"It might be out of order."

"Once you get down there with my wire cutters?" He struggled not to laugh. She was priceless.

She scrunched her nose. "It was only an idea. You know, we are a bed-and-breakfast. If a fellow would like to camp out here for a few weeks of vacation, we wouldn't charge for that and he could get his meals reasonably priced."

"That's a generous offer, Rose."

"Cinnamon rolls as big as your face for breakfast," Grace said quickly, with a hopeful glint in her eyes.

Susanna looked at Grace and Rose and just shook her head. She turned to Joe. "I believe you promised to teach Abby how to care for a horse, buggy and tack. I don't believe your work is done here."

"You, too?"

She wagged a finger in his face. "A man's word is his bond. You offered. Now follow through. Got it?"

He held up both hands. "I've got it. You're right. I did agree to do that. I'll tell my boss I'm staying for a while longer."

"*Goot.* I have work to do."

Rose beamed at Susanna. "I've never been so proud of you, *dochtah*."

A tiny smile played on Susanna's lips. "I find plain speaking solves most problems. Unlike ridiculous schemes."

Rose chuckled. "Ah, but it isn't as much fun."

Grace rubbed her hands together. "Now that you'll be on vacation, perhaps you'd like to come bird-watching with us. It's very exciting. Abby loves it. We're going out this evening if you'd like to join us. Herbert, Bertha and me. I haven't had a chance to ask Abby, but I'm sure she'll go when she hears what we're hoping to find."

"Sure. I'll come along. *Danki.* I'd like to see what she finds so interesting." It might give him the opportunity to apologize to Abby.

Grace and Susanna went out and two gray cats came in from the hallway. One sat by the food bowl and meowed. The other one slipped under the table.

Joe frowned at Rose. "You have two cats?"

"*Ja*, Wilma and her new friend Smokey. She looks just like Wilma, doesn't she? I think they might be sisters. I've seen Smokey hanging around your trailer. Has she been annoying you?"

He shook his head in amazement. "*Nee*, she's a good cat. She caught a mouse in my trailer, and I let her sleep on my couch the other night."

"That must have been the night Wilma got stuck in the basement, because I couldn't find her. I'm glad you're going to spend more time with us, Joe. I promise I won't push you and Abby together anymore."

That was what he'd wanted, so why didn't it make him happy?

He mulled over the thought as he walked to the phone shed. He placed a call to Oliver. His call went to voice mail. "Boss, this is Joe. I'm finished at the Harts Haven Inn. The widows are happy with the job. You've been telling me I need to use my vacation hours so I'm going to take you up on that. I'm going to stay in Harts Haven for another two weeks. Don't worry, I'll still take the job in Oklahoma City if you want me to. I just won't be down for a couple of weeks."

Joe hung up the phone. "That's that."

Now he could teach Abby all she needed to know, if she was still speaking to him, and when it came time for him to leave—he hoped they could part as friends.

On the ride back to the inn Abby had plenty of time to think about what she would say to Joe. She had to apologize. If he was still around. That he might have left without telling her goodbye was too painful to think about. Why had she picked a fight with him on his last day?

Relief filled her when she saw his trailer was still parked under the trees. He wasn't gone. She had a chance to make things right.

She rode up to the back door of the kitchen and leaned her bike against the house. She started to slip her bag off her shoulder when the door opened, and Joe stood there. She dropped her bag and the curtains spilled out.

"Abby, can I talk to you?"

She quickly stuffed the material back in her bag and stood up. She wrapped her arms around it and hugged it close. "I was just on my way to see you."

"Look, I want to apologize. I honestly didn't mean to upset you."

She almost started crying again. "I know. I can say the same thing. I'm sorry I blew up at you. I don't want your trailer to end up with four flat tires."

"I appreciate that."

"Are you done here?" She didn't want him to say yes. Couldn't he stay another day or two days. What would that hurt?

"All done."

"Oh." She knew her voice sounded small. "When are you leaving?"

"I told Oliver I wanted to take two weeks of vacation before I head to Oklahoma. I have that and more coming to me."

Her tears evaporated. She grinned at him, absurdly happy with this news. "I'm so glad."

"As Susanna reminded me, I haven't finished teaching you about buggy horses yet."

"That's right, you haven't. I sort of left in a rush this morning. If Rose hasn't hired a new maid while I was gone,

I have some work to do. I'll come down to the barn after supper."

"Sounds good."

"Great. I'll see you then, and I am sorry for getting angry with you. I don't know what came over me."

"Rose said you're having a stressful time what with hoping to join the church and all."

Abby kept her smile in place. Rose knew what she was talking about. It was a stressful time for so many reasons Abby couldn't share with him.

He shoved his hands in his pockets. "Things will work out. You'll see."

"I have to believe that. So are we friends again?" Maybe she wanted more from him, but she couldn't let him see that.

"We never stopped being friends, Abby."

"Okay."

"Do you want to hear something funny?"

"Does it involve pancakes?" she asked dryly.

He chuckled, then sobered and held up his hand. "Sorry. It turns out that Rose has two gray cats. They look exactly alike. Wilma and Smokey. Smokey went missing the night Wilma got stuck in the basement."

"Are you serious?"

"We should have known. Rose claims that she always tells the truth."

He walked away and Abby watched him until he went into the barn. "Unlike some of us who can't bear to have others learn what that is."

At least she and Joe were back on friendly footing and that was what she dearly wanted and so did he. It should have made her happier but for some reason it didn't. The trick would be keeping her growing affection hidden.

It shouldn't be too hard. She had been hiding a lot more

since the day they met. She went inside to catch up on the work she had missed.

By late afternoon Abby was waxing the final section of the dining room floor when Herbert and Bertha came in.

"Going birding this evening?" Herbert asked. "Grace tells me you go regularly out to the wetlands."

Abby picked up her supplies. "I get away when I can. What are the two of you up to?"

"We thought we would save you a long pedal and take you with us." Bertha smiled brightly.

"You're going out this evening? I thought you had your online birder meeting."

"We've had reports of a barred owl in the area," Herbert said. "They seldom travel this far west into the state. They prefer forest areas rather than our grasslands. We're much more likely to see one of them in the evening so we plan to spend several hours out at the sanctuary tonight and to-morrow evening."

Abby smiled and nodded. She wouldn't get back to her house for several days.

Bertha looked as excited as a child. "They have a dis-tinctive call. It sounds like they're asking, 'Who cooks for you?' Doesn't it, Herbert?"

"Precisely. I shouldn't have a problem picking up their call with my microphone if there are some in the area. What do you say, Abby? Are you game to brave the mosquitoes and do a little nighttime bird-watching?"

"I guess so."

"We have a chance to make another convert," Bertha said with a grin.

"Really? Who?"

"Me," Joe said, stepping in from the kitchen. "Surprise."

Grace clapped. "Isn't it fun. Joe mentioned wanting to

try birding since you seem to enjoy it so much. I've already told Rose we'll be back late. We have a picnic supper in the car so we're off."

Abby kept smiling. Just when she'd managed to put their friendship back on normal footing, Joe was going to be spending more time with her. How much harder was God going to make this for her? She put away her cleaning supplies and joined them outside at Herbert's car.

She found herself squeezed in the back seat between Grace with her picnic basket and Joe. She was pressed against him from shoulder to thigh. He smelled so good, like fresh-cut cedar wood and leather soap. Her heart started pounding. Her palms began to sweat. She tried not to breathe.

He leaned closer. "Are you okay?"

"I get carsick sometimes." The last time was when she was ten, but he didn't need to know that.

"Want me to roll down the window?"

"Yeah, that might help."

The blast of fresh evening air cooled her face and gave her a chance to regain her composure.

He was looking out the window. "Another Kansas farmstead left to rot. What a shame. Think of all the hopes and dreams that were born there."

They were passing her place. "It is a shame," Herbert said. "The gal who inherited it has simply allowed it to fade away. Even the land that goes with the house isn't being farmed."

"That's odd," Joe said. "This is river bottom ground. A farmer shouldn't have trouble raising a crop. Why doesn't she sell it?"

"Who knows. I've tried to buy the marshland she owns

at over market value but all I get is a big fat 'not interested' from her lawyer. Crazy, right?"

"I don't like that word, Herbert," Bertha said. "People who have mental illnesses are sick. Depression and schizophrenia are no different than heart disease or diabetes except what's wrong is in the brain where no one can see it. They aren't crazy."

Abby listened without comment. Was that how Bertha really felt?

"You are exactly right," Grace said. "The stigma of mental illness will never leave our society until everyone accepts that these conditions are treatable, even if we don't have the ability to cure them. People died of infections for thousands of years until penicillin was discovered. The answer is out there. We just have to find it."

"Sorry." Herbert glanced at Bertha. "You are quite right to chastise me."

"I get carried away sometimes," Bertha admitted.

"You are right to be passionate about something you believe in," Herbert said.

Abby managed a stiff smile and glanced at Joe from the corner of her eye. "Not everyone feels that way about mental illness."

Bertha nodded. "You're right. There are still many people who see it as a shameful weakness and judge people affected with mental problems harshly."

"Even the Amish?" Abby asked quietly.

Bertha turned to look at Abby. "Sadly, that is true of some. Changing people's opinions takes time and education."

Abby folded her arms over her stomach. Time wasn't something she had.

Herbert pulled into the sanctuary entrance. "Here we are. Get your bird eyes on."

Grace and Abby set out a quilt and the picnic basket while Herbert got his microphone out of the trunk and showed Joe how it worked. Bertha walked away, looking through her binoculars.

Herbert squared his shoulders. "One of the many things you'll learn about birds, Joe, is not only how they look but how they behave."

Grace chuckled. "Oh, no, his behavioral speech. Prepare to be bored, Abby."

Abby sat on the quilt, pulled up her knees and wrapped her arms around them. "I didn't get that speech. What have I been missing?"

Herbert cleared his throat. "You'll want to notice subtle differences in how the birds move and where they forage. Take wrens, they flick their tail feathers up and down. A woodpecker in flight undulates, flap, flap, glide, flap, flap, glide. Brown thrashers and cat birds will be thrashing around on the ground in the leaves looking for food."

"It that why they're called thrashers?" Abby asked.

"Precisely. Cerulean warblers prefer mature deciduous trees for their habitat. An undisturbed area like this where sycamores, elms and hackberry grow would be inviting to them."

"I saw a cerulean my first time here," Abby said. Maybe Joe would be impressed.

"What did it look like?" he asked.

"It's blue."

"Like a blue bird or a jay?"

"Yes, but rare in this area," Grace said.

"Ladies, please. Joe needs to know these things if he is to enjoy the experience. Cerulean warblers forage for insects high in the tree canopy. You'll see them when they dart out to catch a bug in flight."

"Here it comes," Grace whispered.

Herbert waved one hand through the air. "Accurate bird identification comes from seeing and understanding the whole compendium. I wasn't aware of these things when I started. I learned it from other birders. You'll rarely meet a finer, more helpful group of people."

"Yellow-rumped warblers are called butter butts," Abby added, trying not to smile at Joe's dazed expression.

"Are they?" He looked skeptical.

Herbert nodded. "They have a yellow marking on their back. They're common in this area but they're colorful birds with blue, black and white feathers. If you're looking for a cerulean, you should be looking through the yellow-rumps. They're partial to the same habitat."

"I'm going to be looking for butter butts and blue birds." Joe arched one eyebrow at Abby. She managed not to laugh.

"Not this evening," Herbert said. "We seek a barred owl. We should hear it before we see it. Quiet, please." He put on his headphones and walked away, swinging his microphone slowly from side to side. Grace got up and followed him. Bertha was on the other side of a pond looking at a pair of little blue herons.

Joe sat down on the quilt beside Abby. "So this is what you do for fun?"

"It's not for everyone, but I like it."

"I'm starving. What's in the basket?"

"Your guess is as good as mine." She opened the top. "I see plastic containers."

"I'll pass. Plastic gives me indigestion."

She giggled and pulled out a loaf of homemade bread already sliced. "Bread and water?"

"Don't you think Herbert's lecture was punishment enough?"

"You're right." She unwrapped the foil covering a pan. "Ah, fried chicken?"

"Definitely. Wait. Is it against any bird-watching rules to eat fowl? I'd hate to get off on the wrong foot."

"Domestic birds don't really count to the serious birder."

"Oh, *goot*. Legs, please."

She held out the pan and he selected the piece he wanted, then he leaned back on one elbow and began eating. "It's a pretty evening."

"It is."

"*Goot* company," he added.

"Herbert can be a bit dry, but Grace and Bertha make up for him."

"I was talking about you."

She knew she was blushing. She hoped he couldn't see that in the fading light. He tossed the cleaned leg bone off into the brush. A silent shadow swooped out of the trees, picked it up, then flew away.

Abby and Joe exchanged astonished looks.

"I guess we have the answer to the owl's endless question." Bertha walked up to them.

"What question?" Joe asked.

"Who cooks for you? Who cooks for you?" She imitated the owl's call. "Apparently Grace does."

They all began laughing until Herbert shushed them from the other side of the pond.

Bertha took an apple from the hamper. "I'll go tell him which way the bird went. Until we have a recorded call or a verified spotting with two people we can't post to our group."

"Was it the barred owl?" Abby wanted to mark it off her list.

"I couldn't be sure." Bertha went to join Herbert and Grace.

Joe raised up to see in the basket. "What's for dessert?"

Abby examined the contents. "Looks like a whoopie pie or brownies."

"A brownie as long as the center isn't gooey."

"I can't believe you said that."

"I don't like gooey brownies. I wasn't talking about—"

"Don't say it!"

He cleared his throat. "Other foods."

She selected a brownie from the paper plate and pushed her thumb into the middle of it. "This one is cake-like, not overly moist." She held it out to him.

"But it's squished."

She shrugged and bit into it. "Mmm, very *goot*."

"Can I have one that isn't overly moist or squished?"

"Honestly, Joe, I had no idea you were such a picky eater." She held out the plate.

He grabbed one but set it down. "You know what?"

"You don't care for bird-watching."

"I've only seen one owl and a pair of herons that I could see any day of the year, but that's not what I was thinking."

"What were you thinking?" What kind of jest was he making now?

His eyes grew soft as he gazed at her. He reached out and drew a finger softly along her cheek. "That I'm really glad I decided to stay on for a couple more weeks."

Abby scrambled to her feet before she blurted out how much she cared for him. The plan was to stay friends. That wasn't going to happen if he looked at her like that again, if he touched her face like she was something delicate to be treasured.

She brushed the crumbs from her skirt. "I'm happy you did, too. I'm going to see if they've had any luck locating the owl."

Joe could have kicked himself for letting his emotions get the better of him. He couldn't seem to get it right with Abby. She was always running away from him.

"And whose fault is that?" he muttered.

He made her angry, he frightened her, and she drove him nuts. He couldn't keep a lid on what he was feeling for her. He liked her way too much.

No, *like* wasn't a strong enough word. He was falling for Abby. He was falling hard. He wasn't sure if his feelings were returned. Sometimes he sensed she was drawn to him, too. Like in those seconds before she jumped to her feet just now and ran off. He'd seen something in her eyes. Or maybe he only wanted to see something. He didn't deserve love, but he couldn't stop these feelings he had for Abby. He wanted to be a better man because of her.

If she did care for him, what could he do about it in the two weeks he had remaining? What was fair to her?

Abby had her heart set on settling in Harts Haven. He would always be moving on to the next job because Oliver needed him.

Until when?

The question hit him out of the blue, but once it was in his head it wouldn't leave. When would it be his turn to decide where to work and where to stay? He had let Oliver make those decisions for him. First because he'd been a grieving kid with nothing. Later because he simply didn't care. No one had wanted him except Oliver.

His eyes were drawn to where Abby stood silhouetted against the fading colors of the sunset and perfectly reflected in the still water of the pond. She glanced his way and their eyes met. She didn't look away.

What if Abby wanted him to stay for good? What if she was the sign that he had been forgiven? If that was true, could he forgive himself?

Seventeen

Joe cornered Rose early the next morning before Abby came in for breakfast. She was elbow deep in bread dough. "I need to ask you something, Rose."

"I'm listening."

He hesitated. He wasn't sure how to say this without sounding pathetic. He shoved his hands in his pockets and plowed ahead. "Does Abby like me?"

Rose stopped kneading and peered at him over the rim of her glasses. "I'm sure that is a question you should ask Abby."

"Don't play coy. You've been pushing our match since day one."

"I only encouraged you to see the possibilities in each other."

"Right. So what's the possibility that Abby will let me court her?" There, he'd said it out loud. His next steps depended on Abby's feelings. If she cared for him the way he had come to care for her, he would tell Oliver he wasn't taking the Oklahoma City job.

"Courtship? That's a big step, Joe."

He pulled out a kitchen chair and sat down. "You're telling me."

"I'd say the possibility isn't great at the moment."

His heart sank. "She doesn't like me?"

"Oh, she likes you. Very much."

"You're confusing me, Rose." Not for the first time.

"Abby is the confused one. She has so much on her mind right now that I'm afraid if you declare your interest, she'll refuse you. Your courtship could be over before it even starts."

"So what do I do?"

"Be patient. Be gentle. Be kind. She needs that right now."

"But you think there's hope for me?"

"*Gott* chooses. I just make suggestions. Continue to be her friend. She needs that now more than anything."

"Why?"

"It isn't for me to say. I'm sorry."

"Rose, if I don't know what's wrong, how can I help?"

"You have ears to listen with. You have shoulders to lean on. You have knowledge to share. All these are things Abby needs. She will soon realize just how much if you are always there for her."

"I don't know if I can be just a friend anymore."

"Abby has learned not to trust people. She has been betrayed time and again. You have to be her friend before all else."

What choice did he have? "All right."

"She may push you away if she becomes frightened by her feelings for you. Don't let her. I think the two of you are meant for each other."

"You did this to me, Rose. You'd better be right." He took a deep breath. "I'm afraid, Rose."

"Of what, dear boy?"

"That I don't deserve her affection if she does care for me. I made a terrible choice once, and people I loved died because of me." Admitting that to Rose eased the tightness in his chest.

"You recall what I told you about forgiveness, don't you?"

"You said I must forgive myself as *Gott* forgives us. I'm trying, Rose. It isn't easy."

"Every little step will bring you closer to peace. Do you love her?"

Did he? He sighed. "I'm not sure I know what love is, but I want to be with her. She makes me happy." She could also break his heart if she turned from him when he found the courage to tell her everything about what happened to his family. She had to know someday.

Rose smiled brightly. "That's a *goot* start. Make yourself scarce today."

"What? Why?"

"Because I asked you to, and because you will be on her mind if you aren't underfoot."

"Fine. Where should I go?"

"Fishing. I know you enjoy that. Or a visit to David and Barbara wouldn't be amiss. I'm sure they would love to see you again. Let me know how Micah is doing. You will be careful with Abby, won't you? She's vulnerable."

"I wish you would explain, Rose."

"I wish I could, too. Now, run along."

Joe left the inn feeling more confused and unsure of himself than when he'd walked in, but he was more determined than ever to give Abby whatever help she needed.

Abby's hands were ice-cold as she grasped the door handle of Dr. Bertha's clinic on Friday morning. Only the presence of Rose by her side kept her from turning around and running. "Maybe I could find a doctor who doesn't know me."

"Don't be silly. Bertha has met many unwed mothers in her time, as have I. We don't let it faze us. You'll be made to feel welcome, and she will be as delighted as I am to know you're going to be a mother."

"She'll think I'm irresponsible and shameless."

"Fine. You're a hussy. Do you feel better now?"

"Rose!"

"I'm only giving you what you asked for. You must learn to ask for what you need, not what you think you deserve. Besides, you're a poor judge of character if you believe you're shameless."

"I *am* a poor judge of character. I agreed to work for you, didn't I?"

"Very true. Open the door."

A half an hour later, Abby lay on the exam table waiting for Dr. Bertha to return. Her exam had been thorough and sensitive. The elderly woman was smiling when she came in pulling a small machine behind her.

"Everything looks fine with you and the baby. My estimate is that you're about fifteen weeks along. Does that sound about right?"

"It does."

Bertha smiled at Rose. "Could Abby and I have some privacy?"

"Of course. I'm just along for moral support. I think she's over the hump."

After Rose left, Bertha pulled up her chair and sat beside Abby. She reached out and took Abby's hand. "Okay, what is the plan?"

Abby stared into Bertha's sympathetic eyes. "It's complicated."

"Starting a family always is. What about the father? Is he involved?"

Abby shook her head. "He doesn't know. I will do everything in my power to make sure he never learns about this child."

Bertha leaned back slightly. "That's harsh. The two of you may not get along, but he has a right to know about his child. Legally and morally."

"Logan is not a moral person. He used me for personal gain. I was nothing to him but a means to an end."

"Well, he certainly doesn't sound nice. I can't force you to contact him, I can only encourage it. Having a child is a wondrous event, but it is also emotionally and physically exhausting. A good support system is essential for mother and baby. Do you have family who can help you?"

"I'm it. Rose guessed I was pregnant the first day we met."

"I'm not surprised. Rose is a skilled midwife and as sharp as they come although she doesn't always act that way. I know you are new to this community, but Rose will see that you are taken care of. That's one thing I never have to worry about with an Amish patient. They take care of one another."

She gave Abby's hand a squeeze and then wheeled her

chair over to the small desk, where she began writing. "I'm giving you a prescription for prenatal vitamins. It's important you take them. It's also important that you eat well and get a moderate amount of exercise. I want to see you again in a month. Sooner if you are having any problems."

"There is one more thing I need." Abby clasped her fingers together so tightly they ached.

Bertha paused her writing to look at Abby. "What would that be?"

"I need the name of an attorney. I was hoping you could recommend one."

Bertha's eyebrows shot up. She quickly schooled her features into mild curiosity. "Are you thinking of placing the baby for adoption?"

That startled Abby. "Oh, no, I'm keeping my baby. I need an attorney to help me reclaim some property, and I don't know of any in this area. Harts Haven is a small place. I assume I will have to go to Hutchinson to see someone."

Bertha smiled. "Actually, you do know an attorney here in Harts Haven."

Abby frowned. "I do?"

"Major Herbert Young, US Army JAG Corp, retired, but still practicing civilian law."

Abby stared at Bertha in disbelief. "Herbert? The birdwatcher? He's an attorney?"

"Thirty years as a member of the US Army Judge Advocate General's Corps."

"I don't know what that is."

Bertha waved her hand. "I'm not surprised. It's a military justice system that operates like our courts. The officers are licensed attorneys qualified to represent the army or soldiers in military legal matters. Court-martials and that kind of thing."

None of that sounded as if it applied to her. "I'm not being court-martialed."

"Herbert's duties encompassed a wide range of legal disciplines. Anything a civilian attorney could do. If you have a property dispute, I'm sure Herbert can help."

Abby could see Logan having a field day going up against the kindly old gentleman. "I think I need someone younger."

"Don't underestimate him. He prosecuted some very high-profile cases in the military. He hasn't lost his edge. The only thing Herbert loves more than bird-watching is a good fight in court."

"I guess it won't hurt to talk to him."

Bertha got up to move the machine closer. "Let's listen to your baby bump knocking." She turned on the machine and a low hum filled the room. She picked up a wand and pressed it to Abby's tummy. Harsh static was the first sound. That died away and Abby heard a faint thumping.

Her breath caught in her lungs as wonder overwhelmed her. She looked at Dr. Bertha. "Is that her heartbeat?"

"Or his." Bertha moved the wand slightly and the sound grew louder.

Abby finally had to breathe. She sucked in a ragged gulp of air. It was real. There was a tiny baby with a heart growing inside her. She had known it but until this moment she hadn't felt it in her soul. "It's beautiful."

"I think the same thing every time. One hundred and forty beats a minute. That's perfect."

"She's okay?"

"As far as I can tell, she's fine. Or he is fine. Are you hoping for a boy or a girl?"

Abby blinked back tears. "I'm hoping my baby is healthy and loves me as much as I love her. Or him."

* * *

Abby hung on to the sense of wonder at hearing her baby's heart throughout the morning as she did light cleaning around the inn. She couldn't stop smiling.

She walked past the sewing room and saw the door was open. Susanna was seated at her quilting frame with a lamp beside her. Her needle flashed in and out of the fabric in quick, sure motions.

"You can't see much from back there," Susanna said.

"I didn't mean to interrupt you."

"You aren't. Come closer." She didn't pause in her stitching.

Abby pulled up a chair. "That's amazing. Your stitches are so tiny. How did you learn to do that?"

"Hours and hours of practice."

"Who taught you? That's a silly question. It was Rose, wasn't it?"

Susanna smiled at Abby. "My mother has a lot of wonderful qualities, but she wasn't always a patient teacher. My grandmother taught me how to quilt."

"I can see that you love doing it."

"It's very satisfying. I didn't always like it. I started when I was small because I loved doing things with my grandmother."

"So did I."

"One day I decided I was going to make my own quilt. It was not as easy as I had imagined. My grandmother made it look effortless. I don't know how many times I wanted to give up on those blocks. But every day my grandmother would come over from the *daadi haus* and ask to see it. I had to keep working even though I had started to hate that piece. I begged her to help, but she made me do it myself. Somehow, weeks into it, I gradually began to enjoy the rhythm and the sense of accomplishment that grew with each block I completed. When the whole quilt was nearly done, I found myself stitching ever so slowly."

"Why?"

"Because I didn't want to be finished with it. I was afraid I would never enjoy quilting another one as much as I did the first one I made by myself. Or maybe it was because I treasured my grandmother's constant encouragement."

"I imagine your grandmother was proud of you."

"I think she was. We worked together on many quilts later on, but I always cherished the time she made me do it by myself."

"I told the Hostettler girls and Mary that I would come to Mary's quilting bee."

"It's always fun to get together with the other women in the community."

"I haven't quilted since my grandmother passed away. That was years ago. I'm afraid I will embarrass myself or make a mess of Mary's quilt."

Susanna gave her a sidelong glance. "Do you need a refresher course?"

"Are you offering?"

"Get a needle and thimble out of the drawer in the worktable. There's no time like the present."

"Are you sure you don't mind?"

"Get them." She bent over her work.

Abby opened the door where everything was neatly arranged in small compartments including several sizes of needles. "Which needle should I use?"

"One of the betweens. Start with a nine. I have the quilting thread over here."

"Don't I need a smaller needle?"

"Not until you're used to handling them again. Using a smaller one will only frustrate you."

Abby selected one and a thimble, then came to sit beside Susanna again. She threaded her needle and looked at Susanna. "Now what?"

"You'll start stitching a quarter of an inch in from the fabric seam. Don't try to make small stitches until you get the hang of how the needle feels going in and out."

"You'll have to rip out what I do."

"I don't think so."

"But it's not even or neat. Especially compared to your work."

"I've noticed life is not even and neat. I'll leave your stitches in as a reminder of you."

Abby looked up in surprise. "That's kind of you to say."

"You've made our inn a more interesting place."

Abby shook her head. "Not always in a good way."

Susanna laughed. "We were too dull, anyway. Now try rolling your needle when you come up through the fabric. Like this, see?"

Joe was cleaning out the horse stalls when he saw Abby knock on his trailer door. "I'm in here," he shouted.

She glanced his way and walked over. "Where have you been all day?"

"Did you miss me?" He kept raking the stall floor so she couldn't see how important her answer was.

"I did. I looked for you several times. Where were you?"

He smiled. Maybe Rose knew what she was doing. "I went out to see how Micah is getting along."

"And?" she prompted.

"You'd never know he was sick. Chubby, happy, trying to get his fist in his mouth all the time. He's rolling over in both directions and getting up on his hands and knees. Barbara says he'll be crawling soon."

"That's wonderful."

"Yeah, he's a sweet kid. What have you been doing?"

"Rose and I ran an errand this morning," she said quickly, "then Susanna offered to teach me how to quilt. I mean, I know the basics, but she was amazingly kind, and she taught me so much."

"I guess bird-watchers aren't the only nice people. Are you ready for a horse class?"

"I am. What's on the agenda? Don't say stall cleaning. I know how to do that."

"I had hoof care in mind."

She closed her eyes and put her head back. "Ahh, picking up their big feet that they stomp things with?"

"Yep."

"Okay. I need to know this, right? You're not just doing this to torture me?"

"You need to learn this stuff. I'm not going to teach you to shoe a horse. You'll hire a farrier for that, but you do need to know how to check that the shoes are secure, that the hoof is clean, not infected or split."

She waved one hand through the air. "Accurate hoof care comes from seeing and understanding the whole compendium."

"Something like that. You're in a good mood."

"I guess I am." A funny smile played across her lips. She didn't elaborate and he didn't want to pry.

"I'm glad. Go bring Cooper to the crossties."

"The biggest horse first? You are cruel. Can't I get a goat and cart and skip having horses?"

"That depends."

She looked interested. "On what?"

"If you actually want to go anywhere?"

"Oh. Not good at long-distance trips?"

"I'm waiting for you to get your horse."

"I'm stalling so I don't have to."

He held back a grin. "I noticed. Fine. Go back to the house." He turned away.

"Don't be like that, Joe. I'll do it but I'll hate doing it, and Cooper will know I'm afraid, and he'll shake his skin like he does and it's weird."

"Abby, all horses do that. Get him."

"I'm going." She walked to the next stall and opened the gate. "Nice Cooper. Don't do that skin shivery thing, okay?"

Joe smiled and shook his head. Did she even know how adorable she was? When could he tell her that without having her run off? When could he kiss her? How would he know the time was right? Would Rose let him know? He thought he was a patient man, but he was learning he wasn't where Abby was concerned.

What if she didn't care for him the way he cared for her? He longed to know how she felt about him. If there was a chance for him or if he should just move on.

What if she didn't want anything to do with him when she learned about his part in the deaths of his family? He needed to tell her, but he couldn't do it today.

"I'm waiting," she called out. She had Cooper in the crossties.

"So am I," he muttered to himself. Rose had said Abby was vulnerable. She needed his friendship. He should concentrate on that. She didn't need to be burdened with his life story. Not yet.

Abby made her way through town to Herbert's home later in the afternoon. She had been there once after her first outing as a bird-watcher when he insisted on giving her several of his books. She knocked on the door of the small single-story blue home.

Herbert opened the door. "Abby, how nice to see you. What can I do for you? Are you here for more birding books?"

"Not today, sir. I need an attorney."

"I hope it's not for something serious."

"Actually, it is. Is there somewhere we can discuss it?"

"I was just on my way to my office. I have a little place on Main Street. I like to keep my work and my private life separate. We can walk there now if you like."

"Don't I need to make an appointment?"

He smiled. "My dear, you just did."

Abby walked with him down a narrow sidewalk to Main Street. It was a short four blocks long and there were only a handful of shops, a post office and a bank in what passed for a downtown area. Herbert stopped at a door adjacent to the bank and unlocked it. A small sign above the door read Herbert Young, Attorney at Law.

Inside stood a large mahogany desk and a huge floor-to-ceiling bookcase filled with beautifully bound volumes. The opposite wall was covered in framed prints of various sizes, all featuring birds.

He sat down behind the desk and indicated that Abby should take a seat in one of the leather chairs facing him. "All right, young woman, why do you need an attorney?"

"Everything I say here is confidential, is that right?"

"If you retain me as your attorney, that is absolutely true."

"How do I retain you?"

"Repeat after me. Herbert, will you represent me?"

"That's it? What about your fee? I don't have much money, but I can pay you a little each payday."

"I do mostly pro bono work for the Amish in this community. If they can pay me, that's fine. I don't require it. I am comfortably retired and practicing law is now my hobby."

"I thought bird-watching was your hobby?"

"I have several. I also build and fly model airplanes. If you don't use your mind it gets rusty. Remember that when you get to be my age. Now, how can I help you?"

"I wish to end my father's guardianship."

Herbert sat back in his chair. "I know it's not polite to ask a woman her age, but aren't you over eighteen?"

"I'll be twenty-two in September."

"Then why is your father still your guardian?"

She clutched her hands together, wondering what Herbert would make of the reason. Unless she told him, nothing would change. "Because he had me declared mentally incompetent. He has had complete control of my life since I was sixteen."

"Well, you don't look crazy to me. Tell me what happened."

She flinched at his choice of words. "I became severely depressed following the death of my mother and grandparents within a month of each other when I was fourteen."

"That is completely understandable," he said softly.

She opened her mouth to tell him about her suicide attempt, but the words wouldn't come out. He would see her as a crazy person who needed to be protected from herself as her father had told her over and over again. She couldn't do it.

She swallowed hard. "I was eventually hospitalized and successfully treated for my depression when I was sixteen.

Thanks to the wonderful doctors and nurses who took care of me I got better."

"You were released from the hospital?"

"I was due to be released when my father arrived with his physician, who said I needed continued care. In a home environment. I was locked in a suite of rooms at my father's estate and kept medicated to the point that I could barely stand or speak coherently. I was told it was all for my own good, when I was told anything."

Herbert leaned back in his chair and swiveled slightly from side to side. "There are checks and balances in any guardianship situation to prevent abuse such as what you're describing. Annual reports have to be filed with the court."

"Checks and balances don't matter to my father. He's a powerful man with powerful friends and enough money to buy whatever he needs. Including judges and physicians. And that makes me sound paranoid, doesn't it? Perhaps now you can see the uphill battle I face in proving I'm competent."

"It makes you sound like the victim of a horrendous miscarriage of justice."

Abby's hopes rose. "Then you believe me? You'll help me prove I'm not incompetent?"

"It's not all that simple, but it is possible. You should know I have never handled a case like this. I'm going to have to do some research. Probably a lot. Kansas law is very clear on guardianship. It's not so clear on restoration of capacity other than to say you are within your rights to petition to end a guardianship."

He took a pen and paper from his desk and began to make notes. "Okay, this is what has to happen. First, we're going to file a petition for restoration of capacity. That just means we believe you no longer need a guardian, and we are asking the court to agree."

"I don't. I'm fine. I can make my own decisions."

"You don't have to convince me." He put his pen down and laced his fingers together. "There is one major hurdle in front of us right now. Legally, a person judged to be mentally incompetent cannot enter into any contract. Therefore, you can't hire an attorney."

"What does that mean? You won't help me?" Abby grabbed the arms of her chair.

He held up his hand. "It means the court will appoint an attorney to represent you. In all likelihood I will be appointed as that is your wish. I'm just telling you the steps you have to go through."

She relaxed. "Okay, I'm listening."

"You will need to be seen by a psychiatrist and a physician. I'm sure Bertha will suggest a psychiatrist we can have evaluate you. Once we file a petition, and that means going to the courthouse, seeing a court clerk at a filing window, paying a filing fee and submitting the petition to restore your capacity, then the clerk will set a court date."

"Will I have to appear in court?"

"It will most likely be an informal hearing with the judge. At that time we will present documentation from a psychiatrist and from a physician. If the court does not find clear evidence that you are impaired, the judge will terminate the guardianship."

"Will my father have to know?"

"Oh, yes. He will be notified of the court date as soon as we file. From what you tell me, you will have to be prepared to face him and his accusations. Frankly, termination of the guardianship is difficult if the guardian does not agree to it."

She clenched her fingers together tightly. "Are you tell-ing me to give up hope?"

"Not at all."

"You should know my father is a dangerous man. He'll fight this."

A frown creased Herbert's brow. "Dangerous in what way?"

"The men who came to the inn looking for a runaway daughter were looking for me."

"I had begun to suspect that."

"They were armed. My father's business involves pro-viding security for anyone who can pay to have their prob-lems solved."

"He employs mercenaries?"

"Among others."

"I've dealt with some tough characters in my time. It doesn't deter me. The first thing we need to do is have you see a psychiatrist. Once you have had an evaluation and I have his report in hand we will talk again."

Abby sat up straighter. "Good. My grandparents left their farm to me in their will. For some reason my father didn't tell me about it. I learned the details from someone else. My father has control of that trust. Once his guard-ianship is dissolved, that property will belong to me. Am I right?"

"You are of legal age. Once you are restored to compe-tency there is no need to keep your assets in trust."

"There is one more thing I need. I want to legally change my name to Abigail Martin and get a social security card."

"I see. What is your legal name?"

"Victoria Abigail Worthington."

Herbert sank back in his chair. "Is Victor Worthington your father?"

Had she already lost an ally? "He is. Do you know him?"

"I know of him. None of it good. This puts things in a different light."

"How so?"

"The quicker we move on this the less time he'll have to block us. He's well-connected. I'll speak to a judge I know right away, and I want Sheriff Hart informed. We'll have to arrange to keep you someplace safe until the hearing."

"The more people who know I'm here the more likely Victor is to find me."

"The sheriff is a man of discretion. He won't reveal your whereabouts. I'm going to call Bertha and have her set up a meeting with a psychiatrist for you. Your father will be notified when we file so I'll ask that your case be heard as soon as possible. I'll also ask that you not be required to appear so we can keep you in hiding. I can't promise that, but I'll try. I'll be in contact soon."

"Thank you, sir."

Abby shook Herbert's hand then left his office feeling more confident than she had since she arrived in Harts Haven. Her plan was in motion. With God's help, she would see it through and be free at last. She turned the corner in front of the café and almost ran into a man coming her direction. She sidestepped and looked up to apologize for her inattentiveness. The words stuck in her throat. She knew him.

She dropped her gaze. "Excuse me," she mumbled and walked on.

He had been one of the pilots who flew Victor's private planes. Had he recognized her? She hadn't seen him in years. Not since she was fifteen, but she was sure he had been her father's pilot. What was he doing here?

She wanted to look back, but she kept walking until she

reached the end of the block. Pausing to cross the street, she allowed herself to look in both directions. He was gone.

Sparks of light flashed in front of her eyes. Her legs started trembling. She grabbed the streetlight pole to keep from falling. Now what did she do?

Eighteen

Abby spent the next two days staying close to the inn and worrying. Grace invited her to try out some new recipes. She offered helpful hints as she showed Abby how to make traditional Amish dishes, but Abby couldn't concentrate. She and Susanna worked on their quilt together, but she ended up picking out half her stitches.

Joe taught Abby how to hitch two horses to a wagon instead of just one to a buggy. She went through all the motions while expecting her father to arrive at any second. She wouldn't go quietly. Not anymore.

Joe was the only one who seemed to notice her distraction, but he didn't push her to tell him what was wrong. She appreciated that.

When the third day dawned without her father putting in

an appearance, Abby began to think she had overreacted.
Maybe the man was just someone who looked like the pilot
she used to know. He hadn't stopped her or followed her.
That afternoon she decided to venture out to the farm. She
packed the freshly laundered curtains, sheets and bedspread
into her bike carrier and left a little after two.

Joe noticed Abby's bike was gone when he went to the
kitchen door. He stepped in to get a glass of lemonade.
Grace was in the kitchen making shepherd's pie for supper.
"If you're looking for Abby, she went to the bird sanctuary."

"I saw her bike was gone."

"Today might be a fine day to look for snipes out there?"

"You've got to be kidding, Grace. I know what snipe
hunting is."

"Oh. They are real birds, not just a joke kids play on
each other at night. Did you ever go snipe hunting with a
gunny sack?"

"*Ja.* Didn't catch one."

"Abby has been down in the dumps these past few days."

"I noticed. Do you know what's going on?"

"I don't, but I think she would enjoy the company of another bird-watcher."

He didn't need more urging. "Mind if I take the wagon?"

"Not at all. Enjoy yourself."

An afternoon alone with Abby in the woods didn't sound
like a bad idea. Maybe he could make some progress in discovering how she felt about him? The idea that he might
want to settle down and maybe start a family had been so
foreign to his way of thinking until a few days ago that he
couldn't be sure of what he was feeling.

When Joe reached the entrance to the wetlands, he saw
Abby's bicycle leaning against a tree. She had to be some-

where nearby. He called out and stood to see farther into the marsh. Nothing. Maybe she had gone the other way. The place was over four hundred square acres.

He turned Bendy around and caught sight of Abby's green dress down by the abandoned farm. What was she doing there? The place was posted no trespassing in a dozen places.

She hurried across the road into the vacant field. There was something almost secretive about her movement. What was she up to?

She crawled through the fence nearby and looked up at him in surprise. "What are you doing here?"

"I thought I would come enjoy your company. It's odd that I find you aren't looking for birds at all. What are you doing, Abby?"

"I saw an owl go into that barn. I wanted a closer look."

"You left your bicycle and walked all the way through those weeds instead of using the road to see an owl?"

"There was a pheasant, too."

"I don't buy it. You have cobwebs on your *kapp*. Your apron is damp at the knees and you smell like pine cleaner."

"We shouldn't be here. Someone may see us."

He was getting frustrated. "It's a public place, Abby. What does it matter if we're seen?"

"Please, Joe. Just go."

"I think I'll have a look around first."

"Joe, listen to me. It's important that no one knows I've been coming here."

She wasn't looking at him. He wanted to see her eyes. "Why? Because you're trespassing? Abby, look at me and try telling the truth."

She seemed to fold in on herself as she stared at the ground. "I'm not trespassing. The farm is mine. I inherited it from my grandparents. I'm here making the inside fit to live in."

"I don't understand. Why the secrecy?"

"My father has control of my property. If anyone is watching the place and I'm seen, my father's men will drag me back to Kansas City."

Drag her back to Kansas City? What did she mean? Suddenly a cold suspicion formed in his mind. "Who are you?"

Abby bowed her head. "I used to be Victoria Abigail Worthington. A sad creature. Now I'm Abigail Martin. An Amish maid at the Harts Haven Inn."

His mind was reeling. "Those men who came to the inn. They were looking for you. You're the ill woman they were searching for."

"I told you that was a lie. I'm not ill. My father is a cruel man. He abused my mother and me."

"So you ran away from home?"

"I wanted to return to the place where I was happiest. This is it. It's not much to look at now but once it was a well-tended and well-loved home. My grandparents left it to me. My father clearly doesn't care about it, but he doesn't want me to have it, either. If he discovers I'm here, he'll send people to get me."

"How could he do that? You're a grown woman."

"Trust me when I say he has his ways. I have a plan to recover my inheritance through the courts. When I've done that, I'll make my home on the farm, but for now he can't know I've been here."

Joe wasn't sure what to believe. Every time he thought he was getting to know Abby, she unfolded another secret. Who was the real Abby Martin?

It was too much to take in. "Put your bike in the back. I'll drive you home."

"Are you angry with me, Joe?"

"I would have to know who I'm talking to before I decide if I'm angry with her."

Abby wanted to cry but that wouldn't solve anything. Joe was right to be angry with her. She couldn't blame him. She lifted her bicycle into the back of his wagon and climbed up to the seat beside him. They rode in silence until they reached the river bridge. She had made such a mess of things and she didn't know how to make it right.

"I wanted to tell you," she said at last.

"You had plenty of opportunities. It's not like I'm a hard man to find. I thought we were friends."

"We are."

"Who is my friend? Abby Martin or Victoria somebody."

"Victoria may be my legal name, but she is not who I am. I'm the Amish woman who hung out her window to scold you for being rude the first day we met. I'm the one you helped to get over her fear of horses. I told you once that I said goodbye to Victoria Worthington in Columbia, Missouri, and I meant that. Abby Martin is the woman who wants you to understand that she has come to cherish your friendship more than anything, but she isn't free of her past. Until she is, she must be careful. I'm asking you to trust her."

Abby held her breath and prayed that their bond of friendship was strong enough to withstand her deception.

He cast a sidelong glance her way. "Are there other things you aren't telling me?"

"Yes."

His mouth dropped open. "Unbelievable. You are asking a lot."

"I know that."

"So I'm supposed to carry on as though I didn't just find out you are not who you pretend to be. Until such time as you decide it's okay for me to know the rest. Is that about it?"

"Yes."

She could tell he was aggravated. "I can't believe this. Does anyone else know this about you?"

"Herbert Young, he's my attorney. He's going to help me recover my inheritance and legally change my name. Rose knows everything."

"What about Susanna, Grace and Bertha?"

"They don't know anything about Victoria."

He turned to stare at her. His eyes were hard as stones. "You have to tell them."

"No. The fewer people who know, the safer I am."

He frowned. "Safer? Are you in danger?"

"My father will stop at nothing to maintain control of what is rightfully mine. I don't even know why, but yes, I'm in danger. If he discovers where I am, he will make sure I disappear. He has the means to do it. No one will hear from me again."

He slowly shook his head. "I don't know what to make of this."

She sensed he was relenting. "I'm sorry I had to involve you."

"There's something else. The widows all know you weren't raised in an Amish home."

"You told them?"

"After your pancakes they were working it out themselves."

"Oh, dear. They haven't said anything."

"They see how much you want to be accepted in this

community, so they've decided to help you learn what you need to know."

"My cooking and quilting lessons. Now I get it. Oh, those wonderful women."

"Which is why you should tell them who you really are. They won't blabber it about."

"I can't."

"Look. They already know you weren't raised Amish. Does it really matter that they know your name?"

Abby closed her eyes. She had been so determined to regain her life by herself. Maybe she didn't have to do it alone. Rose knew, Herbert knew, now Joe. Maybe it would be okay. "I just need a little more time. A few more days. By then Herbert will have filed my court case and everything will be out in the open."

Only she had other secrets, too. The day would come when she would have to share those with Joe, and she dreaded it.

"How bad of shape is the house in? The outside is a wreck."

"I have my work cut out, but I'll get it fixed up."

"I could give you a hand," he said grudgingly.

A chill clutched her heart. There was no telling what her father's men would do to him if they caught him with her. "No. I'm handling it. I don't want you there."

"Fine." He pressed his lips into a tight line and didn't say anything else.

Abby looked away. Maybe someday when he knew the whole story, he could forgive her.

Joe kept his mouth clamped shut as the pain of her rejection sank in. She didn't need or want him to be part of her life. Why had he thought she felt something for him? He'd been a fool. He was destined to live his life alone. He knew that now. He'd just forgotten it for a little while. He wouldn't wait the two weeks to leave. He'd get someone to haul his trailer to Oklahoma tomorrow. The sooner he put Abby Martin Victoria somebody out of his life the happier he would be.

When they reached the inn, Abby waited for several seconds. "All I ask is for your understanding, Joe. Please."

He was too hurt and angry to even speak. She jumped down from the wagon, stumbled and fell to her knees behind Bendy. Startled, the horse kicked out, catching her in the side. She crumpled to the ground, writhing in pain.

Joe's heart dropped to the pit of his stomach. He vaulted out of the cart and dropped to his knees at her side. "Lie still. Where does it hurt?"

She was gasping for air and clutching her abdomen. "Get Rose. Hurry. Please, God, don't take my baby."

Joe rocked back on his heels in shock. Baby? What baby?

The door of the inn flew open, and Rose rushed out. "I saw what happened. Abby, are you all right?"

"It hurts to breathe. Am I going to lose my baby?"

"Don't think such a thing. We'll get you to Bertha's office right away. Joe, make room for her in the back of the wagon."

He rose slowly to his feet and stood staring at Abby. Was he going to lose her, too? It was his worst nightmare all over again.

"Joe!" Rose stood and took him by the shoulders. "Abby needs help. Make room for her in the wagon. Now."

He nodded and hurried to the back, where he lifted out Abby's bike and let the tailgate down. He rushed back to Rose's side, feeling helpless.

"Stay with her," Rose said. "I'll get some quilts and pillows." She ran into the house.

Joe sank to his knees beside Abby. She reached for him and he grasped her hand. "It's going to be fine, Abby."

"I'm sorry. I know you must be ashamed of me."

"Don't talk nonsense."

"I wanted to tell you." She turned her face away.

"Now I know. Lie still. We'll get you to Bertha's in a few minutes and everything will be fine." He tried to put as much reassurance into his voice as he could, but he didn't believe what he said.

Rose, Grace and Susanna came out carrying pillows and blankets. Susanna climbed into the wagon and quickly spread them out. "Bring her here, Joe. Be careful."

Like he needed to be told that. His arms were shaking as he gently lifted Abby and placed her on the makeshift bed.

"I'll go phone to let Bertha know you're coming," Grace said and raced toward the phone shack.

Susanna got out of the wagon and helped her mother in. Rose knelt beside Abby and Joe took the reins. Within a few nerve-racking minutes he pulled to a stop in front of Bertha's office. She was waiting at the door and held it open as Joe carried Abby inside.

He laid her on the exam table and stepped back. Her eyes so full of fear sought his. "Bertha will take *goot* care of you," he said. "Have faith."

"I'm sorry, Joe."

What did she have to be sorry about? All she had asked for was his understanding. He was the one who'd let her down the same way he'd let his family down. He turned on his heels and fled the room.

Abby clutched Rose's hand as Bertha examined her. Finally she stood back. "I'm going to get my ultrasound machine so I can take a better look at what's going on. Your baby's heartbeat is still strong but fast."

"Please, God, don't take my child." How could she love someone so much?

"Have faith, Abby. *Gott* is with you," Rose said. "He is your strength."

Bertha returned with a large gray machine with a screen like a television. She put cold gel on Abby's stomach and began moving a probe around. She switched on the sound and the steady rapid beat of the baby's heart filled the room.

Abby started crying. "Is she all right?"

"As far as I can tell, she or he is fine. Would you like to see?" Bertha turned the screen so Abby could view it, too.

There in the grainy gray-and-black picture lay a tiny babe. "I see her. She's stretching." Abby went from tears to giggles in a flat second. Reaching out, Abby touched her fingers to the screen. "She's wonderful. Or he is." She didn't care which.

"The placenta is intact. I don't see any blood clots or leaking but I'm going to want you on bed rest for a few days just to make sure. You've had quite a fright. You are also going to have sore ribs for a few days. Thankfully the horse didn't kick you with its full might. You can get dressed now. Go home and straight to bed. If you feel fine in a few days you can go back to your regular routine. Any concerns, come see me straightaway."

"Thank you, Dr. Bertha."

"You're welcome, my dear." She pushed the machine out of the room.

Abby let her head fall back on the pillow. Her baby was fine but what about her friendship with Joseph? She looked at Rose. "He was shocked, wasn't he?"

"Of course." Rose patted Abby's hand. "Joe is a sensible young man. He knows we all make mistakes. He'll not hold this against you."

"How can I face him? What should I say?"

"You will figure it out."

Abby bit the corner of her lip. Joe had been angry with her for keeping her true identity a secret and now he knew this secret, too. Was he disgusted by her? Would he ever trust her again? Did she even have a right to ask given that she still harbored a horrible secret? She didn't want to see the revulsion in his eyes if he ever learned what she had done.

Joe was sitting against the wagon wheel with his head in his hands when he heard the door to Bertha's office open. He looked up and saw Rose. "How is she?"

"Very frightened. She had the wind knocked out of her and she's going to have quite a bruise on her side, but otherwise she is fine."

"And her…baby?"

"Bertha says everything looks fine, but she wants Abby on bed rest for a couple of days."

"Thank God." He could finally draw a deep breath.

"This wasn't your fault, Joe."

"We were quarreling. I was so angry with her. She just wanted to get away from me."

"There will be plenty of time for the two of you to make up. She is worried what you think about her now that you've learned she is pregnant."

He looked up at Rose. "Honestly, I don't know how I feel about it."

"Then you have a lot of thinking and praying to do. Whatever you decide, know that Abby needs our help and support."

"She doesn't want my help," he said bitterly.

"Oh, Joseph, you have a lot to learn about her. She is as frightened of trusting her heart as you are."

He was scared and with good reason. He couldn't face losing another person he cared about. "I can't do it, Rose. I can't."

"Is it the baby?"

"I won't lie. It was a shock. Do you know who the father is?"

"I don't."

"She needs him, not me."

Rose shook her head. "I don't believe that's true, or she wouldn't be hiding here. She deserves our support. I know this is hard for you but nothing worthwhile comes easily. Please don't turn your back on her."

He raked his fingers through his hair. Rose was right. Abby was pregnant, alone and hiding from her abusive father. No matter what his personal feelings were, she deserved help.

Abby didn't see Joe after he drove her home from Bertha's office. Not that evening or during the next two days, but his trailer was still parked in the same place. He was avoiding her. Who could blame him? Whatever had been between them wasn't going to survive this. She saw that now. Any hopes she harbored otherwise were a fantasy.

Three days after her accident she was feeling good enough to ride out to the bird sanctuary in the afternoon. At least at the farm she felt that she was accomplishing something. She leaned her bike against her favorite tree and turned around as Joe stepped out of the brush. It was the first time she had seen him in days and her heart gave a happy leap before she ruthlessly pushed her happiness aside. "What are you doing? I said you couldn't be here."

"You also said that you were in danger and that your father could make you disappear. It might be harder to do that with a witness. I'm not leaving here until you do."

It was a kind gesture and she adored him for it. There was great comfort in knowing he would be close. "Joe, about my pregnancy."

"It is what it is." He looked so stern.

"I can explain."

"No need. Let's see how much work needs doing to make this place a fit home."

It wasn't what she wanted to hear but at least he wasn't avoiding her anymore. She would accept his help gratefully. "Okay, but you have to follow me and do as I say."

"Lead on."

She climbed through the fence and followed the game trail back to the road. After waiting and checking for any vehicles, she darted across the road with Joe on her heels. She led the way around to the back of the house and touched her fingers to her lips. She listened at the door for a few moments and then eased it open. The flour she'd left sprinkled on the floor was untouched. Only then did she relax. "Come in. The place is still something of a wreck but I'm making progress."

"If your attorney is going to restore this property to you anyway, why risk coming here repeatedly?"

"I can't leave it like this. My grandparents loved this place. The more I get done, the sooner I can move in when it's mine again. I waited years to be back here. I reckon I'm impatient."

"What's with the flour on the floor?"

"Each time I leave, I sprinkle a fresh coat so I can see if anyone has walked in while I was gone."

"That's actually smart."

It felt like high praise coming from him. *"Danki."*

She led the way into the kitchen and pointed to the broken window. "That's where the worst damage is. You can see the floor has rotted away beneath the window."

He moved closer to examine it. "It won't take much to replace the floorboards and the drywall. You should fix the window first."

"My father has someone who drives by to check on the place. I've seen tire tracks where he has pulled in and then left. I saw his truck once. He hasn't come into the house. I don't want him to see any changes on the outside."

"Who is it?"

"I don't know. All I know is that it's someone who lives around here."

"You're playing hide-and-seek with an unknown person who could show up at any moment and whisk you away. You should get out of here and not come back. It doesn't matter that your grandparents loved this place. I'm pretty sure they loved you more. Do you really think this is what they would want from you?"

"Maybe not, but I'm staying. You are welcome to leave."

He took off his hat and laid it on the table then started to roll up his sleeves. "Has anyone told you that you are a stubborn woman?"

"No, but someone once said I had determination and that wasn't a bad thing."

"The idiot didn't know what he was talking about. Let's see the rest of the place."

He wasn't angry. Her spirits rose. Maybe there was some hope for their friendship after all.

Abby took him through the downstairs rooms and then led the way up the steep narrow stairs to the upper floor. "This is where I've gotten the most done."

He walked into each room and then came back to the hall. "Is there only one way up here?"

"Yes."

He went to the windows on both sides of the house, opened them and leaned out. He shut them and turned to her. "That's a long drop. You'd break a leg if you had to jump."

"Why would I jump out the window?"

He didn't say anything. He led the way downstairs and turned to her in the kitchen. "What needs to be done first?"

Seeing him so willing to help in spite of everything warmed her heart. "Joe, thank you for coming. I know I said I didn't want you here but that isn't true. There isn't anyone I would rather have doing this with me."

His expression softened. "And here I thought you didn't appreciate me."

She stepped close and laid her hand on his chest. "I do. More than you realize."

He covered her hand with his. "Abby, you tie me in knots."

She turned her face aside. "I'm sorry." She couldn't think about how much she wanted to be held in his arms. She had to be strong.

"I care about you, Abby. I want you to know that."

She pressed her lips tightly together to keep from blurting out how much she cared for him, too.

A sound caught her attention. "Do you hear a vehicle?"

He tipped his head slightly to listen. "That's an airplane. There's a crop dusting service near here. I've seen them a few dozen times. They always fly low."

Their moment of closeness had passed. Abby moved away. "Herbert has been having a feud with the pilot. He buzzes the wetlands and scares the birds. Herbert thinks he does it on purpose just to annoy him. We should start with the bedroom off the hall."

Joe was able to move the bed in her grandparents' room, allowing her to clean out the pack rat's nest they found behind it. He washed the walls while she concentrated on getting the floor clean. All the while she was constantly aware of him. What would have happened if she had been honest with him from the start? It didn't matter. He would be leaving soon. She was just glad he could find it in his heart to help her after everything he had learned about her. He still didn't know the worst and she prayed he never would. They worked without speaking until he called a halt to the afternoon.

"We have enough light left," she said.

"You've done too much already. You're going home now and that's that." He picked up his hat and left by the back door. She powdered the floor and followed him out.

He loaded her bike in the back of the cart he had parked in the barn and drove the entire way home without a word.

When they returned to the inn, Joe drove off in Rose's cart. He returned a while later but didn't come up to the house. Abby could hear his saw and hammer in the barn. She wanted to see what he was doing but she was afraid he wouldn't appreciate her company. She missed the easiness that had existed between them before. She'd give anything to endure his teasing, to see him smile at her without reservation, to be his friend again, but she had lost him.

Herbert and Bertha came by that evening. They stayed to supper and he showed photos of birds that he and Bertha had taken. Before he got ready to leave, he spoke to Abby. "Is there somewhere we can talk in private?"

"Out in the garden."

She led the way, hoping he had good news to share. She was too nervous to sit on the bench and faced him with her hands clasped in front of her.

"Everything is underway. I've spoken to my friend the judge. He appointed me as your attorney so we're over that hurdle. You have an appointment tomorrow morning for a psych evaluation."

"Tomorrow?" She was shocked.

"Bertha can pull strings like you wouldn't believe. I'll drive you there."

"Has my father been told?"

"Not yet. We won't let that cat out of the bag until the hearing date is set and then you must be prepared to go into hiding. The sheriff will have a safe house ready for you. How are you doing?"

"I'm scared and trying to have faith."

"Faith is the best thing you can have. Sheriff Hart will be checking on you, but you must still take care until we have a judgment."

"I will."

"Okay. I'll let you know the minute we have a court date. Your nightmare is almost over, Abby. You're going to be free."

Nineteen

True to his word, Herbert picked her up at eight o'clock the next morning. She saw Joe and waved to him as Herbert drove out of the yard. Joe waved back and her heart grew lighter. Maybe he wasn't going to stay angry with her.

The visit to the psychiatrist's office went unexpectedly well. She was able to talk about her past and lay out her hopes and expectations for the future. When the visit was finished, she looked the doctor in the eye. "Am I sane?"

"My dear, you have had a traumatic life, but in the lake of psychiatry you aren't even wading in the shallow end. I definitely consider you a competent adult and my report will reflect that."

She shook his hand, knowing she was one step closer to reclaiming her life. If only she could share her good news with Joe. That would mean telling him why her father had her committed in the first place and she couldn't do that. She prayed he would never find out.

Abby was at the farm the following evening working in the living room when she heard a horse and buggy pull up outside. She cautiously peeked out the window. It was Joe. What was he doing? He knew better than to be seen coming to the house. He lifted a large wooden box out of the back of the buggy and came around to the rear door. She opened it for him. "I thought I said no one can know we are working here."

"I haven't seen a soul on this road in all the time we've been coming here. I brought you something." He set the box down on the floor.

"*Danki*, but can you at least put the horse and cart in the shed?"

"I will if you promise not to open the box until I get back."

"I promise." She pushed him toward the door. When he was gone, she stood staring at the beautifully finished cedar box. She could see the top was hinged. She ran her fingers over the smooth surface.

"Did you peek?" He took his hat off and hung it on the peg by the door.

"Of course not. Can I look now?"

"Not yet. It goes upstairs." He picked it up and carried it ahead of her.

At the top of the stairway he looked at her. "Which will be your bedroom?"

"The one I slept in when I was young. The one at the rear of the house that overlooks the garden in back." She went ahead of him and opened the door.

He brought the box in and set it beneath the window. It dawned on her what it was. "Is it a window seat for storage?"

"It's a window seat but there isn't much storage inside. It has another use. Go ahead and open it."

Inside she found a rolled-up rope ladder with wooden rungs. She tipped her head to look at him. "What's this for?"

"It's an escape ladder in case there's ever a fire and you can't get down the stairs." His voice cracked and he looked away. He cleared his throat. "I'll fasten it to the wall. All you have to do is toss the ladder out the window and climb down. There are a couple of smoke detectors in here, too. Put them up before you move in."

It was an odd gift, but she could see it had a great deal of importance to him. It had been made with care. "It's wonderful, Joseph."

"I just want you to be safe. You and the baby." He moved to stare out the window. "I wish I'd thought of it a long time ago." His voice sounded far away.

She realized there were tears in his eyes. "It might help to talk about it."

Joe rubbed his sleeve across his face. He needed to tell her and prayed she would forgive him. Then maybe he could forgive himself. He knelt, pulled his screwdriver from his back pocket and began fastening the window seat to the wall studs. "You're not going to like hearing it."

"Let me be the judge of that."

He cleared his throat. "The night my family died was the night before my wedding. Kara, the girl I was going to marry, didn't have much family so my parents were hosting the wedding. She stayed over to help with the baking and to get things ready. She didn't want my *mamm* to have to do it all."

"She sounds like a sweet person."

"That she was. Sweet and kind to everyone. My folks adored her. So did my sister and especially my baby brother, Henry. Everyone told me how fortunate I was to have found someone like her." He turned to face Abby. "I didn't appreciate what I had until it was all gone."

"You said you weren't there. Where were you?"

"Even back then I worked for Oliver. His company was smaller. We did mostly local jobs. I was the only Amish lad on his crew, but we were all friends. Always joking and pulling pranks on each other. They were a good bunch of fellows."

"They were your friends," she said.

"Yeah. They weren't about to let me get married without giving me an *Englisch*-style bachelor party. They showed up at my house and wouldn't take no for an answer. I went with them for one last bit of fun. I knew they'd never let me hear the end of it if I didn't.

"Oh, I knew it was wrong. I had already been baptized and taken my vows. Such a party wasn't permitted. I didn't realize how late they intended to stay out. It was after three o'clock in the morning when they got tired of trying to keep me at their party and finally took me home."

He fell silent as grim memories gripped him.

"Go on, Joe," Abby said softly.

"I saw the glow in the sky from a half mile away. The house was completely engulfed by the time we got there. Those men tried to help me put out the fire but there was nothing that could be done. Everyone I loved died that night. I don't know why God spared me except to punish me for breaking my vows."

He sighed heavily. "So now you see what a poor excuse for an Amish fellow I really am. I gave in to temptation, and God took them all away."

He couldn't look at her face. He was afraid of what he would see in her eyes. Suddenly her arms were around him and she was holding him close as she knelt beside him. "I'm so sorry, Joe. You're not to blame. It wasn't your fault. You weren't being punished."

He laid his cheek against her *kapp*. "I know that now," he whispered.

He clung to her and let go of his grief as tears rolled down his cheeks until he had none left to cry. He finally drew away from her and wiped the moisture from his face. "The thought of another fire haunts me. So I wanted to make sure you and the baby would be safe."

She was gazing at him with compassion and understanding. "It's a wonderful, fine gift, Joe. I'll cherish it forever."

"I pray you never have to use it."

"So do I."

He sniffled a couple of times. "I meant to ask how your visit with Herbert went yesterday. I saw him pick you up."

She smiled gently. "It was good."

There was so much more he wanted to say now that he was free of the guilt he had carried for so long. He stood and slipped his hands under his suspenders as he took a few steps away from her. "I've decided not to take the Oklahoma City job. I'm going to suggest Oliver ask James Shultz to take the position since I know he can handle it."

"But why?"

He gazed into her eyes. Even if she didn't love him, he

needed to tell her how he felt. "Because I've found a reason to stay in Harts Haven. That reason is you, Abby."

He took a step toward her. Pounding on the front door brought him up short. Abby went deathly pale.

Twenty

Abby caught Joe's arm as he started down the stairs for the door. "Don't open it."

Joe went cautiously to look out the window. Then he pulled the door open. It wasn't her father's man who stood outside. It was Sheriff Hart.

He tipped his trooper's hat. "Evening, folks. Herbert asked me to check in on you."

Abby looked at Joe as relief made her weak. "We're fine."

"Good. I'll take a look around outside if you don't mind. If you see anything suspicious, get word to me. Herbert is going to get you a cell phone."

"Okay." Then Abby remembered the white truck. "There is a hay shed out behind the barn. Do you know someone who might be using it?"

"On this place. No, ma'am. Why?"

"It's probably nothing, but a grass strip has been mowed on one side of the building and I saw a white flatbed truck go into the field and come out fifteen minutes later with a load of straw bales."

"Did you get the make or plate number?"

She shook her head. "I didn't. It was white."

"There's a lot of white trucks in this county, ma'am, but I'll check it out. I also wanted to let you know there's a line of thunderstorms headed this way. Could be severe, but there's no tornado watches yet. You might want to think about getting back to town before you get wet. I noticed the open wagon and the bicycle in the shed. Unless you're planning on spending the night?"

"Nee." Joe shook his head emphatically.

Sheriff Hart smiled and touched his hat brim. "Okay, have a nice evening and keep an eye on the sky."

He walked back to his cruiser, got in and drove toward the entrance to the hayfield. Abby closed the door. "I put my trust in God, but it feels good to have the police keeping an eye on me. Let's finish up and go home."

"Abby, *danki*. For understanding."

"You have carried a heavy burden for a long time."

"I'm grateful that you listened and understood. It has given me hope. Abby, there are so many things I want to say to you. I care for you deeply." There was a hint of uncertainty in his voice.

He was waiting for her to say something. She drew a shaky breath. Joe cared for her. He was willing to give up his job and stay in Harts Haven for her. After all that he knew about her. Did she dare hope for a future with him?

"Joe, there's something else you need to know."

He smiled softly and took her hand. "What burden do you carry that you haven't shared with me?"

There was another knock at the door. Abby reached for the doorknob thankful for the reprieve. "The sheriff must have forgotten something."

She opened the door. Rose stood on the porch. "We brought you company, but Herbert thinks he spotted a barred owl fly into the barn. He and Bertha have gone to look. He has news."

"News about what?" Joe asked.

"That legal matter he's looking into for me," Abby said quickly.

"We brought cookies and lemonade to celebrate," Grace said, carrying a basket over her arms.

"So this is where you've been going every afternoon," Susanna said, looking the place over.

"Yes, Joe has been helping with some repair work. I'm afraid the place is a bit run-down." She took the basket from Grace. "Joe, show them into the living room. Rose, would you help me in the kitchen?"

Once the two of them were alone, Abby pressed a hand to her forehead. "Rose, why did you bring Grace and Susanna? No one is supposed to know about this place until after my court hearing."

Rose took the basket and set it on the table. She began to unpack it. "We are your friends. We are here to help. Just like Joe."

"You know that Herbert is helping me recover this property, but you don't know the reason I lost it in the first place." It was so hard to admit how weak she had been.

"Maybe it's time you told all of us," Rose said softly.

Abby turned away to get some of the dusty glasses out of the cupboard. She carried them to the sink and began to wash them. When they were clean and dry, she turned to face Rose. "I'm ashamed."

"We will understand. So will Joe. He's in love with you, Abby. You know that, don't you?"

Abby wanted it to be true. "He said he cared deeply for me, but he didn't say love."

Rose gave a dismissive wave of her hand. "Men rarely say those things, but I can tell. I can also tell that you're in love with him. There's no use denying it."

Abby took several unsteady steps to the table, pulled out a chair and sat down. She hung her head. "I tried not to fall in love with him."

"Why?"

"Because he's a fine man and a wonderful friend. He deserves so much better than a mess like me."

Rose wrapped her arms around Abby. "You aren't a mess. You are a child of *Gott*."

Herbert and Bertha came into the kitchen a few minutes later. Rose patted Abby's shoulder and went back to unpacking the basket.

Herbert smiled broadly. "It was a barred owl. I captured some wonderful calls."

"We saw the sheriff go by. He seemed in a hurry," Bertha said.

"I must call him when we get back to town. The cell service is terrible out here." Herbert grew serious. "Abby, our request for an expedited hearing has been granted. Your court date is on Monday. We'll meet with Judge Aberdeen at three o'clock."

Abby sat up straight. She couldn't believe what she was hearing. "This Monday?"

"Yes."

"Are we ready?"

"Everything is in order. Your father will be notified tomorrow so you must be prepared to go with Sheriff Hart first thing in the morning."

She could be free in just a few days. Her life would be restored. She could reclaim her property and do anything she wanted with the farm. Most important, she could raise her child without fear.

And she wanted Joe to be a part of that.

She had to have faith that he would understand. She had lacked faith as a young girl and made a terrible choice, but she was a woman now. An Amish woman whose faith must be the bedrock of her existence. God was good and He was her strength.

Abby took a deep breath and raised her chin. "I'd like to speak to Joe alone."

Rose smiled and nodded. "I'll send him in. Bertha, help me take the cookies and drinks into the living room. Herbert, go find a seat."

Joe came into the kitchen a few moments later. "Rose said you wanted to see me?"

She took his hand. "I care about you, too, Joe." Joy filled his eyes. He squeezed her fingers. "But there is something I need to tell you." She opened her mouth and shut it again. This was so hard.

"Okay, take your time."

Abby gestured toward a chair. "I think you should sit down."

The front door banged opened. Startled, she looked that way as her father walked in with two of his men. Herbert and the women rushed in to see what was going on. Victor's cold eyes settled on her. "At last. It's time to come home, Victoria."

Joe stepped in front of her. Abby couldn't find her voice.

"Who is Victoria?" Grace asked.

"Victoria Abigail Worthington is my daughter. Who sadly suffers from a severe mental disorder that leaves her paranoid, delusional and suicidal. I'm here to protect my unborn grandchild from his insane mother in case she tries to kill herself again."

Her knees gave out and she dropped onto the chair. "I'm not insane."

Victor chuckled. "Aren't you? I'm sure you have concocted some story to match the clothing you're wearing. If she has been telling you that she is Amish, she isn't. Which sadly proves my point about her delusions. I am her legal guardian. She is under the care of my personal physician Dr. Weir. I have a letter here stating her condition as well as the papers proving that I'm her legal guardian and that I have the power to return her to her home."

Herbert stepped forward. "I would like to see those documents. I have been appointed Abby's attorney by the court."

Victor nodded to his men. One of them pulled a large envelope from his suit pocket. "Your appointment won't hold up. She has an attorney. Poor, sad child. I'm sorry she has wasted your time with her fantasies. I'm just thankful she hasn't hurt anyone else."

Abby looked at Joe. "It's not how he makes it sound."

"Abigail is not mentally ill," Bertha said firmly.

"And my doctors say she is. She needs to be back on her medications and placed in a safe environment. For her well-being and for that of her baby. Another suicide attempt by her might succeed if she isn't monitored."

Abby closed her eyes and bowed her head. "Please stop."

"Get your things, Victoria. I'm taking you home."

She found the strength to get to her feet. "I don't want

to go with you. I intend to stay here. This is my grandmother's home. She left it to me. You have no right to take it away from me."

"The court documents are in order," Herbert said. "Bertha, would you take a look at the physician's letter."

"Gladly." She marched forward and snatched it from Herbert's hands. She read it over and then handed it back. "This says she suffers from profound depression, delusions and paranoia. I have not seen any of this in the time I have known this young woman. We have a report from our own psychiatrist that says she is fine."

"You think a sane person professes to be an Amish woman while telling everyone about her cruel father? This is part of her long-standing paranoid delusion. I haven't taken anything away from Victoria. Your property remains in a trust overseen by me and my attorney, reviewed annually by the court."

Two more of his men came through the door. Abby's heart fell to her feet. He was going to win. "I have filed a petition to restore my capacity. The court will hear my case."

Her father stepped around Joe and leaned close to her. "Poor Victoria," he whispered in her ear. "They won't."

"I'm not going anywhere with you."

"You don't want to see these well-meaning people get hurt, do you?" Menace coated his every word. "Tell them to leave. This is a family matter."

He straightened and nodded to his men. One of them grabbed Joe by the arm. "Out."

Joe looked at Abby. "I'm not going anywhere."

Rose sat down in a chair beside Abby. "The Amish do not resist evil. Our faith in God's mercy sustains us. We will stay with our sister in Christ."

Susanna and Grace moved to stand by Rose. Her father's men approached. Abby couldn't let them be harmed for her sake. "Please don't. Rose, everyone, Joe. Please leave. This is my father, and I must obey him." The words burned on her tongue.

Her father's smile didn't reach his eyes. He had won and he knew it. "You heard her. You people are trespassing. I am asking you politely to leave."

Joe yanked his arm away from the man holding him and rushed to Abby. He knelt in front of her. "This doesn't change anything. Do you hear me, Abby? It doesn't change the way I feel. It doesn't change what is between us."

She turned her face away from him. She had to make him leave for his own safety. "It wasn't real. It was part of my delusion. I see that now. Please go."

Her father's thug yanked Joe to his feet and pushed him toward the door. Rose took Abby's hand. "*'Yea, though I walk through the valley of the shadow of death, I will fear no evil: for thou art with me; thy rod and thy staff they comfort me.'* The Lord will never abandon you. He is your strength."

"Enough with the prayers, old woman. Be on your way," Victor sneered.

Herbert folded his arms over his chest. "This is kidnapping, pure and simple. She does not wish to go with you."

Abby looked up sadly. "Herbert, please don't make things worse. Take the women out of here."

"I don't know what could be worse than this," Bertha declared, picking up her purse. "All you men are poor excuses for human beings. Terrorizing a young woman. Shameful. Come along, Herbert. We will see what the sheriff has to say about this."

Her father laughed. "He will say I am within my rights

as her legal guardian to return her to the safety of my home. Have a good night."

Tears blurred Abby's vision as she watched the people she loved walk out the door. Would she ever see them again?

The door opened and a small man in a black turtleneck and black pants came in. "We've got a complication, boss."

Victor sighed heavily. "I don't like complications. Handle it."

"I can't change the weather. There's a severe thunderstorm approaching. We aren't flying anywhere until it clears out."

"How long?"

"Maybe only an hour delay if we are lucky."

"Is everything else ready?"

"Yes, the trucks are waiting."

"Then we will just have to make ourselves comfortable."

Joe stumbled as Herbert led him away from the house. Abby didn't mean it. She couldn't. She cared about him. Why had she said it was part of her delusion?

"I don't like this, Herbert," Bertha said. "We have to do something."

"There's more going on than a man who simply wants his daughter back," Herbert said.

Joe looked back at the men who were watching them. "I can't leave her."

Herbert opened the car door. "We're not leaving. Get in so it looks like we are."

"I'm staying." Joe couldn't abandon her.

"Get in the car, Joe," Herbert said loudly. Then he leaned close. "I have a plan," he whispered.

Joe reluctantly got in the vehicle. Herbert started the car

and drove toward the bridge. He stopped where the road curved around the creek. "Get out, Joe, we're going back."

"You can't go back there," Grace said. "You don't know what those men might do."

"We aren't going all the way back to the house. I just need to get close enough to listen. Bertha, as soon as you get a signal on your cell phone, call the sheriff. Even if Worthington has legal documents, I still say he's up to no good."

Herbert opened the trunk and pulled out his parabolic microphone. He closed the trunk and turned to Joe. "We need to get close to the house without being seen."

"I know a way."

"Good. Bertha, drive on. In case they are watching, we want them to see car lights traveling down the road. Hurry."

Joe led the way. The clouds were moving in quickly but a three-quarter moon rising in the east gave him enough light to find his way to the side of the barn.

Herbert put on his headphones and turned his microphone toward the house. Joe waited as long as he could then he grabbed Herbert's arm. "Can you hear her? Is she okay?"

"This is about the planes, isn't it?" Abby stared at her father, trying to see some shred of compassion or caring in his eyes.

He looked mildly surprised. "What about the planes?"

"There's an airstrip on my grandfather's land. You had it built after he died because he wouldn't have sold any part of this farm to you."

"The old goat wouldn't even talk to me."

Abby tried to figure his angle. "It's not about spraying crops. There's not enough money in that to interest you. So what is it?"

"Too bad you didn't take an interest in my business when you were younger. Maybe if you had, none of this would've happened. But you are too much like your mother."

"I take that as a beautiful compliment."

He laughed harshly. "Of course you would. It's too bad you weren't as biddable as she was. She knew her place although I did have to remind her from time to time."

"A bruised cheek, a black eye—those are what you call reminders?"

One of the men came in through the front door. "Radar shows the storm is moving in fast."

"I don't like delays, but if it can't be helped. Make some coffee, Victoria."

She didn't get up.

Her father chuckled. "You might look the part of a meek Amish housewife but you're not one. An Amish *frau* would have already offered us some. Kindness is their calling."

Abby bit back a retort. She got up and went to the stove. "Even if you take me back to Kansas City, I'll find a way to escape again."

"That's why you're not going back to Kansas City."

She spun around. "You're going to let me stay?"

"You are going to a special asylum for the mentally challenged in Mexico. A client of mine runs the place. You won't trouble me again."

Mexico. She knew he was telling the truth. Her hand trembled as she spooned coffee into the pot and shut the lid. "Are you going to tell me why?"

"I guess I have an hour to kill, don't I? Your grandfather was no fool. He made sure I would never get my hands on this land. He left it to you. I needed the use of it. While you were a minor that wasn't a problem but when you turned eighteen you would have inherited it free and clear. I couldn't have that. I had already made a considerable investment in the property."

"The airstrip?"

"Among other things."

"What did you mean when you said Grandpa was no fool?"

"His will was quite specific. In the event of your death, if you had no living heirs, the property would go to his wife's nephew in Ohio. So you see, I couldn't just have you disappear or die tragically like poor Logan. Having you declared mentally incompetent was the easiest, but it was an expensive option. Logan came up with a brilliant suggestion. If you were to have a baby, your child would inherit in the event of your death. Sadly, he was insisting on a bigger cut."

"What did you do to Logan?"

"Car accident. Speed and alcohol kills."

She had never wished Logan dead. "You're a monster."

"I'm a businessman. This property was never meant to be a major source of income but oddly it has become my most lucrative venture."

"Logan said drugs were your most lucrative venture."

"Logan talked too much."

"You're smuggling drugs in on the planes."

"She's finally worked it out. Yes, I'm a silent partner in a string of crop dusting businesses across the central US all the way from the Mexican border to Canada. Low-flying planes that stay under the radar routinely. They are so common most people don't give them a second look. You'll see the same green planes in Texas as you see in North Dakota. From here it's easy to move shipments east and west. The merchandise is hidden in straw bales and shipped out on trucks large and small. We're only an hour from two major interstate highways here. Or the plane can refuel and go as far north as Manitoba. The whole setup was Gilly's idea. We have a crop dusting airfield and a second smaller strip in this out-of-the-way place away from prying eyes. Genius really."

"Gilly. Roger Gilman was your pilot." That's who the man on the street had been.

"A sharp-eyed fellow who can spot a fake Amish woman ten paces away."

"You won't get away with it."

"I already have. I have a business associate flying in tonight. He's not going to be happy with this delay or finding you here. Take her upstairs. Put a guard on her door."

One of the men grabbed Abby's arm. She jerked away from him. "I don't like to be manhandled. I can walk."

"Move," he said.

She went up the stairwell slowly as her mind raced. She had to get away. She wasn't going to let her father ruin her child's life. She paused at her bedroom door. Her guard opened it and gave her a shove. "In."

Once the door closed behind Abby, she sank to her knees and covered her face with her hands. "Please, God. Save me. Save my child. You are my strength."

She heard a rumble of thunder in the distance. The storm was moving in fast. If she was going to get away, it had to be under the cover of the storm. She went to the window and knelt on the window seat to raise the sash. The wind rushed in making the curtains flap wildly. She heard the thunder again, closer this time. She leaned to look out the window. It was a sheer drop. There was nothing to break her fall. Even if she could risk a broken leg by jumping as Joe had said, she couldn't risk her baby's life.

She sat on the window seat and battled despair. Her

father would take her away and she would never see Joe again. And she hadn't told him that she loved him. Why hadn't she said it? She could see his earnest face, could hear his firm voice telling her nothing her father said made a difference. She drew her hand over the smooth wood of the window seat and stopped.

He cared for her enough to give her an escape ladder in case there was ever a fire. She jumped up and opened the window seat. The ladder was neatly coiled inside. All she had to do was let it down and crawl out without making too much noise. God had sent Joe to save her and her baby.

Lightning flashed and thunder crashed again outside. She carefully lowered the rope ladder out the window. The wind lashed it against the side of the house, making it bang. She pulled it back up. Would her father or his men hear the noise? Would they go out to investigate? Would she be climbing down into their arms? She shuddered at the thought.

She had to wait until the storm grew louder and trust God to see her to safety.

Twenty-One

Joe watched Herbert's face as the old man put down his microphone and took off his headphones. "Well? What did you hear? Is she okay?"

"They took her upstairs in one of the bedrooms with a guard outside her door. The storm is too loud for me to hear more. I don't see how we can get her out of there, but I have enough on this recording to interest the KBI and the DEA. I've got to get back to the bridge to get a phone signal though. Come on. The sheriff should be here soon if Bertha got through to him."

"You go. I'm not leaving." Abby was in there. He wouldn't desert her. A brilliant flash of lightning and the crash of thunder proved the storm was almost upon them. He heard raindrops begin hitting the tin roof of the barn.

"All right, but don't give them a reason to panic. Abby is safe for now."

Joe knew better. She wasn't safe. She was alone and frightened the way she had been for years. It had to be tearing her apart. He prayed the Lord would give her the strength to endure the trials she faced. He prayed Herbert would bring help in time.

Be strong, Abby. You're the strongest woman I know. Cling to the comfort our Savior gives to all who believe in Him.

"Please, God, don't let them take her away from me. I know I don't deserve her, but I love her more than my own life. Give me a chance to be part of her life. I will love her child as my own, I promise." He would take her place in a heartbeat, but he was helpless. He balled his hands into fists.

Lightning blinded him. Thunder crashed again, much closer. Cold rain pelted his face. He wiped it from his eyes so he could see the front door of the house and thanked God for the storm that was keeping them inside. *A little longer, please, God. Please don't let them leave with her.* The thought of never seeing her again squeezed his heart with unbearable pain.

The fury of the storm broke around him. Lightning and thunder crashed almost continuously as he huddled against the side of the barn. The next brilliant flash showed him a figure at the side of the house for a barest instant. He stood up straight, not sure if his eyes were playing tricks on him. He peered into the darkness, blinking away the rain.

The next flash and crash gave him another view of the house. There was no one outside. He stepped back against the barn as the rain came in torrents now.

How long would it take the sheriff to get here? Had

Herbert been able to contact him? *Please, God, save her and her child.*

He cringed when a bolt of lightning struck an old tree at the edge of the field. He should get under cover, but he couldn't lose sight of the house. His heart was in there alone and afraid.

A dark shape flew out of the rain toward him. He put out his arms as a body careened into his. He barely had time to recover his balance before arms encircled his neck and Abby burrowed against him. He wrapped his arms around her and held her tight as he sobbed her name. "Abby darling, are you hurt?"

She looked up and he could see the outline of her pale face. "I can't believe you're here."

He clutched her to him fiercely and realized she was getting soaked to the skin. He pulled her toward the yawning blackness of the barn door. When she was out of the rain, he cupped her face in his hands. "Are you okay? Did they hurt you? How did you get away?"

"You saved me."

"Me? I did nothing."

"It was your gift, Joe. It was the rope ladder. Once the storm was loud enough to cover the noise, I opened the window, let the ladder down and climbed out. You saved me."

"*Nee*, darling, you saved me." He pulled her into his arms and kissed her. As much as he never wanted to let her go, he knew he had to get her away. He took a step back. "We should go. We need to get out of here before they find you missing. I'll hitch up Bendy."

He led her to the buggy. Opening the back door, he pulled out a horse blanket and wrapped it around her. Just then he heard a shout.

She grasped his arm. "They're coming."

There was only one road away from the farm. Bendy was a fast horse, but she couldn't outrun their cars while pulling a buggy.

"Can you ride?" he asked, knowing it was a foolish question. She was afraid of horses.

"No. I can't get on a horse."

"You must. I'll keep you safe. I hope Bendy will take a rider. Or two." He grabbed the lines, coiling up the extra length, and swung up to the mare's back. She danced sideways and tossed her head at the unfamiliar burden but quickly settled. He held out his hand to Abby. "Climb on the wheel of the carriage and get up behind me."

"Joe, don't make me do this."

"They'll be here in a minute. For me and your baby you must do it. Show me that determination of yours."

"Oh, God, please help me." She climbed up as he told her and slipped onto the horse, wrapping her arms around him. It was comforting to have her holding him tight.

"Where are we going?" she asked.

"Into the marshes and then we're going to cross the river. Their car can't follow us even if they figure out which way we went. Hopefully, they will think you're hiding somewhere and give us a little lead."

"We can't cross the river. I can't swim."

"Neither can I but the horse can."

"Carrying two people?"

"It won't be that deep. She'll be able to wade across." He prayed he was telling the truth. The rain would swell the river, but it would take time unless it had been raining heavily upstream. He wouldn't know until they reached the riverbank.

He nudged Bendy with his heels and she walked out into the storm. The overgrown brush and trees along with the driving rain would help hide them until they reached the roadway. After that the first flash of lightning would make them visible to anyone looking in their direction until they reached the marshes a quarter of a mile away.

His instinct was to kick the horse into a gallop, but he didn't think he could stay on without a saddle. He hadn't ridden bareback since he was a boy. Instead he urged the mare to a quick walk. Keeping one hand wrapped in Bendy's mane with the coiled lines. He kept his other hand pressed against Abby's arms around his waist.

The storm was moving rapidly off to the east. It wouldn't be long before the rain stopped altogether, and the searchers would have better visibility.

Joe felt Abby's arms tighten. "I see car lights in the lane. Hurry, Joe."

"The marsh is just ahead. We will be safe in there."

Abby knew better. Joe didn't know her father. They wouldn't be safe anywhere. He had found her once and he would find her again. She looked back, but the car lights hadn't moved. They must be searching for her around the buildings. Maybe there was a chance for them.

Inside the entrance to the sanctuary, Joe turned toward the river and Abby slipped sideways. She scrambled to stay on. Joe had to stop the horse to pull her up against him again.

"I'm sorry."

"Don't be. I'm surprised we aren't both on the ground." He clicked his tongue to get Bendy moving again.

The tall reeds and brush scraped Abby's legs as the horse made her way into the marsh. Bendy stumbled once, nearly unseating them. Abby listened for sounds of pursuit behind them, but she heard only the wind and the occasional cry of a night bird.

After what seemed like an eternity, they reached the river. Joe stopped and half turned to look at her. "Are you ready to try this?"

"No." She shivered in the cold night air.

"Courage."

"I think I used it all up already." She closed her eyes and held on tight as Bendy went down the steep bank. A second later the water was up to Abby's knees and the horse was lunging forward. Abby lost her grip and slid off. After everything that had happened, she was going to drown in a muddy river.

She felt Joe's hand grab her arm. "I got you. Hold on. Don't let go."

She was pulling him off with her. He couldn't swim. She had to save him. She let go.

The water dragged her under but suddenly Joe's arm was around her. Her head broke the surface. Joe was in the water, but he had the lines wrapped around his arm. Bendy was pulling them to shore.

Joe found his footing first and pulled her up. The mud under her feet had never felt so wonderful. They climbed the riverbank together. She looked around. "Where are we?"

"Pretty close to the road that leads into town. Come on. I'll put you up on Bendy."

"Joe, I'd just as soon walk."

Red and blue flashing lights were rapidly approaching from the direction of the bridge. Joe hugged her. "I think we're saved."

A deputy sheriff rolled up beside them. Behind him came Bertha in Herbert's car. Rose, Grace and Susanna piled out of the car and Abby was pulled from Joe's arms.

She was swaddled in a blanket and pushed toward the car. She reached for him, but he stepped back. "Go with them. I'll be with you soon."

Abby was safe at the inn and unharmed. That was all that mattered. Joe stood in the garden outside the French doors and watched her being fussed over by Rose, Susanna and Grace. She didn't need him now. She was free. Her father would never trouble her again.

Joe wanted to take her in his arms and hold her close. He wanted to kiss her and tell her that everything would be all right. It would be for her. He was sure of that. Her friends would rally around her. They would take care of her and her baby.

Her baby.

Abby was going to be a mother. He had grappled with that knowledge unsure of exactly how he felt knowing she was going to have another man's child. Someone he'd never met.

What kind of man was he? Did he care about her at all? Had she loved him? Did she still love him?

Joe had wanted to ask her those questions, but he was afraid of the answers. He knew that Abby cared for him. But was that enough to overcome what stood between them?

The storm had moved on, leaving a clear sky overhead where the stars twinkled brightly in the rain-washed air. It would be a good night for stargazing, but he wasn't interested in doing that without Abby beside him. He paced across the patio several times then moved to stand by the roses. Abby had said she loved roses because they had their own thorns for protection. Now he knew what she'd meant. He pulled a bloom off the vine and began plucking the petals, letting them float to the ground one by one.

"You're supposed to say, 'she loves me, she loves me not,' when you do that," Abby said softly.

He hadn't heard the door open. For some reason he was afraid to look at her. He dropped the blossom. "I don't think a flower can answer that question."

"You're right. You're going to have to ask the woman."

He turned around then. "Maybe I'm not ready to hear the answer."

"I see." She looked down. "A lot has changed tonight. I can't blame you for thinking less of me."

"Less of you?" He looked at her in amazement. "You can't be serious. You were so incredibly brave. You didn't need me to come to your rescue. You rescued yourself."

"Until I was almost swept away in the river. You dove in after me. You saved me with your foresight and your kindness in the house and with the strength of your arms in the water. You are a wonderful man, Joseph Troyer. I can't thank you enough."

A wonderful man. That was good, but was he the kind of man she could love or was her heart taken? He had to know. "Okay, I'm just going to come right out and ask you. Are you in love with someone else?"

She cast him a sidelong glance. "You mean someone other than you? Like the baby's father? *Nee*, you're the one."

He straightened. "Wait. Do you mean you're in love with me?"

"Couldn't you tell when you held me in your arms at the barn?"

"There was a lot going on. I know you were grateful that I was there for you. Sometimes things can be misinterpreted in the heat of the moment."

She stepped close to him and cupped his face in her hands. "Okay. This isn't the heat of the moment now, is it? There's no drama. No one's trying to kidnap me. We aren't running for our lives. We're standing alone together in a rain-drenched flower garden that smells heavenly. So you can be sure there isn't any pressure on me right now. I'm going to say it. I love you, Joseph Troyer. No matter what happens, I want you to know that. I love you with all my heart."

He couldn't believe she meant it.

She sighed heavily. "If you don't feel the same, that doesn't change how I feel. I can't imagine that I will ever stop loving you."

"Do you mean that?"

"Yes, Joe, this is where you kiss me so I don't cry."

Joy filled his heart until it hurt. "I can't stand it when women cry." He pulled her into his arms and kissed her gently on the lips. He kissed her cheek and then each eyelid.

She drew back to look up at him in the moonlight. "And?"

"And, Abigail Martin, I love you with all my heart. You are *Gott*'s greatest gift to me. I can't imagine my life without you. I will never stop loving you until the day I die."

"It took you long enough to get around to saying that. I've been in love with you since I saw you comforting David Shetler."

"I'm not a guy who likes to be rushed."

"I'll remember that."

"I want you to be my wife, Abby. Will you marry me? This is where you say yes and kiss me or I'm going to cry."

"Yes." She threw her arms around his neck and kissed him with a passion he never expected. The night faded away until there was nothing but the feel of her in his arms and the taste of her on his lips. He never wanted to let her go. He trailed kisses across her mouth and up her cheek to the corner of her eye. He could taste the salt of her tears. She was crying.

He drew back. "What's wrong?"

"Nothing. Everything's perfect."

"Then why are you crying?"

"Because I'm so happy. You make me happy. Roses make me happy. The stars make me happy. Are you sure that you want to marry me?"

He brushed her cheek with his knuckles. "Why wouldn't I want to marry the most remarkable woman I have ever met?"

She bowed her head and rested her forehead against his chest. "Because I once tried to kill myself."

"God spared you and I will never stop giving thanks for that."

She cupped his cheek with her hand. "Okay, but I'm also pregnant."

Joe struggled to find the right thing to say. He couldn't mess this up. It was another man's child. Had she loved that man more than she loved him? Could he love another man's son or daughter?

From the corner of his eye he caught a streak of light in the sky that flared and winked out. A shooting star. Blazing for an instant and then gone as easily as he could have lost her tonight. His doubts didn't matter. All that mattered was her happiness.

He slipped his finger under her chin and lifted her face so she could see the love in his eyes. "Oh, that. It's a blessing. An unexpected gift from *Gott*."

"Are you sure?"

"Hopefully over the course of our marriage you will be pregnant a number of times. I think I'd like a big family. Five, maybe six kids."

"I was thinking three or four."

"We'll leave it up to *Gott* and take as many as He wants to give us." He knelt and pressed his forehead to the slight swell of her stomach. "Starting with this one. Hello, *liebchen*. I'm Joe. Your *mamm* says I can be your father. I hope you're okay with that."

Abby burst into tears as her heart overflowed with love for Joe. Amazing, wonderful, endearing man. How could she have mistaken what she had with Logan for love. This was pure and selfless. She had no idea why God was granting her such happiness after all her sins, but she would spend her life giving thanks every day for this amazing man.

Joe stood and gathered her close. "I thought I told you I don't like crying women."

"Too bad." She sniffled. "You're stuck with this one. You already proposed and I said yes, so we're betrothed. Got it?"

"Are you ready for a lifetime of putting up with my rude ways?"

She giggled and hiccuped. "I haven't heard a rude word out of you in weeks. I think you've shaken that bad habit."

She sobered as she realized there was still a lot she needed to tell him. She wiped the tears from her cheeks with her hands. "The things that you heard my father say. Only some of it was true. After my mother and my grandparents died, I wanted to die, too. It felt as if the world had been painted black and there was nothing in it to live for. That was wrong. I'm very glad I didn't succeed in my efforts to end it all."

He pulled her close and stroked her back. "So am I. *Gott ist goot.* You don't have to tell me more."

Safe in his arms with the sound of his heart beating beneath her ear, Abby found the strength to go on. "I want to. I want you to understand. When I was sixteen I was hospitalized for severe depression after my failed suicide attempt. It took months of therapy for me to regain my desire to live, but I recovered. That's when my father took me out of the hospital and set me up in my own rooms in his house. I was watched and medicated until I was in a stupor most of the time. One day when a nurse gave me my meds, I guess I was too out of it to swallow them. Hours later the fog started to lift. I found my pills on my pillow where they had rolled out of my mouth. I stopped taking the medications then. After a few days I realized I had been kept drugged, but I had no idea why. The next time the doctor came to see me I told her I thought my father was keeping me prisoner. She said it was a delusion and part of my illness."

"My poor darling. It makes me angry to think how you suffered."

"The nurses and people who came to take care of me wouldn't listen. They all looked at me like I was insane. It's hard to prove you're not when people have been told that you are."

She leaned back to look up at him. "That's why I was afraid to tell you. I didn't want you to look at me the way they had. With pity and repugnance. I hope you can forgive me for not being honest with you, but I was so afraid of losing you."

"I can't begin to understand what you went through. I can't imagine a father doing that to his child for the sake of money. There's nothing to forgive, my love."

She wrapped her arms around him and pressed her face to his chest. "What do you want to know about Logan?"

"Is he the baby's father?"

Abby looked up at him. "No, you are my baby's father. I will never think of this child in any other way."

"Then I don't need to know a thing about him except to say I pity him. He has no idea what he lost when he lost you. My only concern would be that he might try to take this child from us."

"He won't. My father told me that Logan died in a car accident, which I suspect was arranged by my father. I had come to despise Logan, but I never wished him ill. My father is an evil man. I can't believe my mother could have loved him."

"The sheriff said he will be in prison for a long time. He was smuggling drugs. They found a large stash at the hay shed along with an accountant who was happy to share what he knew. We will pray your father repents and asks for the Lord's forgiveness. We must forgive him. Can you do that?"

She nodded. "I know I must. I can't carry hate in my heart when my baby rests under it."

He leaned in and kissed her forehead. "Our child has a very wise mother."

"Say that again."

"You are a wise woman."

She drew back to look up at him. "No, the first part."

"Our child?"

She sighed and sank against him, wrapping her arms tightly around his chest. "I love you, Joseph Troyer. I'm so glad that Rose thought we should make a match of it."

"She and *Gott* seem to work well together."

Abby chuckled. "Never let her hear you say that."

"When will you marry me?"

"As soon as the bishop allows. I have to be baptized first. What if the congregation doesn't want me as a member after all this comes to light? I haven't exactly been a meek and modest Amish maiden."

He took her by her shoulders and gave her a little shake. "Are you serious? Can you imagine how Rose will react if we can't marry? This town will never hear the end of it. Wait! When is your baby due? I want to be married before our son or daughter arrives."

"Dr. Bertha says around the first of November."

"Okay, so a September or October wedding is possible. We'll have to finish getting the house ready. The place still needs a lot of work. The floor in the west end of the kitchen needs to be replaced and so does the drywall."

She smiled at him. "It's fortunate that I know a good contractor. I only hope I can afford him."

"Don't worry. He works for undercooked pancakes."

Her mouth fell open. "You did not just go there! You are never, ever to mention that incident again."

He laughed. "Pancakes, pancakes, pancakes. See how much I love you? I'm willing to marry a woman who can't cook."

"I'll learn."

"I know you will because you are nothing if not determined. Did I mention that I love you?"

"Not in the last few seconds," she said with a small pout.

"I love you. I'll never get tired of saying that."

"Then we are well suited because I'll never tire of hearing it. I love you, too, Joe. Kiss me again."

"I was just thinking that." He bent to cover her mouth with his and tenderly kissed her. Joseph captured her heart beneath the starry sky in a fragrant rain-drenched garden and made all her dreams come true.

Epilogue

"You're late. You know how much work we still need to do at the farm." Abby climbed awkwardly onto the wagon seat beside Joe. Her big belly got in the way of everything and made the simplest tasks that much harder. She would be so glad when her babe was born. Joe's grin said he wasn't the least bit upset by her chastisement.

He slapped the lines to get Bendy moving and drove away from the inn. "I ran into the bishop at the hardware store. He's a hard man to get away from when he's in a talkative mood."

"What did he have to say?"

"Just this and that."

"Nothing about the wedding?"

Joe snapped his fingers. "That's right. I almost forgot. The wedding has to be postponed."

Abby grabbed his arm. "What? Why?" She and the widows had been cooking and cleaning for days getting ready for the ceremony that would be held at the inn and the meals that would follow.

Joe shot her a sidelong glance. "I'm just kidding. You still have to marry me on Thursday."

She playfully pinched his arm. "That was just plain mean, Joe Troyer."

"I admit it was. You should've seen the look on your face."

"I'm having second thoughts about marrying you."

He slipped his arm around her shoulders and drew her close. He kissed her temple. "No, you're not. You've never been so sure of anything in your life."

Her heart melted the way it always did when he was near. "How can you be so sure?"

"Because that is exactly how I feel."

Abby snuggled against his shoulder. "I never knew it was possible to be this happy."

Her life had been filled with joy in the past few months. She had attended *Die Gma noch geh* for the eight-week classes and professed her desire to be baptized before the congregation afterward. The vote to accept her had been unanimous. Joe had been there looking on proudly. The bishop had read the banns to announce their upcoming wedding at the following service.

"I'm happy that you're happy," Joe said.

"Someone else is glad, too." Abby took his hand and laid it against her belly where her baby was kicking up a storm.

"He's going to be a strong fellow."

"Or a strong girl."

He grinned. "That will be fine, too. Boy or girl, it makes no difference to me."

"Are you sure?"

"Of course I am. If I don't get my boy we will just have to keep trying. There is one thing we haven't talked about."

"What would that be?"

"Names."

"I've been giving that a lot of thought."

He bopped the end of her nose with his finger. "Let's hear what you've already decided."

"I haven't decided on anything but…"

"Ja?"

"I thought perhaps, if it's a boy, we could call him Henry after your little brother."

Joe blinked back the tears that filled his eyes. "I think that would be a *wunderbar* name for our son. And if we have a daughter?"

"I was thinking we could call her Rose."

"Isn't that putting too big a burden on a girl in Harts Haven?"

"Why do you say that?"

"If we name her Rose, she's bound to become a matchmaker."

Abby patted his arm. "I know Rose likes to take the credit for getting us together but if it wasn't for this baby, I wouldn't be here at all. I never would have found the courage to escape."

"Okay, if it's a girl we can call her Rose."

When they neared the farm, Abby was surprised to see buggies parked along the road. "What's going on?"

"We're having a work frolic. Everyone has come out to help clean and repair the place and build a workshop for me in the barn so I can get my business up and running. I talked to Oliver this morning. He's going to send some business my way. He said James Schultz is working out just fine as his foreman."

"But I was going to set the place to rights." She wanted to be the one to restore her grandparents' farm.

He stopped the horse and turned to her. "Abby, this is what being a member of an Amish community means. We are a part of the whole. They help us, we help them, and we all worship as God commands."

She smiled. "You're right."

"Finally she admits it." He kissed her and sent the horse forward.

Abby belonged now. To God, to Joseph and to the community she loved. Happiness warmed her like the sunshine on her shoulders. *Gott* was *goot*.

* * * * *

SPECIAL EXCERPT FROM

She moved to Harts Haven to forget her past.
Will she find a future there this holiday season?

Read on for a sneak preview of
A Match Made at Christmas
by Patricia Davids
available October 2022 from HQN Books!

One

"Oh, Karl. Yoo-hoo!"

Karl Graber cringed at the sound of Rose Yoder calling his name. He was in no mood to deal with her this morning.

After burning the oatmeal at breakfast, he discovered his renter had moved out in the night without giving notice or paying his back rent. Now Karl was going to be late getting to the store because his buggy horse was limping.

He decided to pretend he hadn't heard Rose. Maybe the elderly Amish woman who claimed to be the most successful matchmaker in Harts Haven would go pester some other poor fellow.

Bent over Checkers's front foot, Karl noticed a stone lodged between the horse's steel shoe and his hoof was the gelding's problem.

"Hallo, Karl! I must speak with you."

The tenacity of the eighty-four-year-old romance ped-dler was another difficulty Karl had to face this morning.

"I'm not interested in meeting your latest hopeful," he muttered under his breath.

If the stubborn stone would come out, he could be on his way before the elderly woman reached the end of the block and crossed the wide street.

"*Daed*, Granny Rose is calling you." His six-year-old daughter, Rachel, stood up and waved. Rose wasn't related to Karl, but due to her advanced age most of the children in Harts Haven called her Granny.

"She's coming this way," Clara informed him from the front seat of the open buggy. His ten-year-old daughter wasn't any more excited to see Rose than Karl was. She suspected the same thing he did. Rose was on a match-making mission.

"Hallo, Granny Rose," Rachel shouted happily. "We're taking our puppies to the store so someone can buy them. Would you like to see them?"

The offending stone popped loose. Karl dropped Check-ers's hoof. "Got to get the store open, Rose. Can't take time to visit."

When he spun around, it was already too late. She had reached the buggy ahead of him. How did someone her age move so fast? She didn't even look winded.

"*Guder mariye*, Karl. I'm so glad I caught you. There is a chill in the air this morning, isn't there?"

It was the second week of November. Of course, the air was cool. Rose hadn't intercepted him for idle chitchat. He moved to step around her since she was blocking the buggy door. "Customers will be waiting for me."

Rose didn't budge. Other than picking her up and setting

her aside, he had no hope of leaving until she finished having her say. He resigned himself to hearing who she thought would be perfect for him this time. As if any woman could take the place of his Nora.

"Did you find us a new mother?" Rachel's hopeful tone stabbed his heart. Rachel was too young to remember much about the mother who died when she was three. She only knew other children had both mothers and fathers, and she wanted the same thing.

Clara scowled at her sister. "We don't need a new mother. Ours is in Heaven. No one can replace her."

Clara understood. She was old enough to remember what Nora had been like. A sweet, gentle, bright and loving woman. The world was a darker place without her.

Rose's cheerful expression softened with sympathy. "I'm still looking for someone special to join your family. Clara is right. She won't be your mother. Instead, she will be your stepmother, but she will love you and take care of you as if you were her own."

Rachel sighed. "I hope you find her soon."

"That's enough, Rachel," Karl said. "What do you want, Rose?"

"I'm here to tell you about the new teacher. She arrived yesterday. She and her sister are staying at the inn for the time being. They are Grace Sutter's nieces from the Amish side of her family."

Grace was another elderly widow, Old Order Mennonite, and co-owner of the Harts Haven Inn along with Rose and Rose's widowed daughter, Susanna King. The trio were all fond of meddling. A single man stood little chance of remaining unattached in this Amish community unless he avoided the widows. Rose's knowing smile put Karl on his guard.

Rachel clapped her hands. "Yay, the new teacher is here. Now I can go back to school and be in the Christmas program. I hope I get to be an angel like Thea and Miriam Bachman last year. Their mother made the most beautiful wings for them."

Rose grinned. "Your teacher's name is Sophie Eicher. Her sister is Joanna. They are lovely young women."

"Also single and hoping to find husbands in Harts Haven. I know what you're doing, Rose. Not interested!" If his cutting tone didn't drive his point home, maybe his scowl would.

Rose puffed up like an angry little hen. "Don't take that tone with me, Karl Graber. For shame."

He was thirty-two years old, but she made him feel like an errant toddler. "I'm sorry."

She inclined her head. "You are forgiven. I stopped to tell you we are hosting a welcome party at the inn on Saturday so folks can meet Sophie and her sister. Would you kindly spread the word?"

He eyed her suspiciously. Where was the catch? "Sure. What time?"

"We'll start at noon, but folks can come and go as they please." She turned to his daughters. "I know you girls must be excited to go back to school."

"Teacher Becky had to leave to take care of her mother because she got sick," Rachel said. "I only went to school for one week. I don't think I learned much."

"I taught you letters and numbers," Karl said.

Rachel's lower lip jutted out. "Only so I could help at the store. Not to read a book."

There weren't enough hours in the day to run the hardware store, manage the farm work, cook, keep house and still find time to instruct his daughters. Most days, he struggled just to get out of bed. He was doing the best he could.

"How soon will school resume?" he asked Rose.

"The bishop and the school board haven't decided." She leveled her gaze at him. "I know you'll be at the welcome party."

That was the catch. Grimacing, he shook his head. "Social gatherings aren't something I enjoy."

Her eyes narrowed. "It is common courtesy to introduce yourself and your *kinder* to the new teacher. You remember what courtesy is, don't you, Karl?" Rose turned on her heels and strode away.

His conscience smote him. It wasn't right to be rude to anyone, yet alone an elder. He caught up with her in a few steps. "Rose, wait. I'm sorry."

Glancing over his shoulder to make sure the girls couldn't overhear; he lowered his voice. "It hasn't been easy for me. Nora was the one who loved company. It doesn't feel right to do things without her. It just makes me miss her more."

Instantly, he was sorry he had shared that much.

Rose's expression softened. "You have your daughters to think of, Karl. Nora wouldn't want them shut up in the store all day. Nor would she approve of you taking them home straight after church services instead of letting them play with their friends so you can avoid talking to people. I understand grief, Karl. I buried my husband and a son-in-law who was dear to me. We all cope with loss differently, but don't let your grief rob your *kinder* of their childhood."

He focused on his feet. Maybe Rose was right. In his struggle to get through each day, he hadn't always put his children's welfare first. "I reckon I could close early for once. I'll bring the girls to meet their new teacher."

He looked up with a hard stare. "But don't get the idea that I'll go along with any of your matchmaking schemes."

She shook her head. "Sophie needs someone special. You are completely wrong for her. I'm afraid the two of you would be at each other's throats within a week."

He drew back. "If she's hard to get along with, should she be teaching?"

Rose poked her finger into his chest. "You are the problem, not Sophie."

"Me? What's wrong with me?"

"Plenty. You figure it out. Relax. You aren't on my list of potential suitors."

That made him smile. "You have a list already? I thought she only arrived yesterday."

Rose grinned and winked. "There aren't that many single Amish fellows in this area."

Karl watched her walk away with a sense of relief that was quickly followed by an unsettling question. What did Rose think was wrong with him?

He kept to himself, but who could blame him? Losing his wife, his childhood sweetheart, had nearly broken him. Standing by helplessly as cancer sucked the life from her despite everything the doctors tried had devastated him.

His beautiful Nora had endured terrible pain. In her last days, he had stopped praying for her to be healed and only asked that God end her suffering and take her home. The guilt from those anguished thoughts never left him. He couldn't love another woman. He was better off alone. He had his daughters. That was enough.

"*Daed*, we're going to be late," Clara called out.

Clara was trying hard to be his helper at home and in the business the way her mother had been. She worked hard. Perhaps too hard for a child her age. He returned to the buggy and got in. At least he didn't have to worry about Rose trying to set him up with the new teacher. He wasn't on her list.

Her sister, Joanna, barged into Sophie Eicher's room and threw open the curtains. Bright sunlight streamed in. Sophie closed her eyes against the sudden glare. Sometimes Joanna's eagerness to embrace life was annoying. "Will you shut those?"

"In a minute. I'm ready to see this new town of ours, aren't you?"

Was she? What if coming to Harts Haven had been a mistake? She would meet all new people while keeping her secret. Could she pretend she was fine, and that everything was normal? "I think I'd rather rest for another day."

Joanna spun around with her hands on her hips. "Honestly, Sophie, if you're just going to sit in a dark room and contemplate your own death, why did we move a thousand miles to the middle of nowhere?"

"You didn't have to come, and I'm not contemplating my death."

Maybe she thought about dying more than most people, but she had good reason. She had survived breast cancer for now, but it would be back. How many weeks or months would she have? She took her *kapp* from the nightstand, put it on and pinned it in place as she prayed.

Please, Gott, *let my sister return to Ohio before then and if she won't, let me live long enough to see her settled.*

Joanna left the window to kneel in front of Sophie. "I came with you because I wasn't about to let you have an adventure without me. I'm sorry if I upset you."

"You didn't." Sophie couldn't stay annoyed with her sister for long. They weren't related by blood, but they were sisters of the heart. Joanna had been adopted as an infant when Sophie was nine. They looked nothing alike. Sophie was slender, blond, with sky blue eyes and an ordinary face. Joanna was full-figured with abundant dark curly hair that she hated, coffee-colored eyes and adorable dimples. Sophie always felt plain beside her, but she wasn't jealous of her sister's beauty. It was a gift from God.

Joanna grasped the ribbons of Sophie's *kapp* and tugged gently. "You need to start enjoying your new life."

"Please don't pull on my *kapp*." Sophie's hair had finally grown long enough to part in the middle and tuck behind her ears allowing her to look like a normal Amish woman. Losing her hip-length hair during her chemotherapy had been devastating. She checked to make sure her bobby pins were secure.

"You look fine. Let's get out there and discover the best place to have coffee and shoofly pie. And a post office. I want to mail a letter to *Daed*. I need stamps."

Their father had recently married a widow with three young children. It was another reason Sophie had taken the job in Harts Haven. She didn't want to be a burden to the new family when her illness returned. Joanna had refused to stay behind. Perhaps because she knew in her heart that Sophie would need her at the end, even if she would never admit that. Joanna believed Sophie was cured.

"We should go house hunting soon," Joanna announced. "It's wonderful that *Aenti* Grace is letting us stay at her inn, but don't you want your own home?"

Sophie rolled her eyes. "You can't know how eagerly I look forward to picking up after you, cooking for you and doing all the chores, including your laundry again."

Joanna's infectious grin widened. "*Goot*. That's the spirit. We are going to love living here. Just to show you I have matured, I will do my own laundry in our new home. Can we go now? I want to see what Harts Haven has to offer."

Her sister's unflagging optimism had supported Sophie through the devastation of her diagnosis and the worst of her treatments. She couldn't love her more. "Unless I miss my guess, you are more interested in checking out the local bachelors rather than real estate."

Joanna giggled. It was a sweet sound that always made Sophie smile. "We girls never know when the right fellow will come along. It could happen today."

"For you maybe." Sophie looked away. Marriage was out of the question for her. How could she burden any man with what she knew waited for her?

Joanna gripped Sophie's hand. "You can't give up on love because Nate turned out to be a coward."

Sophie flinched at the painful reminder. "Nate was simply being practical when he broke our engagement. He didn't want to be tied to a dying wife." She had hoped for his support, but she couldn't blame him for his decision.

Everyone in their small Ohio community knew Sophie Eicher was a walking dead woman. Breast cancer had killed her mother and her grandmother. The pitying looks, the way people chose their words so carefully around her, had been stifling. It had been like living in a coffin waiting for the funeral to begin, but it had been even harder on Joanna, who didn't share the community's outlook. She railed against it until the bishop reprimanded her for not accepting God's will.

Joanna grabbed Sophie's shoulders and shook her. "You didn't die. Your last scan was negative. You beat your cancer."

Her little sister was still railing against the inevitable.

"You can't say that with any confidence," Sophie said gently.

"Bah! Only *Gott* knows our fate. Until then, live life to the fullest. Have faith in *Gott*'s goodness and mercy. I believe my stodgy older sister will scold me and love me for a hundred years."

"That is unlikely."

Joanna sighed and sat beside Sophie. "You don't want anyone here to know about your illness. I understand that. We came to Harts Haven so you could start over. Here people will see a kind, generous, intelligent woman, not someone who is sick, but only if you go out and meet them. Now, get rid of that anxious frown and let's go."

Sophie might not have years to live, but dwelling on the fact wouldn't change the outcome. Joanna pulled her to her feet. Once she was upright, Sophie pushed aside her reservations about their move. She had made her decision and would stick to it. This was the right thing for her, but more importantly for Joanna. If Joanna refused to return home, then before Sophie left this earth, she would do everything in her power to see her sister happily married and settled. She would need someone to lean on when the time came.

"All right. We'll explore the town, but I want to see the school as soon as possible. There's no telling what shape the last teacher left things in. I sincerely hope she was a good record keeper. I need to know exactly what I have to work with before I meet with the school board."

Work was exactly what Sophie needed. Setting things to right, solving problems, creating order, opening children's minds to the value of learning, those were the things she loved.

"You need to dress warm. It's chilly out. Take your heavy bonnet, a scarf, your winter coat and gloves."

Sophie arched one eyebrow. "Is there a blizzard blowing?"

"I know you still get cold easily."

It was true. The cold affected her more than it used to. She had lost weight during her cancer treatments. And strength.

Sophie pulled Joanna close and hugged her. "You are the best sister ever."

Joanna hugged her back. "I'll remind you of that the next time I do something that drives you up the wall."

"Which will be shortly, I'm sure."

Joanna laughed as she drew away. "O ye of little faith. Let's go."

The two women went downstairs, where they found their aunt in the large kitchen rolling out dough. Grace Sutter was Sophie's father's sister. She had been raised in an Amish home but chose not to be baptized into the Amish faith. Instead, she married a Mennonite farmer. Now a widow, she had come to Kansas and settled in the Amish and Old Order Mennonite community of Harts Haven a few years earlier. The family kept in touch by writing numerous letters. It was Grace who first suggested Sophie apply for the teaching position in Harts Haven. It had been Joanna who had nagged Sophie into doing so. It was still hard to believe she got the job.

Teachers were either in short supply or Grace's recommendation carried a lot of weight with the local Amish bishop. Grace knew about Sophie's past illness, but like Joanna, her aunt believed Sophie was cured and had agreed not to mention it to anyone.

Grace looked up from her work. "Are you off to do some exploring?"

"We are," Sophie said. "Joanna wants to find the best place for coffee and shoofly pie."

"You don't have to go far. Just through those doors to our dining room. You won't find better baked goods anywhere within a hundred miles."

"There," Sophie said. "Now we don't have to go out in the cold."

"We still need to find the post office and the school."

The outside door opened. Rose Yoder came in. Sophie had taken an instant liking to the spry elderly woman with twinkling eyes behind her wire-rimmed glasses when they met the previous evening.

Rose smiled widely at the sight of her guests. "Good morning to you both. I hope you slept well."

"We did, but now we are off to see Harts Haven," Joanna announced.

"Would it be too much trouble to ask you to stop by the hardware store and get a roll of lamp wick for me?" Rose asked.

Grace laid her rolling pin aside. "I thought you got some a few days ago."

Rose waved a hand. "We need more. I was going to get it this morning, but I was sidetracked when I saw—someone."

Grace propped her hands on her hips. "And did you announce your intentions in your usual absurd fashion?"

Rose chuckled. "Of course not. Quite the opposite. On rare occasions, being subtle is better."

Sophie exchanged a puzzled look with Joanna. What were they talking about?

"I'm sorry I neglected to get the wicks," Rose said. "You know how forgetful I can be."

"Uh-huh." Grace picked up her rolling pin again. "I imagine it will get worse before it gets better."

Rose chuckled. "I shouldn't wonder if it will."

Sophie didn't understand the pointed looks that passed between the two older women. "We'll be happy to pick up lamp wicks for you, Rose," she offered. "How wide?"

"One inch. Grace, can you think of anything else we need at the hardware store?"

Grace grinned, but quickly sobered and began vigorously flattening her dough. "Not right now, but I'm sure something will occur to me later."

"I'm sure it will, too," Rose said, with a distinct twinkle in her eyes.

Sophie met her sister's gaze. Joanna appeared puzzled by the odd conversation, too. "We don't mind running errands for Rose and you, Aenti Grace. It's the least we can do."

"Absolutely," Sophie echoed her sister's sentiment.

Rose smiled and patted Sophie's cheek. "That's sweet of you to say. Oh, Grace, we're having a party on Saturday."

Grace tipped her head to the side. "When did we decide this?"

"When I saw you-know-who."

"Who?"

"Honestly, Grace, you astound me." Rose shook her head and left the kitchen.

Sophie nodded toward the door. "We should get going."

Grace went back to rolling her dough. "The road out front will take you straight to Main Street. The post office is on the corner. You can't miss it. The hardware store is two doors down. A party on Saturday. As if I didn't have enough to do. Oh, now I know who Rose meant. How silly of me."

Sophie and Joanna slipped outside. On the covered porch, Joanna grabbed Sophie's arm. "What was that all about?"

"I have no idea."

"I'm not sure we were part of the same conversation as those two. I hope we don't sound like that when we get to be their age." Joanna took off toward the street.

"I don't expect to see that age," Sophie muttered and followed her sister.

The town of Harts Haven was smaller than the village where Sophie was from. Everyone they met smiled and called out a cheerful greeting. The houses were modest and well-kept, but they were connected to electric lines, so the inhabitants weren't Amish. That wasn't unusual. The Amish preferred country living to town life. Sophie's father ran a dry goods grocery but lived on ten acres outside of town to allow grazing for the buggy horses and a large garden.

Joanna had been right to insist Sophie wear her gloves and heavy coat. The sun was shining in the bright blue sky, but the wind stole any warmth from the air. She was used to cold winters, but not to the blustery gusts that seemed determined to pull her bonnet from her head and burrow under her coat.

The walk to the business district didn't take long. The town was only four blocks wide.

Joanna pointed to a small building with a flag fluttering out front. A horse and buggy stood at the hitching rail. "I see the post office."

"And I see the hardware store," Sophie said when she spotted the sign.

"You go on. I won't be a minute." Joanna rushed up the wooden steps and went inside.

Sophie looked up the street and saw a young Amish girl come out of Graber's Hardware carrying a small stool, followed by an Amish fellow with a large cardboard box. He put it down, wrote something on the front and went back inside.

The child sat beside the box and looked in. A moment later, the front paws and head of a puppy appeared. The child lifted the black-and-white dog out and held it, earning a face licking in return. A second and a third pup appeared and began trying to climb out. One red-and-white puppy succeeded and tumbled to the sidewalk.

"Clara, come help me!" the girl called out as she tried to grab the second puppy while a third, this one black and brown with white markings, tumbled out of the box and headed for the curb.

A pickup roared past, alerting Sophie to the potential danger. If the puppy made it into the street, the results could be horrible. She dashed toward the child.

Two

Sophie grabbed the red-and-white pup at the edge of the curb as another car flew past. She held on to the squirming puppy and picked up the black-and-brown one heading for the street, too.

"Oh, *danki*," the child said in relief, putting her black-and-white puppy back in the box marked Aussies for Sale. "I reckon I need something taller."

Sophie nodded in agreement. "You certainly do. Can you find something that will work better?"

"Yup. We have more boxes around the back, but I can't leave my puppies."

As her racing heart slowed, Sophie smiled at the child. "A problem easily solved. Why don't I watch them for you?"

"*Danki*. I'll just be a minute." The child darted into the alley beside the store.

Sophie placed all the puppies back in the box, then perched awkwardly on the small stool and spoke softly to soothe them. It didn't work. Having discovered they could escape once, they all set about climbing over each other to get out. As soon as she pushed one back in, the next one hopped over the edge. She didn't have enough hands. In desperation, she unbuttoned the top buttons of her coat and tucked two of the puppies inside while she cradled the other one.

The coat worked so well that she was trying to get the third one in when Red wiggled his head free and began licking Sophie's chin, making her laugh. Black-and-White got her head out and added her tongue to the assault, going for Sophie's ear. "Stop that. I already washed my face this morning."

"What are you doing?" A man's deep, annoyed voice came from behind her.

Sophie looked over her shoulder to see the same fellow who had brought the box out earlier. He had dark hair and amazing stone-gray eyes rimmed by thick black eyelashes. A fierce, daunting scowl marred his face. Full lips above his neat beard were pressed into a tight line that matched his furrowed brow.

"I'm getting licked by puppies. What does it look like?"

"I see a woman trying to stuff my dogs into her coat. Where's my daughter?"

The black-and-brown pup in her arms joined the kissing session. Sophie tilted her face back to get out of their reach, lost her precarious seat on the stool and fell backward.

The man caught her before she hit the sidewalk. After righting her, he took one pup from her arms.

Flustered by his nearness and grim expression, Sophie forced a smile. "Your daughter has gone to get a taller container. If I wanted to steal your puppies, I would have picked up the box and walked away with them.

His scowl deepened. "It looked odd, that's all I'm saying."

It was hard to maintain a commanding pose while seated with her coat full of wiggling fur balls, but the old Sophie would not have allowed herself to be intimidated on her first day in a town. She drew on her years of teaching experience and the advice of the teacher who had trained her.

Never let them see they've rattled you.

Meeting the man's gaze, Sophie looked him up and down, then arched one eyebrow. "Looks can be deceiving, and baseless assumptions are usually wrong. You owe me an apology."

The rude dog owner looked taken aback. A flush climbed up his neck and stained his cheeks a dull red. He inhaled sharply and then cleared his throat. "I reckon that's so."

It wasn't much of an apology.

When he wasn't glaring at her, he was a good-looking man. There was something compelling about his gray eyes. Their gazes locked. A strange connection passed between them, surprising her and him by the way his eyes widened. She blinked hard and looked away. His beard proclaimed he was a married man. And rude.

"Puppies!" Joanna's delighted squeal alerted Sophie to her sister's presence. "Oh, how adorable."

She took the red-and-white one from Sophie and cuddled him. "Isn't he sweet? Sister, we need a dog. Can we keep one? Please say yes," Joanna beseeched her.

Sophie shook her head. "*Nee*. We can't repay *Aenti* Grace's generosity by returning with a puppy."

"How can you bear to be so sensible? I love this one." Joanna kissed her pup's nose.

The little girl returned with a box almost as tall as she was. "That one is Mick," she said, putting her burden down beside Joanna and stroked Mick's head. "He is my favorite."

Joanna smiled at the child. "Mine, too. I'm Joanna Eicher."

"I'm Rachel Graber. This is our store."

"We were just on our way in. This is my sister, Sophie."

"That's my *daed*," Rachel said, pointing.

His expression softened as he gazed at his child. He was definitely good-looking when he wasn't scowling. He turned his stunning eyes back to Sophie. "I'm Karl Graber. You must be the new teacher."

"I am." She nodded slightly. His gaze remained on her face until she grew uncomfortable with his scrutiny. What was he staring at?

"Can I be an angel in the Christmas program, teacher? Please?" Rachel asked in a pleading voice.

Sophie smile at the adorable child. "I haven't decided on a program yet."

"But Christmas is almost here, and everyone will want to see an angel," Rachel insisted.

"That's enough," her father said. "Don't pester the woman."

Sophie placed her black-and-white pup in the box. The pup immediately started crying.

"Biscuit is crying because she misses her *mamm*. We had to leave her shut up at home so she wouldn't follow us. My *mamm* is in heaven," Rachel said with a catch in her voice. "She died from being sick."

Tenderhearted Joanna hugged the child. "I'm sorry. Our

mother passed away, too. Sometimes I feel sad when I think about her, but I know she is smiling when she sees I'm happy. That's why I always try to be cheerful."

"Granny Rose is looking for a stepmother for us," Rachel added. "I pray she finds one soon. Are you married? *Daed* says you must be here to find husbands."

Joanna blushed and giggled. "If *Gott* has someone in mind for me, I will consider it."

This was something Sophie could nip in the bud. She gazed at the child. "I'm not looking for a husband. Married women can't be teachers, and I love teaching. It makes me happy."

Rachel looked up at her father. "It would make *Mamm* smile if you could be happy again, *Daed*. Don't you think so?"

When he didn't answer, Sophie glanced at his face and saw his eyes fill with pain. The muscles in his jaw clenched.

Overcome with sympathy for him, Sophie stepped between him and his child to take the puppy from his arms. She gazed into his sorrow-filled eyes as he struggled to gain control of his emotions. "I'm sorry," she whispered. "It is difficult to lose someone dear."

His gray eyes turned stormy and locked with Sophie's. His fierce scowl returned. She wanted to help, but his expression said he didn't appreciate her interference.

Karl pushed his pain deep inside the way he always did. He didn't need Sophie Eicher's sympathy. That this stranger thought she understood what he was going through infuriated him. His grief was his own. He didn't want to share it.

"That pup's name is Buck," Rachel said.

"Like the dog in *The Call of the Wild*?" Sophie asked a

bit too cheerfully as she turned away from him. "That was one of my favorite books as a child."

She lifted the pup to look him in the face. "You'll have to grow into a mighty fine *hund* to live up to that name. Rachel, do you know the story?"

Rachel shook her head.

Sophie smiled. "It's a wonderful tale about a brave sled dog in the Yukon. When school starts, I will make a point of reading the book to everyone."

"Oh, I can't wait." Rachel grinned and clapped her hands.

Hearing the excitement in his daughter's voice eased the tightness in Karl's throat. It had been one of his favorite books, too. He was a little surprised that the new teacher made the connection. The story was the reason he had named the pup Buck.

But right now, he had a business to run. He needed to know how soon he would lose Clara's help in the store. "When will school start?"

Sophie cuddled the pup. "A week if everything goes well. I want to get the students back in class before Thanksgiving."

"What has to go well?" A week wasn't much time for him to find a clerk to take Clara's place. How he would pay someone without the rent from the *daadi haus* was another problem he had to solve.

"I'll have to do an inventory at the school. Make sure I have adequate school supplies and books for the students. Then I need to review all the students' records and make sure they are current because I understand the last teacher left abruptly. Lastly, I want to meet with the parents and families to get an idea of what they expect and let them know my expectations. In other words, a lot, but first on my list is finding the school."

"That's easy," Rachel said. "It's across the road from our house."

"That's *goot* to know," Joanna said. "But where do you live?"

Buck started barking furiously and struggled to get free. Karl saw what had the pup's attention as Sophie tightened her grip. Three half-grown lambs were trotting toward them up the sidewalk.

"Not again." Karl clenched his hands into fists. "Rachel!"

"I locked the gate, *Daed*, I did." Her lower lip quivered as the young sheep surrounded her, butting her for attention and bleating. "I don't know how they got out."

"If I've told you once, I've told you a hundred times to make sure it's latched tight." He didn't have time for this. Now he'd have to close the store and lose a morning's worth of business to take Rachel's pets back to the farm.

Sophie laughed as one lamb nibbled at her apron hem. "Mary had one little lamb, but Rachel has three as white as snow."

"And everywhere that Rachel is, the lambs all try to go," Karl finished dryly. "One problem with letting your child raise bottle babies."

Rachel hung her head. "I can take them home, but who will watch my puppies?"

"I will," Joanna offered quickly.

"Is that okay, *Daed*?" Rachel asked.

"That's fine. I'll close the store and take you to the farm as soon as I finish with these customers."

Rachel could easily walk that far. She did it all the time,

but it was too far to send her by herself with the sheep. There wasn't much traffic on their rural road, but having the lambs along might distract her when she should be paying attention.

Sophie handed her puppy to Joanna. "I can walk Rachel home, make sure the miscreants are safely locked up again and visit the school since it's nearby."

Rachel tilted her head. "They aren't miscreants. I don't know that breed. These are Rambouillet sheep," she informed her teacher solemnly.

Sophie hid a smile behind her hand, but quickly recovered her composure. "My mistake. I'm not familiar with sheep."

Rachel smiled at her. "That's okay. They're about the most popular breed in the world because they have really soft wool."

"I see." Sophie's grin returned. "May I walk your daughter and her Rambouillet flock home for you, Mr. Graber?"

Two *Englisch* customers entered the store, tourists by the look of them. He didn't like the idea of being beholden to Sophie, but she was going to be his child's teacher, and it was turning out to be a busy morning. "Fine. If you have the time to spare."

"I do. Joanna, will you get the item Rose needs?"

"In a minute." Joanna held the puppy close and rubbed her face in the dog's fluffy fur.

Sophie rolled her eyes. That was always Joanna's answer when she didn't want to do something. "Never mind."

She turned to Karl. "Rose Yoder asked us to get a roll of one-inch lamp wick for her. Do you know what kind she prefers?"

"Sure." He walked into the store, then stopped and turned to stare at her. "Rose sent you?"

"That's right."

"Rose bought a roll of wick two days ago. Why does she need more?"

Sophie shrugged. "I don't know. She asked if we would pick some up since Joanna and I were going to the post office. I distinctly remember her saying that she had intended to pick some up herself this morning but forgot about it when she ran into someone she knew."

"Hmm." Why send the teacher to his store today on such a questionable errand? Was Rose up to something? She could be crafty. Some folks thought she was addled. He knew better.

Sophie tilted her head to the side. "Is something wrong?"

Rose said he wasn't on her list of prospective husbands for this woman, so he didn't need to worry that she was matchmaking, but something felt off. Perhaps Rose had simply mislaid her wick roll. She was getting older.

He eyed the new teacher closely. Rose said Sophie needed someone special, but why? He saw nothing out of the ordinary about her. She was a pleasant-looking slender woman. A shade on the skinny side but she had an attractive smile when she wasn't chiding him.

She brushed her cheek with one hand. "Do I have something on my face?"

"*Nee.* Why?"

"You keep staring at me."

"Sorry." He turned away, determined not to look at her again. He quickly found the brand of lamp wicks that Rose preferred and handed them to Clara at the counter. "This is your new teacher, Sophie Eicher."

Clara barely glanced at Sophie. "Rachel's silly sheep are outside."

He nodded. "Don't worry about it. Teacher is going to take Rachel and the lambs back to the farm."

Despite Clara's dour expression, Sophie smiled at his child. "I'm delighted to meet another of my scholars. Are you excited to return to school?"

"I'm not going back. *Daed* needs me here."

That surprised him. He did need her, but they hadn't discussed keeping her out of school.

Sophie glanced from Clara to him. "Finishing your education is important. I'm sure your father will agree."

"He'll homeschool me. That will be four dollars." Clara held out her hand.

"We'll talk about it later." He didn't want to have the conversation in front of her teacher. His *Englisch* customers left without buying anything.

Sophie pulled a five out of her purse and handed it to Clara. "I hope you'll decide to come to school. Learning with your friends is always more enjoyable."

Clara ignored Sophie. "We're getting low on sheet metal screws. Shall I add it to the order form for next week?"

"I'll take care of it." He had meant to order those last week.

Sophie took her purchase. "It was nice meeting you, Clara. And you also, Mr. Graber. I'm sure I'll see you around."

He walked her to the shop door. "The girls and I will be at your party on Saturday, but not until late."

She gave him a puzzled look. "What party?"

"Rose is giving a welcome frolic for you and your sister. She asked me to spread the word."

Sophie chuckled. "I heard her tell Grace that they were having a party Saturday, but she failed to mention it was for us. Grace was none too pleased at the short notice."

"Rose travels a zigzag path of her own. The rest of us don't even try to keep up. I should warn you that Rose thinks of herself as a matchmaker. Don't be surprised if she introduces you to single fellows left and right."

Sophie's smiled faded. She looked away, but not before he caught a glimpse of pain in her sky blue eyes. "Rose won't have any success with me. I'm not looking for a husband."

He heard a deep sadness under her words. Why? "Well, I have warned you."

When she looked at him, her expression was serene once again. "*Danki.* I intend to devote my life to teaching. If Rose wants to find a husband for Joanna, that would be *wunderbar.*"

He rocked back on his heels. Okay, now it was making sense. Rose had him in mind for the younger one, not the teacher. He knew something was up with Rose needing another roll of lamp wicks. Well, she was going to be disappointed in her matchmaking. "Thanks for seeing Rachel and her sheep home. Make sure the gate gets latched this time."

"I will. Please give careful consideration to Clara's schooling. I know you'll do what's best for her."

She walked out the door. He watched as she followed Rachel and her miniflock around the street corner and disappeared.

She was a nice woman. Helpful. Maybe a bit outspoken, but that was to be expected from someone who had to keep students in line. He glanced at Joanna, holding a puppy in her arms while she talked to a boy who seemed interested. Rose was slipping if she thought he'd fall for that one. She was prettier than Sophie, but she was far too young for him. He found her mature sister more appealing.

That Sophie wasn't husband hunting was the most attractive thing about her. Only why wasn't she? She had claimed she wanted to devote her life to teaching. If that were the case, what had caused the sadness he'd glimpsed? Had she lost someone she loved?

He surveyed the store. Clara had started restocking the shelves. There weren't any customers. He wasn't needed now. He really should make sure Rachel got her sheep home safely.

"Clara, I've changed my mind. I'm going to go with Rachel. Your teacher has things to do to get ready for school. She doesn't need to be looking after your sister."

"I can manage here."

She could but he hated leaving her alone.

"Mr. Wilson is next door if I need anything," she added, giving him a look that said she didn't require anyone's assistance.

"Okay." He walked outside and told Joanna where he was going. She quickly offered to keep an eye on Clara and the dogs. Relieved, he headed down the block at a quick pace.

Sophie followed Rachel as she skipped along with her sheep following. The child was adorable, bright and talkative. "This lamb is April. That's May, and that one is June."

Sophie couldn't tell them apart. "Does your father raise sheep?"

"*Nee.* These belonged to our neighbor, but their mama rejected them. He didn't want to have to bottle feed them. He asked if I would take care of them. He said I could keep any that lived, and they all did."

"You must have taken very good care of them."

"Clara helped. *Daed* says we will sell them in the spring.

Clara and I get to keep some of the money. He says that is only fair 'cause we did a lot of the work."

Karl Graber sounded like a generous father. One lamb stopped to nibble at a patch of alfalfa. Rachel kept walking. Sophie looked at the lagging lamb and waved her hands at it. "Go on. Shoo. The others are leaving you."

Rachel was a dozen yards ahead. Sophie called to her. "Rachel, this one isn't following you."

The child stopped. "That's April. She'll come. Give her a push."

Rachel resumed waking as Sophie stared at the straggler. She had no experience with sheep. What part did she push on?

She shoved against the animal's side. It stepped over but kept eating. "Rachel, I think you should come back. She doesn't want to go."

Sophie was startled when Karl jogged up to her. "I decided you might need a hand in case the sheep had other ideas about going home."

She grinned with relief. "This one certainly does. I can't get it to move."

He grabbed a handful of wool near the shoulders, lifted her slightly, and then shoved her in the right direction with a knee to her rump. April decided she wanted her friends more than her next nibble and ran to catch them.

Sophie chuckled. "I guess I need to be more persistent. *Danki.*"

"You're welcome."

She fell into step beside him as they followed Rachel. He shortened his stride to match hers.

"The school is across from my lane. You can see it from here. It's the white building set back from the road."

"Did you go to school there?" she asked.

"I did. My grandfather donated the land for it. I remember the summer the community raised the building. I must have been five. I wasn't eager to go to school."

"Like Clara?"

He nodded. "She wants to continue helping me at the store, but I haven't made up my mind."

One of the lambs stopped to eat at the side of the road. Sophie nudged it firmly in the rump with her knee. It trotted ahead.

"You catch on quick." There was a hint of laughter in his voice.

"I've dealt with a few reluctant scholars in my time. I can be persistent." She wanted to see him smile, but he didn't oblige. Was he normally a somber man?

"Have you been a teacher long?" His tone was serious again.

"I taught for four years back home." Happy years that had ended abruptly with her diagnosis instead of with her marriage.

"You enjoyed it?"

She smiled. "I did. Very much so." It had been a wonderful and fulfilling career.

"Then why move here?"

Grim memories replaced Sophie's happy ones. "Things change."

Unwilling to share more, she quickened her pace to catch up with Rachel.

The school turned out to be just over a mile outside of town. It was a single-story building with white clapboard siding and four large windows along each side. Sophie nodded in satisfaction at the sight. They would provide plenty of light inside for her and her students. A school bell hung from the porch ceiling just outside the front door. Her fingers itched to ring it for the start of class. She had missed teaching during her treatments. When she was surrounded by eager young children again perhaps she could forget her own troubles.

A red storage shed with white trim stood behind the school. The wide lawn appeared neatly kept. A playground consisting of several swing sets of various heights, a tee-ter-totter, a tetherball pole and a ball diamond with a wire backstop completed the school grounds. The community obviously took excellent care of the property. It was an encouraging sign.

Sophie looked at Karl. "Is the school building locked?"

"It is, but I know where the spare key is kept. Rachel, wait here."

"Can I swing?"

"You may but keep an eye on your lambs."

As they walked toward the shed, Sophie looked back toward the town. "I'm surprised April, May and June went all that way to find her."

"When they were too little to be left home alone all day, I took Rachel and the lambs to the store with me. So, they know the way."

"How funny."

"Not to my way of thinking. Three sheep wandering along the road are just asking for trouble. Rachel needs to be more responsible when she feeds them." He opened the shed door. Inside were two stalls for horses and a room for coal storage. He took a key off a hook just inside. "Look around all you want."

He took her hand and placed the key in her palm. "Keep this one until you get your own set from the school board."

When his fingers touched hers, a startling sensation raced across Sophie's nerve endings like a wave of warm water sweeping over her skin. Glancing at his face, she saw his eyes widen with shock. Did he feel it, too?

Sophie took a quick step back as Karl did the same. She couldn't stop staring at him. He looked away first and cleared his throat. "I need to get these sheep home and get back to the store."

"I need to—" What did she need to do? Her mind was a blank as her heart hammered in her chest. She'd never experienced such a startling reaction to any man's touch. Not even with Nate, and she had been ready to marry him. It made no sense. She barely knew Karl Graber.

He spun on his heels and walked away. "Rachel, let's go."

Sophie watched them cross the road and walk down the quarter-mile-long lane. Just before Karl disappeared behind the cedar trees surrounding his farmstead, he looked back, and her heart started racing again. Rachel waved. Sophie raised her hand and waved, too. Karl didn't. He turned around and kept walking.

When they were out of sight, Sophie crossed the brown grass to the steps of the school and sat down abruptly. What had just happened?

In the past, her chemotherapy had left her with what the nurses called "brain fog," but this was different. Maybe it was a delayed reaction to all the medications she had taken, but she had finished those drugs six months ago.

Had her cancer moved to her brain? That might explain her unexpected reaction. Or maybe it was because Karl was a handsome and compelling man.

This would never do. She was here to be a teacher, not to get involved with Rachel's father.

She drew a deep breath and blew it out slowly. There would not be a repeat of this. She would make sure of it.

Avoiding Karl in such a small community would not be possible, but she wouldn't be alone with him again.

Sophie looked at the key in her hand where a sense of warmth still lingered. What she needed to do was stop thinking about Karl Graber and get to work on the job she had been hired to do.

Don't miss
A Match Made at Christmas *by Patricia Davids,*
available October 2022 wherever
HQN Books and ebooks are sold.

www.Harlequin.com

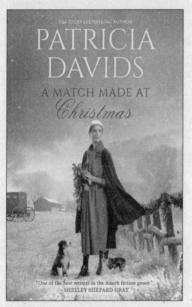